Beyond the Memories

by

Jeanette Sferes

Jeanette Sferes

BEYOND THE MEMORIES

Published by:

J. Hammer Publishing
202 US Route 1
PO Box 140
Falmouth, Maine 04105

Cover Design by Philip Candelmo

Library of Congress Catalog Card Number: 2004097997
ISBN: 0-9755154-0-3

Printed in the USA by Morris Publishing
3212 East Highway 30 • Kearney, NE 68847 • 1-800-650-7888

In memory of my husband, Paul, who personified all that was best in a man. He was my hero.

PROLOGUE
1958

After looking back on that night when my life changed forever, I wondered if it was simply destiny. If I had left my hotel room in Athens a few hours or even a few minutes earlier or later, would it still have happened? It is one of the great mysteries of life, whether our life is preordained or whether it evolves for no reason at all. I had never really given it much thought before. The irony is that such a catastrophe should befall me for the most mundane reason. I was only doing what women were born to do—I went shopping.

FOR SOME UNKNOWN REASON, we are prisoners. I strain to identify the others in the semi-darkness of the room. I count seven including myself—all are young, all are female. Only one girl is awake and whimpering; the rest are unconscious, sprawled haphazardly on the gritty cement floor. Another is slumped against a wall like a tossed rag doll; the full skirt of her dress is in disarray, displaying gangly legs as awkward as a foal's. She wears white cotton panties with pink polka dots, the kind I once wore before I grew up. I crawl over and pull down her skirt to cover her. She wears only one sandal, and it bothers me. What happened to the other one? Why is she here? Why are we all here?

I force myself to breathe—somehow, I have forgotten how to do it. I take deep breaths, willing myself to relax. If I don't, I'll panic, and that frightens me almost as much as being a captive. Every nerve in my body is taut, and I try to ignore the drumming of my heart. It's all just a bad dream, I tell myself. I pinch the flesh on my arm until it hurts and shake my head until it rattles. I am not asleep—this is for real. I feel doomed and helpless. *Oh, God! What is happening?*

The girl nearest to me, the one crying, is pitifully young, has eyelids at half-mast, and chattering teeth. The horror on her face is a mirror image of my own.

"Jesus, Mary and Joseph. Where am I?"

"Who are you?"

She stammers in a thick Irish brogue, "Bridget…I'm Bridget Donahoe, from County Cork, Ireland."

Fearing that we might just disappear forever, she wanted someone, anyone, to know who she was and where she came from.

"I'm Suzanne Conti, an American."

In an adjoining room, I can see light peeking under the door. Male voices chortle in a foreign language that is not Greek. My guess is Arabic or Turkish. In the background, I hear a radio blasting out Greek music.

Was this a prison? Perhaps we were being held for ransom, or maybe we were hostages. I couldn't escape the reality that each of us were young women, some only girls. I shuddered to think what that suggested—white slavery. This can't be happening. Abductions do not occur in civilized countries like Greece, or do they?

Slowly, my memory returns. I recall when I last saw my husband of only two weeks. He was in the shower, and I peeked in on him and kissed him playfully on his lips—his head slathered with shampoo, its lemony scent still locked in my mind.

"I've got some last minute shopping to do. The hotel shops are still open. Is it okay?"

He grins in his quirky lopsided way. "Sure kiddo. Don't spend too much money, and pick up the *Herald Tribune.* I'm dying to know how the Red Sox made out against the Yankees."

I wipe the soap off the tip of my nose with the back of my left hand and salute him sharply with the other. "Yes, boss!"

I left our suite on the concierge floor, and rode the elevator down ten floors to the lobby along with three men all dressed meticulously who reeked of aftershave. Their black, brilliantine hair was combed straight back like gangsters. All had mustaches and wore diamond rings on their pinkies. My feminine intuition told me something was wrong, but what? Anxious to leave the elevator, I hurried off, but one of the men rushed past me, turned around, and said, "*Signomi, Kyria.*" I acknowledged his apology with a nod and rubbed my hip. I felt a sting—had something bitten me? I sashayed through the lobby of gleaming marble floors and walls, glittering chandeliers, lavish floral arrangements, and plush, white leather couches. Sophisticated and stylishly dressed people were about, ready for an evening out in Athens—which always began late. Only Americans and babies ate before nine.

I glanced at the assistant concierge of the hotel. As I walked past his desk, he lifted his bushy eyebrows, his tongue stroking his mustache like a cat ready to pounce on a mouse. Although annoyed, I was used to it—young Greek men were *so* bold, especially when they saw an attractive blond female of any age. I laughed at this *buffus*, proud that I had added one more word to my limited Greek vocabulary, even if it didn't exactly mean buffoon. Without warning, everyone around me seemed to be walking in slow motion. Sounds faded out. After that, nothing.

Bridget clasped her hands together and prayed. Tears traced her cheeks. "Hail Mary full of grace, the Lord is with thee—" I envied her. At least she believed in her religion. My sparse visits to my Episcopal Church at Christmas and Easter and for funerals and weddings did little to comfort me. My spirituality was something I always intended to work on someday.

One by one, the slumbering bodies sprung to life. We were all Caucasian, blond or redheaded, except for one, who was startlingly beautiful with long black hair and sooty eyes. We exchanged our stories and suspicions. Five of us had been kidnapped from Greece—two from Turkey. Moreover, we had been stripped of all possessions: passport, photographs, cosmetics, money. My treasured wedding and engagement rings, my sapphire necklace, were gone, probably forever. As the early morning light filters in through the lone barred window, we stare at each other in disbelief.

We guess that we had been given a drug or an injection that made us semi-conscious, yet responsive enough to walk with assistance. Aha! The mysterious insect bite. Whatever it was had obliterated all our memories of the abductions.

Bridget clung to my side like a younger sister. Her snarled, russet hair hung over her freckled face like a shroud. "I took me a job to be a servant by a rich family in Turkey, and this is what becomes of me. I wanted to help me family." She continued to sob and I felt sorry for her. I patted her on the back. That's all I could do. I was as scared as she was.

Alice, a young Bostonian, had been snatched in Turkey. She was confused, and her bright, dilated pupils spelled only one thing—drugs. Sheepishly, she confessed that a Turkish man gave her hashish when they spent the night together. She wasn't sure, but she thought that was the day before.

The German girl, Veronica, had straight flaxen hair that looked like the boy on a can of Dutch Boy Cleanser. Her pale blue eyes were slits beneath swollen lids. Her jaw was bruised. It was obvious that someone had beaten her up. She was livid. "I'm a prostitute working the bars of Piraeus, outside of Athens," she told us. "Should have stuck to the American sailors! I knew I wasn't worth that many friggin' drachmas to a Greek."

The young teenager wearing only one sandal is named Elizabeth, another American. A pretty, baby-faced girl, about sixteen, with large brown eyes, pink chubby cheeks, and pouting lips. "Why didn't I listen to my parents? They warned me about things like this. I came to visit a classmate in Athens, but something strange happened at the airport."

Alexandra, the dark-haired beauty, was the daughter of a French, Catholic mother and a Lebanese, Muslim father who was a professor at the American University in Beirut. She said she was raised as a Catholic. She spoke four languages, for after hearing her say that French was her primary language, I heard her speak German to Veronica, and she conversed with me in English. My initial suspicions were confirmed about our captors when she listened at the door and told us they were speaking in Arabic. That she understood their language gave us a feeling of some power, and we agreed that it was best that we keep that to ourselves. Alexandra's creamy skin was flawless, except for a tiny mole on her left cheek. Her almond shaped eyes were dark and mysterious—fringed with long lashes and thick brows that slanted upward. A shock of sable hair fell down to the small of her back. It was impossible not to stare at her—even for me, another woman. I could only imagine what she did to men. There should have been a law against anyone being that beautiful.

The last member of our group was Marilyn, another stunning woman about my age. She was tall and fashionably thin, with green eyes and long hair the color of corn silk. Her generous bow-shaped mouth encircled perfect white teeth. She bragged that she was a model from New York. At first, I didn't believe her, but her appearance suggested that she could be telling the truth. She had the look of a model. The way she strutted, the way she stood.

"Those creeps don't know who they're dealing with. I'm the niece of Senator Moore from New Jersey. I was on a shoot at the Acropolis for *Vogue*. I was going to be on the cover, and now this shitty nightmare," she muttered.

Veronica snapped, "Sure you are, and I am the bloody Queen of England."

"Listen, you, I am who I say I am," answered Marilyn, her green eyes blazing. "Keep your mouth shut, or I'll shut it for you."

Veronica kept quiet. She was short and chunky and no match for Marilyn, who rose from the floor, towering over her, her long muscled legs planted apart, her arms folded like those of a captain on a ship.

Alexandra intervened. "Stop it, both of you! *We* are not the enemy—*they* are, those men on the other side of the door. We must stick together." After that, everyone quieted down. She was right.

Marilyn pulled me aside, and whispered: "We need a plan to escape. There's only one barred window and one door out of this place. We have to figure out how many men are outside, and when they come and go. Are you with me on this?"

"Of course."

"I knew you were the one to approach. I've been watching you. We've got one crazed hooker, two children, one druggie, and one half-Muslim. I like her, but I don't trust her yet. I want you, my American compatriot, to help me with a plan."

"Okay. You've got it."

Our conversation ended when the door burst open. Two men, swarthy and bearded, entered the room. Without a word, or a look, they brought in pails of water, soap, combs, toothbrushes, personal necessities, and towels. They left and then returned with a mat and a blanket for each of us. A third man followed, pushing a cart that held bowls of steaming rice, pita bread, fruit, and tea. After they were gone, we devoured the food; it had been at least a full day since we had eaten last. Only Alice hesitated, her hands shaking so badly that she could hardly hold her cup—a clear enough sign that she needed a fix. She begged us to do something. "Please, tell them I've got to get out of here. I'm a diabetic and I need my insulin. I could die." None of us believed her.

When we finished eating, we washed and groomed ourselves. It didn't change our dire situation but we did feel better. Alexandra eventually persuaded Alice to eat. She munched on a peach and sipped her tea. In every crisis, a leader emerges, and I knew that person was Alexandra. "I'm the only one here who has lived in a Muslim country," she said. "It is best that we act modestly. These men will respect us if we behave ourselves. They don't want to touch us. It offends them, and I don't think they intend to hurt us."

She was the first to use the primitive toilet in the darkest corner of the cellar. It was a hole in the ground with metal footprints on which to place your feet while you squatted above the hole. There was no privacy, so we averted our eyes. I was the second to use it, and had to cover my nose with a cloth to keep from gagging from the revolting smell. A wave of queasiness hit me, rising to my throat, and I was afraid I'd vomit. I held my breath and finally relieved myself. The others followed. The last to use it was Elizabeth, who when finished staggered back and collapsed on her mat.

IN THE LATE AFTERNOON, an attractive middle-aged woman entered the room; a trail of perfume followed wherever she stepped. Her jet-black hair was coiled into a French twist. As she stood in front of us, her gray eyes darting laterally, she appeared to be much taller and more ominous than her diminutive size.

She spoke English with a strong French accent. *"Bonjour, Mesdemoiselles*, I am Madam Boudreau. Pardon my English and I will do my best to make you understand me."

Taking a gold cigarette case and lighter out of her black Chanel handbag, she lit a long cigarette. She offered the pack to each of us.

Veronica, Marilyn and I each took one. She lit them for us. I spotted a huge, emerald-cut diamond on her ring finger. Her long lacquered nails were the color of blood.

"This is not personal," she said. "This is the way I make a living, and I choose to live well. Women who are beautiful or different fascinate my customers: light skin, blond or red hair, blue or green eyes. It is my job to have you examined by a physician. If you are diseased, you are worthless to me. If you are sexually experienced, you'll be of some value. And if you are a virgin, and someone finds you *desir,* I mean to say desirable, you will be worth many francs."

She paused, inhaling deeply on her cigarette—the smoke shooting out of her nostrils like a dragon. She tilted her head and looked us over. "Some of you are much better than average—*tres* better."

There was no longer any doubt about why we were there. I looked around at the others and saw the panic in their eyes. Their hands covered their mouths in disbelief. Our worst fears were just confirmed.

I shouted, "How dare you say this isn't personal! It's personal to us! We're human beings, not animals to be bought and sold. If you have any mercy, Madam Boudreau, any mercy at all, please help us. *Please!"*

"I am not a monster. We can't always select our professions. None of you have been through a war and suffered as I did, or seen your husband executed by the Nazis because he was in the Resistance. I have responsibilities to my children and my elderly parents."

Four-inch, stiletto heels clicked and echoed as she crossed the concrete floor, leaving a slammed door in her wake.

Just before she left us, she had a final conversation in French with Alexandra. We asked her what she had said. The Lebanese girl answered sadly, "She told me that I would make her so rich she could retire. She said I was the most beautiful woman she had ever seen, as if that were going to make me feel better."

"That goddamn bitch!" said Marilyn.

We could hear Madam yelling at someone through the closed door. I put my ear to the door so I could hear the conversation. "Everyone be quiet!" I said.

She was reprimanding a man who spoke English. "Are you sure

the Arabs left?" she asked.

"Yes, Madam. They went to pray."

"You idiot! Why did you take a famous model, and why Americans who are well educated and one that's married? I have told you before, only young Caucasian women who would not be missed—country girls—immigrants—nobodies."

"I know, Madam, and I am sorry, but these women are worth a fortune. My client wants beautiful women for special customers. This is a one-time deal."

I recognized the voice—I had heard it before. It was *Yanni,* that slimy worm. I wanted to kill him for ruining my life. Now I knew that I had not been randomly selected; however, I didn't share that information with anyone or that I was married.

"What's done is done, and we can't change it, *c'est fini,*" said Madam Boudreau. "I don't like working for Arabs, but what choice do we have? They want the women, and who has more money than they do? After that, the voices became more distant, and eventually we couldn't hear anything at all.

Everyone was despondent except Veronica who snarled, "Men are swine. What does it matter who I sleep with? They are all the same," and she rolled over onto her side, pulled her blanket up to her shoulders, and shut her eyes—snoring within minutes.

I tried to sleep, but the air was close and muggy and I was distracted by a naked light bulb dangling from the ceiling. I rolled over onto my stomach to blot out the light and pulled the blanket over my head in spite of the heat. The flies buzzing around my face were driving me crazy.

I wondered if I would ever see my husband or my family again, and then the tears came in a deluge. As I sobbed, I tried to muffle the sound when I felt a hand reach out and grab mine—it was Alexandra. I wasn't alone. Eventually, I willed myself to hear the sound of the sea crashing against the beach, telling myself that I would see it again, my beautiful family home in Cape Elizabeth.

Chapter 1

SUZANNE
1941—1958

Portland Headlight was built by the order of our first president, George Washington, and is possibly the most photographed lighthouse in the United States, but it is not in Portland; it is in the town where I grew up, Cape Elizabeth, Maine. People traveled from miles around to see it, even from foreign countries, but it is a familiar sight to me. All I had to do was look out of my bedroom window, and there it stood.

When I was a little girl, I would trace my finger on an atlas and fantasize where I would land if I sailed my father's boat from Cape Elizabeth, Maine, past the offshore islands of Casco Bay and straight out across the Atlantic Ocean. Maybe Spain—more likely Portugal.

I adored that vast, ever-changing mass of water and color that was the Atlantic Ocean. I would breathe its salty scent until I thought my lungs would explode. What could be lovelier than to live in such a bewitching place?

As a teenager, I was a dreamer who relished reading romantic and scary books like *Wuthering Heights* and *Rebecca* while nestled like a seagull in some rocky, windswept cove. I would imagine encountering someone like Heathcliff, or Rhett Butler, or even Mr. Darcy, but I never did. The only young men I knew did not have dark hair and raven eyes, and would never dream of being as romantic as Heathcliff, or as mocking as Rhett Butler, or as arrogant as Mr. Darcy.

I wasn't always thinking of the seductive heroes of my favorite books. Sometimes I would look for sea glass and bits of broken pottery—pretending that it came from a sunken ship or a foreign land. *That was my trouble*, my mother said; *I was a dreamer, not a doer.* She wanted me to study harder, practice longer on the piano, and have perfect manners... *Well! If she only knew the real me.*

Within our town lived an exclusive group of families, *The Elite.* Over the years, the membership has remained much the same. Nearly all were Caucasian, Protestant, Republicans, and of old money. At the top of the list, and meeting all requirements, was the Mason family, of which I was a member.

I GREW UP IN A GATED estate called Cornwall, overlooking Casco Bay, with a sweeping expanse of ocean, islands, and lighthouses. My house, a white, Georgian mansion, was trimmed in black shutters, with two Ionian pillars and a half-moon shaped balcony that hung over the front entrance. Three stories of mullion-paned windows with white tie-back curtains faced the front of the house. Manicured evergreens and thick hedges dotted the landscape. Variegated, climbing ivy covered the four brick chimneys with a thick cushion of greenery.

On the back side of the house, French doors opened to a flagstoned terrace that looked over long, emerald green lawns and stone walkways that led down to the water's edge. At the shoreline stood a gray-shingled boathouse and a boat landing extending sixty feet into the water.

A second building consisted of two apartments, housing Rosie, the housekeeper, and Charles, the gardener. Beneath it was a four-car garage, which contained three cars—Mummy's old Buick convertible, Daddy's Chevy, and Charles's pick-up truck.

However splendid our house was, our parents preferred unpretentious, American-made cars.

I once overheard Rosie tell her sister, Agnes, on the telephone: "...tis a Yankee thing, so the Mason family wouldn't be confused with those new folks moving in with their new money. Mrs. M. said they should stay near their Catholic Churches and Jewish Synagogues, and drive their Cadillacs and fancy foreign cars somewhere else. 'Tis the truth I tell you. They'll just tear down these old houses and put up modern ranch houses that Mrs. M. says look like big house trailers…I know, Aggie, and I'm being a good Catholic, too, but I know me place, and I wouldn't belong out here either if I weren't working for the Masons. I'd be up on Munjoy Hill or on the West-end if I lived on me own…Yeah, I know what you mean—"

However much I loved my house, I admit I felt guilty living in such a privileged way, but this was the only place I had ever lived, and I wasn't sure that I wanted all those new people moving into our neighborhood. I liked it just the way it was. I especially enjoyed sitting in the window seat in my bedroom and looking out on the ocean. To the left, stood Portland Headlight, and to the right, the lighthouse at Fort Williams.

The sea was seductive and my whole family was seduced by it. When my father, an obstetrician, was not on call from the hospital, he would take us out in his thirty-foot wooden sailboat, which was designed and built in Maine, from somewhere Downeast.

"Kiddos, if you can handle the Maine seacoast, with its fog and rocky coast, you can sail anywhere in the world," said Daddy. Together, with my younger siblings, Jane and Robby, we practiced rigging, tacking, and coming about, until our arms ached and our hands swelled from handling the lines. We wore yellow slickers to keep us dry when we tacked through the roll and swell of the waves, never minding the spray of water that made us look like drowned rats. When we had our fill of sailing, or when the wind grew wild, or the fog rolled in, we docked—my job was handling the lines at the stern. We were cautious, and only sailed on the clearest of days when there was a good gust of breeze, but on the Maine seacoast, things can change fast and frequently did.

Daddy could have lived in leisure, or dabbled in banking or investments as many rich men did, but instead he became an obstetrician/gynecologist—the most demanding of all the medical specialties. As a result, we had to share him with his patients who were all women. This was a major problem for my mother. He was incredibly good-looking with dark brown, wavy hair, peppered with gray. His twinkling blue eyes and easy smile made every woman feel special, as if *she* were his favorite patient. Mother was probably a little jealous, and I can still hear her saying, "I know you prefer to be with those young women who think you're a god," but he would take it with good humor and wink at one of us kids.

When she was in the "dark pits," as Daddy called it, he would warn us, "Mummy isn't feeling well today, so be good." Then, he would shrug, pick up his black medical bag, and hurry off to the hospital.

We hardly ever had a holiday dinner without an interruption. Daddy would usually say, "Sorry gang, it's time to go. Babies decide when they're coming," which was usually in the middle of the night. When my mother complained, which was often, he'd say, "Edith, when will you understand that when my patients need me, *they* come first?" We, his children, understood perfectly the demands of his profession, but my mother never did.

I was proud when one of my friends said, "Your dad brought me into the world, and my mom thinks he's wonderful." He delivered thousands of babies, and some parents named their sons Robert after my father, Dr. Robert Alden Mason.

My father broke with medical tradition, and delivered me, Suzanne Meredith Mason, as well as my younger sister, Jane, and Robert Jr., the baby of the family. When people asked why he did this, he would justify it by answering, "Who could possibly care more for them than I?"

My earliest memories of my mother were happy ones. She would giggle like a child when she thought I did or said something funny. She would wrap her arms around me, and nuzzle the back of my neck. She'd pick me up and twirl me around until we were dizzy, collapsing to the floor in giggles. My mother was my whole world, but after Robby was born, she got sick, and I lost my fun-loving mother forever.

She was tall, almost as tall as my father, with a regal bearing—a classically beautiful, blond woman with blue-violet eyes that were large and brilliant. She could function and be charming when she played bridge, golf, tennis, and all the other country-club stuff. She liked shopping and enjoyed traveling with Daddy *alone*. We made her nervous, she said. We even had moderate periods of tranquility, but my mother's capacity to love anyone more than herself was beyond her. Her chronic depression had crippled her ability to love others, or so it seemed.

Mummy was thrifty, the way some rich people are about money. It wasn't a problem when she bought something for herself or her family, but for others, she was stingy. We were embarrassed when she left a ten-percent tip, or even less. When we didn't turn off the electricity after we left our room, we'd get a lecture about wasting money. She was proud of her Yankee thrift.

I knew we were millionaires, although our parents never discussed it with us. Mummy had drilled it into us. "Never talk about money, the fact that you have it—or that you don't have it. Nobody wants to know if you're poor, and only the *nouveau riche* talk about money."

However, my father, the quintessential crusader, taught us about fairness, tolerance, and generosity. My parents had many arguments because he refused to bill his poorer patients.

"Edith, how can I send a bill to someone who has just had a baby and can't even afford a crib?"

"It's not your fault there's a Depression. The City Hospital is free—send them there."

"I'm their doctor, Edith. We don't need the money. I won't send my patients to another hospital."

"THIS IS STILL THE WORLD OF THE WASP," said Mother. "You'll never see a president who isn't a male, white and Protestant."

"It's not fair," said Jane.

Mother often belittled us, desperate to fit us into her mold of who her daughters should be.

"Don't be so naïve. What's fair about life? We *are* different. We speak, think, and vote differently. Stop denying who you are and be thankful that you're lucky." I thought about it, and what she said was true. We did speak differently, and we recognized each other by the way we spoke and what words we used. In our house, drapes were always *curtains*. Couches were *sofas*. Yachts were *boats*. We lived in *houses,* not homes. People were rich, never *wealthy*. We had our own language and we learned it from childhood.

As children, we didn't care what Mother thought. We had Rosie, the housekeeper, a stout, Irish Catholic woman who mothered us like her own. The queen of clichés, and her favorite one was, "God never closes one door without opening another." She had gray, kinky hair, eyes the color of moss, and she wore horn-rimmed glasses and a cheap silver cross around her neck. She had multiple chins and a wart on her left cheek with a hair growing out of it; but to my eyes, she resembled an angel. She became our refuge when our mother was unreachable and our father was at the hospital.

There were times Mother and Dad acted like sweethearts. Often, on balmy summer nights, I would see them strolling down the stone pathway, holding hands, walking to the water's edge. Sometimes they would stop, and I would see my father pointing up to the sky, probably identifying a star, then lean over and kiss her. I knew they loved one another, but I just couldn't figure out why my mother was angry so much of the time.

OUR GARDEN WAS INFORMAL, English Cottage in style, a kaleidoscope of color, like an artist had carelessly splashed paint on a canvas. As the seasons changed, so did the landscape, but my favorite, was always spring. I chose it for its rebirth: the sight and sound of migrating birds, the return of greenness to the landscape, the less chilly breezes, the bursting spring colors—yellow, white, purple.

By summer, after the lilacs had lost their bloom, clusters of rosebushes and day lilies blossomed, turning the grounds of Cornwall into a botanical paradise. Amid this setting, we watched the sea, its palette changing from a dull gray to a brilliant blue, dotted with sailboats like tiny toys tangoing through the waves. At low tide, we could see the seals with their shiny black coats, reclining like sunbathers on the jutting rocks. At high tide, the crashing surf cascaded over the boulders that abutted the inlet. Our family would swim on that stony little beach on hot summer days until our lips (the children's) turned blue from the frigid water. Daisy, my dog, would lick the salt off my face as I lay giggling in the sun, drying off.

In the spring, Jane and I would wade through fields of buttercups and thick stalks of purple lupine, with the pungent smell of pine from the trees blotting out everything else. We'd make bouquets of wild flowers, and Rosie taught us how to dry them. We led an idyllic childhood with our sixty-year-old playmate Rosie, with her ponderous bosoms and her belly that shook like Jello.

In the autumn, Maine changed her coat to scarlet, persimmon, and gold. It was hypnotic, and years later, when I was far away, the memory of it would haunt me. By Halloween, Charles would rake the fallen leaves into huge piles—then burn them. Our family, neighbors, and friends would gather together, drink cider, and eat Rosie's pumpkin cookies as we watched the leaves crackle and burn. We danced around the fire in our Halloween costumes, dressed as witches and devils and cats and everything else that was scary, while our two family dogs, Jack and Daisy, barked at us as if we were crazy.

Winter was long, too long, but at times, nothing less than magical. I would watch the snowflakes float down to the ground, then press my nose against the cold, frosty windowpanes. After a heavy snowfall during the night, the next morning would be sunny and bright. The trees and shrubs, encased in ice, resembled a fairyland. In the shadows, the snow was actually blue-gray, a color I had never seen anywhere except in Maine. Two or three times a year, a "nor'easter" would come roaring up the coast. We would hear it before we saw it—the wind howling and whistling like a phantom train. Blinding snow, which we called "a whiteout," would streak horizontally by the windows. We'd be thrilled—no school that day—and maybe not the next one either.

ALTHOUGH OUR HOUSE WAS LARGE, it had a feeling of warmth and charm usually found in cozy, smaller houses. This was due mainly to my mother's excellent taste and fondness for family antiques, and lots of silver framed photographs and piles of books everywhere. Flowered chintz slipcovered nearly every piece of upholstered furniture in the house. When needed they were replaced with the same fabric if possible, but only when they became threadworn. Mummy didn't like changes. She would preach: "I like a house that looks lived in. It says who we are."

When I grew older, I discovered that there was a name for this; Mother and her friends called it "understated elegance," while others were more disdainful and dismissed it as "reverse snobbery," and nobody did it better than wealthy Maine Yankees, not even the Boston Brahmins. New houses, with new furniture and new people spelled only one thing to my mother, *Nouveau Riche*.

I never realized until I was old enough to visit friends' houses how unique our house was in comparison. Whenever I brought new friends home, they'd stare in awe at the soaring stairwell. Usually they'd say something like, "Wow! I never saw a home like this. It's so-o-o-o big!"

"My grandfather built this years ago. It's just an old house," I'd say.

The foyer was striking; black and white squares of marble covered the floor like a checkerboard. A shimmering antique Aubusson carpet lay on its surface, and suspended from the high ceiling was a Baccarat crystal chandelier that sent off every color of the spectrum. How many times had I slid down the banister with Jane and Robby following my lead, while portraits of dour-faced ancestors hung from the walls staring down at us? The last time Robby did it, he got a splinter in his ass and let out a howl that was heard throughout the house. My mother gave him a stern lecture as Daddy dug it out with tweezers and painted it with Mercurochrome.

Above the library mantel hung a portrait of Mother in her twenties. A light above the frame illuminated her shoulder length, golden hair. She wore a lilac-blue velvet dress that matched her eyes, with a deep oval neckline and a three-strand pearl choker. Her eyes followed you everywhere. No wonder Daddy married her. I would never be *that* beautiful. It didn't occur to me until years later, after the frizz turned to curls and the blemishes on my skin disappeared, that I inherited her incredible eyes as well as her golden hair. At the age of thirteen, I thought I was ugly.

My parents had separate bedrooms that were connected by a large bathroom. I thought it was strange that they didn't sleep in the same room, as other married couples did, but Mummy said it was because Daddy was in and out of the house all hours of the night, and he didn't want to disturb her. I knew they slept together sometimes, because my little brother, Robby would burst in on them when he had a nightmare.

Mother's room was painted yellow with white woodwork. Her French Empire lounge placed in front of a large bay window overlooked the sea. Her prize possession hung on the wall in her bedroom: an original Monet of water lilies, which had been bought in the late forties for only seven thousand dollars. Years later, it would be worth millions.

The only photographs in her room were of dead people, a small one of her parents, and another of her brother Peter, who died in the Second World War. It was as though *we* were not her family. My Meredith grandparents died together in an accident when I was a toddler. The details remained a mystery. My mother never spoke of them, and I envied my friends who had grandparents who fussed over them. My Mason grandparents were gone too, but they had been older and died of natural causes.

My room, with its panoramic view of the ocean, was my sanctuary. Hearing the waves splash against the shoreline lulled me to sleep at night. My collection of dolls and stuffed animals were my little family, as well as my dog, Daisy, a West Highland terrier, who always slept at the foot of my bed.

Mother thought every educated young girl should study music, and so Jane and I took piano lessons. She was gifted, I was not. Week after week, I struggled with the same old piece. I hated piano lessons. On one occasion, Jane and I were practicing a duet for a recital to take place a month away. It was a simple little piece, so Jane agreed to do it for my sake. While playing on the baby grand in the living room, with forty feet of French doors and windows that scanned the Atlantic Ocean, I became distracted—no, bored is more like it. Jane was twelve and disciplined, and although I was two years older, I was not.

"We have to practice, Suzy! If not, we'll look like a couple of fools. You remember what Mrs. Johnson said, don't you?" said Jane.

"Yeah, yeah. I hate playing Beethoven. It's too hard. It has too many flats."

I got up from the piano bench and walked over to the coffee table to get a mint. In front of the fireplace, twin love seats faced each other, divided by a white marble coffee table. Every couple of days, mother arranged a spray of fresh flowers amid neat piles of *National Geographic, Smithsonian, and Vogue* on top of the table.

We heard our parents in the hallway, and I knew they were coming into the living room, as they always did when my father came home from the hospital. Except for summer, there was always a blazing fire in the fireplace by late afternoon as there was on this day. They usually had a martini together and talked. It was their private time.

"Let's hide on Mummy and Daddy behind the Chinese screen and surprise them."

Jane giggled, and we hid.

I heard my father say, "Edith, I have something to tell you, and it's going to be difficult for me, so please listen."

"Good heavens, Robert! After all these years, you aren't going to tell me that you're involved with another woman, are you?"

"Of course not darling," he replied. "How could you think such a thing? I've never cared for anyone but you."

"Well, you're scaring me. What is it then? You look upset."

"I did something. I think it's morally right, but legally it's wrong. I performed…an abortion…I had no choice."

"Are you crazy? It's against the law. I don't understand."

"A patient of mine came in to see me. She's a poor woman living in poverty you've never seen or could imagine. While she was pregnant with her last child, her husband raped their thirteen year old daughter, and she became pregnant as well."

I covered my mouth with my hands so I wouldn't make a sound. Jane was bug-eyed, listening intently.

"Edith, she was just a child. Her mother sent her to live with her grandmother. She'll be all right…The abortion went well."

"Does anyone else know?"

"Just you. I did it in my office after hours. There's something else. This wasn't the first time," he admitted.

"I can't believe you're saying this. Why are you telling me?"

"Because I want you to understand; the law is *wrong.* I did it before, only twice, but that's all. They were poor women who had large families and had suffered previously from postpartum depression just like you, only much worse. They had both tried to kill themselves."

"Are you saying you did this for me?"

"In a way."

"Are you going to do it again, Robert?"

"I don't know. I hope I don't have to. No promises. I *hate* abortions. It's against everything I've been taught, but I also made an oath to do no harm. In my heart, I felt that I was morally right. I saved two women and one child from terrible consequences."

"I'm going to tell you something, Robert. Something even you don't know about me."

Oh, my God! Is she going to tell him that she had an illegal abortion before she met him? Jane's mouth was wide open, and I was afraid of what else we were going to hear. I heard my mother get up from the sofa and pace around the room.

"My freshman college roommate, Elsa, performed an abortion on herself with a wire coat hanger. I never saw so much blood in my life. She was in the bathtub, and if I hadn't found her in time, she would have died with a punctured uterus. I never told anyone except the doctor in the Emergency Room. If I had, she would have been ruined. She dropped out of Wellesley, and the last I heard, she was at Smith. I haven't seen or heard from her in all these years."

My heart was pounding. I couldn't possibly imagine my mother in a situation like that. She was always so proper. Daddy just listened. I'm sure he was as stunned as we were.

"Robert, you did what you had to do. Someday they'll change the law, and some abortions, the necessary ones, like those for incest and to save the mother's life will be legal. I just hope they don't go too far."

"You're amazing. You saved your friend's life. You do understand."

"Robert, promise me one thing. You must be careful, and it must always be because there is no alternative. I don't want you to end up in jail and lose your medical license. Even though I complain about being a doctor's wife, I'm actually very proud of you."

"I promise, darling. Let's go take a walk down to the water. I have more to tell you."

I heard the sound of the French doors opening to the terrace, and then closing. They were gone.

We stood there, hardly believing what we had heard.

"Holy Shit!" I said.

Suzanne, swearing is a sin," lectured my sister.

"Who *cares* if I swear once in a while? What's the big deal, Miss Goody Two Shoes? Do you realize what we heard? Daddy could go to jail, locked up like a criminal."

As daughters of an obstetrician, there was little that we didn't know about the facts of life, and it was still hard to imagine that my parents did *that*. It sounded horrible and must be terribly embarrassing. I spent many a rainy afternoon looking at his medical books about conception and childbirth.

Jane said, "I'm hungry. Let's go see what Rosie cooked for dinner."

SCHOOLS IN CAPE ELIZABETH weren't up to Mother's standards. She had gone to the Spence School in New York City, Northfield Boarding School for Girls, and later, to Wellesley College. Both my parents were sent away to boarding school, but hated it, so we attended the only private school in Portland that wasn't Catholic: Westview.

We wore boring uniforms: pine green jumpers and white blouses. Boys wore chinos, blazers, white shirts, and green ties. What was the good of savoring our fashion bible, the magazine *Seventeen,* if you never got a chance to wear the latest fashions to school?

On weekends we went wild and wore what *we* wanted: jeans rolled up to our calves, bobby socks, saddle shoes, and best of all, our fathers' white shirts.

My mother was horrified. "Why in heaven's name are you wearing dungarees like a farmer? And leave your father's shirts alone."

"Oh, Mother, please! Nobody calls them dungarees anymore."

On Friday and Saturday nights, we held pajama parties, drank coke, smoked cigarettes, put our hair up in pin curls, and at parties jitterbugged to the music of Bennie Goodman, Louie Armstrong, and the late Glenn Miller, whose music was more popular than ever.

My two best friends at school were Lorna Heinz and Elena Lucca. Mother didn't approve of them. Elena's parents were first generation Italian-Americans and even worse, Lorna's parents were German-born. Mummy lost her younger brother, Peter, during the invasion in Normandy. He was a Ranger, killed on deadly Omaha Beach. His commanding officer sent a letter to his wife praising him and his heroism. His remains were buried in the American Cemetery in Normandy. That, combined with the horror of the Holocaust, convinced my mother that many Germans were inhuman and evil. Only six years had passed since the war ended, but to Mummy, it was like it happened yesterday.

Mother spoke to Lorna with icy cold politeness, causing her to ask me if my mother liked her. At first, I was going to lie, but I decided to be honest with her.

"It's not that she doesn't like you personally, it's that her brother was killed by the Germans."

"Well, that's no reason," she shouted. Her hazel eyes narrowing to slits. "I lost my German relatives in the war too, but I don't hate Americans. War is war."

"Yes, but *they* started the war, and because of it, millions died."

Once, at the Heinz seaside cottage at Higgins Beach, Lorna's mother said, "The Jews got exactly what they deserved." I froze on the spot. She recounted the Depression following the First World War when she lived in Germany. She blamed the Jews for the inflation that ruined the country.

She claimed, "A whole wheelbarrow of money would buy only one loaf of bread. People were going hungry until Hitler came into power. Jews owned all the businesses. They brought it on themselves."

"Why did the Germans kill all those people in concentration camps? Old people, women, children, and even little babies," I asked—I wanted an explanation.

"That's a Roosevelt lie!" she yelled, "The allied bombers killed them—Americans and British."

I bit my lip, afraid of what I might say next. I was brought up to respect my elders. I knew I had a big mouth, my mother told me often enough. Personally, I had always thought of Mrs. Heinz as being kinder and more hospitable than her own daughter, Lorna. After that, I wasn't so sure. Did she really believe that stuff? Although my own mother was prejudiced, there was no malice or hatred in her, only her own misguided ideas about people she didn't know or understand.

However, my classmates were not the least bit prejudiced. Both of my friends were the most popular girls in the class. Lorna was pretty, buxom, and blond—an unbeatable combination with boys. Her long blond hair, so light and shiny that it almost glowed like platinum, was the thing that made her stand out. She wore it in a pageboy with part of it falling down over one of her hazel eyes, thus dubbing her the "Veronica Lake" of our class. Almost everyone liked her, except a few jealous girls who called her names behind her back, such as "Eva Braun" or "Big Boobs." I always defended her and considered her my second best friend.

Elena was first and we met as small children at the Portland Boy's Club while taking swimming lessons. At Westview, we became reacquainted. She was the smartest girl in our class, and one of the most popular. Elena always shrugged it off and explained that she was blessed with a photographic memory, which made memorizing long passages of words easy for her. She aced all her tests. Her sparkling personality and diligence made her the darling of all the teachers, except for one who complained to my mother that Elena was never wrong, and that was very intimidating to a young teacher. She was thoroughly Italian looking, small-boned with dark eyes and hair, and a slightly prominent nose. Like me, she was not considered in the same class as Lorna when it came to the looks department. Neither of us as yet had "developed," which is a very big deal when you are teenager. I finally wised up and bought a padded bra.

Although I was blond and blue-eyed like my mother, I inherited my father's tawny complexion, wavy hair, and heart shaped face. Mummy said that I got my skin color from some unknown Black Irishman on my father's side. I asked her if it meant that I had colored blood. She laughed, and said, "Oh no, dear! In the sixteenth century, during a war with England, sailors from the Spanish Armada jumped ship in Ireland and intermarried with the Irish. Your father has a little Irish in him, so I like to kid him about it."

One night, I got into an argument with my mother. She criticized me for biting my nails, which was in her estimation a major crime. Then she started in on my grades at school. They weren't good enough. She was never satisfied. I ran into my room and slammed the door as hard as I could.

I wished I had the courage to say, "Shut up," to her. I was furious.

I flung myself on the bed, about to have a good cry, with Daisy licking my face, when my telephone rang. It was Lorna. "Hi Sue, guess what?" Without waiting for my answer, she continued, "I've got a dreamy guy for the senior prom at Portland High School, and he's got two friends who need dates. They're both swell fellows, just shy. I thought of you and Elena. She's going—"

I stammered, completely forgetting all the melodrama with my mother, and asked, "What about *my* date? Who is he? Wait a minute. I need a cigarette, I'm so-o-o-o nervous." I reached under the bed for the ashtray and cigarettes, and quickly opened both windows to let out the smoke. If my mother came in and found me smoking, I'd be dead—grounded forever.

"Go on, tell me more." I puffed nervously, but didn't inhale because it made me dizzy. I had only begun smoking a few weeks earlier.

"He's a cousin of Michael's, who's my date. His name is Jim Aliberti. He's never been to a prom before, so you'll both be in the same boat." She paused, and then continued, "He's not so great looking, but he *is* the center on the basketball team."

"What do you mean? What's wrong with him?"

"Well, he's tall…and thin…and has big feet, but he's a nice guy. You don't have to worry about him. Michael said he's a real gentleman."

I hesitated. He didn't sound like my type, whatever that was. "Gee…I don't know if I should. I could get in big trouble with Mom."

"That never stopped you before. *Please*, Suzanne. It'll be lots of fun."

"…Okay, I'll go. If Elena is willing to go, so will I." As soon as I hung up, I called her.

She was as excited as I was, but apprehensive also, as neither of us had ever been on a date. I kept thinking, what if he tries to kiss me? What will I do? The only boys I had ever kissed were at parties when playing spin-the-bottle.

We were juniors, only sixteen. Portland High School, the inner city high school, was made up mostly of students from blue-collar and ethnic families, people I didn't know. I knew I would have to lie to Mother, but that wasn't anything new. She automatically said no whenever I asked her if I could go anywhere. Sometimes, I got a maybe, but never a yes.

The big night came, and I told her that I was going to a slumber party at Elena's house. Charles drove me there with my suitcase containing my secret contraband: gown and accessories. Elena's mother, a former beautician helped us with our hair and make-up. I couldn't believe that I had mascara and rouge on my face. If Mummy could see me now, she'd have a bird.

At the beautiful ballroom of the Eastland Hotel, I met Michael Conti, Lorna's date, and for the first time in my life, I had a crush on a guy. My heart almost stopped beating. He was gorgeous: a cross between my two favorite movie stars—Tyrone Power and Gregory Peck—who both had a widow's peak and gorgeous black wavy hair. Michael's dark brows rested straight across almost to the bridge of his nose, over honey-colored eyes with long bristly lashes—and when Michael smiled, which was all the time, I was *dazzled.*

My date, Michael's cousin Jim, towered over me and was even thinner than I had imagined—a real beanpole. His face was covered with little bumps from acne and he'd cut his face shaving. He stunk of cigarettes. Forcing a smile, I listened as he droned on about basketball. "I scored twenty points when we played Deering, and twenty-five points when we played Cheverus." *What a bragger!*

His clumsy feet ruined my white satin pumps, only my second experience with high heels. He was a terrible dancer and when he tried to jitterbug, he sent me flying across the floor smack into another couple. I was so embarrassed. Those big clodhoppers tore the hem of my very first evening dress—a strapless gown of lilac silk and white toile, and now it was ruined. My mother bought it at Bonwit Teller in Boston for my Cousin Amanda's formal wedding.

Michael didn't see me at all—I was invisible to him. He laughed with Elena and her date, David Bennett, Michael's best friend. I watched him gawking at Lorna as she swung her platinum hair off her face and teased him with her hazel cat's eyes. Midway through the evening, Michael politely danced two obligatory dances with me, while, all the time, his eyes were darting around the ballroom seeking out Lorna. I only reached up to his shoulder. I inhaled his clean scent, which I was sure was Old Spice, the same as my father's after-shave lotion. We exchanged small talk but we never made eye contact. I was too shy and he wasn't looking at me anyway. I said stupid things like how much I hated playing the piano. He added, "I'm not good at music either."

Lorna had bragged that he had lettered in three sports and was the most popular boy in the senior class. I also knew he was smart—the valedictorian of his class, as well as the class president. My God! He was just too perfect. Far too perfect for someone like me.

There was no doubt that they were the best-looking couple on the floor, and all eyes were on them. He wore a black tuxedo, and she wore a waltz-length gown of pale blue. I thought that Lorna was a lucky girl to have Michael for a boyfriend.

Later that evening, the tempo changed and I was doing the boring box step with Jim like eighth graders; he didn't know how to do the fox trot. We were only a few feet away from Michael and Lorna. They couldn't see me, but I overheard Michael say to Lorna, "Too bad that beautiful dress was wasted on your friend. It would have been sensational on you."

Lorna retorted, "What's wrong with *my* gown?"

"Hey! I'm a guy. What do I know? Your gown is beautiful, too. I just meant it's a sexy dress, and she still looks like an kid."

"Well, okay, if that's what you meant." Lorna started to giggle and said, "I shouldn't tell you this, but the gown probably would have fallen down if she hadn't been wearing a padded bra. She doesn't have the figure for a strapless gown. Isn't that hilarious?" He obviously agreed, because he laughed and laughed. I turned my burning face away from Jim, so he wouldn't see my eyes fill with tears.

Lorna continued, "Her parents are loaded. You should see her house; it looks like a goddamn museum, and her mother is the biggest snob I ever met."

Michael snickered, and I hated both of them.

Jim pretended that he hadn't heard anything, but I knew that he had. I was humiliated, and wanted to disappear. To his credit, Jim tried to distract me with a funny story about his little sister and I laughed through my teary eyes.

After the dance ended, Jim asked me if I wanted to go to a party. He hinted that they might have a "real" drink there. I said no, and I knew that he was relieved because he wanted to get rid of me. He drove me back to Elena's house in a pouring rain. The latch that held the convertible top down was broken, and I tried to hold it with my hands, but the wind kept catching it. I was soaked, my hair was plastered to the sides of my face, my ugly corsage of carnations drooped, and my gorgeous dress was ruined.

He snarled, "What a lemon! I'll never borrow this car again," as the muffler roared back at him. I shivered from the cold as I watched my date from hell lose his temper.

He didn't try to kiss me goodnight. If he had, I would have slugged him. Only tramps kissed on the first date and, as far as I was concerned, there would never be a second. The feeling was mutual, because Jim never called me again. When Charles picked me up at Elena's house the next morning, I told him the truth and asked him not to tell my mother. He winked at me, and I knew I was safe. He had been with us forever, even before Rosie. Because he was a man, I was never able to talk to him as I did with Rosie; however, I trusted him completely.

The next day, after hearing about Michael and Lorna's remarks, Jane was livid.

"That witch is no friend of yours, and he sounds like a big jerk."

I listened as I hung my head over the side of the bed hoping to stretch my neck so I could look more like Audrey Hepburn, my idol.

Nevertheless, in time I forgave Lorna, never dreaming that Jane's opinion of Lorna was true. Although hurt, from Michael's cruel remark about me being a kid: and from his insinuation that I was flat chested, I still felt giddy thinking about him—after all, you can't fight chemistry. I asked Jane if she believed in love at first sight. "No, of course not," she said. "I'd have to know someone a long time before I could fall in love."

I wasn't so sure. I couldn't think of him without my stomach flip-flopping. At night, in bed, I remembered the songs we danced to. *It Had to Be You,* and the other, *Moonlight Serenade*. I bought both records and must have played them a hundred times, shutting my eyes and fantasizing that I was again dancing with Michael. Knowing

Lorna, I knew that it wouldn't last long. She was after bigger fish to fry than someone whose father was a barber.

Someday I knew we'd meet again and I would accomplish two things—I would even the score, and he would be as enamored by me as I was by him. Of this, I was certain. However, I didn't know that it would take five years.

When I graduated from Westview a year later, I was accepted to every college to which I applied. I decided upon Radcliffe. Lorna and Elena would be nearby at Boston College.

The entire graduating class consisted of thirty-eight students. Our picture appeared on the front page of the society section of the *Sunday Telegram.* All the girls wore floor-length white dresses and held long-stemmed red roses. The boys wore green blazers and ties, with a white carnation in their lapels. Mummy said that we were now members of society, and everyone who picked up the newspaper would know it as well. Daddy muttered, "Edith, don't fill Suzanne's head with such nonsense."

"When I was a young lady of eighteen, I made my debut—"

Jane cut her off and said, "We know Mummy. You made your debut in New York City, one of six girls, your escort was the son of the governor, and the party was at the Ritz. Blah, blah, blah."

"Robert, how do you expect us to get any respect when you encourage her to be rude?" she asked.

"I would rather have my children be rude than think they are better than someone else just because they've had had more opportunities."

I MADE SOME FRIENDS at Radcliffe, young women my mother found acceptable, but nobody replaced Lorna and Elena. I was disenchanted listening to the debutantes discuss their coming out parties, or whether this boyfriend had *real money*, or if the family was just *well-to-do*, and to which elite clubs their boyfriends belonged. Most of the students had known one another from boarding schools like Miss Porter's, Madeira, or a prestigious day school like Brearly in New York City. Meeting them, I finally understood the world from which my mother came. Fortunately, I made friends with other girls who were more down-to-earth.

In its entirety, Radcliffe changed my life for the better. Finally, I knew who I was, not who someone else expected me to be. My fondness for books and writing blossomed. I decided that I wanted to become a journalist. If Jane could dream about becoming a doctor, why couldn't I chase my own impossible dream?

Socially, I was average. In my freshman year, I spent most of my time on my studies. That first year I dated rarely, and by my sophomore year had gained a reputation of being aloof with boys. The truth was, I was still shy and unsure of myself. By my junior year, something miraculous happened: I met Andreas and fell in love for the first time.

Chapter 2

FOREIGN INTRIGUE

At the end of my junior year in college, my family took a six-week Grand Tour of Europe. In New York City, we arrived at Pier Ninety and saw the huge white letters—*QUEEN ELIZABETH*—across its enormous blue hull. This was our first trip to Europe and we were eager to board her, the largest and grandest ship afloat. She was the ultimate—a majestic floating city.

Each evening, we dressed formally for dinner in the first-class dining room, providing my mother with the opportunity to show off her gowns and jewelry, especially when dining at the Captain's table. Few young women were passengers, so Jane and I were much in demand as dancing partners by the junior officers.

Robby met a Spanish girl slightly older than him and she tried to teach him the tango. He just couldn't get the hang of it; his legs kept getting tangled up in hers. We almost collapsed with laughter watching him. Gamely, he attempted a dramatic ending to the dance. He bent her backward, her long dark hair touching the floor, her high-heeled shoe pointing towards the ceiling, and then—he accidentally dropped her on her bottom. Everyone laughed. Robby, red-faced and flustered, helped her to her feet, and apologized profusely. Without missing a beat, she grabbed him and kissed him on the mouth like she meant it. Then everyone applauded her for being such a good sport. My silly brother looked as though he was going to die from happiness as they slipped away together for a stroll along the deck or something more adventurous.

I heard my father say to my mother, "Robby's only seventeen, but I think he's a chip off the old block."

"Robert, *you* were a good dancer," my mother said with a dead-pan face.

Jane and I whispered together about Robby. We wondered what would happen with the Spanish number. "Do you think he's done *it* yet?" asked my sister. Even though we were older, we were girls and had not done *it* yet. The rationale being that it was okay for boys of a certain age to have a little experience—that is, unless he got someone pregnant. And then he would be in big trouble. I'm sure, knowing my father, that Robby had been told to keep his fly zipped.

"I don't think so. But he probably will before this trip is over. European girls are much more uninhibited." Of course, I didn't know what the hell I was talking about, but I think I impressed my younger sister with my worldliness. The next morning at breakfast, Robby was strangely quiet with a stupid grin on his face.

The ship had many decks, some as long as a football field, and it was impossible to see and do everything. The ship's hospital was even equipped for surgery and that really impressed Daddy. Jane and I were more interested in the spa. My parents played shuffleboard and bridge, and wrapped themselves in blankets on the deck chairs on the starboard side, which was the sunniest, while we crossed the frigid waters of the North Atlantic. I felt a chill when one of the ship's young officers pointed out the place where the Titanic had sunk. We spent five luxurious days being pampered and entertained before we landed in Southampton, England.

I hadn't expected London to be such a beautiful city. It was a wonderful surprise to see the many parks with stretches of emerald green lawns and colorful beds of flowers. Wonderful old churches and museums were everywhere. At Westminster Abbey, I noticed a plaque honoring Henry Wadsworth Longfellow, poet laureate born in Portland, Maine, and the only American poet so honored. Also, I was fascinated by all the famous historical figures that were entombed there, especially Queen Elizabeth and Mary Queen of Scots.

On a day trip to Canterbury we visited the old Cathedral, and I stood on the very spot where Sir Thomas Beckett, the Archbishop, was assassinated, and later, awarded sainthood by the Catholic Church.

My love of history was paying off. I could almost see the bloodstains upon the ancient stone floor on the exact spot where Beckett was murdered. (Or so the guide told us.)

Like all tourists, we walked the route of the pilgrims in *The Canterbury Tales.* I had never appreciated Chaucer before, but I vowed to reread the book when I got home. We had lunch at a local pub in this quaint little town before returning to London on the train.

The next stop was Paris, "The City of Lights." The wonderful museums, the *Louvre* and the *Jeu de Paume,* the broad boulevards, the Eiffel Tower, and the Seine River that divided the right and left banks of the city. It was even more enchanting and romantic than I had expected. One of the most beautiful places was the ancient *St. Chapelle,* which glittered like a jewel box with its fifteen stained-glass windows, so brilliant, the colors shimmering in the morning sunlight.

No trip to Paris would be complete without a visit to *Nôtre Dame*, with its grotesque gargoyles and exquisite rose windows. I could almost see the hunchback peering out of one of the gargoyles. We enjoyed its beauty a second time while dining at the legendary *La Tour d'Argent* which stood across from the church. We chose the specialty of the restaurant, duckling in orange sauce, as we viewed an illuminated *Nôtre Dame* in the evening.

It was all so romantic when Daddy lifted his wineglass and made a special toast, "To my lovely wife Edith on her forty-sixth birthday." Then he kissed her cheek and handed her a jewel box. She opened it up and took out a gold *Cartier* watch. She gasped, "Oh Robert! It's so lovely. Thank you, darling," and then she leaned over and returned his kiss—on the lips. Robby gave us his parents-are-so-embarrassing look, Jane rolled her eyes, and I glanced around to see if anyone was looking. After such a rare display of affection by my parents, we were a little self-conscious, but we shouldn't have been—this was Paris.

Another must in Paris for a woman of elegance was a fashion show. We went to the House of Chanel where Mother bought a suit for herself costing an enormous amount of money. The models had no imperfections that were obvious and looked like living mannequins.

Jane said, "Who would want to be that thin? They look like they just got out of a concentration camp. Anyway, the clothes are much too expensive. It's obscene to spend that much money on one outfit. I could have bought a car for that amount of money."

"What do you know about clothes? These are originals by Coco Chanel. Of course they cost a fortune," I said.

"Coco Chanel was a Nazi sympathizer. She socialized with their generals," said my sister who read more than novels.

Mother interrupted, "Girls, behave yourselves. This is supposed to be fun. And another thing, Jane, is there anything you *don't* know?"

"I know I wouldn't buy a suit for ten cents from a Nazi lover," answered Jane.

"Jane, you always have to have the last word, don't you," said my mother. That shut her up. No way was she going to prove that mother was right.

On our last day, Robby went with Daddy to the Military Museum, and Mother took us to lunch at the Ritz, in the beautiful square, *Place` Vandome.* Surrounding the square were the most exquisite shops of Paris. Inside the hotel, we walked down the long corridor of endless display windows filled with the treasures of Paris—correctly called "Temptation Walk." We drooled with envy.

At *L'Espadon*, where everyone who was anyone went to dine and be seen, we saw at least a dozen gorgeously dressed women in designer outfits. Even Mother and her snooty friends back home would have looked dowdy compared to them. However, on this occasion, my mother wore her new Chanel suit and combed her hair in a French twist. She wore diamond earrings and a string of gold chains. She looked as elegant as any other woman in the dining room.

"Mother, look," I said as we were being seated. We saw Coco Chanel holding a long cigarette holder peering into the eyes of her much younger escort. When we passed her table, she put down her cigarette and gave my mother the once over.

I whispered to Mummy, "That's her, Coco Chanel, and she's looking at *you.*"

"Hush," she said, while faking a smile. As we neared our table following the maitre d', she spoke to me again—this time through gritted teeth. "What is wrong with you? Do you want her to think we're hicks from Maine?"

After we were seated, the Duke and Duchess of Windsor were guided to a nearby table and I heard the waiter address her as "Your Highness." Her voice was mannish and she did the ordering. "We're just having something light today, maybe just a consommé, a filet of sole, a green vegetable and some champagne. You know what vintage we like, Philippe."

"Of course, Duchess, as you wish," responded the waiter. He bowed slightly, backed away, and left. The Duke sat there smiling at his wife adoringly as he smoked his cigarette. Jane gave Mother the elbow, and whispered, "stop staring."

"Oh, yes dear, you're right. It's just that I never thought I'd see *them*."

Jane remarked, "God! He's such a little man, and she looks even thinner than the models. She's not very pretty, and she's so old."

Through clenched teeth, Mummy said, "For God sakes, will you *please* stop criticizing people!"

Although I was exasperated with both of them, I was more concerned for my mother and her fragile mental state. "Mother, calm down. This isn't good for you." I glared at Jane and she got the message. *Keep your mouth shut.*

"All right, all right, I *am* nervous, but one doesn't see people like them every day. Both of you are too young to know that he gave up his crown for her. He was a king, and she was a commoner, a twice-divorced American. It's one of the great love stories of the twentieth century."

Suddenly I became interested in what she had to say. I asked, "Did he do the right thing?"

"I don't know...He did it for love…Whether it was the right thing or not, it changed history, and his brother became the king."

THE NEXT DAY, WE RENTED A CAR and drove to Giverny in Normandy, to see Monet's home and gardens. There were two gardens, one surrounding the lily pond and another in front of his house. We were all struck with the beauty of the pond and the many varieties of lilies. It was a dazzling display of color.

The Japanese Bridge looked exactly as it did in his paintings. Rain started to fall at the pond, combining with the croaking sound of the frogs; it was almost like music.

Daddy said. "Darn it. The rain will spoil my pictures."

"No Dad," replied Robby. "They'll just be much more interesting."

My father wiped his camera lenses and clicked away. "You're right again, son. I think they will be."

We toured Monet's house, which was charming though small and modest. It was what we saw surrounding it that was so extraordinary. Broad beds of red, yellow, white, and blue flowers stretched out horizontally in front of his house. The floral bands of color were as inspiring as his paintings. We had missed the spring flowers, but the early summer ones were blooming. It was as though we were strolling through one of his paintings.

Mummy was eager to go to the American Cemetery in another part of Normandy, to visit her brother's grave as a family pilgrimage. It was the tenth Anniversary of D-Day. Nothing could prepare us for the beauty and the sadness of thousands of white crosses and stars of David. It was quiet and peaceful, and off in the distance was the ocean. We heard the comforting sound of the waves hitting the beach. Peter had died on that beach, on D-Day.

My father took out a copy of the letter sent to Peter's wife, Lisa, from his breast pocket and read it. It was from Peter's commanding officer.

Dear Mrs. Meredith,

As you know, Peter was a member of the elite Second Ranger Division, an all-volunteer outfit that belonged to C Company. Company A had landed earlier and had been virtually wiped out by the German machine guns at the top of the cliffs, so our company knew what we were heading into. By the time we landed, it was high tide on the western edge of Omaha Beach, and there was virtually no beach for a foothold, and what was there was too narrow with no place to take cover. Ahead of us was Pointe-du-Hoc with cliffs about one hundred and twenty feet high. Of the sixty-eight Rangers who landed, only thirty-one reached the base of the cliff. Peter was one of them, but he was shot before he reached the top. He died instantly. I know, because I was right beside him. He did not suffer. Lt. Peter Mason was my friend and a true American hero. He is with the Almighty and the rest of his comrades now. Bless you and your family.

Most Sincerely,
Capt. James Killinger

We viewed the beach with a renewed, quiet respect. It seemed an appropriate setting for Peter's final resting-place. I watched Mummy weep at her brother's grave, and leave a bouquet of violets.

"He was so young, too young to die. If you had only known him as I did," she said to us. "I guess he was too good for this world. Aunt Lisa was such a young widow with those two little babies, both still in diapers when he died. How he would have loved to see them grow up."

"Why don't we see them anymore?" I asked.

"Since Aunt Lisa remarried, we don't visit each other. Carol and Johnny have a new Daddy," said Mother.

Mother and her sister Marie were much older than Peter. After their parents had died, they had become his guardians. I remembered when Mother got the call from Lisa. She collapsed to the floor and cried until she was exhausted. When Daddy finally got her up, she fainted. She lived on sedatives for nearly five days. It took her two months to recover. She had suffered *another* nervous breakdown.

I remember overhearing Mother tell her older sister, Marie, "Thank God our parents are not alive. I don't think they could have stood it. Remember when they were in their forties and thrilled to finally have a son? And how happy we were to have a little brother?"

Marie answered wistfully, "Maybe it's a blessing they died together in that terrible car crash, and they don't have to go through this. No parent wants to survive their child. It's their worst nightmare."

"I know, and I'm thankful for that. But I can't forget that they died in a fiery explosion. Remember, Marie, we never saw their faces again."

It was the first time I had ever heard in any detail of how my maternal grandparents had died. I knew it was an accident but nothing more. She rarely talked of Peter either, except to curse the Germans. I began to wonder if my mother was afraid to love anyone. After all, she lost both her parents and her brother in premature deaths.

We spent a brief time in the south of France. It was lovely, full of happy people swimming and sunning themselves on the pebbly beaches with hundreds of brightly colored umbrellas and blue and white striped cabanas. The sea was dotted with white sailboats and speedboats pulling water-skiers. Women in skimpy bikinis were everywhere. A few bold women were even topless. Mummy said, "The French are too lenient about these things." Robby's male eyes were everywhere, not knowing which young girl to look at next. My father and brother exchanged looks the way men do.

The spectacular scenery in the hill towns, such as St. Paul de Vence was enchanting, but the memory of the rows and rows of crosses at Normandy haunted us. The pain of it was fresh in our minds, so we left for Italy and a change of scenery.

Whereas the French were aloof, the Italians were gregarious and cheerful. Even if they ostensibly had nothing to be happy about, they still laughed. Our tour guide in Rome pointed out the largest bank and said that it was going broke. Mother responded sympathetically. "That's too bad. I'm so sorry."

"Don't be, *Signorina*, it's normal. Ha, ha, ha," he laughed, his belly shaking like gelatin. "What do you expect? *This is Italy*."

I would need a hundred pages to describe the wonders of Rome, the charm of Florence, the excitement of Venice, the mystery of Pompeii and the beauty of the Amalfi Drive, with the blue-green water of the Tyrrhenian Sea, and the smoking Mt. Vesuvius—still threatening. With the cliffs and hanging pastel villas on one side of the road and the sea on the other, the scenery was breathtaking.

Robby asked the driver, "When do they expect another eruption?"

"Only God knows. It could happen any time, but when it does, it will be much worse. So many more people. All of Naples will be covered, but we don't worry about these things. Why worry? It does no good. I lived through the war. As you can see, I'm still here."

The guide raced the van along the twisting road and hairpin turns while he serenaded us with an aria from an opera by Verdi. We knew it was part of the tourist routine, but he did have a good voice. Of course, he honked his horn to warn anyone who might be turning the corner, but that did little to comfort me. We nearly went off the side of the cliff, or so it seemed. I heard the screech of brakes and the sound of my mother's scream. Was that tourist entertainment too, I wondered?

"Jeez! What a ride," said my brother. "The only thing better than this would be a ride on a motorcycle."

"Don't worry *Signorina*, I'm a good driver," he said as he turned around to reassure Mother who had gone white in the face.

The last country on our itinerary was Greece, and for me, it meant seeing my boyfriend, Andreas. Only Jane had met him. My parents didn't know he existed.

We spend three busy days in Athens, and take a day trip to Delphi, followed by an island cruise. I fall in love with the Greek Islands, especially Santorini, which some believe to be the lost Atlantis.

We go ashore in a speedboat that services the cruise ship. In the entire world, Santorini is unique—the only inhabited island built on volcanic residue. High up, built in tiers, cliff-side cave houses glow in incredible whiteness; the blue shutters that protect them from the winter wind and the blazing sun of August, are now open. Lacy curtains flap in the breeze. Terra cotta pots filled with red geraniums and other flowers sit on every step. The scent of lemon trees and jasmine follow us. Hundreds of feet below, our cruise ship appears no larger than a toy boat anchored in the turquoise bay.

In Crete, Greece's largest island, we rent a car for the day. Along the hillsides are cypress trees and twisted trunks of stone-gray olive trees. We catch the fleeting aroma of basil, sweet and intoxicating, and watch the bare-footed peasant women wearing black headscarves leave the olive groves riding their over-loaded donkeys. With their little sticks and high-pitched voices they urge the beasts to move along. "*Ella. Ella.*"

We find a cove, stop the car, change into our bathing suits and run to a deserted, pristine beach. The warm water, so salty we barely had to swim to stay afloat. I hear a conversation between my parents, "Edith, this is the best vacation we have ever had with the kids."

"I know, Robert, if only it could stay like this...There is no stress here. It's so peaceful. I get confused at home...and I can't cope.

Sometimes I don't like myself very much, and I know I've hurt my children."

"It's not your fault! Everything will get better. This trip has changed us both. I wasn't home enough, but now that will end. I can change. I know I can."

"I hope so Robert, I really do...And I'll try too."

I kept my eyes shut, pretending to sleep as I lay on my stomach on that sandy beach listening to my parents bare their souls.

UPON RETURNING TO ATHENS, I telephoned Andreas who summered on the island of *Hydra.* He and his family had dual citizenship though Andreas and his sister were born in the United States. He asked me to join him for lunch on his boat the next day. He wanted me to meet his sister and some of his friends. I was delighted because, although we had been dating nearly a year, I had not yet met his family or any of his Greek friends.

I told my parents I was going to visit a classmate on Hydra for the day. Mummy protested as usual. "We are in a foreign country, and you don't speak Greek. I don't think it's such a good idea. Who is this person anyway?"

"It's a friend, just a good friend. His name is Andreas Moustakis."

"What a mouthful," Robby said.

"Be quiet, you little creep," I said.

Mummy said, "Robert, I don't think it's a good idea."

Daddy came to my rescue. "Edith, she's a grown woman. We have to let go sometime. Besides, Suzanne is a sensible girl."

"Well, okay, if you say he's a friend, you can go, but be careful. The taxi drivers are crazy over here."

I met Andreas at the end of my sophomore year. He was a junior at Harvard. Although he was not handsome, he was interesting looking, with brown eyes, sandy hair, and a short-clipped mustache. I was more impressed with his mind than his looks. He knew so much about so many things, and he had traveled everywhere.

I took the ferry to Hydra out of the port of Pireaus, and about two hours later, I arrived. As we approached the island, I spotted the picturesque horseshoe harbor with its bright colored awnings, sidewalk cafes, and marina filled with boats—a mecca for local and visiting artists and boatsmen.

Andreas was there to meet me at the dock. He greeted me with flowers and a kiss. He clasped his arms around me, squeezing me tightly, and again kissed me, three times, first one cheek and then another. His mustache tickled my lips—it had been months since we had seen each other.

He whispered in my ear, *se aga po.* I smiled and answered, "I love you too, and missed you—more than I expected."

"Not more than I missed you." He kissed me again, this time for real. I was happy. Andreas *did* love me.

Together we walked to his boat, a cabin cruiser. I was surprised because it was much more elaborate and larger than I had expected.

"My father just bought it a few months ago because I told him you were coming for a visit…Only kidding, *Kukla.* My father hopes to use it for business entertaining, so don't be too impressed."

"I am impressed, but with you. You're so tanned. You look like a Greek god."

"Don't you mean a goddamn Greek?"

"No, I mean like Poseidon, God of the sea, if I know my mythology," I said.

He was wearing a Harvard sweatshirt, dark sunglasses, boat sneakers, and a skimpy European-style bathing suit that left nothing to the imagination. I could see that he was generously endowed.

"Are you staring at me?" he asked.

"No, of course not." I could feel my face getting hot, and I averted my eyes.

"Don't lie, Kukla. You *are* embarrassed. Don't be! Americans are too puritanical. We Greeks love the human body. Haven't you noticed that most of our statues are nude?"

An incredibly handsome young man helped me into the boat. His eyes were black and glinting like those of an Arab. He was dressed in white linen pants and a black silk shirt open at the neck. Like all Greek men, he wore a gold cross. "Welcome to Hydra, Suzanne, I'm Nikos."

Andreas introduced me to the others. "Suzanne, I want you to meet my friends Stellious, Spyro, Nikos, whom you have already met, my sister, Zoe, and my little cousin, Katina."

"*Yassou, Yassou,* Suzanne," they replied enthusiastically. They were all dressed in similar nautical outfits and looked far more cosmopolitan than I did in my jeans. For a while we sat in the marina and talked, laughing all the time. They all spoke English, though occasionally they slipped into Greek. They were mostly a cheerful group that made me feel welcome.

ANDREAS TOOK THE WHEEL, Spiro and Nikos untied the lines, and we left the charming harbor of Hydra.

His sister, Zoe, less animated than the rest of the crew, gave me only the hint of a smile as she fidgeted with the gold bangles on her wrist. His male friends and Katina, a teenager, were very friendly and, before long, we were at sea, singing Greek songs and drinking beer. Andreas took my hand and guided me to the bow of the boat so we could be alone. He asked Stellious to take the wheel. The water was calm, but the speed was exhilarating. We talked a little, but mostly we were lost in each other's arms. The wind was blowing my hair forward into my face, so I grabbed my scarf and tied it on in an Audrey Hepburn style, with the ties bound at the back of my neck. Andreas went to the cabin to get his hat and another beer, leaving me temporarily alone until Zoe came along and sat beside me.

"You can never marry him you know," she hissed.

Startled, I looked at her, seeing the hatred in her dark eyes.

"That's not an issue. He hasn't asked me."

"He will though. All he talks about is *you.* Even the boat is named *Andreas's Girl.* Of course, that's you."

"You don't seem pleased about it."

"To me, it makes no difference. To our parents, it means everything. He is going to be a diplomat and marry a Greek girl whom my parents approve of, like my second cousin Katina."

"Don't you think she's a little young for him?"

"She won't be in five or six years, and by then he'll be in the government. You will be just a memory. King Paul is my father's friend, and he has already requested my brother's service. An American wife would be most detrimental to him."

"And, what if I choose to ignore your parents' wishes? He doesn't want to become a diplomat. In fact, he hates the whole idea. He would much rather become an engineer and live in the States."

"You don't understand. You are not a Greek. He will lose his inheritance and his social position. My parents will never forgive him, and you will have ruined his life and theirs. Have fun together, but keep your head. It is impossible."

"We'll see about that, Zoe."

"Don't say I didn't warn you."

Andreas returned wearing a Greek sailor's hat, and Zoe said, "Suzanne and I had a nice talk. I'm sure we'll become good friends."

I felt as though I had met Medea.

He said, "So, tell me. What do you think of Greece?"

"It's wonderful—magical. I love the climate and the people, most of them."

"Could you live here?"

"I don't know. I'm an American. Even though it's 1954, in many ways this is still a third world country."

"Not if your name is Moustakis. We live very well. My family is prosperous and well respected. Baba knows King Paul personally, and Mama has had tea with Queen Fredericka."

"Well, I can't say that my father knows the president or my mother has had tea with the first lady, but we are a good family."

He dismissed my sarcasm as irrelevant and said, "I'm sorry you can't meet my parents but they're in Athens," said Andreas.

He was lying. I heard Zoe ask Katina to come back to the house after the boat ride to see her aunt and uncle.

Instead I said, "So are mine, and my mother will be convinced that I've been kidnapped if I don't get on the next boat."

Something like that is impossible here. Crime is practically non-existent," he said.

Before leaving for Pireaus, Andreas said, "I'm glad you and my sister hit if off. I have to have someone in my family on my side."

He cupped my face in his hands and kissed me. I returned his kiss, but in my mind I was thinking, *do I really love him enough to go though all this Greek tragedy stuff?*

I couldn't tell him the truth about his sister. I didn't know what the truth was, even about me. I wasn't sure about my own feelings.

He had too many faults, and he had just added another one—lying. He was an odd mix—insecure one minute and arrogant the next. Also, he drank too much, even for a college student. I don't think I ever saw him without a can of beer in his hand.

"Adio. I'll see you back in Boston," he yelled as the ferry left the dock. I waved and waved, and stood on the deck for a long time, until the island became a blur on the horizon. Like Ulysses, I was spellbound by the wine-blue waters of the Aegean; the magical sea of the Gods; wondering, *what the hell is love anyway*?

Chapter 3

ALL SCORES SETTLED

I began my senior year at Radcliffe on an Indian-summer day in September, uncertain in which direction to go after college. I could see that the traditional role of women was changing for some as we entered the second half of the twentieth century. By 1955 women were beginning to tire of being ingenious in the classroom and restricted in the workplace, only to move on to marriage and being mothers, as if it were their only option. Among my classmates were some young women who would choose a different path and become trailblazers in their chosen field. Corinne was going to be a trial lawyer; Nancy was going to be a biochemist; and Peggy, a colored girl, dreamed of a political career, with two obstacles to overcome. I was impressed with their fierce determination and energy—they were like my sister, Jane. I wanted to be done with school. Or did I? One more year and I would be free of studies, housemothers, and living with parents, but Columbia School of Journalism loomed in my mind too. Which way to go? If only I could decide.

Lorna could hardly wait to tell me about her latest conquest, Billy James, a fellow classmate at Boston College. Elena rarely dated, and as usual studied judiciously, although she majored in psychology, which some considered an easy ride through college. It was not as if becoming a psychologist was in her plans.

Upon returning to Radcliffe, I could hardly wait to see Andreas, despite his sister's warning. Zoe had delivered me a challenge, and I rarely passed one up. What was once just a college romance had turned into something else—a tug of war between his family and me.

Andreas was probably the first person who ever really listened when I spoke. He was loquacious, and we would chat for hours and never become bored. We argued and played devil's advocate, especially when discussing politics. We loved jazz, walking along the beach at Cape Cod, the Red Sox, and skiing. We took our first ski lessons together. We were both terrible, but we loved it anyway.

He thought I was very funny. While sitting with him and some friends at a pub in Boston, I asked, "Why can't they put draft beer in bottles?"

Everyone was in hysterics; all laughing at me, but no one laughed harder than Andreas. I felt like Lucy Arnez on the *I Love Lucy* television show, but I joined in along with the rest of them. Ironically, years later, someone did get around to putting draft beer in cans and bottles, so maybe I wasn't so stupid after all.

I was naïve about some things, particularly alcohol, and its effects. For Andreas and his friends, the main objective at a party was to get drunk. I shudder when I remember how many times I sat in his car when he drove while intoxicated. I thought, *he's all right; he's not slurring his words or staggering around.* However, looking back on it, how could he not be—after drinking eight, nine, or ten more beers? I hardly drank at all. I justified it by reasoning that all young guys drink. He'll change, I know he will. When he proposed marriage to me, I was stunned. At first I thought it had something to do with the drinking, but the next day, he repeated his proposal only more enthusiastically. We had known each other for several years, and gone from friendship to love, and although our sexual attraction was torrid, we never crossed the line. Andreas was always a gentleman. We both believed in celibacy before marriage.

There were too many things against us: we were still in school, we were both young, neither of our parents would have approved. Somehow, all of that now seemed insignificant. Without thinking, and disregarding all the danger signs, I foolishly accepted his proposal. I thought that love would conquer everything; we both wanted the same things—marriage and a family.

"Let's elope," he said. Once we're married they'll have to accept it."

"No, Andreas. I intend to marry only once, and I don't want to run away like we did something wrong."

"My parents will go ballistic, and I'll lose my inheritance, but that's okay—we'll still have each other. With my degree I ought to be able to get a job at something."

We agreed that he would tell his parents first—they were the toughest. I knew that I would have resistance too, but with my father's influence on Mother, it would come out all right.

It would be a test for him. Was this an act of rebellion, or would he be man enough to stand up to his family? I think I always knew it would never work out. I was an American, not a Greek. Also, my own doubts lingered. Was I in love with him enough to marry him, or was I just trying to prove I could get him?

When he went to Athens for Easter, he told his family and all hell broke loose. Relatives and friends came from all over to talk him out of it. The whole fiasco lasted only weeks. They wore him down, and eventually he succumbed. There would be no wedding.

When he returned to Boston, we sat in his car overlooking the Charles River. He looked terrible—tired and defeated like a whipped dog. His voice trembled, "I love you…but I love my parents, too…My father said he'd take a gun and shoot my mother and then kill himself."

I almost laughed—it was such a farce. Andreas actually believed that they would do it, which was even more ludicrous.

He was near tears, but I was angry. How dare he break my heart and humiliate me like that! Although my parents were in the dark, our close friends knew of our plans—we had told them. I guess we needed the moral support. That incident dictated all my future decisions—romantic or otherwise. Never again would I be so rash.

Greeks always had a flare for drama; after all, they invented it, though this was a bit extreme. A Greek-American friend informed me that this was standard behavior when you were romantically involved with a non-Greek or even another Greek that your parents found unacceptable. Her mother took to her bed and fainting spells when she wanted to marry an Armenian. It had worked. Helene, my college friend, had broken her engagement to her college sweetheart and ended up marrying a Greek-American doctor who was bald and ten years older. These were reliable, old tricks that Greek parents had used to keep their children in line and to marry whom *they* chose.

Andreas made his choice—and it wasn't me. Although it was corny, he told me, that it was better to have loved and lost, than never to have loved at all." Original, he was not. He dropped me off at my dormitory, and I dramatically slammed the car door with all my strength, hoping that one of the windows would break.

He had declared war on my pride. Damn him! Lorna invited six of my best girlfriends, including Elena, to her summer home at Higgins Beach that next weekend. We popped bottles of champagne, made toasts, and I vowed, "I'll never date another Greek."

I threw everything that reminded me of him into the hearth of the stone fireplace. A pile of pictures, cards and letters. Even gifts of semi-precious jewelry, including the scarab earrings that I rather liked. That night all my respect and love for Andreas went up in smoke in more ways than one. My friends applauded and cheered me on, chanting, "Andreas is a rat! Andreas is a rat!"

For several months, I was heartbroken and humiliated. Rejection hurts. Word got back to me that he was equally miserable…and drinking…more than ever.

He admitted to all our friends that he still loved me—couldn't get me out of his mind. After many months, he heard I was dating someone else, so he called me on the phone and asked to see me. We met in a Cambridge restaurant and had a coffee together.

The minute he walked in, I knew I no longer was in love with him, but I did still care about him. Although he was not my first infatuation, he was my first love. After a few awkward moments, he said, "Suzanne, I hear that you're dating someone pretty regularly. Is it true?"

"No. I date only occasionally. I'm concentrating on graduating from Radcliffe, which is enough of a challenge for me. Two more months to go and that's it."

"I know what you mean. Graduate school is a bitch, but I need it if I'm going to be a diplomat."

"What happened to engineering?" I asked.

"Ah, it was just a dream, just like you were a dream."

"Fight back, Andreas. Live your own life."

"I could do it if I had you," he said, his sad, brown eyes blinking behind his glasses. I knew he was blind as a bat without them. He continued, "Please, Suzanne. I was wrong to give you up. I'd propose again if I thought it would make a difference."

"No, it would *not* make a difference. It's just too difficult, too complicated. I love you—I'll always love you—but I can't be *in love* with you."

This time, I refused him and, strangely enough, I felt sadness instead of revenge. I didn't enjoy hurting him. I watched his face turn white, and he said, "I'll never love anyone the way I love you."

"Yes you will." *And she'll be Greek.*

His face crumbled. As I watched him disintegrate, I almost weakened, so before I could change my mind, I sprung up from the table and ran from the restaurant—out of his life forever.

For months I was numb—not wanting to be in love with anyone. It was too painful. Maybe I would be a journalist after all, if I could get a job at a newspaper after graduation. If not, maybe graduate school at Syracuse or Columbia. Then one day Lorna said, "You'll never guess who I bumped into at the museum?"

"Not wanting to play her stupid games," I said, "I give up. Who?"

"Michael Conti, my high school boyfriend."

I never relived that unforgettable night at the senior prom with Lorna, or anyone except my sister, Jane, and Elena. Never told her how angry she made me, or how hurt I'd been. Above all, I never clued her in on my crush on Michael, and I made Elena swear on a Catholic bible that she would never tell. Lorna continued the conversation giving me a list of Michael's achievements. He graduated from Bowdoin College, Phi Beta Kappa, Magna Cum Laude, and was now at Harvard Medical School.

"What did he do? Give you a run down of all his accomplishments?"

"No. Carrie Nichols told me. She was in his class in high school. Michael's not a bragger. If I had known then what I know now, I wouldn't have broken up with him. He was the best darn boyfriend I ever had, and boy, could he kiss!"

I thought it strange that Bill James, her present boyfriend, hadn't made the top of her list.

She continued, "He's still unattached. Imagine that!"

My heart jumped. We had only met once, and yet, even after five years the thought of him made me light-headed. I never told anyone, but several times over the years I had dreamed of him and they were not nice little girl dreams. Perhaps we would meet again, though I doubted it, and if we did, I was convinced that he wouldn't even remember me. Until now, I had forgotten about my vendetta with him, which now, five years later, seemed so foolish.

Jane was a student at the University of Maine in Orono, which offered a nursing degree as well as one in the liberal arts. Mother would have preferred one of the Seven Sisters colleges, but they compromised. It was a double major, but if anyone could handle it, it was my sister. My mother had hoped for better things for Jane—and being a nurse wasn't one of them. That's what ordinary people did, not a Mason.

Robby, in his first year at Yale, majored in partying. His first semester grades were not good. Daddy felt they would get better after he settled down. With all of us in college and out of the house, life was less stressful for my parents, and their marriage was the best it had ever been.

I was ecstatic when I graduated from Radcliffe. I made it and I had had my doubts as to whether I could do it. My parents were proud of me even though I didn't graduate with any special honor, for I had done the best I could. It was one of my happiest days, and to celebrate Daddy took the whole family to dinner at the Ritz Carlton, Boston's most venerable restaurant. The food and setting was beautiful, although the waiters and especially the wine steward were pompous and intimidating. There was no way that my mother was going to pay fifty dollars for a bottle of wine from France. She settled for a good Californian Chardonay.

TWO WEEKS LATER, ON A SUNDAY afternoon, my world collapsed. Sitting cross-legged on the floor with Lorna and Elena blowing smoke in each other's face and sipping wine in our newly shared apartment, the phone rang and, surrounded by unpacked boxes, Lorna stretched the telephone cord and handed me the phone. "It's Jane," she said.

"Oh, Suzanne, I'm so sorry...Daddy died...of a massive heart attack. He didn't suffer; he died instantly." She started to cry and I could hear my mother wailing in the background. Without answering, I dropped the phone. I opened my mouth to scream, and nothing came out. Not a sound—it was as though I were frozen. Lorna picked up the phone, and off in a distance, I heard her say. "What's wrong Jane?" Seconds later, I regained my voice and screamed, "*Nooooo! Nooooo!*"

In Elena's comforting arms, great gulping sobs took my breath away, and for the first time in my life, I experienced the agony of losing someone I really loved—in the most final way of all—in death. There would be no second chance to tell him I loved him, or to touch his face and feel the warmth of a living person, or to see his eyes look back into mine. There would be no parting words for me, and I felt cheated. I lost my anchor, my protector, my wonderful father. He was dead, and I wondered if I'd ever be happy again.

The funeral remains a blur. The service was as brief as Reverend Scott could allow, with a moving eulogy by Dad's best friend, Dr. Harry King. He even told a funny story about my father, but I didn't laugh; instead I sat in the front row and stared at his closed casket draped with a blanket of white roses, his favorite flower. In his coffin, I left a photograph of us together. Mother left a letter, and Jane and Robby left other personal keepsakes. In the row behind me, Rosie was sobbing and blowing her nose. I did not cry—there were no more tears left. At the church, every seat was filled with fellow doctors, nurses, friends, patients and, of course, family. He was loved and respected by people I didn't even know.

As requested in his will, the burial was private, and so we were a small group. It should have been raining, the wind should have been howling, and lightening should have been crackling in the sky. My father was dead—only forty-nine years old—a tragedy. Instead, it was a radiant June morning—the sky was a brilliant blue and birds were singing. Didn't they know my father had died? I took one of the white roses from the casket, which I later pressed into my Bible on the page containing the twenty-third psalm. My mother didn't want to leave. Although he was the one who died, my heart ached for her as well—she was so lost. She kept saying, "I don't want to live without

Robert. Why does everyone I love die?"

Uncle Hubert half-carried her back to the car. Jane and I remained, not wanting to leave. Robby stood nearby crying, the tears streaming down his young face. Rosie ran back to us, her heavy bosom heaving, her face swollen from crying.

"The dear man is with the angels. They'll take care of him." She put her soft comforting arms around us and steered us away. "Tis a sound that will haunt you forever if you stay and watch them shovel dirt over the grave. I saw them do it to me Pa. I've never forgotten it. Come away with me girls, and you too, Robby."

I REMAINED AT HOME FOR A MONTH. My new employer, *The Boston Post,* was very understanding, perhaps because the editor was also Aunt Marie's brother-in-law. Robby went off to Europe to travel with his college friends. My last words to him were, "Don't ride a motorcycle. Give me your word. One more tragedy and Mummy won't survive."

He nodded, gave me a hug, and said, "Don't worry about me. I'll be fine, and no bikes, I promise."

Mummy seemed to age overnight since Daddy died. She lost weight, and her hair was becoming more gray than blond. Her depression had returned, and we prayed that she would not have yet *another* nervous breakdown. She was so angry with Daddy for dying and leaving her alone, that some mornings she refused to get out of bed. Together, we forced Mother back into the world of the living with the help of an angel named Margaret.

A joyous event had occurred earlier in the year. Just one month before Daddy's death, his younger brother Hubert, a confirmed bachelor of forty-seven, had finally married. Hubert was now married to one of the richest women in America. Only Barbara Hutton and Doris Duke were richer. They had been introduced to one another at the Kentucky Derby when her horse, "Thunderbolt," won the race for the roses.

They married aboard her yacht in Monaco, and though none of us attended their private wedding, we delighted in his choice, even Mummy.

Margaret Bowes, an old-maid (Rosie's word) of forty, was petite and shapely, funny and gregarious. She had merry green-gray eyes and short-cropped hair the color of a copper penny. It was impossible not to like this ebullient woman who lit up any room she entered.

"Imagine that, a woman of her age, and most likely still a virgin," said my mother who still lived in her own world where women never engaged in sex before they married."

Rosie winked at us, "Oh, yes, Mrs. M."

My sister and I locked eyes—we had made a pact as teenagers that if we were still virgins by the time we reached thirty, we would definitely have an affair. There was nothing glamorous about being a thirty-year-old virgin.

All of us were fascinated with Margaret, and it gave Mummy a new focus and a new friend when she needed one badly. She even persuaded Mother to touch-up her hair and become a blond again, and to stop wearing black.

She said, "For God sakes, Edith, you look like a professional mourner. Do something about it!" She had found my mother's weakness—vanity. Mother never wore black again unless it was to a cocktail party.

Margaret and Hubert purchased the estate next to us, which was nothing more than a big old summer cottage on the ocean's edge with seven acres of land. When they got through remodeling it, adding a horse stable, a tennis court, and a swimming pool, it was without a doubt the most palatial estate in all of Southern Maine. Margaret named it, "Stonehedge." I was ecstatic—my house was no longer number one—and I was no longer *different*.

Stonehedge had twenty rooms, decorated by the famed interior designer, Sister Parrish, who had a reputation for making everything look like it was thrown together, sort of cottage-like and understated. However, the end result was always lovely. Within this setting, the walls were covered with priceless paintings: Winslow Homer paintings, John Singer Sargent portraits, and some of the best Impressionist paintings in the world, including a Renoir, which her father bought years before it soared in value.

"I just buy what I like," she said, but I think she had an eye for good art and recognized it when she saw it. Her favorite painting was Van Gogh's *The White Iris*, which she hung in her bedroom suite.

She told me it was so magnificent that she would never sell it while she lived. "Someday, if they build a proper museum in Portland, it will hang there and belong to the world."

She owned other homes as well: a Kentucky horse farm, a Palm Beach estate, two apartments, one in New York City and another in London. Her dominion also included a hundred and fifty-foot yacht that she moored in Monaco, as well as a private plane and innumerable commercial properties. She told Jane that this year she was giving up her Aegean cruise to spend more time in Maine to finish the remodeling and to help Mother.

Her two handsome brothers, Buddy and Thad, were international playboys, with glamorous second wives who nearly always made the best-dressed list. Margaret dismissed them as "useless," except when they raised money at charity balls, but she still held out hopes for her two Gatsby-like brothers.

Apart from her art collection, she bought and sold companies, served on corporate boards, gave gratuitously to countless charities, and still managed to keep her common touch. Even Alice Roosevelt Longworth liked her, and *she* disliked almost everyone.

Margaret, the heiress, and Rosie, the housekeeper quickly became friends and often played poker together, with pennies just to make it interesting. They had two things in common—they were both outspoken and they both loved to gamble. We warned Margaret that Rosie cheated. Margaret cupped her hand over my ear and whispered, "So do I."

Her stories mesmerized us. She knew almost everyone who was important. Margaret was a friend to presidents, celebrities, and people we just read about: Winston Churchill, Averill Harriman, Greta Garbo, and Aristotle Onassis. Mother almost swooned when she heard Garbo's name, and asked, "What is she like, really?"

"She's beautiful and boring. A really dumb Swede."

Hubert looked a lot like Daddy, though he was shorter and stockier than his older brother. They were completely different in personality. Hubert was a sportsman who dressed meticulously. His suits were all custom-made by Saville Row, and his shirts by Turnbull and Asher in London, whereas my father often wore mismatched socks. Nor was he as cultured as my father had been, but he did ooze charisma. Always laughing, revealing his teeth, which seemed a little too large for his mouth, and he had that white, pinkish skin with a brow covered with freckles that was so common with the descendants of the Mayflower. Unlike my father, no black Irish genes had emerged in Uncle Hubert.

Margaret never minced her words. I recall one afternoon when we sat on the terrace and discussed Margaret's earlier days when she competed in equestrian events. I heard words I hadn't heard since my dormitory days at Radcliffe. She'd say, "I spent my girlhood with the grooms mucking out the stables and cleaning tack."

To my mother, it sounded like a foreign language. She asked, "What do you mean? I don't understand."

Margaret replied, chuckling mischievously, "You know Edith, shoveling up the horse shit. Didn't you ever ride when you were a girl?"

Mother answered, "I've always been afraid of horses, but I would have liked to have been a rider."

"You wouldn't have liked shoveling shit, though. Of that, I am sure."

Mother smiled in spite of herself.

Margaret could say anything and get away with it. She, as well as Hubert, laced their language with four letter words, especially when losing a horse race or at cards. Still, nobody would ever call Margaret anything but a "lady."

Rosie interrupted, as she often did: "Anyone for a nice cup of Earl Gray tea and homemade scones with cream and jam?"

"Make mine a scotch on the rocks," said Margaret.

Out of the blue, she addressed my sister. "Jane, become a doctor if that's what you want! Never mind emptying bedpans and taking orders from men. Go to medical school. You're smarter than ninety-five percent of the men I know. You can do it. I know you can." Mummy's mouth shaped itself into a perfect O, but she remained silent. I suspected she had the same dream for Jane and found an ally in Margaret.

Jane sighed, "You're the first person to tell me what I always wanted to hear. Daddy said it would be too tough on me emotionally. There was just one woman in his class, and the professors and most of the other students made her life miserable. She ended up hanging herself."

Margaret's gray eyes blazed. She poked her finger into Jane's breastbone. "Well, you apply and make *their* lives miserable, and you damn well better not kill yourself. I won't come to your funeral if you do. I don't like cowards."

A FEW DAYS LATER, I returned to my job at the newspaper reporting weddings and other social events. It was typical fare for a female cub reporter.

Our apartment in Boston was dreadful, but we loved it. Radiators creaked and hissed, waking us up at night. Bookcases were nothing more than bricks and boards, and the coffee table was an old lobster trap. The wooden floors were scratched and worn, and the kitchen linoleum was ancient. The people on the floor above us partied half the night, but who cared? The three of us were finally free. Free to stay up half the night, to gossip and smoke. Free from classes, from housemothers, from nosy relatives, from all the things connected to the past.

That weekend Elena invited me to the opening night of her church's "St. Rocco Festival," which was celebrated every year in honor of their patron saint. The strung lights were twinkling in the red and green colors of Italy. It reminded me of Christmas, only this was a hot summer night with a full yellow moon. There was so much to see: games, trinkets to buy, knitted sweaters, delectable foods of all kinds: pizza, grilled sausages, Italian cookies, candy cotton, puffs of dough doused in powdered sugar. Throngs of people crowded the booths. Lots of young women resembled Elena, with their southern Italian characteristics: petite with dark eyes, and slightly prominent noses. The younger girls were dressed in their Sunday best frocks with bows in their hair, and were wearing white ankle socks and Mary Jane shoes. Golden crosses draped their necks. The little boys were running around like hordes of little puppies.

Elena and I got caught up in the ambiance and the excitement of the street fair. I had never seen anything like this in Cape Elizabeth. Our church affairs were so sedate. Elena handed me a piece of pizza. The aroma made my mouth water. The recipe was a secret and straight from the old country. I knew it was true because the woman who served it to me said it was her grandmother's recipe. "No mozzarella cheese in our pizza. That's American style. No good."

Plump women without waists and others as thin as skeletons were dressed in black, huddled in groups gossiping. Elena filled me in on them when they spotted us as we walked by. She said they go to mass every day, but these old ladies from southern Italy and Sicily were nothing but troublemakers. She said that they made up lies about her mother, though she didn't elaborate.

The most exciting thing about the festival was a greased pole with a hundred one-dollar bills at the top. Teams of boys and young men climb the pole, time after time, only to slide back down again. Every time someone came close to the top of the pole, the crowd cheered. The Italian parish priest, with his bushy mustache and dressed in a long black tunic yelled, "*Bravo, molto bene.*" He tapped my arm lightly with his hand and said excitedly, "Vincenzo, up there on the top, he's the head altar boy. He will be the one."

I laughed—I didn't have to pretend. It was funny. The climbers were covered with grease. Their faces were smeared with it, and for the first time since Daddy's death, I was having fun.

I felt his eyes on me before I actually saw him—it was an unexplainable thing, as if the hairs on my body were standing up on edge, and I knew someone was watching me. He clutched my bare arm with a firm grip until I turned around. For me, the moment was electric, but I hid it well. After all, he could not see my heart beating out of my chest. I had been preparing for this meeting for a long time, and I knew exactly what I was going to do. Basically, to ignore him. Michael stood there looking at me with his mouth open. I had waited five years to see him again, and there he was—the quintessential dreamboat. He was older, even better looking—his shoulders had broadened, his high-school persona lost in time. If he had changed little, I knew that I had changed a lot. Growing up, a metamorphosis had occurred and I had finally, finally become the butterfly.

"Suzanne!"

I had seen it in the eyes of other boys I had grown up with. I could read his thoughts even before he said anything.

"Boy! Have you changed! He flushed and stammered, "I mean

you've grown up…and look so much older."

"That's because I *am* older," I said. "I forgot your name…Jim, or is it…John?"

"Don't you remember me? I'm Mike Conti. You know—my senior prom at the Eastland Hotel with Lorna Heinz. You and I danced together. Jim was *your* date."

"Oh yes. Now I remember. It's been a while."

"You're looking great too, Elena," he added. I could hardly believe that this was the same person, once so confident and cocky. Elena couldn't help grinning. She knew me from cover to cover.

Elena rambled on with small talk, asking him about his lifelong friend, David Bennett, and what had become of him. Michael said his friend had moved to New York City and was at Columbia Law School, and was now engaged to a Jewish girl, someone of his own faith, a fellow law student.

By this time, someone had reached the top of the pole, clutching the prize money in his greasy hand. The crowd applauded, whistled, and cheered, especially the members of his team. To my amazement, I spotted Jim (my date from hell) as he slid down the pole. He was still thin, but had added a few muscles and his skin had cleared up. I was surprised that he looked as good as he did. Who would have guessed it?

Michael said, "Excuse me for a minute, and *don't* go away." He ran over to Jim and patted him on the back. We heard him say, "Nice job, Cuz. I'm glad you guys won."

Jim smiled and said, "Yeah, isn't it great?" Michael returned, and wiped some grease off his hand with a handkerchief.

We continued our conversation, and Michael told us that he was now at medical school and loving it.

"Oh, how nice for you," I said in a monotone. I was being a bitch, but I didn't care. I still had a score to settle.

"Yeah. It used to be just a dream, now it's true. You know, I read your Dad's obituary in the paper. I'm sorry that he died so young. He was a good man."

"How did you know him?" I asked.

"He was there when I was born. My Mom told me about him. She thought he was swell—not cold like some doctors. And he didn't even send her a bill."

"I didn't know that."

"Hey, I was even named after him! I'm Michael Robert Conti." Actually, it's Roberto...but I like Robert better. This is America, not Italy."

"My father would have been honored, especially if he knew you were becoming a doctor."

I was so glad I was wearing my lucky red dress. It seemed that every time I wore it, something exciting happened. I had chosen it to be comfortable; the August night was hot and sultry. The low, scooped neckline and cap sleeves showed off my small cleavage and bronze tan. I wore short white gloves and white high heels. Michael's eyes stared admiringly at me, as he once did with Lorna.

"Where are you living now?"

"Boston. I live on Marlborough Street with Elena and Lorna. We share a third floor walkup. It's small, but better than a dorm."

"Where did you go to school?"

"Radcliffe, so I could be near all those Harvard boys."

"And did you meet many Harvard boys?"

"I met my share." I answered.

"I had no idea you were so nearby. I knew Lorna and Elena were at Boston College, but I didn't know you were in Cambridge. We were both on Harvard campuses last year, and I never had a clue. I should have realized that you would have ended up at a prestigious college like Radcliffe. It's a wonder that we never met at the Co-op or at Harvard Square." He hesitated for a second and then said, "Do you think we could get together sometime?"

"Get *together*, like on a date?"

"Well, yeah. That's what I mean," he mumbled, obviously uncomfortable.

I wanted to say yes, but my pride wouldn't let me. Why did he continue to insult me? I resented his remark about me ending up at a prestigious college. I knew I wasn't a brain like him, but I wasn't a moron either.

I looked at him as if I were looking at a bug under a microscope and answered, "I don't think so. I've been busy, but maybe sometime later."

He was disappointed and frowned, but so what? I had waited a long time to see him again. Now, let *him* wait. It was fated that we would see each other again—and on my terms. I was never more certain of anything in my life. Never had I felt such a strong attraction to anyone, even for Andreas. Perhaps Jane was mistaken and there was such a thing as love at first sight.

He walked us back to my red Chevy convertible, a graduation present from my parents. He shifted his weight from foot to foot, brushing away imaginary wisps of curls from his forehead and said, "I hope I'll get to see you again. I mean…both of you…Goodnight girls."

Elena and I got in, and I drove off, jamming the gas pedal to the floor. He stood there watching. I saw his puzzled expression from my rear view window. A little voice in my head said, *"Suzanne, one—Michael, zero."*

Elena could hardly wait to speak. "Boy, why are you playing so hard to get? You know you want to go out with him."

"It could be that I've finally learned how to play the game. Indifference is a magical potion."

"If you say so."

After a week back in Boston, Michael called on the phone. The first two times he called, I told him I was busy. On both occasions, it was true and it nearly killed me to say no. But, rejection only seemed to encourage him. I hadn't meant to go *this* far. The next time he called, I accepted, and we went to a small Cambridge theater and saw *Casablanca*, a film that I had never seen. I always thought Bogie was ugly. But when I watched beautiful Ingrid Bergman standing in the shadows with her face aglow, her heart breaking, looking at Bogie for the last time, I wept and wept—and was mortified. Michael looked at me and grinned as I dabbed my eyes with tissue.

After the movie, we went to a pub in Cambridge to have a drink. He was nice, but definitely defensive. Going to Bowdoin and Harvard with all those privileged students had left its mark.

Later, as I recalled our conversation, I remembered his thoughts about some of his fellow classmates.

"I'll be glad to be finished here. If I hear one more guy say, 'When my father was a student here,' I'm going to throw up. It'll be a relief to get it over with. My father is an immigrant and a barber without any formal education. I'm the first in my family to graduate from college, let alone attend medical school. Can you understand what I'm saying?"

"I'm trying, but be fair. Don't evaluate people by their family background. Even affluent people can be nice."

"You mean like you?" he said.

"I'm not always nice, but I do try most of the time. As for understanding about you being the first to go to college, I admit my family always had it easy and college was just waiting for us. It was expected."

After that, he had a second beer and he relaxed. I nursed my Tom Collins and we made small talk. I told him funny stories about my family and the people I worked with. He spoke a lot about his brother and growing up in the city.

"Hey, it was a good experience. Every Saturday morning I went to the library and checked out books, then we loaded up on candy at Woolworths. After that we went to the movies, found our friends, and sat through the whole thing twice, no matter what the movie was, and they gave us free dishes. I went to so many movies that my mother had a whole set."

"It sounds like fun."

"It was. After school, I practically lived at the Boys Club and played all kinds of sports. I had a good childhood—then we moved to the suburbs."

"What was that like?"

"It was different, and from then on I spent a lot of time on a bus, or hitchhiking to Portland High."

"Why didn't you switch to Deering?"

"All my friends were at Portland, and they were athletes. I thought Deering was a snobby place, but then at Bowdoin, I met some Deering guys and they were okay. High school kids are so discriminating."

The jukebox was playing *And the Angels Sing,* and we discovered that we were both Ziggy Ellman fans.

He said, "I took trumpet lessons and was so bad that my father paid me five bucks to stop."

"Oh, my God! That's funny. You sound just like me. My sister is a pianist; I mean she can *really* play. I just make noise. My teacher was so relieved when I quit. I think we have something in common—we're both musical zeroes."

He started laughing and threw his head back revealing a mouthful of Pepsodent white teeth. He eyes twinkled—they were warm and seductive, but in a nice way. Everything about him pleased me and his manners were impeccable. The time seemed to fly by and I didn't want the evening to end. There was one other thing I noticed—he drank only two beers. I didn't want another Andreas.

DUE TO MICHAEL'S HEAVY schedule, we only saw each other about every five days. Sunday afternoon, we strolled along the Charles River, held hands, and even hugged a few times. On the third date, he kissed me goodnight. After that, I stopped dating others.

Eventually, Lorna's name came up. He told me that, initially, he liked her, but in time found her too controlling. His exact words were, "She's too bossy." Elena and I found living with her frustrating—Lorna was a neatness freak. We had had enough of dictatorial mothers and relished our new laid-back lifestyle. We were both slobs.

Lorna had become increasingly sharp and argumentative with me, always trying to contradict whatever I said. I sensed it had something to do with Michael.

When I asked Elena about Lorna's behavior, she found it incredulous that I hadn't guessed the reason.

"She's jealous of you—how can you be so blind?" she said.

"But why?" I asked.

"It's mostly about Michael—he was once *her* boyfriend. But it's really about everything—you have a better job, you travel, you come from an old respected family, and you're rich—really rich. Before, when we were in high school, Lorna was the queen bee—now she's just like everyone else. And you know down deep that you've gone the other way. She can't stand it when anyone says how glamorous you've become.

I was struck dumb trying to comprehend everything.

Lorna's boyfriend, Billy James, a student at Boston College Law

School, was an okay guy. He was bright, good looking, easygoing, but nobody thought that he was extraordinary or in the same league as Michael. She was accustomed to having the best of everything, including boyfriends.

Elena continued, "Lorna hates her job at Little-Brown doing line editing which is so boring, and she would love to have your job. You make more money and write for a metropolitan newspaper."

"Writing up weddings and engagements isn't exactly being May Craig."

"Who?" asked Elena.

"May Craig. She's the most famous woman reporter in Washington; she wears crazy hats and writes a column for the *Portland Press Herald.* Elena, you were the valedictorian of our class. Don't you think it's about time you started reading a newspaper or a book?"

"I never have time. I only read what I have to read and nothing more," she replied.

I was angry with her. "Jeez, if I only had your photographic memory, I'd go for the whole enchilada—I'd be a lawyer or a scientist or something great."

She continued, ignoring my last comment, which was always a touchy thing with her.

"Let's get back to the subject," she said. "Okay? Lorna never talked behind your back before, except to say, 'Poor Suzanne, when will she find a boyfriend who isn't a loser like Andreas?' Now, she says, 'I don't see what Michael sees in Suzanne, unless it's her money.' I think she wants to take him away from you.'"

"Elena, that's ridiculous. She loves Billy. They're even talking about becoming engaged. Why would she want Michael when she has Billy?"

"I don't mean she wants to marry him. After all, Billy comes from a big bucks family, and you know what that means to her. She wants Michael to show some interest in her, and then, after you get jealous and hurt, she'll drop him. You know Lorna—she just wants what she can't have. That's the bad part of Lorna—but there's the good part, too. It's just the way she is."

"What kind of a friend are you anyway? You think it's okay to try to take a friend's boyfriend away. It isn't going to happen. Michael was right when he said Lorna peaked at eighteen and has been heading downhill ever since." I stormed off to my room and slammed the door.

I was disappointed in Elena for not clueing me in sooner. My naiveté had always been my downfall. I believed they were my best friends, and yet Jane had warned me about them, especially Lorna. For the time being, I'd have to put up with them.

I'd always considered Elena to be my best friend and told her everything, but I knew she was not always straightforward with me, especially about her troubled family life. Elena uncharacteristically hinted of it, when she said that the Old Italian gossips told lies about her mother. Michael, who was up on the Italian gossip around town, filled me in on the details. Her parents' marriage was an arranged one, which was common with Italian immigrant families and doomed from the beginning. To the shock of the Italian community, after a number of years in an unhappy marriage, her mother had taken a younger lover.

Three months after my father died, Elena's father filed for divorce. Her father's departure left her alone to deal with her difficult mother. If Elena resented her mother's boyfriend, she never let it show. I wished she could have trusted me enough to discuss it, though I realized that it must have been a painful subject for her. That was the mystery of Elena. You never knew what she was thinking when it pertained to her family life. However, I did respect her for not acknowledging her mother's indiscretion. She had always been good to me and I had no right to make moral judgments about others—I left that to God.

Elena's previous boyfriends had always been intellectually beneath her, but recently, she met Keith Kelly, an Irish Catholic. He graduated from Bentley and worked for a well-established accounting firm. Their romance was on the fast tract and she wore his fraternity pin. His family adored her, but no one loved her more than Keith. He wasn't handsome, but pleasant looking with inquisitive eyes, curly brown hair, and a cleft chin. She thought he looked a lot like Kirk Douglas. Although not tall, he towered over her. She was only five feet tall. Once, I asked her how she knew she loved him. She replied, "I fell in love with his mind first, and the rest followed."

RETURNING HOME FOR THANKSGIVING, Rosie made her usual delectable turkey dinner for just our family, and two of Robby's school chums. Charles had gone home to be with his brother in New Harbor. Hubert and Margaret were in Kentucky, and I missed them. Without Margaret's high spirit and humor, there wasn't much to laugh about, and having our first Thanksgiving without Daddy, nothing was the same.

It was about this time that something began to trouble me. Mummy seemed to be misplacing things, repeating herself, and reading books, seemingly without turning the pages. I blamed it on Daddy's death, thinking she was still grieving. Jane noticed it too, but said, "It's probably just menopause."

I returned to Boston after the holiday and got busy with the details of our upcoming Christmas party. We had talked of it for months. I took care of mailing the invitations and buying the decorations. Elena bought the snack food and planned the menu (not that any of us could cook), and Lorna cleaned the apartment until it sparkled.

The Saturday morning of the party, we set up the Christmas tree and decorated it in blue and white sparkling lights, complete with silver balls and tinsel. Collectively, we prepared a variety of sandwiches and hors d'oeuvres and bought beer and wine—lots of it. I splurged on a new dress, and had my hair and nails done at Pierre's.

To add to the excitement, both Lorna and Elena were convinced that this Christmas would bring them engagement rings, and they couldn't stop speculating about it.

The evening of the party was mass confusion! Friends were arriving so quickly we barely had time to make introductions. As for the space problem, there wasn't any. We were over fifty people jammed into a small apartment. It was standing room only. As we were a generation of smokers, including all three of the hostesses, the cigarette smoke engulfed the apartment. A forty-five-speed record player was spinning out Christmas carols while some of us were singing along.

Michael arrived late. He found that most of us were slightly drunk and a few others very drunk. Giggling, I kissed his cheek and said, "Where have you been?"

"I just delivered my first baby. A woman came in the Emergency Room and barely got through the door and on to a gurney. She never would have made it to the Delivery Room. What a thrill to hear that little boy cry, and to see the mother looking at me as if I were Jesus Christ Almighty. Of course, I had a little help from her and the nurses."

"My father said that it was always like a miracle, and he delivered hundreds, maybe thousands."

"He was right. I'll never forget it."

I handed him my glass of beer, and said, "You need this more than I do."

He replied, "I can use that. I've got of a lot of catching up to do."

Later, we switched to popular music, dimmed the lights, and danced to the songs of Elvis Presley who was new on the scene and old favorites like Frank Sinatra and Nat King Cole. The party had been a success though our apartment looked like a battlefield. About three in the morning, the crowd finally left. Keith, Billy, and Michael stayed and helped us clean up.

Although he had kissed me goodnight many times before, that night he *really* kissed me. I heard him whisper, "You're so beautiful." He had warm soft lips (not wet, sloppy ones like some guys) and he held me in his arms as though he never wanted to let go. I loved his fresh clean smell. Most of all, I liked what I thought I saw in his eyes. Tonight his eyes were not twinkling—they were intense. I wanted to believe that I saw love, but I wasn't sure. As he turned to leave, he told me, "I'll call you soon."

I wanted to say, "Yes, I can't wait to talk to you tomorrow," but instead I said, "Please do that." I was still hesitant to reveal my true feelings. I didn't want to scare him away. Suddenly, he became serious and gripped my shoulders.

"Look Suzanne, if there's anyone else in your life, please, tell me now, because I've got a feeling that this is going to get very, very serious, and I don't want to waste my time."

"No, there's only you."

He kissed me again, this time more passionately, slipping the tip of his tongue between my lips. My heart pounded, my knees weakened. He kissed the hollow in my throat, and I felt his lips sliding down my neck and beyond.

Abruptly, he stopped, and then he laughed and said, "Wait a minute. Perhaps, we're moving too fast. I'm sorry."

"Don't be," I whispered. I wanted you to do it…I've never been kissed exactly like this before." I wondered if he knew that I was lying.

"That's exactly my point. I know you haven't, and that's why we're going to be careful. I want this to be perfect."

I felt a little guilty that I had never mentioned Andreas, but, then again, that was in the past. I wasn't the innocent that he thought I was. At our age, it would have been naïve for either to think the other never had a prior love. My father had always advised me to be mysterious and private about my life—he said it would make me more interesting.

Keith and Billy had left, and Lorna and Elena were already in bed. I looked out my window and watched Michael walk up the street to his car; a heavy snow had begun to fall, and I could see his footprints on the ground by the light of the lamppost. I thought to myself, *if he turns around, looks at me, and waves, it would be a sign.* As if it were predestined, he did all three. Blissfully, I undressed, slipped into my bed, pulled up the covers, giggled, and relived the night repeatedly in my thoughts. Finally, overcoming it all, I zonked out.

Elena and Lorna had guessed right. Both received engagement rings for Christmas. Michael presented me with a black and white male kitten that we named Noel. I gave him a beige cashmere scarf, which I wrapped around his neck while pretending to strangle him.

Michael said, "I have something else for you. Close your eyes."

I felt his fingers fumbling on my sweater. *What's he doing?*

"Okay, you can open them."

I looked down, and pinned to my white angora sweater, was his fraternity pin. He kissed me and said, "Merry Christmas, Suzy Q."

Now we *were engaged* to *be engaged*, which was what a fraternity pin symbolized. We kissed to finalize the deal. My long ago dream was coming true, and yet he still hadn't said the right words. I said, "Michael, you have never said that you love me."

"Neither have you. Besides, I never said it before to anyone. It's hard for me to express myself…you know I do."

"I need to hear it, Michael…to hear you say it."

"I do love you, Suzanne. I think I'll always love you."

"Always is a long time."

"This isn't something I haven't thought about seriously. I wouldn't have given you my pin unless you meant the world to me."

"I love you, Michael, and I have for a very long time."

We sat on to the couch, and after a few more amorous kisses, I realized that I had to tell him about Andreas, so I told him the whole story which probably sounded like a soap opera to him. He listened, then gave me a quirky lopsided grin, and said, "I'm glad you didn't marry that mama's boy."

"What would you have said if your parents didn't want me?"

"I would have said, if you don't want her, you don't want me."

When I heard that, I knew he was the guy that I'd end up marrying. He asked me a few more questions, and then confessed that unlike me, he had *never* been in love and he was *not* a virgin, but gave me no names or details. He was definitely not a kiss-and-tell kind of guy, which I admired. "That's all in the past tense. From now on, it's just the two of us."

He held my face in both his hands and kissed me like he thought I would break—first my eyelids, then my cheeks, the tip of my nose, and finally, my lips. I returned his kisses with equal tenderness. It was magical. It was too special to mix up with passion. That would come later, but not tonight.

We returned to Maine for Christmas. I had to tell someone my fabulous news, and that person was Jane. My wonderful sister listened as I told her everything.

"I don't know how I'm going to tell Mom. She has never met him, and I know what she's going to say. You know, too, don't you?"

"Yeah, I do. She'll say he's not a Protestant. He's penniless. She'll ask what his father does for a living. I know all of that, Suzanne, don't worry…Think positively…Think about what he has to offer…What she'll like about him."

As usual, Jane calmed me down.

Michael and I drove back to Boston two days before New Year's Eve. While driving, I said that I had told Jane about us.

"Well, we're even. I told my brother, too."

"I'll wear the pin in Boston, but when I go home, I'll have to take it off. I need time to prepare my mother."

"Prepare her for what? For me?"

"Michael, you have to understand about her. My father just died, and she's still not over it. She doesn't even know that I date you. I've tried to tell her about you, but it's hard."

"Why is it hard? Jesus! I'm not a criminal. Is it because my last name ends in a vowel? You don't have to tell me. I already know. She'd think I wasn't good enough for you. I'm not well off and I'm not a WASP. I'm just an ordinary guy."

"You are *not* ordinary. You are everything I've ever wanted. I told you my mother is a little narrow-minded, but I'm not. She thinks our Anglo-Saxon heritage has to go on forever. She's so proud of it and our family history. Just give me a little time...Whatever happens, if I'm ever forced to choose between the two of you, it will be you." He remained unmoved.

"We rode in silence; the absence of sound was deafening. To make matters worse, it had started to snow—big, fluffy, snowflakes that covered the windshield, making the visibility terrible. I listened to the sound of the windshield wipers flapping back and forth, back and forth. Suddenly, we felt a thud and Michael slowly stopped the car nearly skidding off the road. He opened the door, got out, and then slammed it. I saw him kick the tire. I don't know if he was madder at the car or madder at me. He opened the trunk, took out another tire, a jack, and tools. The heater was off, and I sat there shivering.

I was sure that Michael would get back in the car and tell me it was all over. I started to cry. I rummaged through my purse looking for a handkerchief. As usual, I didn't have one. I opened the glove compartment, and found some tissue. Hidden behind the box, almost out of sight, was a package of condoms. I sat there, frozen physically and mentally; my perfect guy was not perfect after all. He was a rat, even a bigger one than Andreas!

Ten minutes later, he got into the car; his head, shoulders and eyelashes were coated with snow. He shut the door and looked at me.

"What? Okay, now you know...I have a temper...I'm sorry I made you cry. It's not your fault about your mother. Forgive me for being such a jerk?"

"No, I'll never forgive you!" I threw the package of condoms in his face. "I've been seeing you for four months. I'm wearing your fraternity pin, and you've been…screwing around. I hate you!"

"Suzanne, you're wrong…They're not mine."

I screamed, "You liar!" I drew back and slapped him across his face as hard as I could.

He looked surprised. I saw him draw his hand back, his eyes aflame. "Don't you ever call me a liar," he said in a voice that made me fear him.

He didn't strike me, but I felt my legs go numb. If I had been standing, I would have sunk to the ground. How could I have been such a fool? He wasn't the gentleman that I thought he was. I should have known better. Mummy told me that Italian men always hit their wives.

He took a deep sigh. "Suzanne, listen to me. I know I scared you. I can take the slap, but don't ever call me a liar again. There is nothing you could say to me that would make me angrier. I almost hit you, and I have never, *ever* hit a girl. I apologize…Now, I'm going to say this slowly and calmly so you understand perfectly…the condoms are not mine. I repeat, they are not mine…I have not been unfaithful to you."

"But they're in your car," I whimpered.

"Yes, but I'm not the only person who drives it."

"You mean Arthur or one of your friends?"

He stared at me and shrugged. "Either you believe me or you don't, and if you don't trust me, this thing between us isn't going to work."

I hung my head, crying, and dabbed my nose with tissue. The tears wouldn't stop. I was shaking, shivering from the cold, and tried to think of an appropriate response. Could I trust him? He reached out to touch my face, and wiped the tears off my cheeks gently with his gloved hand. His looked sad, disappointed.

After what seemed like an eternity, I spoke, in a little girl voice: "I believe you, I do. Did I hurt you?"

He leaned over and kissed my cheek. Then I put my head on his shoulder. He put his arms around me and held me close. "Hey kiddo, that was some whack. He laughed to himself and said, "I didn't know you were such a spitfire."

He turned on the ignition. The warmth of the heater filled the car, and the warmth of his words filled my heart. His temper had frightened me, but I knew that I was the one to blame. I went too far. I would never question his honesty again. If he was lying to me, he should have been an actor—it was an Academy Award performance. I believed him because I loved him and I wanted it to be true.

When I got home both Lorna and Elena were already there. I took off my coat, proudly sticking out my chest, displaying Michael's fraternity pin. Elena grinned and kissed me on the cheek. "Hey gal, you did it!"

Lorna smiled and followed with a hug as well. "Michael is a terrific guy. You two make a great couple." She seemed to be genuinely happy for me, and I was puzzled. For some reason, after the Christmas party, Lorna seemed to change back to her pre-Michael days.

Noel slunk out of my bedroom and rubbed up against my leg. I missed him so much. I picked him up, stroked his back, and cuddled him. "I missed you, baby. I hope those drunks upstairs fed you enough."

The last night of the year was bitter cold. Both my roommates were out celebrating with their boyfriends at the Totem Pole, a popular nightclub. Michael and I chose to have dinner at a romantic, Italian restaurant in the north side of Boston. A few hours later, we returned to my apartment to welcome in the New Year with a cheap bottle of champagne. Michael asked me how long we had been dating.

"You know how long, since August."

"That's five months, Suzanne. I've been doing some thinking, and I don't want to wait forever to be with you. Five months is long enough for me to know my mind and my heart. You know how I feel. Will you marry me?"

I was stunned. A second marriage proposal out of the blue. We had only been pinned a week. He took my silence as a rejection; I could see that his feelings were hurt by the expression on his face.

"You're not sure are you? It's too soon. I blew it, didn't I?"

I took his hands and guided him to the sofa. "Oh no, no Michael.

It's not what you think. I want to marry you. I do. I'm ready to get married. I'm twenty-three, old enough to know what I want…You just surprised me…that's all. The truth is that I've loved you for so long, from the first time I saw you. I know that it's hard to believe, but it's true."

"Sue, are you saying yes?"

"Of course, yes. Yes! Yes! I will marry you."

"Wow! You've made me a happy guy. I feel wonderful. This summer, we'll get engaged and next June, after I graduate from med school, we'll get married. I'll never be a millionaire, but I promise you, I'll always take care of you."

"Michael. I don't need to be a millionaire. I just want you and a family of our own. Let's keep this to ourselves for a while. We can't tell anyone until my mother knows. This spring, before June, I'll tell her. I promise."

"Okay, kiddo. If that's the way you want it, that's the way we'll do it."

He kissed me, but this time it was different. I wasn't merely kissing my boyfriend; I was kissing my future husband.

DIZZY WITH DREAMS of the future, I vowed to keep my secret from Lorna and Elena. Being pinned was one thing, but being engaged was another. Besides, I didn't want my happiness to distract from their upcoming weddings. Our time would come.

The months flew by. I wore Michael's fraternity pin, always careful to take it off when I was with Mother in Maine.

By the end of March, the pristine snow had turned into slush the color of dirty white socks, and slowly the long-awaited spring arrived. Those of us from places with long, stormy winters and short days know what that means. It was like coming alive again. Flocks of birds in flying formations returned from the south, crocuses in the muddy ground sprouted in clusters of purple, yellow, and white, and I spotted my first robin.

Jane decided on the plan of attack. She would have a party to celebrate her college graduation and Memorial Day, the unofficial beginning of summer. She told me to invite Michael. The rest was up to me, but I needed allies—who better than Margaret. She had met

Michael in Boston when she and Hubert took us out to dinner.

Margaret told me privately, "I like Michael, he's got character and he's some looker. But you had better tell your mother soon. She wants me to introduce you to my nephew, Freddy. She doesn't know he's the black sheep of the family—a compulsive gambler, and the father of an illegitimate child."

"Mummy only sees two things—old WASP families and money. But that's going to change," I said with bravado.

Memorial Day arrived and the weather was perfect. The lilacs, flowering fruit trees, and azaleas were all in full bloom. Beds of tulips blazed in bright spring colors. Charles had worked very hard to make the grounds look lovely. On these occasions, he would assist Rosie serving drinks and canapés and attending to the needs of our guests.

Jane invited lots of family friends, fellow graduates, and a smattering of relatives, including snooty Aunt Marie, Mummy's sister from Greenwich, Connecticut, and Uncle Liam.

Jane made a special effort to look good. She wore a yellow shirtwaist dress and high-heeled pumps. Being tall, even taller than Mummy, somewhere in the past year, she had lost her lanky look. With her fiery auburn hair pulled back into a ponytail, and her sea-green eyes sparkling, she was beginning to get the looks from guys that I was used to getting, though she didn't seem to be aware of it. She went so far as to wear lipstick and. her small pink-tinted pearl earrings and necklace. Make-up and jewelry was not my sister's forte. Usually she wore slacks and a tucked in man's white shirt. Jane would never be beautiful, but at twenty-one, she had become exceedingly attractive. Better still, she had grown up and stopped being a know-it-all.

Jane introduced Michael to my mother as my friend from Boston, and threw in a few, selected key words that would impress Mother. *Harvard* always scored big time with her.

I saw my mother press her lips together when she heard Jane say, "Michael Conti." She hid it well, smiled, and shook his hand limply. "How nice of you to come, Michael."

"Mrs. Mason, surely you're kidding! You look like an older sister, not their mother, but I do see a family likeness."

My mother interrupted, "Which one? My daughters don't look anything alike."

He faltered for just an instant. "Actually, they each took their best features from you." Mother smoothed her hair back away from her face, unable to hide her vanity in spite of herself.

"Jane should have added charm to your many fine qualities," she retorted.

Michael blushed.

Mummy gave me that you-don't-fool-me look. She saw right through us. He told her about Daddy bringing him into the world, and that in another year, he too would become a doctor. I thought he was pouring it on a bit thick, and tried to pull him away, but she kept asking him questions. She wanted to know how long we'd been seeing each other, and he answered, "Over a year."

"*Reeeaaally*. I had no idea. Suzanne never told me." She fumbled with her earring and it dropped accidentally on purpose, and when Michael stooped down to pick it up, she glared at me. I read her thoughts. *How dare you surprise me with a boyfriend and not tell me about him first?*

Michael never looked better. He wore his blue blazer, light gray trousers, a pale blue shirt, and an Italian silk tie that I had given him for his birthday. His dress shoes were shined to a high gloss. He was the most handsome young man at the party. Mother often said that as a young man, my father was as good-looking as a movie star. She wasn't blind and I think she recognized the similarities. Michael and my father could have been father and son. They looked so much alike. Both were tall. Both had dark hair with distinctive hairlines. Both had beautiful seductive eyes, though my father's were blue and Michael's were brown. And of course, both chose doctoring as a career. I often wondered why I fell in love with Michael. Was it because he reminded me of my father?

Jane's plan turned out to be a success. Just the right mix of people—not so many that Michael would be overlooked. A four-piece band supplied the music as we danced on the flagstone patio. Michael danced with my mother and sister. Hubert whirled Margaret around like Fred Astaire. She had invited Senator Norton, our senior senator, as a guest, and Mummy was ecstatic when she danced with him. All eyes were on Robby's date, Ashley Mortimer, a stunning redhead from Sarah Lawrence College. Robby cut in to dance with Mother, and Senator Norton's eyes almost popped out of his face when Ashley drifted into his arms.

Looking back on the party, I could see that my mother was outnumbered. Everyone fussed over Michael, especially Aunt Marie, who tittered like a schoolgirl when he boogied with her. Mother could play the spoiler, or she could accept my choice of a husband graciously. To this day, I don't know what Jane and Margaret and Marie said to her, but the next morning she told me that we had her blessing and that we could become engaged.

She approved of Michael, but, and it was a big but, there would be "no Catholic wedding." I was so relieved that I told her she could plan the whole thing. "Don't think I won't. I have to live in this town, dear, and I want the wedding and the reception to be done correctly." She kissed me, and I was never happier. If only my father could have been there, my happiness would have been complete.

That June, Michael gave me an engagement ring. As I might have guessed, the ring disappointed Mother. It was a small round diamond in a tiffany setting, but Michael said he would replace it someday with a diamond so big, that even Mother would think it vulgar.

We wanted neutral territory for our engagement party, so we chose a quiet restaurant. I didn't want to intimidate Michael's family with our house and servants. Surprisingly, our two families got along well. The two mothers complimented each other, exchanged air kisses and praised each other's child. There were lots of laughs and thanks to Robby and his jokes and Michael's witty comments, everyone was at ease.

Mr. Conti made a toast in remembrance of my father, "To Dr. Mason who brought both of these wonderful young people into the world so they could find happiness with each other." Mother's eyes filled with tears, and she whispered to me, "Michael's father is such a gentleman." I was proud of Mummy. Finally, I felt the closeness that had so long eluded us. Robby, grinning from ear to ear, added another toast. "To Mike, a future brother, whom I desperately need for moral support in a house full of women, and as a new mate to handle the sails." Rachael rose her glass, her dark eyes shining with happiness and said, "*La Chiam.* To Life."

"Hear! Hear!" we cheered.

ALL THREE OF US MARRIED within one chaotic year after a flurry of bridal showers, luncheons, rehearsal dinners, bachelor parties, and the hottest June and July the fickle state of Maine had managed in years.

In June 1957, Lorna married Billy James of Weston, Massachusetts. The wedding was small and simple with only Elena, the maid of honor, and Billy's best friend, John Davis, as the best man. Lorna wore a tea-length blue silk dress and carried a bouquet of daisies. She was a beautiful bride and Billy was thrilled to be her husband.

After the ceremony, a dinner was held at a local restaurant in a private room with a pianist playing background music. There was to be no dancing nor alcoholic beverages served except the champagne toast. The dinner was one course, and the desert, the wedding cake.

Mrs. Heinz grumbled, "I wanted my only child to have a big beautiful wedding, but she wanted the money instead. You know my daughter—stubborn and frugal like my mother-in-law." Lorna whispered to me when they left for their weekend honeymoon at Bar Harbor, "It's so wonderful to start our marriage with a nice bank account, and all of our furniture paid for."

Elena married three weeks later, with July temperatures soaring to over ninety degrees. In contrast to Lorna's wedding, hers was large and held in the Italian Catholic Church with a large wedding party.

Lorna complained that the bridesmaids' dresses were more expensive than her own wedding dress, and that she would never wear it again. It was a heavy, pink taffeta dress, with a matching floral headband and pink dyed pumps. Elena's mother had picked it out and we all hated it.

I'd never seen so many baskets of flowers at a wedding. There was an archway decorated with pink and white roses and carnations, which all the wedding party had to pass through before stepping up to the altar. The aroma of the flowers and incense was overpowering, and made several of us queasy.

Then, disaster struck! Elena fainted. She lay in a heap in her gorgeous, long sleeved wedding gown. Keith tried to pick up his bride, but she was deadweight. The priest requested that all the guests leave the church for a half-hour. Four fans were set up facing the wedding party. Elena was revived, and the wedding continued, the priest saying the words so rapidly that we could barely understand him, which hardly mattered since most of it was in Latin anyway.

At the reception, Mummy said to me, "In their white dinner jackets, the groomsmen looked like a bunch of waiters. I never saw so many people drunk. You can be *sure* your wedding will not be like this."

To which I answered, "Yes, Mother."

The bride and groom finally left in a white limousine to spend the night at Portland's finest hotel. The next day, they left for Europe: it was the Kelly's wedding gift.

Before long, it was 1958. The months flashed by, faster and faster—within seven weeks, Michael would be a doctor and we'd be married. I was busy with my job and all the preparations for the wedding, talking daily on the telephone with Mummy. Finally, it was time to send out the invitations. There were the usual arguments about who to invite and who not to invite to the wedding. Michael gave me a list of about fifty relatives and about twenty-five family and school friends. The relatives included twenty-six cousins?

Mother said, "Those *Eyetalians* certainly have a lot of children." To which I replied, "One third of them are Jewish."

"Oh my God, we're finished," said Mummy.

Chapter 4

MICHAEL
1932 – 1958

I had the misfortune of being born in 1932 in Portland, Maine, during the worst of times—the Great Depression. Or so I was told a million times by my parents, Rachael and Frank Conti. But, they were wrong—there had been worse times.

Growing up at the bottom of Munjoy Hill, in a neighborhood teeming with immigrants and the children of immigrants, I had no inkling of the history of Portland and, more importantly, of my own neighborhood, until I read about it as a child from a book in the children's section of the Portland Public Library.

In 1689, in Portland, then known as Falmouth, a raging battle lasting five days took place between the settlers and the Indians at Brackett's farm (which later became known as Deering Oaks) and continued at Fort Loyall at the foot of King Street (which became India Street) resulting in the burning of all dwellings. The Indians scalped and slaughtered the whole village population while their collaborators, the French, looked the other way. The dead remained unburied for two years and there were no white settlers left alive.

Holy Cow! I'd gone skating at Deering Oaks, and walked down India Street hundreds of times, and I never knew that any of that stuff had happened. It was more exciting than the movies. It was just like *The Last of the Mohicans*, one of my favorite books. I continued to read more about the settlers now that my curiosity had been aroused. Why hadn't our teachers told us?

By 1727, in a third attempt to create a town, forty families tried again. The Reverend Thomas Smith wrote in his diary, that some of them were even respectable. They settled in the same general area; there was peace with the Indians. But life was hard, and ten years later, in one cruel, harsh year, seventy-five people died of an illness called "throat distemper."

It was kind of interesting, but I preferred action, and so I scanned ahead to the good stuff.

By the time of the Revolutionary War, Portland had the best natural harbor on the eastern seaboard and was thriving in lumber, fishing, and shipbuilding, but serious problems started with England in 1765. The English decided to tax the American colonists by passing the "sugar act." The Falmouth merchants refused to pay a duty and dumped molasses into Casco Bay.

Hey, wasn't this before the colonists in Boston threw the tea into the Boston harbor? As students, we learned about "the Boston Tea Party," but nothing about what happened in our own city. Ten years passed with all kinds of trouble with the English, and then in 1775, the English retaliated.

Falmouth was bombarded for twelve hours by four English warships for refusing to hand over cannon and small arms. Their sailors landed and burned 414 of 500 buildings to cinders. Then it rained for three days. Winter was approaching, and poverty and hunger swept the colonists. Despite that, Falmouth sent many men to fight with the Continental Army who eventually beat the English and gained their independence.

After that, the fourth of July was not just another holiday to me, another excuse to light firecrackers and shoot off Roman candles. Those settlers were tough, and I admired them. I questioned my teacher about it when my classmates couldn't believe such exciting things had happened in Portland. They wanted to know more, and they kept raising their hands to ask more questions. The teacher's face reddened and I could tell that she didn't know the history of Portland. She changed the subject, and after a while, I got the message. I could have embarrassed her further and asked about the "Great Fire," but I was sure she didn't know about that either.

By 1786, the neck of the peninsula called Falmouth, separated from Falmouth proper and changed its name to Portland. With a population of only two thousand, it remained smaller than three other nearby towns, but Portland had a seaport. In 1790, The Portland Observatory was built on Munjoy Hill, with its rolling green lawns and unobstructed view of the sea. A perfect vantage point to spot ships in distress.

My brother and I would pack a lunch, and work up a sweat running up Munjoy Hill—to swim with our friends at the Eastern Promenade Beach. How many times did I pass the Portland Observatory and hardly give it a glance? Now I did. Ships and lives were saved because of it? When I told my brother Auturo, he said, "Jesus! Mikey, if you keep this stuff up, nobody is going to walk with us. What are you trying to be, a walking encyclopedia?"

The town prospered and grew and, in 1807, the president of Yale, Dr. Timothy Dwight, said: "Few towns in New England are equally as beautiful and brilliant. Its wealth and business are probably quadrupled." Fortunes were made, banks were built, businesses thrived, and the city expanded to the west. And with wealth came mansions, most of them built in the new western part of the city in an area called Bramhall Hill.

At that point, I lost interest. I didn't care about banks and mansions, but I sure was interested in the sea and who came to port on those big sailing ships from all over the world. Portland's own poet, Longfellow, born on Fore Street, in a house that overlooked the ocean, would later write:

> *I remember the black wharves and the slips*
> *And the sea-tides tossing free;*
> *And the Spanish sailors with bearded lips,*
> *And the beauty and mystery or the ships,*
> *And the magic of the sea.*

By 1832, one hundred years before I was born, Portland had grown to thirteen thousand people and prospered.

Portland's commercial fleet was the largest on the East Coast—bigger than Boston—bigger than New York. Her magnificent, sheltered harbor, the timber she exported and the fish caught from the ocean, was the envy of the nation. The age of sail was Maine's golden era.

Impressed, I continued to read until I came to the section referring to the Civil War.

Harriet Beecher Stowe, from Maine, wrote "Uncle Tom's Cabin," and was referred to by President Lincoln, as "the little lady who started the big war."

I checked the book out of the library, and I agreed with her—slavery was wrong. However, I didn't know that she had never been to the South, but reasoned that historians hadn't been here when Columbus discovered America, but they still wrote about it.

When Fort Sumter was fired on, the Civil War officially began, and President Lincoln called for seventy-five thousand volunteers from Maine—more men proportionately than from any other state.

I couldn't understand why most of my friends didn't like history, because I loved it. It's just a story about another time. I bet my friends would have been interested to know what happened in Portland just after the Civil War ended, July fourth, in 1866.

The city was preparing to celebrate Independence Day with parades, fireworks, and a balloon ascension, when disaster again struck and Portland suffered the greatest fire calamity the country had seen up to that time. A firecracker started a small fire in a boatyard on Commercial Street. It spread to a lumberyard and then to Brown's Sugarhouse on Maple St. The building became a roaring inferno. A strong south wind whipped the flames to uncontrollable fury, sweeping diagonally across the heart of the city from Commercial Street to Back Cove and to Munjoy Hill, where it finally burned out. Eighteen hundred buildings were destroyed, nearly ten thousand Portlanders left homeless. The fire gutted old family mansions as indiscriminately as it did the tenements of the poor. A tent city sprung up on Munjoy Hill, and relief supplies poured in from all over the United States.

Longfellow, visiting Portland a month later, wrote, "I have been to Portland since the fire. Desolation! Desolation! Desolation! It reminds me of Pompeii, the 'sepult city.' "

So great was the public effort and enthusiasm for reconstruction, that Portland seemed to rise from the ashes like the legendary phoenix, a more modern and impressive city than she had been before the holocaust.

It suddenly occurred to me that my whole neighborhood had burned down. What had been there before? I would never know. The only thing that remained in its entirety was the cemetery, which was directly across from our apartment on Congress Street, Portland's main street, which ran east to west and stretched more than eight miles from the Eastern Promenade to Union Station and beyond. At the midway point was a bigger-than-life-size bronze statue of Mr. Henry Wadsworth Longfellow, Portland's most famous citizen, world-renowned poet, and my not-so-far-away former neighbor. There he sat in the square named after him, content to have pigeons perch on his head and shoulders and do what pigeons do best. But, my world was on the East End of Congress Street, and I knew every inch of it.

As the decades passed, new residents came and went, changing from a sprinkling of prosperous families to middle class families to immigrants and first generation Americans—one of which was my family—the Conti's.

My earliest memories were of looking out the front window of our apartment across the street from the old East Cemetery, a sometimes-playground and scary place at night, especially on Halloween, where graves went back to long before the Civil War. To the right of the cemetery was the North School—my school—and because I lived across the street from it, the school yard was my playground and I never had an excuse for being late.

I was very young when we first moved there, so my memories are almost like dreams: The milkman delivering his goods from a wagon pulled by a horse that clip-clopped down the street with tinkling bells on his harness; the iceman, his back bent to his waist, struggling up the stairs to deliver ice; the colorful trolley cars that clanged up and down Congress Street. As time passed, we bought our milk from a store, purchased a refrigerator and traveled on a bus.

Blizzards came more often and the snow seemed so much deeper when I was a child. Or was it because I was small and everything and everyone was bigger than I in scope. After a storm, giant machines called loaders would scoop up the snow onto a moving vertical belt, chop it all up and dump it into a truck. Swept up with the snow was a little kid who hid in a snow cave and was mangled to death. After that, those of us who remembered never played in the snow banks again. Nobody wanted to die like little Bobby Delaney.

The block that we lived on was a mix of people with diverse ethnic backgrounds—Jews, Italians, Irishmen, Greeks, and a handful of other nationalities, including a few families who had been here a couple of hundred years. The one common denominator was our economic status—at best, we were a notch or two above the working poor, and we were all of the white race.

Included in the neighborhood were the local businesses: MacDonough's Drugstore, Garborino's Fruit and Produce, Pat's Meat Market, and Cohen's Dry Goods. All of them, and the eleven other tenants who lived in our building, became our surrogate parents, with all the duties, and privileges that came with it. Nobody asked them to do it—they volunteered.

Everything I did or didn't do was the neighborhood's business. My parents, Rachael and Frank Conti, would learn about it within minutes, especially my father, working in his barbershop. If I bought a comic book at Charlie Weiner's store, I was looking at "girly" magazines. If I spent more than ten cents on candy, the druggist told me my teeth would rot and fall out. From Officer O'Malley, the neighborhood cop, to Daisy Maietta, the local hairdresser, a network of intelligence was in place that could have matched the Federal Bureau of Investigation.

I could read before entering elementary school. (A mystery even to me) Books were my passion and provided me with a magic carpet, taking me all over the world, allowing me to enter fantasy lands where I could become anyone from "Kim" in India, to "Marco Polo" in ancient China. Saturday morning meant a trip to the library and six new books to read that week. That's how I discovered the history of Portland, and no thanks to the school curriculum. I loved school, and because I did, my friends thought I was nuts. They loved recess.

Miss Murphy, my sixth grade teacher, asked me what I wanted to be when I grew up. I told her a fireman. "Michael, you are insulting your fine intelligence. Do you have any idea how smart you are? You could be a doctor, or a scientist who discovers cures for terrible diseases. A fireman! *Please*!"

She told my mother, who was her seamstress about our conversation. After that, my mother was on a mission—her younger son was going to college.

MY FATHER HAD RECEIVED only an elementary education in Italy, and my mother had to drop out of high school at the end of junior year to work in a dress factory. Mom was an excellent student, and I remember how ashamed she was telling me that she had never graduated from high school, as if it were some horrible disgrace. That this should happen to my mother, who was smart enough to have won the state spelling championship in grade school, made me angry. Hearing my mother recall how she accepted the gold medal from Governor Baxter while wearing a borrowed dress that was too large for her, convinced me that life was not always fair. *Come hell or high water*, (One of my favorite expressions from seeing so many war movies). I was going to beat the odds for my family, and I vowed that someday, I would amount to something and buy my mother a closet full of dresses.

My brother, Arturo, hated school, but we both loved sports, especially boxing. We looked a lot alike, although he was smaller boned, and had lighter hair. He was five years older and my personal hero. Nobody bothered me when he was around. He never stuck his nose in a fight when I was equally matched, but if any older or bigger boy picked on me, there was hell to pay. He was one tough customer. It wasn't that we looked for fights; they were just there. In all fairness, it was like that for every other guy too. We had to do it just to prove that we weren't sissies. Eventually, everyone in our neighborhood knew that you didn't mess with the Conti brothers. My Dad, an amateur boxing coach, gave us four rules: never hit girls, never hit anyone weaker or smaller, never hit below the belt and never fight dirty, unless of course your opponent did.

I developed a tough skin. One day, I was called a WOP which I learned was an abbreviation for Italian immigrants "without papers," or a dago, and the next day, a dirty kike. I never learned where dago and kike came from. Even at a young age, I recognized ignorance, and felt more pity than contempt for them, because I knew that someday I would amount to something, and they would remain nobodies.

Our apartment was a railroad flat—four rooms and a bath. Our kitchen faced the back part of the building and an adjoining, magical porch. There, my brother and I became pirates, circus performers, campers in the wild of Maine, or anything else we could dream up in our wild imaginations. The porch looked down on an ugly dirt and concrete yard that was a graveyard for cats. I discovered that when I tried to plant some flower seeds. Yuk!

If we were poor, we never knew it. We were never hungry or cold—our apartment was immaculately clean, warm and comfortable. On the coldest days, we would come home with red cheeks and frozen mittens. The air would fill with the smell of wet wool as the mittens dried on the radiator. Mama would serve us steaming cocoa to warm us up. Then we sat at the kitchen table, snug and content, playing board games or cards.

Being "on relief," as it was called then, was a disgrace, and only for the lazy, the handicapped and desperately poor people. It was never a choice in our family, even in the worst years of the Depression. Some nights, when I pretended to be asleep, I heard my mother sigh and say, "Frank, I don't know if we have enough money for the rent this month."

He would usually say, "Don't worry Rachael, business will get better. Now that the war has started, people will have more money to spend."

My heart would sink, and to take my mind off the rent money we didn't have, I'd read with a flashlight under the covers. I had to be careful, though, 'cause I shared a double bed with Arturo. He would draw an imaginary line with his hand down the center of the bed and say, "If you roll over on my side of the bed or even if one toe touches me, you're dead."

EVERY CHRISTMAS EVE, we hung up our stockings on the water heater in the kitchen. Each year was the same—a stocking filled with candy, an orange, and a one-dollar bill. We always received two gifts from Santa Claus, one practical gift like a sweater, and another one that we *really* wanted. One year it was ice-skates, another year a sled, and then, my favorite gift of all, a roll-top desk.

One stormy Christmas Eve, I caught my parents doing Santa's work, and they were stunned to see me. Dad looked tired and shrugged his shoulders, and my mother looked as if she wanted to cry. They defended themselves by saying, "There *really* is a Santa Claus. It's three o'clock in the morning, and this year, he's so busy, he asked us to help him." I believed them, mostly because I *wanted* it to be true. If you believed in Santa Claus, anything was possible. Even Arturo swore there was a Santa Claus, though all my friends said it was a bunch of bull.

We never had Christmas trees or wreaths in our home because my mother was Jewish. I missed not having a tree, but I never admitted it to anyone. I didn't want to hurt my mother's feelings. Only once I asked, "Mom, why don't we have a Christmas tree like everybody else?"

She replied, "It means Christ is in your home."

In my Italian grandmother's house, Christ was everywhere. There were pictures of him bleeding and nailed to a cross. Some of the pictures were scary and frightened me. After that, I didn't want a Christmas tree.

ARTURO HAD A GIRLFIEND WHO had big tits. I had heard his friends say it, so I repeated it to him. He gave me two Indian burns on my wrists, a knuckleball on the head, and told me to keep my dirty little mouth shut. I was bewildered. "What did I say? What are tits?" He educated me. Surprised, I said, "Jeez, I thought they were pimples."

He laughed, and said, "You're thinking of zits, you little shit. Don't you know anything?"

His romance with the girl with big tits lasted two weeks.

I remember skating with Arturo at Deering Oaks. My feet hurt and were so cold and numb that I started to cry. There was a small-enclosed shelter where people put on their skates and warmed up, but it was filled. Arturo managed to muscle-up a seat for me, and removed my skates and socks. He rubbed my feet until they were warm enough for us to walk back home. Someday I'll have a car with a heater in it, and my kids won't have to be cold. He kept saying, "Mikey, we'll be home soon and Mama will give you some hot cocoa. You can do it."

I wasn't sure I could make it; I couldn't feel my feet, and the biting, cold wind stung my eyes. With the snot running from my nose and my eyes filled with tears, I cried, "I can't do it. I'm too cold."

"Oh, yes you can! Don't be a sissy.

He wrapped his scarf around my neck, covering my nose and mouth. Never once, did I think of how cold *he* must have been until Mama said to Arturo, "You poor boy. Your ears are turning blue." Although he was the big brother who bossed me around, and I was the little brother who was always a pest, we looked out for each other.

I never really appreciated him until years later. My life was much easier than his, but Arturo never seemed to resent it, nor the fact that I was smarter, a better athlete, and that I would probably go to college and he would not.

WE HAD LOTS OF oddballs for neighbors. Mr. Cohen, who owned the dry-goods store, sold more sanitary napkins than any place in town. Girls came from miles around, not for the best price, not for the quality of the product, but because Mr. Cohen was devoid of any personality whatsoever and also because it was not a drugstore, there were no young boys hanging around. To him, each sale was an important business venture and little else. He would tell my father, "You take care of the pennies, and the pennies take care of themselves."

The girls felt comfortable buying their unmentionables from him. He was as bald as a bowling ball, wore wire-rimmed glasses, and he spoke with a Yiddish accent. He never looked them in the eye, which was all right with them. After all, what decent girl would want any male to know that she was having her period?

Mr. Gallo, another local character, was a fat no-neck man with a huge belly that he camouflaged with a white apron. He worked at the produce store and liked to gamble on the numbers game, commonly referred to as "nigger pool," a term that no one in *my* family would ever use. While selecting some penny candy at MacDonough's Drugstore. Mr. Gallo said, "Aaaaay Mikey, you look lucky today, give us a number."

"Sure Mr. Gallo. How about 4.6.9. The next day, he won more than four hundred dollars…a fortune…and *I* gave him the winning number. A few days later, he patted me on the head and gave me fifty cents, enough for the movies and popcorn. When I told my dad, he yelled, in his usual way of combining his swear words to increase the insult, "That cheap son-of-a-bitch-bastard! That's all he gave you? Why can't you give *me* a winning number, just once?"

I couldn't, because I didn't know how I did it. After that, everyone was always asking me for numbers, and sure enough, some of them hit the jackpot. From then on, I was called the lucky kid—lucky for everyone but my own family.

Although my father swore, he never allowed us to even say *damn*, and he never used words with sexual connotations. One of his favorite expressions was, "I'm your father. Even if I'm wrong, I'm right."

One day, while I sat at my roll-top desk doing homework, I saw a blurred figure drop outside my open window, followed by the sound of a sickening loud thud. I knew something terrible had happened. I looked out the window and saw Ed Johnson, who lived on the third floor, sprawled motionless on the cement pavement. He had been washing the windows for his pregnant wife. Unbeknownst to him, the window frames were rotted, and he plunged to the ground.

Even though Ed was a big man, and my father a small one, my Dad carried him up three flights of stairs; the rest of us, including Mama and Daisy Maietta followed. When Ed died, lying on the couch where Dad had placed him, my father shook his head in disbelief. "He just had a little blood on his foot. He *can't* be dead." But he was. I stood there and watched my father cry—something I had never seen—something that scared me almost as much as the accident. Mom struggled to hold Ed's hysterical wife in her arms as she screamed and screamed.

After that, my first experience with death, the memory of seeing his falling body haunted me for years. Sometimes I would dream about it. Two weeks after Ed's death, his wife gave birth prematurely to a baby girl: Edna Marie, named for her father. All the tenants felt the landlord was to blame for Ed's death.

MY FATHER'S SISTER, AUNT GRACE, and her family lived in the suburbs. To me, their home was like heaven with an apple green lawn that smelled so clean you wanted to roll in it forever and flowers and fruit that you pick without breaking the law. Every second Sunday, Uncle Albert would pick us up in his big, shiny, black Lincoln. He would drive around his neighborhood with four or five of us kids standing on the running board. We hung on to the car taking turns sitting on his lap, tooting the horn and turning the steering wheel.

The Lincoln car was off limits, but Uncle Albert always had a second junky car that his kids would practice on. Using the stick shift wasn't easy. The only cousin who could drive (in her own fashion) was twelve-year-old Ursula. We would prop her up with pillows so she could peep over the windshield, and still take drags off her brother's cigarette while he sat next to her barking out orders. Drivers and passengers in other cars always gave us a double-look. Sometimes they couldn't see her head peeking over the steering wheel. Routinely, a couple of times a month Ursula would put the car in the wrong gear, or not slam the brakes in time, and it would shoot like a bullet through the garage wall or the garage door. Poooooooow!

"You goddamn kids are going to drive me crazy," yelled my uncle. His five children would mock him and taunt him repeating his own words back to him—then run away laughing. Eventually he would break down and laugh himself. Aunt Grace would shake her finger at him, "What kind of a father are you? Albert, you are all bark and no bite."

On Sunday dinners we ate lasagna, spaghetti or stuffed shells, and green salads with lush tomatoes picked fresh from the garden—planted by my grandfather. Deserts of Italian pastries and fresh pies completed the menu. After dinner was over and the kitchen cleaned up we'd go downstairs to the rumpus room and perform song and dance routines, opera arias, and comedy acts. Jeanette and Guy thought they were Ginger Rogers and Fred Astaire. Patsy, the fatso, thought he was Mario Lanza when he wasn't playing the parish priest, and if he didn't get his way, he'd have a tantrum. Ursula, the toughie of the family liked to belt out Fanny Brice songs. *Someday he'll come along, the man I love, and he'll be big and strong, the man I love...* Our parents and grandparents would laugh so hard they cried. Always, they praised us. Faithfully, on cue Aunt Antoinette always said the same thing. "It's so funny, I think I'm going to pee my pants." At the end of each show, because I knew nothing else, I would sing *God Bless America*, salute, and stand at attention like a soldier. After all, we were at war.

We were lucky. We were too young to fight, and our fathers were too old. One uncle was in the navy, but he was safe. He never left town. He was stationed in Portland, and even then, he once went AWOL for a full day to take a girlfriend to Old Orchard Beach. He was young and a hopeless romantic. He did, however, after a good tongue lashing, learn his lesson and received an honorable discharge at the end of the war. Another uncle was a medic in Hawaii treating the wounded from the Pacific.

Dad's barbershop, with its revolving red and white striped pole outside the door, became the meeting place for paying customers and neighborhood characters convinced that they could solve all the world's problems. It was there that I first heard the words: *The Depression, The War, Churchill, President Roosevelt, Hitler,* and *the Japs*.

When the Japanese attacked Pearl Harbor on December 7, 1941, there were mixed emotions. Grief for the thousands who died there. Anger at those sneaky Japs. There was also the exhilaration that the general population felt—that we were *finally* in the war. Hundreds of thousands of young men volunteered to fight—many lying about their ages. The rest, except for those who were 4-F, would be drafted soon enough. Women became army nurses or joined the newly formed Women's Army Corps or the Waves. We became 100 percent mobilized and committed to winning this war, despite the fact that sixteen other countries had larger armies at that time. Never again would we be isolationists. In the shipyards of South Portland, thousands of men and women poured into the area to build hundreds of victory ships. My father, my uncle and two of my aunts were among them.

Windows with blue star plaques hanging in them were our daily reminders of the war. Nearly every window had one. Some windows had two or more stars. Whenever I saw a gold star in the window, I felt sad because it meant some young guy was dead. I had known a few like Bennie Davis, a Marine who lived in the apartment building next to ours, and Mario Pellegrino, a paratrooper with the 82nd Airborne who had been a star quarterback at Portland High School. We lost so many of our best young people. When the five Sullivan brothers perished and went down in one ship, the United States Congress passed a law protecting the last son in the family and exempting him from the draft. In most cases, it didn't matter, because almost every young man in American wanted to fight and end this terrible war.

It wasn't all bad news. In Dad's shop, I would discover who would be the next brave or reckless fighter to take on the World Heavyweight Champion, Joe Lewis. Everyone was waiting for a white fighter who could beat him, depending on who was talking. Some wanted him to be Italian, others preferred an Irishman. One oddball said it wasn't fair because the Negroes had bigger nostrils, which allowed them to suck in more air. The guys argued about it, but most of them didn't believe it. Before long, Joe Lewis went to war himself and became everyone's hero.

OTHER FAVORITE TOPICS were who won the local numbers game, and, of course, women. I would hear remarks such as, "Hey guys, look at that broad with the big ass walking by in overalls…Dames dressed in pants and doing men's work at the shipyard…and they make fifty bucks a week, too. Can you believe it?" My mother said they should keep their big mouths shut because these women were doing work that was grueling and dangerous, often working fifty or sixty feet above the ground. Such women would gain the title of "Rosie the Riveter."

Always, there was the local gossip, which included some topics discussed only in hushed voices. I knew it was about sex or a dirty joke whenever my father would halt the conversation, and yell out, "Mikey, go run to the bank and get me some change for the cash register."

Dad had no idea that I knew about the facts of life. Except for sports, my friends talked of little else. Arturo gave me a little information, but I think he was uncomfortable talking to his little brother about girls. He had nothing to worry about; I didn't particularly like them. It seemed to me that we didn't have much in common, and that girls were silly and boring. They didn't do anything but jump rope, play hopscotch and giggle. The only exception that I knew of was Lucy.

Lucy.

Lucy dressed like a boy with a boy's haircut slicked back with Brylecream, smoked Camels and could outswear any boy on the block. She was Arturo's age when I saw her beat up a sailor who was bigger and stronger than her. When the locals laughed and told him that he'd been fighting a girl, he gulped, his Adam's apple bobbing. "For Christ's sake, are you *sure*? She's as fast as Willie Pep and hits as hard as a rock," he said in his drawling southern accent, holding a handkerchief over his bleeding nose.

After the fight, Lucy beamed and flexed her arms like superman. The only thing that gave her away was her big rear-end. However, if you weren't looking for it, you probably wouldn't have noticed it, because she always wore loose shirts. We called her a tomboy, but years later, I figured that she must have been a lesbian. If I had heard the word then, I probably would have thought that her parents came from Lesbia: even though I got an A in geography, I didn't know all the countries.

WE WERE AT WAR and everything was rationed: gasoline, butter, meat, and leather shoes. Products made of rubber, tin, and silk were nonexistent; however, the ingenious American scientists invented nylon and artificial rubber. Like most good Americans, we obeyed rationing rules, bought war bonds, collected tin cans and rubber, planted victory gardens, and sent care packages overseas. Local men became air raid wardens, and when the sirens went off, the shades came down and we dimmed our lights. We tried our best to do our part, however small. Nobody cheered louder at the movies than I did when a German or Japanese plane exploded in the sky and went down in flames.

We had so many heroes. Aside from our great generals, Eisenhower, Patton, Bradley, MacArthur and Marshall there were others. Movie stars like Clark Gable and Jimmy Stewert were flyers, and were being shot at for real. The Englishman, Leslie Howard who portrayed Ashley Wilkes in *Gone with the Wind* was in the RAF during the Battle of Britain and died a hero, as well as a whole generation of his country's best and brightest young men. They had emptied the universities of England and they had become heart of the RAF.

Their losses were astronomical. The late President, Teddy Roosevelt's eldest son, Brig. General Theodore Roosevelt, Jr. was, at the age of fifty-six, the oldest man in the invasion. He went in on the first wave at Utah beach on D-Day and died of a heart attack two days later. Millions of others gave up their lives as well to fight in the greatest war the world had ever known.

During the latter part of the war, it was rumored that German U-boats were in Casco Bay and dropping off spies. We were the nearest port to Europe, and a city teeming with sailors and ships, and an island with huge oil storage tanks. Charlie Kelly, one of the local drunks boasted, "I'm heading for the Eastern Promenade with my binoculars. If the *Krauts* are there, I'll spot the bastards. Then I'll get the Coast Guard to blow their asses out of the water." Everyone made fun of him, including me, but years later, we discovered that he probably was right. Someone wrote a book about a couple of German spies who lived on one of the islands and were captured by the FBI. Who knew what was real and what was a rumor?

DURING THOSE WAR YEARS, Dad was recruited for night work at the shipyard, but before he started the job, he taught Mom the fine art of barbering. She filled in for him when he needed a few hours of sleep in the afternoon. My mother was a no-nonsense-in-and-out-barber. When one customer left, she shook the hair off the barber's bib with a smart snap. Then, she swept the hair out from under the stool and yelled out, "Next."

I knew the customers would be glad to see the war end and get my dad back fulltime, especially *Little Louie*, who wrote up the illegal numbers game. He didn't worry much 'cause some of his best customers were policeman. Mom put a stop to that; even Dad couldn't change her mind. Little Louie was out of business in my Dad's shop. Mom's presence made the customers nervous. No more swearing, no more grinding their cigarettes out on the floor. She'd put her hand on her hip, and then glare at them with her accusing eyes. Nobody broke her rules more than once.

Even the complainers were quick to admit that my mother was beautiful. I used to stare at her perfect teeth—so straight and white that they didn't look real. She had black curly hair, brilliant dark eyes, high cheekbones, and perfectly chiseled features. She had the appearance and mannerisms of someone who was well educated and she could mix with anyone. She was always a lady. Her only real fault was her fiery temper, which matched my father's. Although it was always verbal, always in the privacy of our home and over quickly, they scared the living daylights out of me. They were both born under the sign of Scorpio, the most passionate sign in the zodiac and it showed in their emotions. Although they were never demonstrative in front of us, I knew that they loved each other—intensely.

My Dad was my mother's equal in the looks department. He was small, slim and dapper. He sported a Clark Gable type of mustache, and had black wavy hair. A Roman nose complimented his handsome face. His nickname was "The Sheik," which he acquired in his bachelor days for his elegant clothes, his adeptness on the dance floor and his likeness to Rudolph Valentino, the matinee idol who caused more than one woman to commit suicide when he died.

I was in the barbershop when I heard someone yell in the doorway, "Hey, Sheik, did you hear—the president died." I saw grown men including my own father cry like they lost someone in their own family. This man who had given so much, including his own fragile health, who could not even walk, did not live to see the war end. Also, everyone was afraid that our new president, Harry Truman, would be in over his head.

As kids, we had no idea that we were living in a time when more history was being made than ever before. War had been waged on five continents. The largest invasion the world had ever known became known as D-Day. That day, June 6, 1944 was also my twelfth birthday. Auturo was almost seventeen, nearly old enough to fight. He begged my parents to sign the papers so he could enlist. They refused. Other events remain in my memory: the deaths of Mussolini and Hitler, V-E Day, Hiroshima and Nagasaki, and finally, the unconditional surrender of Japan. The war was over, and the world would never again be the same.

Our country, our city, and our neighborhood erupted with unabashed joy. Bonfires lit the streets on most street intersections, and people celebrated well into the night and early morning. Thousands of sailors and civilians were getting drunk, blowing party horns, and kissing everyone—including me. A fat lady with arched penciled eyebrows, a mustache, and heavily rouged cheeks grabbed me, and gave me a big wet kiss on my mouth. I ran home disgusted and scrubbed my face until it hurt. I stunk of her cheap perfume and lipstick. Unfortunately, it was my first kiss, but I knew that things could only get better from now on.

Finally, the world was at peace. We were the most powerful nation in the world, and we thought that war was over forever. There was, however, an ominous cloud on the horizon. It was called Communism.

MY WEEKENDS WERE unlike those of most people. My parents were of two different religions; my father was a Roman Catholic and my mother an Orthodox Jew. It started with a meatless Friday and confession with my Catholic friends (I only watched) progressed to Shabbut dinner at sundown with my Jewish grandparents, and climaxed on Sunday with a visit to my Italian grandparents. Because of the mix, both families disowned my parents, but after their first child, Auturo was born, the two families grudgingly accepted each another.

The only other person I knew who had the same dilemma was my best friend David Bennett. His mother was Irish Catholic, and his Dad was Jewish. He was also my biggest rival academically. His dream was to be a lawyer. Having little time to practice, he wasn't much of an athlete. His father preferred that he spend his time at Hebrew School, studying for his Bar Mitzvah.

David was the only one who understood my confusion about religion. It wasn't just about choosing a faith—it was about choosing between parents, something I couldn't do. My Catholics friends told me I would go to hell because I never went to confession. Five minutes after they confessed, they would start committing sins (real and imagined) until the next Friday. My Jewish Uncle Louie, who was only five years older than I, and so much wiser, told me that holy water was actually piss, and to add further insult, he said it came from the priests. After that, every time I went into the Catholic Church, I eyed the "holy water," and watched as my friends put it all over their faces and chests when they entered the church and made the sign of the cross. I would shudder with revulsion as I watched them, and was glad I wasn't a Catholic. Another time, my Italian cousin, Guy, got mad at me, and even though we were as close as bugs, he called me a Jew-boy and said I killed Christ. Hell, I didn't even know him. When I was older, I realized that prejudice existed in all religions, and I wasn't sure if I ever wanted to join any faith. It was enough that I believed in God and the Ten Commandments.

My dad emigrated to the United States from Vieste, Italy, a small fishing town on the Adriatic Sea, with his family in 1916, during the First World War. While on the ship, he watched for torpedoes and whales. He said he had a great time while my Grandmother and Aunt Grace were below deck, seasick. My Grandfather waited for them in New York to bring them to Portland.

My grandparents and others, who came to Portland from Vieste and other southern Italian towns, lived on Deer Street, or nearby. It was called "Little Italy." Behind the fences, gardens flourished, and the new immigrants made wine in their dark cellars just like they did in Italy. To the new Americans, it was a way of reminding themselves of their homeland. Across the street was Cremo's Bakery where bread was baked exactly the same way as in the old country. My grandparents never felt the necessity to learn any more than rudimentary English: on Deer Street, everyone spoke Italian.

They owned a two-family house. They lived downstairs, while upstairs was the younger son, who was now married, out of the navy, and busy making babies. Grandpa made the wine and Grandma sold it by the glassful, managing to become, by our standards, a wealthy woman. It never bothered her that it was against the law. My Dad claimed that she had thirty thousand dollars hidden in her house—she didn't trust banks. The whole family was in awe of her—and her word was law.

Grandma's hair was jet-black, and her eyesight was so good that she sewed without glasses until she was an old woman. Her face was round with a double chin, and her skin remained as smooth as a woman half her age.

Her home was immaculately clean with starched, crocheted doilies on every arm and headrest of her velour stuffed furniture. She owned an expensive seal coat, which she never wore except on Christmas, as she was certain one of her jealous neighbors would give her *the evil eye.* She had a magic piano that played by itself when you put a roller in it and pedaled it with your feet. Once or twice a year, she would let us play it, but only if she was there, watching us with her stern dark eyes. She was, however, generous, and loved to hand out five-dollar bills to her many grandchildren on Sunday visits or holidays. We would line up for inspection—she would feel our upper arms to make sure we weren't too thin, then give us the money and kiss us on both cheeks.

My grandfather was a laborer, a gardener, a lover of animals, and the best darn smelt fisherman that ever set foot on the Portland Harbor wharf. He was a simple man. He lived to be eighty-nine, dying peacefully in his sleep of old age.

Friday nights we would visit my mother's family and celebrate the beginning of the Sabbath. Climbing the long dark stairs in the hallway, I held my breath trying to block out the smell of cat urine and cabbage. Once inside, it was like entering the world of a *shatetl* (a small village) where everyone spoke Yiddish; the men dressed in dark suits with prayer shawls around their necks and wore scull caps called *yarmulkes* on their heads. It was a gloomy place, a world submerged in poverty, and I hated it. I once asked my mother, "Why do they wear hats when they eat?"

She answered, "To show reverence to God."

I never received long explanations from my mother, just the facts.

Often, there would be strange looking and bad-smelling bearded men joining us for the Shubutz dinner of chicken soup, *gefilte* fish, potato *koogle* and *tsimious*, and *chullah* bread. I gingerly ate the food, and completely avoided the gefilte fish. Why would anyone want to eat a ground up fish ball? I had to admit I loved the bread and the potato koogle. *Zadie*, my grandfather, would bring men home from *shul* after prayers if they had no other place to go. *Bubbe,* my grandmother would lecture him,"*Ve* are a poor family. *Vhy* don't you think of your own family first?"

On Saturday, nobody did anything. The men walked to the synagogue and the women stayed home. It was the day of the Lord, and they were not allowed to cook or even to turn on the light switch. Again, I asked my mother, "Why can't they turn on the lights?"

She responded, "Because in the old days, it meant lighting a fire, and that was considered work, something you don't do on the Sabbath."

My Jewish grandparents could speak English, but with an accent—they had both come from Eastern Europe and could speak several other languages as well. However, their accent annoyed me, so I asked my grandmother, "Why do you say *vhy* and *vhat* instead of *why* and *what*?"

"*Vhat* are you talking about?" she would shout.

Although I wasn't fond of my grandmother, I felt sorry for her. She lost dozens of relatives in the Holocaust, including her parents. In all, about forty people. She was born in Austria, and her brother brought her to this country when she was fifteen to work in a sweatshop, in New York City. When she was sixteen, she married my grandfather who was a widower with five children. When the war ended, every couple of months, my mother would contact the Red Cross to see if anyone had been found alive. I used to visualize all those people being herded into gas chambers—even little babies—and they were *my* relatives. Although I never met any of them, it made the war more personal to me.

In both of my grandparents' homes, everyone talked at the same time. You had to be quick as lightning to get in a word, amid all the arguments and interruptions.

My family, of Mediterranean and Eastern European origin, was more emotional, more melodramatic, and more intrusive into family affairs than other families. If they were angry, they yelled. If they were sad, they cried. My mother's family was so unpredictable that they sometimes laughed while they were still crying. If they hurt, they complained—a lot!

My grandmother spread misery like an atom bomb spread radiation. Maybe she had never experienced happiness. She never forgave my mother for marrying my father, a gentile. She told me that she wished my mother, her own daughter, would get cancer. When she said things like that I hated her, and for the way she looked at me with indifference because my brother and I were *goyiem.* She never smiled at us like she did with my red-headed Jewish cousin Lennie from Hartford, Conn. who spent summers with my mother's divorced sister, and had become like another brother to me. Looking back on it now, I see her for what she was—an uneducated, intolerant, pathetically poor woman who just didn't know any better.

Whenever relatives came from out-of-town to visit, she would say, "Here come the *mashuganas.*" It was her favorite Yiddish idiom. Ironically, she called others crazy people, and although she wasn't crazy in the true sense, I think she was incapable of experiencing or giving joy. However, Zadie, the most religious of all my grandparents, truly loved me and I loved him. According to my mother, he was a direct descendant of Aaron, Moses's brother. How they knew that for sure, after all this time, I didn't know, but they seemed to know it at the orthodox synagogue where he was held in high esteem. His only sin was having more children than he could afford and for turning his back on an occupation he hated—tailoring. If he had done that, my mother would never have grown up poor and without a high school diploma that meant everything to her.

In spite of their different religions, or maybe because of it, my parents each remained steadfast to their own religion and their marriage. As for me, more than anything, I just wanted to be an American. I didn't want to hear foreign languages, or eat strange foods, or be confused about whether Jesus was the son of God or a false messiah, so I vowed that when I had a family, we would be of one religion, and be so normal and so American that my children would never feel different.

Chapter 5

MOVING TO ROSEMONT

Catastrophe had struck! When the Second World War ended, our economic status moved up a few notches, which was good. As a result, we moved to the suburbs, which was bad, but only for me. In fact, there was a mass exodus for families like mine. It was ironic, but true, that only because of a war were we finally able to afford a home of our own. No more struggling to pay the rent. No more groveling to a disdainful landlord for more heat, or better lighting in the dark hallway, or safer windowpanes that prevented people from falling to their death. But this was my parents' dream, not mine. I was selfish—I didn't want to leave Portland High and all my gutsy buddies who weren't afraid of anything. I couldn't imagine being at Deering High with their mediocre teams and all those upper-class kids; many of whom went to college. Maybe they won at tennis and other lightweight sports, but at Portland High we were always contenders in football, basketball and swimming.

After a long hassle, I was allowed to remain, but only because I had completed my freshman year at Portland High School and my basketball coach fought for me. As a freshman, I had made the varsity basketball team as a guard, and was the only left-handed pitcher on the baseball team. David beat me out for president of the class, but being vice-president was still an honor.

The first night in Rosemont, I couldn't sleep—it was too quiet. I missed the sound of rumbling trucks and fire engines and late night chatter on the sidewalk below our apartment. I didn't miss the drunks urinating, swearing and fighting in the alleyway that separated our apartment from the next building. However, there was one redeeming factor which outweighed all others. At last, I had my own room, and I could snore or do all the other obnoxious, distracting, and private things that people do when they're alone, including staying up half the night reading without my older brother punching me out.

The first visitors we got were Aunt Grace and Uncle Albert, and their five kids.

My aunt said, "Oh, Rachael, you have a real fireplace and such a modern kitchen. I love the breakfast room, and it's so sunny! And all those gorgeous lilacs in the yard."

"It is. I really love it here, but it's so quiet. I don't know any of my neighbors. I hope they're friendly."

Dad took Uncle Albert outside to show him the garden and the garage, which had no car in it. That would come next year.

I took the cousins upstairs to see my bedroom with the sundeck that swept over the kitchen. My devilish cousin Ursula said, "Hey, Mike, that's a great place to sneak a cigarette without leaving the house."

"I don't smoke, remember, and I don't plan to start. It's not good for you. Look, what it did to you—you're a runt." Good-natured as always, she and her brother Guy laughed their heads off along with my cousin Lennie who practically lived at our house on his summer visits. Now that Lennie had grown up, my grandmother wasn't too fond of him either.

After they left, Mom was in a dither. The youngest child, a real hellion, had spilled lemonade on her brand new couch, and she was furious. "Those wild Indians!"

Next to the house was a beautifully landscaped lot that belonged to us. Because it was a duplex house, we were landlords and had a tenant that paid *us* rent. Mom was overwhelmed with happiness, and Dad, as usual, was afraid that he was in over his head–the Depression had intimidated him, possibly for life. Our white Colonial house with an entrance adorned with two pillars at the entrance was the largest and the best-looking house on the broad tree-lined street.

Not only did we move out of the old neighborhood, but eventually, most everyone else did too. Our new address never had the warmth or the intimacy of our old one, as all of our new neighbors minded their own business. It wasn't that they weren't good people, just that they were different.

A few years later, we did less visiting and more staring into an illuminated box called a television set. From the comfort of our sofa we watched The *Howdy Dowdy Show*, *Roller Derby*, the *Red Sox*, *the American Playhouse*, and everything in between. It was still a miracle to us. We watched the news of the world nightly; the planet's greatest celebrations and calamities invaded our living rooms, ensuring that our lives would never again be the same.

I GRADUATED in June, the class of 1950, the same month and the same year that we went to war with Korea. It was a year of mixed events—we were the state champions in basketball, the New England champions in swimming, and we beat the hell out of Deering in football on Thanksgiving Day. I was the Valedictorian of our class, David Bennett, the Salutatorian. I chose to speak about "duty to country," as my valedictory theme.

On the day of my graduation exercises, I looked out at a sea of wavy faces and prayed that my rubbery legs would hold me up and that I wouldn't forget my speech.

"Today is the culmination of four years, the day we seniors have been waiting for…Our hope is that we can make a difference in the world…Now, our country is at war…Our generation, as all past generations have done, must answer the call—"

When I finished, there was a hush; and then the audience exploded into applause, but none more than the Conti family, especially my brother who probably would be drafted and have to fight in Korea. At that moment, I remembered what my mother had said many years before: "Michael, you are special. You can be anything you want to be."

At the end of the graduation ceremony, my class, almost three hundred and fifty strong, sang the "The Battle Hymn of the Republic," with fervor. Boys and girls that had never sung before together became sopranos, altos, baritones, and tenors. Under the direction of two dedicated female teachers, we came close to sounding as good as the Mormon Tabernacle Choir.

As captain of the basketball team that had won the Class A Maine State Championship. I was flooded with college applications. I had to make a decision fast. The problem was money—I had none, and neither did my parents. Despite my academics, it was understood that to be granted a scholarship, I would have to play basketball, which was okay with me because I loved the game.

Bowdoin College offered me something close to a "full boat," so I gratefully accepted it. I figured that if the college was good enough for such famous people as Nathaniel Hawthorne, Franklin Pierce, Joshua Chamberlain, and Henry Wadsworth Longfellow, then it was good enough for me, though scholarships at Dartmouth and Princeton were tempting as well. David was also accepted, thus continuing our streak of being together since kindergarten. Everything would have been perfect, if only Arturo didn't have to leave for basic training in the army within the month. I told him he should have enlisted in the navy before they got him, but he said, "What the hell difference does it make? It's my duty to go."

I DIDN'T HAVE MUCH TIME for girls, though I did date one. Her name was Lorna Heinz, and she was a "hubba, hubba girl," whom I took to my senior prom. She wanted to go steady, and we did for a little while, but I still had my dream, and she wasn't in it. When she started suggesting what courses I should take and how many nights she wanted to see me, I balked—she was too bossy for me. That is not to say that my hormones weren't raging like every other eighteen-year-old guy. But with my father lecturing me about "ruining my life," I decided to err on the side of prudence. There was no way that I was going to spend my best years pumping gas and burping a baby.

That summer I worked in the produce department at a supermarket to earn enough money to buy a second-hand car. It was a blue Ford coupe with a rumble seat, a broken heater, bald tires, and a badly dented fender. It wasn't much, but it would get me where I had to go. By comparison, David's car was a little better than mine, but not by much.

I arrived at college with a packed car stuffed with clothes, a new Smith-Corona typewriter, a record player, a few framed pictures, and my treasured baseball glove.

Dave and I were to be roommates, which took the pressure off sharing a room with someone I didn't know. Leaving home for the first time made me both excited and apprehensive. Bowdoin was a little Ivy League college and I wondered if Dave and I would fit in.

Everywhere I looked, shiny automobiles were loaded with luggage and bicycles. Parents, siblings, and students all looked like they had just stepped out of Brooks Brothers. Girls in dark wool Bermuda shorts and Camel's hair coats kissed their brothers and boyfriends good-by. Guys dressed in white, v-necked tennis sweaters, chino pants, and sporting white buck shoes spelled trouble to me. I wasn't dressed right, nor was David.

Eventually I saw one guy in front of my dorm who looked more like us. He had a beak of a nose, unruly dark brows, and swarthy skin. At first glance, I thought he might be a foreign student, so I walked over to him as he struggled to get his trunk off the top of his car. I heard him muttering some choice swearwords that were strictly American.

"Could you use some help? I'm Michael Conti," I said, and extended my hand.

"Hi. I sure could. I'm Andy Maroulian from Lewiston, and I know who *you* are, you son-of-a-bitch. You're the guy who knocked us out of the Western Maine quarterfinals. But I'll shake your hand anyway."

He grinned from ear to ear. He pumped my hand hard, and I knew then that I had found a buddy.

While having lunch in the cafeteria the next day, Andy complained, "What an asshole I've got for a roommate. He's never in his room—which is okay with me. Most of the time he's wandering around the campus looking for someone from Exeter, or St. Paul's, or some other private school. All he talks about is drinking, skiing, broads, and a lot…I mean a bucket load…of bullshit. He asked me what my father did for a living. I told him 'He's a baker.' That prick then had the nerve to ask me how a guy like me could afford Bowdoin. I told him it's none of his goddamn business."

"He sounds like a real jerk," I said.

"I could have told him that my old man employs fifteen people, but I didn't—I don't give out information to people I don't like."

"What are you going to do about it?"

"I'm going to switch roommates as soon as I can. He doesn't like me either. There's a Jap kid here that nobody wants to room with, but he's a hell of a lot better than that creep. In fact, I like the Jap. He was just a kid when the war was on."

Years later, Andy Maroulian would become a United States Senator from our state, Clifford Potter Howe the 3rd, his first roommate, would be struggling to sell stocks and bonds to his rich relatives and their friends; and Andy's new Japanese roommate would become the CEO of a Japanese company as big as Sony.

When parents' weekend arrived, I was nervous. I wanted them to feel comfortable, for it was their dream as much as mine to see me in college. Dad was dressed meticulously in his only suit, a blue pinstripe. Mom wore a new dress that she had made from a Vogue pattern. I thought they looked great until I noticed that all the other parents were dressed more casually. The only colored boy in our class was with his parents, and they were also wearing their Sunday best. Anyway, I didn't give a shit. I thought that my folks looked fine. I introduced them to the president of the college, and although he was a bit condescending, he was polite. They didn't pick up on it, so no real harm was done. My parents enjoyed the visit, and that's what mattered.

I was well prepared for Bowdoin. I knew I lacked some of the social skills but academically, the teachers at Portland High had done a good job. By the end of the first semester, both David and I were at the top of our class—not too shabby for two kids from working-class families. The best news was that I'd be receiving a full scholarship the next year, including room and board, if I could maintain the same average by the end of my freshman year. My parents were thrilled beyond words because money was tight, and they hoped I could do it. To me, it was a done deal.

David and I were initiated into different fraternities, neither of which was one of the upper echelon Greek letter societies. David's fraternity brothers were predominately wealthy Jewish boys. He got along, but his parents weren't from Brookline, Massachusetts, or White Plains, New York, and his father wasn't a doctor, a lawyer, or an owner of a chain of furniture stores; so he had his own demons to deal with. Also, most of his Jewish friends gave only lip service to their religion, whereas David was a devout Orthodox Jew.

My fraternity included the jocks, few as we were. Although it wasn't as snobby as the DEKS, where the best-looking and most insufferable characters lived, it was bad enough. Being a studious athlete helped, but ultimately, it was because of the support I received from another Italian, Freddie Russo. He was one hell-of-an-athlete. He came from the North-End of Boston, where his father owned a shoe repair shop. We met at basketball practice, discovered that we had much in common, and subsequently became friends. Shortly after that, I received an invitation to join Kappa Sigma.

Being a pledge along with the whole initiation process was a pain-in-the-ass, and they made us do a lot of stupid things. My tough upbringing served me well. Compared with the guys of my boyhood neighborhood, these college guys were creampuffs. When it came to toughness, not one of them was in my league, though I admit I didn't like getting my ass whacked. Was it my imagination, or did Andy and I get it a little harder and a little longer. Maybe I was just getting paranoid. I went along with the hazing and the other shenanigans, and chalked it up as another rite of passage.

That first year I waited tables and endured all the indignities thrown my way, especially the ones reserved for those of us on financial scholarship. "Hey, Conti…you *guinea*, how about another glass of milk?" Or "did you hear the joke about the WOP who—" It never bothered me when another Italian or a close friend used those slurs, but hearing it from anyone else pissed me off. I wondered what would come my way when they found out I was half Jewish. Somehow, cracks about Jews always seemed more threatening and sinister.

Like they say about elephants, I had a great memory. I took mental notes on what was said to me and by whom. I learned their game, played by their rules, and waited for the day when I could tell them all where to go.

Being of Armenian ancestry, Andy heard the same thing. "Hey, Andy, did you sell any rugs today?"

At first, he held his tongue. But once he became a brother in the fraternity, he usually would say, up yours, or worse. Andy didn't take any bull from anyone. After a while, we made some friends. We were fraternity brothers, but some of the guys never let us forget that we were different. Deep down inside, we were offended by their remarks, but we kept that to ourselves.

This was not the case at the State University, where there were more of *us* (including tons of veterans) and less of *them*. Bowdoin was an elite college full of WASPS. The important thing was that we received a premium education at a great college—a way to open the doors to politics and to the presidential offices of corporations, banks, and colleges. Andy, David, Freddie and I, and the other token minorities and poor kids were there, and we weren't going to disappear. That was what was important. If we made some friends along the way, it was a bonus. The rest was bullshit.

One young man within that group of rich preppies was different. The first time I saw him, I had to look twice. He looked like a young Charles Lindbergh, tall, fair-haired, and blue-eyed. Everyone was fond of Cammy, the quintessential All-American boy. He was going to become a doctor for all the right reasons. In comparison to him, I felt like a fraud. I envied him for all his ease with people. Unlike me, he had no resentment towards anyone, no chip on his shoulder, and he didn't have the vaguest idea that he was anyone special. Because of Cammy, who became my friend, I began to view my fellow classmates with more tolerance and even with a degree of camaraderie.

One weekend when I went home, my parents had a letter from Auturo. He usually wrote cheerful letters, but this one scared the hell out of us. He wrote, "In case I don't make it back, remember that I love you." My parents cried, and I left the room. Alone, I held Auturo's boxing gloves close to my chest. How many times had he jabbed them in my face? I'd have given anything to have that "big schnoz" back home with me.

Korea was gripped in a brutally cold and snowy winter. The casualties were mounting, and President Truman was facing an unpopular war, which he called "a police action." When the North Koreans retreated, waves and waves of Chinese poured over the borders and joined the North Koreans. There was no end to the Chinese troops, and the news kept getting worse. We suffered huge casualties. Would my generation ever know peace?

By the end of my sophomore year, a letter arrived from the War Department telling us that Arturo had been wounded. We thanked God that it wasn't life threatening, but he would have to spend some time at the Walter Reed Hospital near Washington to recuperate and receive some rehabilitation. My parents didn't know what to expect. Maybe he was worse off than he said.

When Arturo returned home, Mom, Dad, and I were at Union Station to greet him. From a distance, we saw him grimace as he slowly negotiated the train steps and made his way onto the passengers' platform. With a cane in his hand and a duffel bag slung over his shoulder, he limped towards us. Although he looked as though he had aged five years, it didn't matter; my brother was home and alive.

We shouted his name and waved our hands jubilantly while racing towards him. He dropped his bag and held out his arms to Mom and Dad, who covered his face with kisses. Auturo wrapped his arms around both of them.

In my family, fathers and brothers saying, "I love you," or kissing and hugging each other, happened only on special occasions like getting married, surviving an illness, or in this case, returning from a war. For all other occasions, including high-school graduations, a handshake was enough.

Arturo finally turned his attention to me, and grabbed me, blinking back tears. "I'm so glad to see you, Mikey, you little stinker—you'll never know how much." I towered over him and he hugged me so hard I thought he'd crack my ribs. My face was wet, but I was too darn happy to be embarrassed.

During the first few days, I must have asked him at least a dozen questions about his war experiences. He didn't want to talk about them. There was one question I had to ask—it was driving me crazy.

"Artie, did you ever have to kill anyone?"

His face drained of color, and I knew the answer regardless of what he told me.

He took out a pack of Camels, tapped one out, and lit it with his lighter, both hands shaking. "No…not that I know of…killing isn't always close up."

It was a stupid question, and years later, it haunted me that I could have been so insensitive. Eventually, he did tell me about a place called Pork Chop Hill, where enemy gunfire sent him home with a bad leg and a Purple Heart. He was visibly shaken when he said, "I lost a lot of good friends there. They all had families, many were married, and some even had kids. I saw my best friend's face blown away."

Arturo buried his face in his hands. I hadn't seen him really cry since we were both little kids. I tried to console him by touching him on the shoulder. I desperately wanted to say something, but I couldn't find the right words. Silently, I cursed my ineptitude, leaving us with nothing to do but to share the silence.

Arturo cleared his throat and said, "I pray to God that you never have to go to war. It's a nightmare, a living hell, worse than anything you could ever imagine. Remember that, when some big time politician tries to convince you that America needs to go to war—make sure it's the right war for the right reason like the Second World War which had to be fought."

"Do you think you went to war for the right reason in Korea?" I asked.

"That's not for me to say. Let the historians figure it out. They usually get it right eventually."

After awhile, we fell back into our usual routine. Nothing had changed between us. Arturo, though he now asked us to call him Arthur, was still my best friend, toughest critic, and staunchest supporter. After he got home, he never missed a home game at Brunswick. I personally had some good games, but Bowdoin would never have to worry about one of their players going to the NBA.

THE NEXT TWO YEARS whizzed by, and I continued to play both varsity basketball and baseball, maintaining a high point average in my academics. I dated girls from Colby and Westbrook Junior College when I needed a date for a special weekend like homecoming or a house party, but never the same one more than a couple of times. It was safer that way. I continued to receive my full scholarship as the president of the college had promised. In my senior year, my adviser tried to talk me out of applying to Harvard Medical School.

"I say, Conti, Harvard hasn't accepted a Bowdoin student in over three years. Don't you think you could be a little less ambitious?"

"No sir, I don't think so. That's where I want to go."

"But, why, Conti? There are many good medical schools."

"Because. Harvard is the best."

"Yes, yes, Conti. I suppose you're right. Harvard is Harvard, after all."

My friends thought I was slightly nuts. There were many jokes and wisecracks, but that all came to an end when I received my acceptance letter. Everyone seemed surprised—that is, everyone but me. The guys even gave me a party to celebrate the event. That night I got stinking drunk. I was, undoubtedly, the sickest and happiest guy in the world. The next day in one of my classes, Cammy told me that he too was bound for Harvard. The two of us had beaten the odds, though Cammy's Dad was Chief of Surgery at Peter Bent Brigham, and that couldn't have hurt. As equally unexpected and satisfying was the news that David Bennett was going to Yale Law School. I think the preppies were a bit jealous, though some of them got into top-notch graduate schools as well—the difference being that David and I did it against greater odds. There were no alumni paving the way, no generous monetary gifts given to the college, no letters written on our behalf. Euphoria was the only word to describe my parents' reaction to the news. Not only was I the first of my family to graduate from college, but also, I was now going off to medical school. As word got around, my family and I became minor celebrities within the large Italian community. It meant something big, not only to our family, but also to the Italian population at large. Although there were well over a hundred doctors in Portland, only two were Italians. Now there would be three. My Italian grandmother pinched my cheeks and planted a kiss on each of them. In the week that followed, she spent much of her time strutting around the Italian neighborhood telling everyone she knew that her grandson was going to Harvard Medical School like *gli Americani ricchi.*

DEAR OLD BOWDOIN, "the college beneath the pines," had been relatively easy for me. After graduating Magna Cum Laude and Phi Beta Kappa, it could be said that I was a big fish in the small pond. But the famous medical school in Cambridge, was a far different story. Enrolled there were only the brightest of the bright, and not just from the United States, but from all over the world. Suddenly the pond had become an immense lake.

I quickly discovered the benefits of studying both Latin and

Greek. My advisor had said, "To make everything a lot easier, Conti, at medical school and beyond, give Latin and Greek your best effort. Most medical terminology is derived from these languages."

I loved Cambridge: sitting on the banks of the Charles River watching the rowers, strolling through Harvard Square, the old ivy-covered buildings, the Yard, and of course Radcliffe—even though it was on the other side of the Charles River.

We didn't see much of the Cliffies or even had much time for them, but it was pleasant to know they were nearby. I had neither the money nor the inclination to date any of them. Radcliffe gals dressed in cashmere sweater sets, wore real pearls, and dated guys who had decent cars. I doubted they'd be interested in me. I had no long pedigree of rich and prominent relatives, nor was I a member of the Porcellain Club or any other eminent Harvard social organization that could set me up with "the right people" for the rest of my life. I could wait; I had learned to be patient. Nothing on earth was more important than earning my medical degree—all other pursuits, including the search for my dream girl, would have to wait.

Seeking my personal idol was far easier. Every spring through fall he could be seen knocking homers out of Fenway Park. The thrill of seeing Ted Williams, the greatest hitter who ever lived, was not to be taken lightly—nor was the fact that he started "The Jimmy Fund," for children with cancer. Little did I know that some day, his favorite cause and my life's work would be one and the same.

ONE SULTRY NIGHT IN AUGUST, I returned home to Maine for our annual vacation of one whole month for myself. I went to St. Peter's church festival—the annual St. Rocco's Day Bazaar near my old gritty neighborhood. It was there that I again saw Suzanne Mason. She dated my cousin Jim at our high school senior prom. I had danced with her at the prom, but couldn't recall one word of our conversation. The only thing I did remember was Jim calling me the day after the prom, telling me a bunch of nonsense.

"Boy, do I have some news for you. My date, Suzanne Mason, spent the whole damn night asking me questions about you. There's no doubt about it, she's got a crush on you, cousin."

I think I told him that I wouldn't be interested in her in a million years—she wasn't my type.

I thought about that as I watched Suzanne laughing as boys and young men struggled to reach the top of a greased pole for the one hundred-dollar prize. Nearly everyone at the festival was looking up and cheering them on, but my eyes were locked on her. Wearing a red dress, she resembled many of the coeds from Radcliffe with that same air of confidence that made them seem untouchable. Astonished by the change in her, I stood completely captivated, spellbound by her appearance as she stood in the midst of ordinary looking people.

After walking over to reintroduce myself, I tapped her on her arm. Startled, she turned her blond head, and I stared into wide-set blue eyes that were bright with surprise.

"Oh yes, I think I remember you. You are Michael…I'm sorry, but I can't recall your last name." She coyly tilted her head and gave me the who-the-hell-are-you look. Either she had a terrible memory or she was lying. I didn't care which, but it did throw me off my guard.

I felt like a fool and blurted out, "Conti. My last name is Conti…Boy, Suzanne, have you changed!" I was so embarrassed that I can't even remember what she answered. That part of the conversation has become a blur.

I already knew she lived in a seaside mansion in Cape Elizabeth. Anyone who could read a newspaper knew of her family's existence and of their prominence.

Her aunt and uncle were world famous for their philanthropy, their art collection, and their political ties. Within only the last two years, I had read that they pledged millions of dollars towards building a new wing on the hospital. The only connection that I had with her was that her father, a prominent doctor, brought me into the world. There was even a park named after them. No one had to tell me that Suzanne Mason and I came from two different worlds.

In the past, information such as this would have sent me running. "She's out of my league," I would say. Well, maybe not this time.

Suzanne was a little standoffish, but still friendly enough. We talked for about fifteen minutes before she told me that she had graduated from Radcliffe, and I wondered why we had never bumped into each other. It was then that I learned the two of them were roommates with, of all people, my former girlfriend, Lorna. I found out where Suzanne lived, and when I discreetly asked for their telephone number, Elena slipped it to me on the inside of a matchbook.

When she and Elena left, I watched as she drove off in her snazzy red convertible. Strangely, the exhaust fumes lingered far longer than normal. Perhaps it was just my imagination.

When I walked back to the festival, Jim taunted, "Little Suzanne finally grew up. She's even got titties."

I told him to shut his mouth, and playfully jabbed his upper arm, "She didn't even speak to you, you moron."

"That's because her evening with me was unforgettable, a complete disaster. She even admitted to me that I was her first date. I didn't dare to try to kiss her. I was afraid she'd cry."

"She probably was shy."

"Look, Mike, I know you. I can see it in your eyes, the way you looked at her. You're going to ask her out."

"Probably."

"She's not for you. She's not one of us. Christ, those people think we're from another planet. I did some landscaping at their fancy estate, and that mother of hers was a big pain in the ass. She kept looking at us like we were going to steal something. I know these people."

"Thanks for the advice, Jim-bo, but I'm a big boy now."

Two weeks later after calling her for a date twice, and both times been refused, I called again. Usually, my pride would have prevented me from calling a third time, or even a second, but I couldn't get her out of my mind. I called once more and finally got a yes.

We went to see a rerun of *Casablanca*. Like every other girl there, Suzanne wept when Bergman and her husband left Bogie standing in the fog at the airport. Frankly, I preferred Humphrey Bogart playing the role of a crazed killer. I think Suzanne was a little embarrassed when, wiping tears from her eyes, she said, "You must think I'm a sentimental fool, but it was so romantic."

"Oh no, I agree. It was romantic. When my mother saw it, she cried her eyes out." I was secretly amused.

"Not my mother," she said, wistfully.

After the movie, we went to O'Riley's Crimson Pub at Harvard Square for a few drinks. She sipped on a Tom Collins while I had a couple mugs of beer. I had misjudged her at the bazaar. Although the sight of her blew me away, I did sense that she was bit aloof. But I was wrong. She was really quite down-to-earth and uncomplicated like most Mainers. She liked being a reporter and living the single life in Boston. The only time she got serious was when she talked about her father passing away. I could tell that she was still hurting. It had only been a few months since his death.

When the conversation turned to me, I was straight with her. I told her of my limited means and that, because of medical school, I owed my life to the bank. We talked for a while, and she listened attentively without commenting. I ended by saying, "Now you know my life story."

Before I could add another word, she lit up a cigarette, smiled at me, and said, "I have a confession to make. I already knew nearly everything you told me."

"How?" I asked.

"Lorna," she replied. "Lorna knows everything about everybody."

"That figures." I said, and took a final swig of beer, "A word of advice, watch your back with her. Lorna can be vindictive when things aren't going her way."

"Oh. I'm sure you're wrong about her. But I'll be careful."

"Good."

Later that same evening, as we stood beneath a lamppost that lit up the front of her apartment building, I said, "Can I see you again, soon?"

She answered, "I'd like that. Call me, but just make sure it's not on a Thursday. That's my night to do volunteer work at the Children's Hospital. I rock babies to sleep and read stories to the older ones."

I gazed at her through a veil of admiration. The distance that separated our two worlds didn't seem important anymore.

FOR THE NEXT THREE MONTHS we dated many times, or, to be more precise, about as much as my finances and free time would allow. By this time, we had become a couple. About a week before Christmas, I went to her apartment for a party.

I arrived late, around ten o'clock. Hearing the music from the ground floor, I ran up three flights of stairs, two steps at a time. The party was already in full swing and noisy.

Lorna greeted me at the doorway, the back of her hand resting on her ample hip. She was wearing a green velvet dress with a low neckline that revealed her deep cleavage. She caught me off guard—I was gawking at her breasts. *Jesus, I could feel my face burning.*

She shut the door behind her, which left us alone in the hallway. "Merry Christmas, Michael. Let's just imagine that we're standing under mistletoe." She leaned forward and pressed her body into me. She kissed me teasingly on the mouth, and I knew she was smashed. Her musk-scented perfume was so intoxicating that it buckled my knees. I felt guilty for thinking how damn sexy she looked; I tensed my lips and did not return her kiss.

She whispered into my ear, her warm breath exciting me: "It's not too late for us, Michael. I think about you all the time. I saw the way you looked at me—as if you wanted to eat me all up. Let's meet and talk about this before we both make a terrible mistake."

I was dumbfounded but figured out what was going on. She turned me on, but it had nothing to do with my feelings for her, which were zero. She wanted to break us up. I eased her away, "Suzanne doesn't need enemies, does she Lorna? Not with a friend like you. Stick with Billy. He doesn't mind having a leash around his neck."

She sneered, "I loathe you!"

"Sure you do."

In an instant, her behavior changed like a chameleon and she called out in a singsong voice. "Suzaaaaanne, Michael's here."

Seconds later, Suzanne appeared—effervescent and glamorous. This was a Suzanne I had never seen. She wore a bluish violet dress that matched her eyes, and it rustled when she moved. I was sure that the milky pearls around her neck were the real McCoy. Suzanne was definitely not a Filene's basement shopper.

Uncharacteristically, she threw her arms around my neck and said. "It's so late, I thought you weren't coming." I gently pulled myself away from her not wanting her to feel my hardness.

"I had something I had to do, but I'm here now. I had to deliver a baby—a boy."

"I thought only doctors did that."

"That's what I thought. But he wasn't going to wait for anyone." I told her the whole story, thankful for an interlude, which gave me time to settle down before taking off my coat and entering the apartment.

ONCE INSIDE THE APARTMENT, we could hardly hear each other talk. She grabbed my hand, and led me into the living room—packed from wall to wall with the movers and shakers of my generation. Guys and gals, young and vivacious, were partying as they did in the fifties. Booze and cigarettes were the vices of choice and everybody was doing it. The romantic music in the background had lured several couples onto the dance floor, their bodies glued together. Other couples were kissing each other, oblivious to those around them. It reminded me of a typical frat party back at Bowdoin.

I was glad I had worn my blue blazer and gray pants, as everyone else was dressed to the nines. I was quick to identify a few of my classmates who, when seeing me from across the room, raised their glasses in recognition. Suzanne had given me her beer, so I acknowledged them in a like manner.

A small Christmas tree stood in the far corner of the living room. I stared at the twinkling lights that brightened the silver balls and tinsel, and was struck by the thought that I probably appreciated the tree more than any other person in the room. I felt like a little boy who had been given a wonderful gift. The visual splendor was vastly different from looking at a few stockings hanging from an old water heater. Under the tree were some stuffed animals and a bunch of brightly wrapped packages. Later, I discovered that one of them had my name on it.

Suzanne held my hand firmly and seemed pleased to introduce me to her friends. She called out, "Hey, guys, for those who don't already know him, I'd like you to meet Michael Conti, my boyfriend and another Mainer."

A chorus of voices greeted me, and I performed a mock bow. Suzanne stayed at my side, leaving only a few times to greet latecomers. Each time she left, several young women glanced at me and smiled seductively. Elena came over and kissed me, but on my cheek. "Hi, Mikey, you are *so* cute." she said, a clear enough indication that she too was a bit sloshed.

I think I was the only completely sober person in the place. The clarity of my mind told me it was a great time to be young. America was not at war. There was no Depression. I was doing exactly what I always dreamed of doing and, best of all, for the first time in my life, I was in love.

I stayed late, very late. My offer to help clean up the apartment was gratefully accepted. Lorna excused herself, saying she didn't feel well and went to bed. I wondered which it was—the booze or me.

I was the last to leave. It was three o'clock in the morning. Suzanne walked me out into the hall, and I kissed her goodnight. As we held each other, she whispered, "It's been a wonderful evening. I hate to have it end."

While inhaling her flowery scent, I said, "Yeah, me too. It's been swell. I liked the part about you calling me your boyfriend. Did you mean it?"

"Kiss me and you'll find out."

The kisses of the past were innocent—these were not. We were crossing a line, and I knew from now on, Suzanne would be vulnerable and probably willing to do whatever I asked. In the past, I did my utmost to bring a girl to this point, but this time I resisted that temptation. Instead, I said, "I've never felt like this before about anyone. Honest."

"I feel the same way," she said.

When she gazed up at me, I hoped it really was love that made her eyes mist, and not the smoke that filled the apartment.

Finally, we said goodnight, and I descended the stairs slowly, savoring those last few minutes. After buttoning my coat and turning up the collar, I stepped out onto the old cobbled-stoned street and into the biting December night. Huge snowflakes had started to fall and in the glow of the lamplight, they looked like diamonds. I looked up at her window. As I had anticipated, she was watching, and I waved to her.

The following day, I paid for my late night in spades. My head was pounding and I was late for class, and unprepared. Never had this happened to me before. I arrived in the lecture hall, tip-toed down to my seat, and heard Dr. Stein announce to the class, "How nice to have you with us, Mr. Conti."

I sat down red-faced and opened my notepad. Then the professor shocked us. After a brief lecture, he wished us the happiest of holiday seasons and quickly dismissed us with the flick of his fingers and the word, "Go." It was the first time he had ever shown any sign of warmth. He added that he had to catch a flight to New York to spend Hanukkah with his parents. Religious beliefs aside, we all applauded.

Prior to returning to Portland, I brought Suzanne a kitten. She said, "If it's okay with you, I would like to call him, 'Noel.'"

"What could possibly be more appropriate?" I answered. She handed me a handsomely wrapped box, which I quickly opened. Inside was a beige cashmere scarf. She took it from the box, wrapped it around my neck, pretending to strangle me.

"That's a great gift! I've got something for you, too. Close your eyes and don't open them until I tell you to."

"What is it?"

I took my fraternity pin and carefully attached it to her sweater over the left side of her heart. "Okay, now you can open them."

"It's your Kappa Sigma pin. Oh Michael, thank you."

"You do know what it means, don't you?" I asked.

"It means we are engaged to be engaged."

I finally did it. After playing around with words, I said, "I love you, Suzanne. I'll always love you."

The rest of our time together, I said all the things that a guy tells a girl when he's in love with her. She divulged her secrets, including the fact that she had once loved someone else, but had remained a virgin.

"How do you feel about him now?"

"Michael, believe me, what I felt for him is nothing compared to the way I feel about you. I haven't seen or heard from him in almost a year."

"Okay. I'm glad you told me. I don't want any secrets between us. I'm *not* a virgin, but unlike you, I've never been in love." (Not wanting to spoil my image, my male vanity prevented me from divulging the fact that I had had only a few sexual encounters. I had never been anyone's lover.)

"Do you know that I told my sister five years ago that I loved you?"

"You were just a kid then. You just thought you loved me. This is real."

WE RETURNED HOME for Christmas. As usual, my family's activities were kept simple, as we didn't celebrate Christmas. We made certain, however, to visit all of the relatives on my father's side. There was plenty of food, laughter, and gossip to go around. On Christmas Eve, we all stuffed ourselves on elaborately prepared dishes of lobster and shrimp. I wasn't sure if it was a religious observance or just a family tradition, but the seafood was always a part of the meal. As usual, my paternal grandmother was handing out twenty-dollar bills (she had upped the amount as we grew older) to all the grandchildren. I couldn't help thinking: here's my money for New Year's with Suzanne. It wouldn't pay for caviar and champagne, but it would cover a simple evening out on the town. Before I left for Boston, my Dad slipped me another twenty.

While at home, I had a beer with Jim at our favorite bar. He was doing landscaping in the warm months and plowing snow the rest of the time. Our lives had taken different paths, but we were still close.

"Hey, Cuz, are you getting anything from Suzanne?"

"If I were, I wouldn't tell you," I answered icily.

"Come on—nice girls put out, too."

"Jesus Christ, you're an animal, Jim."

"Yeah, I know I'm a pig. Oink! Oink!"

"Look, Jim, I *love* Suzanne, so get this straight. I don't want to hear anymore from you."

"Gottcha—but could I say one more thing, seriously?"

"Sure, but be careful what you say."

"That rich girl is going to hurt you—she's gonna break your heart. Her kind, and our kind, we don't mix. You're a Wop-Jew. You tell me one other guy that we know that ever got a rich society girl like her."

"You forget, Jim. I'm going to be a doctor, and that levels the playing field. Thanks for the advice. I'll watch myself."

"Okay—end of lecture. I'll keep my trap shut from now on. One other thing, could I borrow your car tomorrow night? Mine's in the garage and I've got a hot date."

"Sure, I'll use my Dad's if I go out."

On the drive back to Boston, Suzanne and I had our first real argument. It was all a misunderstanding, and it shook me up so much that I really lost my temper. She thought I was cheating on her, all because Jim had borrowed my car, went out with some tramp, and left Trojans in the glove compartment. She thought they belonged to me. I explained, without naming Jim, and finally convinced her that they weren't mine. I had made her cry and I felt very bad about that, but I said if she didn't trust me, then we had no future together. I assured her that whatever faults I might have, lying would never be one of them.

That evening she called me on the telephone, apologizing again. I told her that I had already forgotten about it and that everything was perfect. She had news: Lorna and Elena were both engaged. Then she blurted out, "Maybe next year it'll be us."

I suspected that she was just being straightforward and saying what she thought. Then it hit me. Why did it have to be next year? I was twenty-four years old—old enough to know my own mind. I loved her; she loved me. Why couldn't I propose on New Years Eve. So I said to myself, *do it, ask her.*

The last night of the old year was electric—with my big secret still locked in my head. Suzanne looked gorgeous, all dressed-up in a sexy, black dress. Her waist was so small I could almost encircle it with my big hands.

We spent a quiet evening having dinner at Giovanni's, a small Italian restaurant on Hanover Street. We left at about ten-thirty and went back to her apartment. There, Noel greeted us with his playful antics, running around the room with a catnip-stuffed toy mouse in his mouth. We praised and petted him as if we were his doting parents.

We danced to a Jackie Gleason album appropriately entitled, *For Lovers Only*. The melodious sound of a soulful trumpet was featured in all of the songs, including one of my favorites, "My Funny Valentine." As I held her in my arms, I realized that I probably would remember it as one of the most beautiful nights of my life, and only one word could describe it accurately: "magical."

Midnight arrived, and we greeted the New Year with the tinkling of our champagne glasses, ending with a long, lingering kiss. There were no more doubts. I was completely in love, and I was going to propose.

I finally did it. I gave her all the reasons why we shouldn't wait any longer to become engaged. She hesitated, and I thought she was going to turn me down, but she didn't. She accepted my proposal and agreed to be my wife.

Suzanne took me by the hand and led me into her bedroom. What was going to happen? I hadn't expected this. She unzipped her slinky black dress and let it fall to the floor. She was wearing lacy black underwear. I stood there watching, my heart going like a jackhammer. We got on the bed together, and she took my hand and guided it to the inside of her bra. I touched her breast and kissed her neck. I heard her whisper, "I've told you I'm a virgin. I want to be one until we marry. Is that okay with you?"

"If that's what you want, it's what I want."

"Oh, Michael, you're so good. I can't risk getting pregnant for both our sakes. We can make love in other ways. I want you to be happy."

I unhooked her bra clumsily, silently cursing my ineptness. I thought I heard her laugh. Then I buried my face in the softness of her breasts. I brushed my lips against the silky, smooth skin of her midriff. I snapped the waistband of her panties, and she slapped my hand. This time, we both laughed—I knew the ground rules. I ran my hands down the curves of her hips and thighs. I had played around with other girls before, but this was different. This was something sacred; she was going to be my wife, the mother of my children.

JANE, SUZANNE'S YOUNGER SISTER, planned it all. A party would take place on Memorial Day, and I would finally meet Suzanne's mother. I thought she couldn't possibly be as difficult as Suzanne had indicated or as bigoted as Jim said.

I was speechless when I saw Suzanne's home and the surrounding grounds. The view of the sea, several lighthouses, the rocky shores, and the gardens blew me away. I had always observed the ocean from public property, and never from the vantage of a grand estate overlooking the ocean. The differences were immeasurable, and my stomach did flip-flops.

Suzanne took me on a tour of her home and introduced me to her old dog, Daisy, which helped lighten things up. I tried not to react in a way that would make her feel uncomfortable. God, my mother was so proud of her new furniture. Here everything was old—antiques that had been in Suzanne's family for generations. Portraits of Mason and Meredith ancestors lined the walls and stairwells—arched eyebrows over cold eyes, sharp chins that could only belong to New Englanders. I was not prepared for it. I felt insignificant, and unworthy of Suzanne. I could never give her anything like this. I told her so.

"Oh Michael, you're such a fool. We'll be fine. I never told you, but I have a sizable trust fund that will help when you're a poor intern. I don't have to live in a mansion, but I do have to be with you. Someday, we'll have a home of our own. I can wait."

"Suzanne, I didn't know about your trust fund, but you can keep that for the extras that will make you happy. I intend to support my wife. Let's go join the others. I'm all right now. Oh! I forgot. I wanted to tell you one more thing."

She looked startled, like I was going to tell her something awful.

"Your dead relatives look like they could use a good laxative."

She punched me in the arm and laughed. "Show some respect for the dead. One of those faces was my grandfather and he was a sweetie. He built this house."

The party was wonderful and everyone was friendly and not the least bit intimidating. I had to admit it…They were normal people after all.

I had no idea that I would find Edith Mason so charming. That her mother was a beautiful woman didn't surprise me in the least. What did surprise me, however, were her occasional memory lapses in the middle of a sentence. My medical training told me that she might have early onset dementia.

Later in the afternoon, I talked to Jane about it. I felt comfortable with her, as we had already formed a friendly relationship with one another. I'd met her many times. The fact that she had been trained as a nurse was an additional consideration as to whether I should bring up the subject of her mother's health. We talked, and what surprised me was her answer. She said, "Yes, that's exactly what it is. My Dad told me before he died. He asked me not to tell Suzanne—she would discover it soon enough." She added, "My poor mother has always had problems. First, a severe bout of postpartum depression after Robby was born, a couple of nervous breakdowns, and now, this dreadful thing."

I admired Jane tremendously. Sometimes, I thought *she* was the older sister. Suzanne seemed more dependent, not nearly as sharp intellectually as Jane. However, Suzanne suited me perfectly. I wanted a wife, a friend, someone who needed me as much as I needed her. I might have found Jane intimidating.

She continued, "And now, for my news. Would you believe that I've decided to make the transition from nurse to doctor? I'm thinking in the area of neurology, partly because of Mother, but mainly because it's what I've always wanted to do. So I'm going to just go ahead and do it."

I had received two surprises, Edith's health being the bad one and Jane's plans for her future being the good one. "You'll make a fine doctor," I said. "You have the mind and heart for it. I've already met too many who are in for either the prestige or for the money."

"I don't need those things. I'm doing it for me—to prove something to myself—to my dead father and for all the women following me. And of course, for us crazy guinea pigs who will be among the first, especially in the fields of neurology and surgery. That is if I make it."

"You will. Go for it."

The family members knew they were in for a rough ride. Edith Mason was only fifty, and may only have five or six coherent years left, but they would be difficult ones. For the first time, I was glad that Suzanne's mother was financially secure. At least she would be guaranteed the best of care. Her three loving children and, eventually, a staff of professional caregivers would see to that. Nevertheless, it made me sad. It was a devastating disease.

Before I left, Mrs. Mason asked me if I could talk to her privately.

I got a sick feeling in the pit of my stomach; now I was going to meet the real Edith Mason, the one I'd been warned about. We went into the library, which was empty, and we sat down together on the sofa.

"Michael, I hope I'm not being presumptuous, but after looking at you and my daughter together, I can see that it's becoming serious. Am I correct?"

"Yes, Mrs. Mason. We love each other."

"In that case, I will be frank with you. My husband is dead, and, therefore, I think it is my place to speak for him. We hardly know you, but you seem to be a fine, upstanding young man who has a profession and a bright future. You are aware, I'm sure, that Suzanne has a considerable trust fund and will someday be a very wealthy woman."

"Yes, I am aware of that, but before we go any further, I must tell you, I am not in love with Suzanne because of her money. I would still love her even if she were penniless."

"That makes me very happy. I hope you are not offended, because that was not my intention. I just want to be sure that my daughter will be loved as my husband loved me. I would greatly appreciate it if you did not tell Suzanne about our little talk. I know it would upset her."

"Yes, it would. I won't tell her a thing. I promise you."

We left and rejoined the party. I was angry and felt belittled. Once again, I felt as though I didn't belong, as though I was reaching out for something that I wasn't entitled to. This woman was going to be a problem. For someone who had dementia, she certainly spoke to me plainly enough. I felt that she would probably talk to Suzanne, and try to put doubts into her mind. On the other hand, I understood her concern. She was a mother who was trying to protect her daughter from a possible gold digger. After all, she didn't know me. I would prove to her that her doubts about me were unfounded. I promised myself I would keep my oath. I would never tell Suzanne about our conversation.

The next day was dismal, with gray clouds and a pounding rain. The telephone rang, awakening me from a deep sleep. I looked at the clock—it was only 6:15. I groaned, "Oh, Jeez, who's that?" I said, "Hello."

"Oh, Michael, it's so wonderful! Mother said yes. She likes you. She *really* does! She doesn't like most people, at least at first. There's just one catch. Are you ready?"

"Okay, what is it?" I said with my eyes still closed,

"It's not much, considering how demanding Mother can be at times. She wants to plan the wedding, an Episcopalian one. Would that be all right with you and your parents?"

Suddenly I was wide-awake. Did I hear correctly? "You mean she said yes. We can become engaged and get married next year?" *I must have passed the test.*

"Michael. I'm as surprised as you are. I know she liked you, but I didn't think she would agree so easily. After all, she just met you."

"As for my parents, they have never been a problem, you know that. They've known for years that I would take my wife's religion. As for planning weddings, I'm sure your mother knows more about these things. Just one thing, though. My parents want to give us a honeymoon in Greece as a wedding gift. I told them it's your favorite place. After hearing you rave about the Greek Islands, I want to see it for myself."

"They know about us—the part about getting married?" she asked.

"Yeah. I know I said I'd wait—"

"That's okay."

"So it's the Greek Islands for us, one year from now."

"Michael, it couldn't be more perfect, but how can they afford it?"

"My parents are proud people. They want to do this for us. They know that you're the best thing that ever happened to me. It's their wish, so we should let them do it."

I asked how her mother had been so easily persuaded. We had expected some resistance.

" I think Aunt Margaret, Uncle Hubie, and Jane sold Mummy on you, not that it should have been hard. I saw how she looked at you. And Rosie called you a dreamboat."

I didn't know what to say. It had been too easy. Of course, Suzanne knew nothing of my conversation with her mother, which may have convinced her that I was an okay guy. However, I fully realized that it was only because I was becoming a physician that made it all possible. Nice guy or not, she never would have agreed to me becoming her daughter's husband if I had been just a carpenter.

"Suzy, baby, can I please go back to sleep? I'll call you later after I have some coffee and wake up."

As the rain came down in a torrent, thunder shook the house, and I could see the lightning flashing through the window. From downstairs, I could smell coffee percolating. My Dad was an early riser. I wondered if I was dreaming. If I was, I didn't want to wake up. My childhood worries of money, college, and even my conversation with Mrs. Mason ceased to bother me. I listened to the rain hammering the sun deck. Never had my bed felt so comfortable. The rain lulled me back to sleep.

In June, my father gave me three hundred dollars and I bought Suzanne an engagement ring—a three-quarter karat diamond. A week later, we celebrated the event with our two families. The get-together went well. We took everyone to a nice restaurant for brunch. Suzanne wore her new engagement ring, which she kept eyeing. We all drank Bloody Marys and made a few toasts. It was a happy occasion for both families.

I WAS IN MY FINAL year of medical school and was lucky enough to be spending it at one of Harvard's teaching hospitals. Also assigned to the facility was Cammy. We had become best friends. His dad was Chief of Surgery, but that only made things harder for him. He had to prove himself to his demanding father. I was fortunate. I didn't come with any baggage.

The hospital was as demanding and exciting as any place could possibly be. Most of the time, I was mentally and physically exhausted, but always thanking my lucky stars to be there. There were days that we worked as much as thirty-six hours straight, catnapping whenever we could. Sometimes, I was so tired that I could hardly stand. There were no exceptions and no excuses. We were the lowest of the low and at the beck and call of all the doctors and nurses. I knew how the system worked—everyone had to pay their dues. The important thing was the end result—the M. D. after my name.

Though no one told me, I knew that I was at the top of my class.

After going through most of the rotations, I discovered that I enjoyed working with children, something I hadn't expected and I was particularly interested in hematology. Later in the year or during my internship, I would make a decision about specializing.

It was 1958. I had graduated with honors, and we celebrated as families usually do. Within my extended family, the completion of medical school was the ultimate accomplishment. After the graduation ceremony, I joined Suzanne and my happy family.

We had accomplished the American dream beyond our humble expectations: my parents owned their own home, I was a doctor, and Arthur was in his last year of college at the University of Maine through the G. I. bill. The next generation of my family would have it easier.

My Dad lectured us as he had many times before: "That is why we worked so hard, so you would have a profession and be respected and not have to work for peanuts. God bless America, this wonderful country, and God bless you, my son."

Mom's lovely face glowed. "Our dream came true! You did it! Just like I knew you would. Just like your teacher, Miss Murphy, said you would." Arthur stood to one side grinning at me, and next to him was Suzanne with a rose in her hand. She handed it to me, and sealed it with a kiss.

In one week's time, I would marry Suzanne. I had no way of knowing what the future held for us, only the expectation of a happy and productive life with the woman I loved. Nothing could have prepared me for what happened. Even if a psychic had looked into the future and told me, I would not have accepted the prophecy—it was beyond belief.

Chapter 6

THE WEDDING
1958

On the morning of my sister's wedding day, I heard a knock on my bedroom door. I stumbled out of bed, fearing that I had overslept. "Who is it?"

"Jane, it's Mother. It's eight o'clock, and Rosie has breakfast ready. Get up, dear."

"Okay. I'll be down in five minutes."

I put on my ratty chenille robe, bunny slippers, and scuffed into the bathroom. I stared in the mirror. I looked terrible, with dark crescents beneath my eyes and the rise of a pimple on my chin. Why today, of all days? Suzanne and I had stayed up half the night reminiscing about old times. I asked her a question that was driving me crazy, and I had to have an answer. "Why," I asked, "are you having Lorna in your wedding when you know she's not your friend? Or Elena, either for that matter."

"I made a stupid promise when the three of us were in the seventh grade. We agreed to be in each other's weddings. I couldn't back out—it was a question of keeping my word."

That was Suzanne: impetuous, trusting, but above all, true to her word. Knowing my sister, I should have guessed it was something like that.

Rosie called from the bottom of the stairs, "Jane, your breakfast is ready."

I splashed cold water on my face, brushed my teeth, ran a comb through my tangled hair, and dragged myself to the end of the hall and down a long tier of steps to the foyer below. I was exhausted.

Suzanne sat in the kitchen, bright eyed and smiling, sipping her coffee and scanning the morning newspaper. Unlike me, she looked as fresh as the morning dew. Robby was up, too, although he looked even worse than I did. Rosie bustled around the kitchen, but Mother was nowhere to be seen.

Robby rubbed his forehead. He looked at me and said, "What a night we had. I hope Michael feels better than I do. His friend Andy got plastered, but boy can he drink. It's a wonder he could even walk."

"'Tis your own fault, Mr. Robby. You should be coming home after the rehearsal dinner like the rest of the family did."

"Hey Rosie, that's what guys do the night before a wedding. It was Mike's last night of freedom."

"Please pipe down. I'm not awake yet," I said. I poured myself a cup of black coffee. I couldn't believe that in only three hours there would be a wedding.

"Janie, are you getting a zit on your chin?" asked my brother.

"She is," said Suzanne, suddenly looking up from her newspaper. Brothers, who needs them! I drank my coffee and prayed that the guardian angel of pimples would have mercy on me and make it disappear.

The beautician was due to arrive in an hour, and the photographer an hour later. I was getting nervous. "Suzanne, how can you be so calm?"

"Nothing happens until the bride arrives. This is my day, and if I'm a few minutes late, everyone will forgive me."

"Well, I won't," said Mother, as she swept into the kitchen with her arms full of yellow lilies and white peonies that she handed to Rosie to be displayed in the foyer.

"Suzanne, this is your wedding day, and you will not be late. It's rude to keep people waiting, especially on a hot day like this. We have a schedule. It's all written down on my list. Now let's get started!"

I gulped down my coffee, grabbed a piece of French toast, and ran upstairs to take a shower.

FOR THE NEXT TWO HOURS our home was a madhouse. Slowly,

however, everything fell into place. The beautician had worked miracles on me and all imperfections were camouflaged with make-up. I couldn't believe what I saw in the reflection of the mirror; I hardly recognized myself. My eyes were bigger, my lashes longer, my nose smaller and my lips fuller. My billowing yellow gown and picture hat reminded me of Scarlett O'Hara in the first scene of *Gone with the Wind*, when she bedazzled the Tarleton twins.

"Suzanne, you look gorgeous," I exclaimed upon entering her room and saw Mother helping her clasp her necklace.

"Look who's talking. You look pretty sensational yourself."

Suzanne was already dressed in her wedding gown of silk and lace. The bodice, with its portrait neckline and tiny puffed sleeves, clung to her twenty-two inch waist with a voluptuous skirt that was yards and yards of shimmering white silk. Her golden hair fell in ringlets down the back of her slender neck that was now draped with the diamond and sapphire necklace given to her by Uncle Hubert and Aunt Margaret as a wedding gift. She had borrowed my diamond stud earrings and laughingly pulled up her dress and revealed a blue garter. She put her hand over her heart and said, "I have a petal of a white rose from Daddy's funeral in my chemise. It makes me feel like he's here with me."

"He is," said Rosie. Your saintly father is with the good Lord now, but he's watching down over his family. 'Tis a happy day for everyone, including the good man himself."

Mummy stood in awe as the photographer snapped away with his camera. She said, her voice filled with admiration, "Wait until Michael sees you."

THE STAINED GLASS WINDOWS in the church glowed as the late morning sun shown through them. Exquisite white calla lilies and baby's breath adorned the ends of the pews. The organist played the music of Bach and filled the church with glorious intertwining melodies.

Rachael Conti, her black hair styled in a poodle cut, looked radiant in a mauve lace dress as she walked down the aisle smiling, holding the arm of the usher, Cammy.

Mother, escorted by my brother Robby, wore a lilac silk dress, her newly rinsed blond hair drawn back in a chignon. She wore her trademark pearl necklace with her diamond and pearl earrings. As always, she looked elegant.

The men in the wedding party, outfitted in traditional gray morning suits, looked quite handsome, but no one more than Michael.

I was the last to enter before my sister, following the six bridesmaids, each dressed in a gown and picture hat identical to mine, only theirs were in the color of an iris.

The organ's voice reached a crescendo as it played the beginning of Wagner's Wedding March, announcing the arrival of the bride. Everybody rose from their seats, their eyes focused on my sister. Uncle Hubert, bursting with pride and a little sad that his brother wasn't there, escorted Suzanne down the aisle. Beneath the veil that hung to the floor like a white mist, the bride was sentimentally lovely, a vision in a white cloud. She carried a bouquet of ivory roses with trailing ivy.

I watched Michael's mother in the front row as she dabbed her eyes with her handkerchief, smiling through her tears and squeezing her husband's hand. He whispered to his wife, who glowed with love and pride as she looked at their handsome son. My mother showed no outward emotion, but that was just her way. I knew she was happy as well.

After Uncle Hubert lifted Suzanne's veil, he kissed her cheek and joined Mother and Margaret in the front pew.

The bride and groom looked at each other in wonderment: she was nervous and misty-eyed while he was solemn and protective, holding her trembling hands. Reverend Scott read passages from both the Old and New Testaments. Throughout the service, their eyes never left each other. I watched Suzanne's lower lip quiver, and I was afraid she would burst into tears. Her demeanor had changed dramatically since the morning when everything was a lark. I had never seen her look so serious or so in love. *Would anyone ever look at me the way Michael looked at her?*

They repeated their wedding vows clearly and without faltering, exchanged wedding rings, and were pronounced husband and wife. They kissed each other—a whispered kiss—then parted. I heard Michael say, "We made it." Then he gave her a second kiss that was much longer.

Reverend Scott raised his eyebrows and coughed twice. The wedding party burst into chuckles, and we sighed with relief—the pressure was off. Once again, the music of Bach filled the church with the glorious sounds from both the organ and the trumpet.

I arranged Suzanne's gown and veil and returned her bouquet to her; she took Michael's arm and almost danced up the aisle. I had never seen my sister so happy. I linked arms with Arthur, the best man, and the others followed.

THE RECEPTION WAS FLAWLESS. I'll give my mother, the perfect planner, her praise. No detail, however small, escaped her scrutiny. An overhead tent, precisely positioned, big enough for dining and dancing, faced the calm, navy blue sea. The weather was balmy with just a slight breeze. The garden was dazzling as it always was in June. At the center of the garden, a three-tiered, Italian fountain bubbled and gurgled. Even Mother Nature wouldn't have dared to upset Mother's plans.

Beautifully displayed on an array of round tables were hors d'oeuvres of smoked salmon, caviar, oysters, and other Epicurean delights. The guests mingled, pursed their lips—planted air kisses on one another and sipped champagne. Down by the water's edge, the bride and groom were being photographed. In the gazebo, a string quartet dramatically bowed Vivaldi's *The Four Seasons*.

Mother turned to me and sighed. "It's all so lovely. I wish your father were here."

I squeezed her hand. "Me, too, Mom."

While circulating through the diverse group of guests, I heard bits of conversation.

"Jesus H. Christ, Jim, can you believe this place? Our cousin Mike hit the jackpot."

"I'm selling my place in Palm Beach. I know I can get a million for it. It's gotten too flashy, too public, and they're letting anyone move in as long as they have money. I'm moving to Hobe Sound where the blood is bluer than the Atlantic Ocean."

"Rachael, I just met a senator. Can you imagine a big shot like that coming to our son's wedding?"

"But Robby, I don't know you well enough for that."

The most astounding thing of all was hearing Michael's immigrant Italian grandmother conversing in Italian with the Italian ambassador, a houseguest for the weekend at Stonehedge. I didn't know what she was saying, but it obviously charmed him, and he planted a kiss on her plump hand. I saw Mummy staring. What she was thinking?

Everyone was seated forty-five minutes later, and the wedding party made its entrance and sat down. Pinging crystal sent a hush throughout the tent. Arthur, the best man, was to give the first toast. He rose from his chair next to me, and I could see that he was nervous. He kept drumming the fingers of his right hand on the table. I doubt he had ever spoken before a large group of people before; but, once he cleared his throat and began, he was fine. He had a deep baritone voice.

"When my brother was a little boy, he had lots of dreams, but they weren't the usual dreams of a child. When he was only eight, he told me that someday, when he finished college and had a good job, unless he became a fireman, he was going to marry a beautiful girl—more beautiful than anyone I had ever seen. He made it a point to tell me that (everyone laughed), and then he said, 'But she will be have to be nice, too (everyone laughed again), but most important of all, is 'that she share her toys and books with me.' (That brought a cacophony of applause, whistles and chuckles.) Now, raise your glasses—To Michael and Suzanne, his boyhood dreamgirl, may they always share everything: the happy times, the tough times, and all their toys: a home with a mortgage, a house full of kids, a marriage blessed with love and happiness."

The applausc was genuine and enthusiastic. Arthur blushed. I looked at him through new eyes. He had delivered a sweet toast with aplomb, and sunk into his seat, relieved of his final obligation as best man. Other brief toasts followed, some more witty, others more serious, but none more sincere than Arthur's. The string quartet performed Mozart as the waiters served a sumptuous, three-course dinner.

My mother didn't believe in chance. She cautioned the photographer to shoot only candid shots of the two hundred guests—they were not to be bothered. There was no stampede of embarrassed girls reaching for the bridal bouquet, no groping hand searching for the bride's garter, and no boring receiving lines—three wedding customs that my mother could not tolerate. She encouraged Michael and Suzanne to go to each table and greet the guests personally. It all seemed spontaneous, but it had been prearranged down to the last detail. Suzanne went along with everything—she had made a deal with Mother.

MICHAEL AND SUZANNE DANCED their first dance to *I Only Have Eyes For You.* I watched as Michael whirled his bride around the dance floor, pausing several times to kiss Suzanne when their friends baited them with the sound of tinkling glasses.

Rosie had splurged on a new dress and she overflowed in a print of green and white silk. She dabbed her eyes with her lacy handkerchief. *Her little Suzanne was a married woman.* Charles stood next to her, looking slightly embarrassed, but pleased. The old bachelor from Downeast Maine had always favored Suzanne, but then, she always went out of her way to say something kind to him.

The orchestra switched the tempo of the music to swing, and soon everyone was on the dance floor. Most of the men had removed their jackets and were dancing in their shirtsleeves. The temperature had soared to the high eighties. Robby discovered Michael's cousin Ursula, and they were the most athletic of all the dancers. He swung her between his spread legs, and then bounced her round bottom off of both of his knees. All eyes were on them. Even the older crowd joined in, including Margaret and her playboy brother, Buddy. His attractive second wife, Gloria who was best known for making the best-dressed list, stood on the sidelines looking bored. Perhaps she was thinking that Cape Elizabeth wasn't quite as exclusive as Tuxedo Park.

I watched the dancers with delight, and was surprised when Michael's gorgeous friend, Cammy, pulled me onto the dance floor when the next number, a slow one, came on. He had it all—a rare combination of looks, charisma, and intelligence, and unlike the rest of us mortals, he didn't seem to sweat. I get a little nervous when my dance partners are better looking than I am. We circled the dance floor to the *Tennessee Waltz* and I began to feel more confident as we seemed to float around the dance floor. He was a smooth, accomplished dancer, and I was astounded when he said, "You dance beautifully. You're as light as a feather."

"I don't know you well enough to call you a liar, but I do enjoy dancing."

Jim Aliberti approached Mrs. Mason. "Hey, Mrs. Mason, are you pleased with the work we did here?"

"What work is that, young man?"

"The gardening. I'm the one who put the geraniums around the fountain."

"Oh! You're your one of those...*Eyetalian* boys I hired. The place looks very nice—you did a good job."

"Glad you liked it. Remind yourself to tell the boss. We could use a raise. The champagne is super-duper."

"*Really!*"

When they played a tango, Michael's parents glided across the floor, cheek to cheek, like Rudolph Valentino and Pola Negri. Later they changed partners with Edith Mason and Hubert, who also knew a thing or two about the tango. All of the younger couples took this opportunity to get a drink and watch the older crowd put on a show. As Cammy and I stood there watching, he said, "I hate to miss the rest of this, but I'm on duty tonight and have to get back to Boston. Would it be all right if I called you sometime?"

Surprised, I nodded. "Sure. I'd like that." He walked off grinning, his jacket slung over his shoulder. *Why would he want to date me when he could have had anyone?*

Lorna and Billy changed partners with the bride and groom. I kept my eyes glued to Lorna, as she threw her head back, laughing, tossing her long blond hair, trying to make eye contact with Michael, but he was indifferent and hardly looked at her. After one turn on the dance floor, my sister was back in his arms. I couldn't help smirking at Lorna whose eyes riveted back at me. We never did like each other.

Later, with Charles at the wheel of Margaret's Rolls Royce, the wedding couple left for the airport to fly to New York. They would spend their wedding night at the Plaza, then fly on to Greece. Suzanne looked lovely in her pink Palm Beach suit and straw brimmed hat, and Michael was handsome in his new suit. Their happiness showed in their faces like a glow from within. The two families and the wedding party threw kisses and waved good-by to the newlyweds. Suddenly, Mummy and I looked at each other and hugged, tears streaking down her cheeks. It was disconcerting—my mother rarely showed emotion, except when grieving. Like a detective tracking a criminal, I looked for signs of the dementia—there were none. Mummy was simply reacting like a mother.

Suddenly, I needed to be alone. I raced down the stone walkway to the water's edge onto the boat landing, and gazed out on the ocean teeming with seagulls. I inhaled deeply, hoping it would cure me of the blues. Then, the tears came in a rush. What was wrong with me? Suzanne was the sentimental one, not I. My dreams were not her dreams—I wanted to be a doctor like my father. *I was jealous of my own sister because I felt an attraction to Michael. Did that make me evil? Was it incestuous to think of such things?* I didn't want to believe it, but my mind told me it was so. Angry with myself, I was determined to put it out of my mind, convinced that it was possible. I wiped the tears away from my face with the hem of my gown, pulled myself together, and ran back to the house to join the others.

While the catering company was packing the glassware and the musicians were loading their van, we sat in the gazebo. Rosie, Margaret, Mother, and I kicked off our high heels, stretched our legs, and flexed our swollen feet. After polishing off another bottle of champagne, we dissected the guests one by one.

Margaret addressed Mother: "That sister of yours, Marie, is a daring one, she is. And who ever told her that she could wear a strapless dress at her age, with those floppy upper arms?"

"I know. She's always been a showoff," said Mother, her head bobbing.

I couldn't let that one go by. "Margaret, what about *your* sister-in-law, the one married to Buddy? How many face-lifts has she had? And I think she's a bigger snob than Aunt Marie. She didn't speak to anyone."

"That's because she doesn't speak to anyone but God and Mrs. Astor," answered Margaret.

We all got the giggles and laughed even harder when Rosie

asked, “Who the hell is Mrs. Aster? I never heard of her.”

“She’s a friend of mine, and the queen bee of New York society,” said Margaret.

“Huh,” sniffed Rosie, unimpressed.

The men, including Charles, puffed on long Cuban cigars, and I didn’t even know that Charles smoked. At first, he resisted, and didn’t want to join us, but even this modest man could not resist an invitation by Mother when she refused to take no for an answer. On this special day, Rosie, and Charles were family.

We drank a final toast to the bride and groom, made by Margaret.

“To Suzanne and Michael, may they have a great marriage and give us some babies soon.”

“Well, I’m not exactly sure how I feel about being a grandmother yet, but I guess it’s not up to me," said Mother.

Rosie, slightly tipsy, added boldly, “That’s right, Mrs. M. That’s one thing you can’t do for her.”

Mother seemed tired, but happy. Not once during the whole day did she lose her train of thought or stammer over her words. I silently prayed that the dementia would be held at bay at least for a few more years.

As though she read my thoughts, she said, “You know, it would be fun to have a grandchild.” She patted my hand. “I’ve noticed you’ve been very quiet. Don’t worry, some day you’ll fall in love too.”

Chapter 7

ATHENS
1958

After a long, exhausting flight for the passengers on Olympic flight 631, the aircraft finally neared the Athens airport. Aboard were an eclectic group of travelers: businessmen, crying babies, black-clad women chattering in Greek, and a fairly large group of second-generation Americans returning to the homeland of their parents.

"Greece is a photographer's dream," Suzanne said. "Everything is illuminated; it has something to do with the lack of humidity."

As the plane gradually descended, it bumped through the clouds, and the travelers got their first glimpse of the Aegean; a mix of blue and green water with a smear of land sitting on the horizon. They felt the thud of the wheels being lowered and the pull of the air breaks as the plane neared the terminal that was surrounded by the lavender and golden hills of Attica. The aircraft dropped lower and lower until it was only a few feet above the landing strip.

Michael squeezed Suzanne's hand as the airplane bounced down hard on the runway. One passenger yelled out, "Greek pilots land planes like they make love." The honeymooners laughed, everyone applauded, and the religious or more frightened passengers made the sign of the cross three times in the tradition of the Greek Orthodox religion.

The captain's voice boomed over the intercom, "Welcome to Athens, the land of the Gods. The temperature is 90 degrees; the local time is three o'clock. Please remain seated until we have come to a complete stop, and thank you for flying Olympic." He repeated the announcement in Greek, only much more rapidly, or so it seemed. Lively Greek music followed the announcement, stirring lethargic minds and bodies after the long transatlantic flight. Stewardesses scurried up and down the aisles assisting the elderly and passengers with babies.

The Greeks, not known for their patience, rose from their seats instantly and clogged the aisles as they awaited the landing platform. After five or ten minutes of waiting in the hot airplane, tempers rose and one man called out: "What are we—cattle to be left here like animals?" An obese young man, perspiring profusely under the strain of a guitar strapped to his back and carrying two parcels, pushed his way forward, and curses followed. But, by far, the most lethal were little old ladies who used their elbows to finagle their way down the aisle. Suzanne complained to Michael that this wasn't at all like first class where passengers were pampered—this was bedlam.

Clad in a sleeveless, white linen dress and Greek leather sandals, she finally reached the stair ramp. Michael followed. He wore a white short-sleeve polo shirt, chino slacks, and tasseled loafers. Both donned dark sunglasses as they stepped out of the plane under the warm, Greek sun. The breeze off the sea felt refreshing.

"Dr. and Mrs. Conti, enjoy your holiday in Greece," said the immigration officer as he stamped their passports. He smiled broadly, his teeth clamped around a cigarette, and slid their passports back to Michael.

Suzanne complained about the crushing crowds who pushed against them as they left the restricted area. "Let's get out of this madhouse before I drop. It's *so* hot." Perspiration beaded her face; tendrils of golden curls escaped from her ponytail.

"I know it's rough. We've been up nearly thirty hours," said Michael. They quickly learned to elbow their way through the mob of waiting Greeks who gave no quarter.

"I don't think the Greeks use deodorants," Michael whispered.

"Ssssshhhhhh! Someone might hear you."

"I never saw men kiss and hug each other like these people," added Michael.

"The Greeks kiss everyone, not once, but three times, and are even *more* passionate than the Italians."

"And how would you know, my little Yankee WASP?"

"I wasn't just reading books all those years before we met."

"Bragger. Well, neither was I. Anyway, it's too late now. We're married, kiddo."

Michael put his arm around her neck and pretended to strangle her. A child standing nearby pointed his finger at them and said, "Mama, that man is hurting that woman."

The boy's mother grabbed his hand, pulled him towards her, and scolded him, "Mind your own business, and hang on to your things. Wait until *Yia Yia* sees you. The first thing she is going to say is that you're too skinny, and it's your fault because you never eat what I tell you. Now come with me. *Ella! Ella!*"

"How would you like a kid like that?" said Michael.

"Our child will be perfect, just like your mother said you were."

"My mother lied."

After a half-hour, with their luggage collected and their money changed from dollars to drachmas, they were finally riding inside an air-conditioned taxicab. The ride into Athens from the airport was an eye-opener. Billboards lined the highway leading into the city. For the most part, Athens was an ugly capital, a mix of Middle-Eastern style buildings and other more modern nondescript edifices. Somewhere along the way, throughout the centuries, the Greeks had lost their genius for architecture. Maybe six hundred years under the Ottoman Empire, two World Wars, and a Civil War were hard to overcome.

Other capital cities like Paris, Rome, and London revered their churches, their war heroes, their memorial arches and parks. Athens's allure was in the remnants of the ancient past, a pagan city that honored its mythical gods and goddesses with temples that were some of the world's most beautiful architecture.

"Look, Michael! There it is, the Acropolis!"

The chalk white temple of Athena, the Parthenon, stood resplendent and ageless, high on the hill that was called the Acropolis.

"Wow! It's magnificent. More impressive than I expected," he said.

"Michael, architects consider the Parthenon to be the most perfectly constructed building ever created. There is not one vertical line in it. Wait until you see them up close, the Caryatids, the Herod Atticus Theater, and the Acropolis Museum."

"That's first on our sight-seeing list."

"Michael, I think we're getting 'the long ride.' When I was here last, the airport was south of the city, and the Acropolis is in the center of Athens. It didn't take us this long before."

Michael laughed. "Taxi-cab drivers are famous for this. You should see what they do to the tourists in Boston."

"Hush, he might understand you," she whispered.

"He doesn't. I'll prove it. *Tee Karnees?*" Michael said to the cab-driver.

"Ah, you speak some Greek. How good, *kala, kala, efkhardeesto polee*." He repeated in English: "I am fine. Thank you very much. Where you from?" He was swarthy with a bushy mustache. Blue worry beads and baby shoes swung over his rear view mirror. A big sign on the back of his front seat said in English, "*No smoking and please don't slam the door.*"

"So, he doesn't understand English?" taunted Suzanne.

"We're from Boston," answered an embarrassed Michael.

"Oh! Bostoni, I visit my sister seven years ago. Her husband makes much money in his pizza business. Maybe in a few years, I go again."

He rambled on about politics: the cursed Communists, the King and Queen of Greece, Paul, and Fredericka, who, he said with distaste, were actually Germans. He further commented on a variety of subjects: the lack of crime in Greece, and how much the Greeks relished their fresh fish, although it was very expensive and, most of all, how much they loved babies, and of course, Americans. After all, the American president, Harry Truman had saved the Greeks from Communism.

The couple politely listened. "Bravo!' the driver said. "*The Athens Heelton*. Everyone who is important stays here." The taxi drove up the long circular driveway parked with Mercedes and Jaguars and stopped in front of the modern entrance. "The best hotel in Athens. It is very beautiful—the only one in Athens with a swimming pool."

Michael paid the fare, adding fifteen drachmas for a tip. Instantly, the cabdriver became enraged and cursed Michael in Greek. In English he added, "Another cheap American. As bad as the Germans."

He threw the coins to the ground, dumped the luggage on the pavement, and slammed the door. A few seconds later, he quickly reopened the passenger door, and pushed in a bewildered Japanese businessman. He slammed the luggage into the trunk and drove off, the tires screeching.

The doorman shook his fist at him and yelled: "*Boofus*, don't come back here again, you animal!"

"Michael, you gave him next to nothing," said an annoyed Suzanne. "I thought you knew the rate of exchange."

"Jesus, I got confused. I thought I gave him about fifteen percent. I'm a doctor, not a mathematician."

"Welcome," said the now smiling red-coated doorman with golden epaulettes on his shoulders. He snapped his fingers. Immediately a bellboy ran out and loaded the luggage onto a carrier. Two more tips followed, but this time, a more generous amount.

Their suite consisted of two rooms—a bedroom with a king size bed, and a spacious sitting room. A bottle of ouzo, an arrangement of flowers and a basket of fruit were on the coffee table. On the desk lay two cablegrams; one was from Suzanne's family, wishing them a wonderful honeymoon, and the other from Margaret and Hubert, with similar greetings.

"How sweet they all are. The flowers are from your parents. That was thoughtful of them," said Suzanne wistfully.

The black marble bathroom was large and modern, with an enormous bathtub, shower, and bidet. The balcony overlooked the pool, and off in the distance, the incomparable Acropolis loomed above the city.

"Incredible! What a view," exclaimed Michael as he stood on the balcony. "Mom and Dad really came through this time. Someday, I'm going to send them on a trip to some great place. They've never been anywhere except New York. They didn't even have a honeymoon. In fact, they eloped. There weren't many honeymoons during the Depression."

"I think that's a swell idea," said Suzanne as she joined him on the balcony. "They deserve it. Just as soon as my husband starts making some money."

"Boy, that's a nice thought. I've been broke all my life, and probably will be for a few more years, but when I do make some money, that's at the top of my list."

They sat on the balcony, jet-lagged, admiring the view for almost a half-hour. A few children below splashed in the swimming pool. The afternoon was quiet and the streets empty. The outside cafès were closed, as well as all the shops. The silence was soothing. It was the Greek siesta, and everyone was asleep. A few unknowing tourists walked the scorching sidewalks along with stray, skittering cats looking for tidbits.

Sitting there, Suzanne recalled their wedding night at the Plaza in New York City. She remembered her anxiety—her fear. Michael had always been gentle, but having full-blown sex for the first time was different. At first, he kissed her tenderly, then when he thought both were fully aroused, his hands and lips were all over her, stroking, touching, kissing, and then he guided her trembling hand to his body. "He whispered, "I promise you, I'll try not to hurt you."

The new bride discovered that having sex was not unpleasant, but thought, "*Why aren't the bells ringing?*" She was glad to have it out of the way. It wasn't as bad as she had imagined or as wonderful as some romantic novelists had written. This was a subject that *no one,* including her married friends, had ever volunteered to discuss with her.

When it was over, he said, "Next time, it'll be better. I haven't had much experience at this myself."

She clung to him and said, "I'm not disappointed, so you don't have to apologize. We have a whole lifetime to learn together. I do love sleeping with you, cuddling up and feeling all your warmth—you're like a teddy bear." She purred as she twirled her fingers through a patch of hair on his chest. "As for the sex part, you just watch, I'm a fast learner."

It felt strange to be lying next to a man in the same bed when she awoke in the morning. For a moment, she had forgotten where she was. She had awakened first, observing him as he slept. His thick, sooty lashes lay like crescents on his cheeks. His brow was as smooth as a woman's; his hair, in inky, black waves curled up on his forehead. *My God! He's so beautiful.*

Carefully, she slid out of the bed, tiptoed into the bathroom, and looked into the mirror to see if she looked different. Nope, she looked the same. She took a quick shower, brushed her teeth, combed her hair, put on a fresh nightgown, spayed herself with perfume and slipped back into bed. She kissed his cheek, and he woke up.

"Wake up, sleepyhead."

"Can you make it worth my while?"

"Try me."

They made love again. This time it was better.

The shrill sound of the ringing telephone jolted Suzanne back to the present, back to Athens. Michael got up and answered the phone. He called out, "The manager wanted to know if we needed anything."

"Sleep. That's what I need," she said. "But first, I'm taking a shower."

"Not alone. I'm coming, too."

They took off their clothes, and showered together, intending to only freshen up and cool off. Predictably, as soon as their wet bodies touched, they melted in each other's arms. Suzanne protested, "Michael, you promised."

"I know, I lied."

With her back to him, he caressed her soapy breasts with his hands. She arched her back and closed her eyes. Then she turned and faced him saying, "Let's make love, here in the shower."

Michael grinned, "Sounds like a good idea to me."

AFTER CLOSING THE DRAPES, darkening the room, they climbed into the bed that was luxuriously outfitted with Egyptian cotton sheets and fluffy down pillows. Suzanne sighed. "This bed feels just like heaven, so soft and cool, and I'm exhausted." She quickly fell asleep to the droning of the air-conditioner.

Michael was unable to sleep; he was wide-awake. He found it comforting listening to the tranquil and steady rhythm of his wife's breathing as she lay next to him. Even now, he could hardly believe that she belonged to him. He watched her small breasts rise and fall in her blue chiffon nightgown. She was so lovely, her long wet hair spread out on the pillow in a halo of golden ringlets. Her lips were parted like those of a small child.

He rose from his bed, and got a glass of ice water. He glanced around the spacious suite, remembering his tiny room at medical school. Wealthy students paid more for larger quarters—Harvard Medical School was not a democracy. Now the internship at Boston Children's Hospital awaited him, and he would actually be paid a meager wage to do it. He loved medicine so much that he would have paid *them* to intern at such a prestigious hospital. He thought himself a lucky man—to have Suzanne and his profession.

Three nights later, the honeymooners strolled through the ancient Plaka, walking in the same streets where Aristotle and Plato had left their footprints. Although it was eleven, people were still dining. Under a crescent moon the color of an apricot, and a pitch-black sky teeming with twinkling stars, they first caught the sound of the bouzouki.

"Why do you suppose the moon seems so much larger and the stars so much brighter than at home?" asked Suzanne.

"I think it's because we're closer to the equator," said Michael, "But, I'm not sure."

They followed the music inside a taverna and ordered the local favorite, ouzo. They agreed that the milky colored aperitif tasted like licorice. After two more tavernas and more than a couple of ouzos, Suzanne wanted to dance. Michael declined, but encouraged her, clapping his hands in unison with the other spectators as Suzanne danced with one of the waiters. Men on the sidelines of the dance floor smashed plate after plate after plate to the ground—a Greek tradition, yelling, "*Oppa! Oppa!*"

It became obvious to Michael that the handsome young man who introduced himself as Yanni was not just employed as a waiter, for his dancing was professional, his demeanor arrogant, his eyes dark and seductive. With both arms raised above his head, Yanni snapped his fingers and moved his body deliberately and gracefully like a matador. As they danced, they conversed. Michael watched them. What were they talking about? The music of the bouzouki was passionate and more exotic than its sophisticated distant cousin, the guitar. Michael sensed that the music and the ouzo were affecting Suzanne as he watched her flirt—something she had never done before. When the dance ended, Michael stepped onto the dance floor, took

Suzanne's hand, and led her off.

"It's time to go back to the hotel—now."

"I want to dance some more with Yanni. It's sooooo much fun."

"He has to dance with someone else. You're coming with me."

"Just because I married you doesn't make you my boss."

"We'll see about that, Suzy Q."

"Hey! Let the pretty girl stay and have a good time," said Yanni."

"Back off, you jerk," Michael growled.

"Okay, American cowboy—take your woman and go."

It mattered little to Yanni that Suzanne was with a man who was probably her husband. Contemptuously, he watched Michael lead Suzanne out of the taverna. His sneering grin enraged Michael. The dancer continued to eye Suzanne until she left the taverna.

Michael was furious with the Greek, but even more so with his wife. He sat there, stone-faced, his arms folded across his chest looking out the window of the taxi.

"Michael, it doesn't mean anything. Greek men are flirtatious. So are Italians, the French, the Spaniards, but it's harmless. It's just a game to them. First they ask you if you want to sleep with them, and when you say no, they laugh and say, 'Well then, would you like to have a cup of coffee?'" She waited for him to laugh, but he didn't.

"Okay! Give me the silent treatment! Yanni didn't do anything wrong. He just asked me my name, and if I liked staying at the Hilton. Please, don't be mad at me."

"It's not that easy Suzanne. I'm pissed off. You are drunk, and you encouraged him. I almost got into a fight over it."

"Oh, for god's sake! It's a sensuous dance like the tango. We weren't doing a waltz."

Michael saw the cabdriver's ears sit up on his head like a birddog's. "When we get back to the hotel we'll settle this. I don't want to talk about it now."

It was nearly dawn when they returned to their room. Michael remained distant, and Suzanne kept trying to change his mood. Nothing worked. They undressed in silence. The only thing he said was that she should learn to behave herself.

"I'm not your child—I'm your wife."

"Then act like it."

When they got into bed, she felt as though Michael was a stranger. This was their first quarrel since before they became engaged, and she felt guilty—down deep she knew she had gone too far.

As soon as the lights were out, Michael reached over and started groping her. There were no kisses, no signs of affection, just lust, or so it seemed. He rolled over on top of her.

"Michael, get off me!"

He lifted himself above her and looked at her as if she were crazy.

"Look, I'm a little drunk myself...a lot jealous...and a lot horny, but that's all. You act as if I'm about to rape you. Come on, Sue. I won't touch you if you don't want me to."

"I'm sorry, Michael. I didn't mean to yell. You just seemed so different, you scared me. I don't want to fight, and I'm sorry if you think I've done something wrong. You know how much I love you. *Please be nice.*"

"When I saw you with him, it made me crazy. Let's start again. I want to make love to you."

"Then stop talking and do something about it."

His kisses were long and amorous and they stirred her in a way that was different from anything she had ever known before. She felt a rousing within her body. She wanted him, needed him. He had seen the look on her face when she danced with that Greek; she wanted this kind of love and he would give it to her. He forced her mouth open with his tongue and she surrendered unconditionally, not timidly like before, but boldly, giving as much as she got.

Everything changed that night for Suzanne. She felt wave after wave of something she had never experienced. It surged, moving higher and higher. She gripped his shoulders and dug her nails into his skin. She knew she was hurting him, but she couldn't help it. It was beyond her control. She concentrated on a tense point of sensation, which suddenly expelled itself in a fluttering spasm. She made sounds—little screams of pleasure—and she was surprised that they came from her. As she lay there looking up into his eyes he grinned, "You just had your first orgasm, and it was libidinous in medical terminology—a beauty. Did I please you?" She nodded slowly, and he gazed into her eyes, deep pools of blue-violet. She panted, "I never knew how wonderful it could be—like a miracle. Michael, I'm going to love you *forever*."

"Forever is a really long time."

"A lifetime."

"Do you still want to be the mother of my child?"

"Yes—do it."

"Are you sure…you want to get pregnant…so soon?"

"I'm sure."

He had held back as long as he could; now he would take *his* pleasure, and, hopefully, give her the child they both wanted.

When it was over, they lay together exhausted and giddy, tangled in the sheets and with each other. Later when Suzanne drifted off, and somewhere, between consciousness and repose, she heard his voice say softly, "I love you so much—I don't think I could live without you."

THE NEXT DAY THEY DROVE down the coast to the Temple of Poseidon where, like thousands of other tourists, they found Lord Byron's name etched in one of the white marble columns of the temple, which overlooked the horseshoe beach and the turquoise Aegean. After returning to Athens, they marveled at the ancient sculptures and other treasures at the Archeological Museum, and later they shopped in the flea market buying sandals, linens, and copper pots. Like all tourists, they were intoxicated by the low prices, buying things they probably would never use. They even learned to bargain. It was expected, and nobody paid the price asked. It was their last full day in Athens. The next day, they would begin their Aegean cruise.

At the port of Piraeus, they boarded their cruise ship, the *Stella Maris*, and settled into a small, cozy cabin.

They visited the islands of Mykonos, Santorini, Rhodes, and Crete—all equally lovely and distinct with their own special charm. Aboard the ship, they shared drinks and dinners with some fellow Americans and a few other European tourists. They too were as bewitched by the Aegean as others had been for centuries. At night they stood on the deck and watched the moonlight dance on the silvery water.

Crete was the last port of call, and because it was the largest island, they were given a full day to tour it. They rented a Russian-made car and drove by groves of olive trees whose gnarled, twisted trunks looked like gray stone. When the breeze blew, it carried hints of sharp citron, the delicate scent of almond, and other spices.

The sea was on the opposite side of the road, in bands of color, sapphire on the horizon and, nearer the shore, a vivid turquoise. Driving along the coastal road, they discovered a deserted, partially hidden cove. They parked their car, peeled off their clothes down to their underwear, raced down the sandy beach, and dove into the gentle lapping waves. Beneath the surface of the water, they clutched each other and kissed as long as they could until their lungs screamed for air. They were completely alone, except for the colorful fish that darted through their legs. As they walked out of the water, still embracing, Michael said, "This is our private paradise, and some day we'll come back."

"We'll come here again on our tenth anniversary with our children and see if it will still be the same."

"I hope it's sooner than that," said Michael.

That night in their cabin, as they made love, Suzanne flung her arms around his neck and whispered in his ear, "I want you to—"

"Do you mean it?" he asked.

"I do."

This would be his first taste of erotica beyond rudimentary sex, and because it was his wife, it was a gift—one that he had not expected so soon—or that *she* would be the first to suggest it. He kissed the instep of her slender foot, and ran his lips in a row of kisses up to her knee and beyond. She cried, "I love you. I love you, I love you," until the words ended in a whisper. He had stirred something wild in her, and it occurred to him that he had awakened a sleeping tigress—perhaps one that he could not please. It troubled him, causing him to wonder if his passion would ever match hers.

Tomorrow the cruise would end, and the Crusader fortress of Rhodes, the windmills of Mykonos, the cliff side cafés of Santorini, and the magical beach of Crete would soon become an indelible memory.

ON THEIR LAST NIGHT IN ATHENS, the new Mr. and Mrs. Conti dined early in the hotel restaurant and then spent their final hour drinking gin and tonics (they had had enough ouzo) on the terrace of the rooftop cocktail lounge—enjoying one last look at Athens at night. A warm balmy breeze caressed them as they watched a light show being performed at the Acropolis. The ancient ruins were aglow as the colors changed from red to blue to yellow to white. It was mesmerizing and a lovely way to end the final night of their wedding trip.

By nine o'clock, Suzanne had finished packing and Michael was in the shower. She opened the shower door, and said, "I'll be back in about an hour. I want to do a little shopping in the arcade for the family, and I saw a pair of earrings in the jewelry store that I *must* have. I'll have to hurry. It closes in about an hour."

After she left the bathroom, he yelled, "Would you pick up the *Herald Tribune* for me?"

"Okay. See you soon," said Suzanne.

After about ninety minutes, Michael dressed, and went downstairs to the lobby. He looked everywhere for her, questioning the shopkeepers who were closing up for the night, but nobody had seen her. When another hour passed, he felt panicky.

Mr. Spanos, the hotel manager, was reassuring and calm. "Perhaps she stepped outside the hotel to shop at a jewelry store, or went to the hotel across the street to shop. Some shops stay open later. You know women. They love to shop."

"You don't know my wife. When she says she'll be back in an hour, that's what she means. Something is wrong! I know it. Call the police."

"Where is her passport?"

"She carries it with her. She needs it for identification when she cashes her traveler's checks."

"You know, Dr. Conti, in our country an American passport is very valuable. Sometimes they are stolen and then sold for a lot of money. Perhaps she lost it or someone forgot to give it back to her, and she is just trying to find it. Or maybe, she's at a sidewalk café having a late snack—there are several around here. Everything will be all right. Athens is an extremely safe city." The manager tried to sound convincing.

"It's *not* all right. She doesn't speak Greek. She's in a strange city. We're supposed to leave on an early flight in the morning. It's nearly midnight. Help me find her. Call the police—now!"

"Yes, of course. Also, I'll call security and then we'll check the entire hotel. Maybe, she is ill in one of the ladies' bathrooms."

"I never thought of that. I'm sorry I yelled at you, but I have a terrible feeling about this."

Within fifteen minutes, two policemen arrived at the hotel. Everyone at the front desk was in frenzy.

After Michael had shown them a picture of Suzanne and described her clothing, they asked the usual questions. Did they have an argument? Was she feeling well when she left? Did she have any mental problems? Did she meet any men while she was in Athens? Michael answered no to all of them.

"Wait! There was one man who flirted with her at a nightspot in the Plaka."

"What was the name of the place?"

"Ahh, let's see, it was the Achilles Taverna."

The older policeman did all the talking. "That place! What did he look like?"

He was good looking, medium height, slender but muscular, black curly hair, black eyes, and he had a tattoo on his right forearm. It said something in Greek with a rose."

"What did he wear?"

"Black pants, very tight, white shirt, also tight, opened to the third button down. His chest was hairy, and he wore a big golden cross on a heavy chain," described Michael.

"Did he have a mustache?"

"No, he didn't."

"Dr. Conti, you just described half the young men in Athens. The other half have mustaches. Do you know his name?"

"Yes, it was Yanni."

"That means John and that name is as common here as it is in America, but we will check it out. Don't worry. We will find her."

The younger policemen offered his opinion, "Is it possible that she went to meet him somewhere?"

"No! It's not possible." Michael said angrily. "We are leaving for the United States tomorrow. My wife wouldn't do that!"

The older policeman took charge again: "Dr. Conti, why did you let your wife dance with this man?"

"I saw nothing wrong with it. He danced with other women before my wife. I thought it was just part of the entertainment."

The officer continued, "I must tell you Dr. Conti, no Greek husband in his right mind would let his wife dance with one of these…what do you call them in the states…oh…gigolos. Here we call them animals. They prey on women, especially blond, blue-eyed women. Some of the Scandinavian and German women and others throw themselves at these men because they have no morals, but these men can't always tell the difference."

"You are not describing my wife. We are on our honeymoon."

"Of course. You are right. We will come back tomorrow. Tonight we will look for your wife. We will do our best. *Adio*, Dr. Conti."

Michael saw the policemen laughing, as they paused to light up cigarettes as they passed through the opened entrance of the hotel. He stood there dismissing them as fools, his fists clenched in tight balls jammed in his pants pockets, fighting his own helplessness.

The next day, after the longest eight hours of Michael's life, Suzanne was still missing. After he talked to the Greek police the next morning, they confirmed that nobody named Yanni worked at the Achilles Taverna. They said he must have been a customer. The waiters did remember him dancing, but they didn't know his name, or so they said. But this time, the police seemed genuinely concerned. Michael insisted that they call Interpol. They said that they would discuss that with the Chief of Police.

The junior official at the American Embassy was indifferent, a typical bureaucrat, and said it was in the hands of the Greek police, and he couldn't interfere. Michael asked to see the ambassador and was told that was impossible. He was in Washington.

"*What an asshole,*" he muttered as he left the building. He looked up at the American flag that was snapping in the breeze and then at the marine guard at the entrance of the embassy and wished to God that he had never left the United States.

It was as though the earth had swallowed her up and she had never existed. The church ceremony, the reception, their wedding night at the Plaza, their Greek cruise...all a mirage.

Michael telephoned the Mason family with the horrible news. When he spoke to Jane, he heard her gasp.

"Oh, my God! She's what—" Then he heard the sound of wailing—it was probably Suzanne's mother or maybe Rosie.

"I'll call you back. I can get a flight and join you—I'll let you know when I'm arriving," Jane said, her voice shaky.

"Okay. I could use an ally. I don't know what else to do," said Michael and then his voice broke. Jane could hear it—great, choking sobs that split her heart in two. Tears rolled down her cheeks. She had been strong until now. There was nothing that was more heartbreaking to a woman than the sound or sight of a man crying.

"I'm sorry...I can't talk," he cried.

Jane put the phone down; she looked at her mother who had thrown herself on the sofa and was beating the pillows with her fists. "Why? Why? Why does everyone I love leave me?"

It's my fault. I was jealous of my own sister and now God is punishing me.

Margaret called Senator Moore, a longtime friend, whose niece Marilyn, a famous model from New York City, was also missing in Greece and had been for four days. It was an inconceivably frightening coincidence since Greece was known to have little crime. Senator Moore assured Margaret he would pull every string he could to find them. He called Interpol, having little faith in the Greek police who weren't exactly Scotland Yard.

Michael tried to sleep, but sleep didn't come that first night, or the second. Finally, after three days, he was so exhausted he couldn't stay awake. He dreamt of a swirling tunnel of mist; at the end of the tunnel was Suzanne, in her blue chiffon nightgown, her eyes frantic, her arms reaching out to him. He woke up in a sweat and said aloud, "Oh, Suzanne, what's happened to you?"

When Jane returned his call to tell him she was coming to Athens, he said, "No. Stay with your mother. I can only remain a few more days and then I have to return home. There isn't anything you can do here. I'm sorry I lost it when I spoke to you—I'll be all right.

I need to be strong for Suzanne—she's somewhere, and they'll find her."

On his last night in Athens, he got a visit from the older policeman who had interviewed him on the night of Suzanne's disappearance. As Michael silently packed his clothes in the suitcase, the policeman said his name was Demo Vamvakias. He told Michael his story.

In 1922, when he and his family and hundreds of thousands of Greeks and Armenians were fleeing the burning Greek city of Smyrna in Asia Minor, he lost his younger sister, Anna. Some said the fleeing Greek Army burned the city. Others said it was the Turks. It didn't matter; his only remaining living relative had disappeared. In the craziness of mass hysteria, fire, looting, and the murdering Turks, her hand had slipped out of his in the crowd. It was his fault, he said. He should have held her hand tighter. He looked everywhere—amongst the dead, the raped, the wounded, the starving. The Turks had mutilated many women's bodies—breasts cut off. In a sea of faces of people who were going mad, he looked for her in her green silk dress. She had wanted to look pretty when she boarded the boat for Athens. Pregnant women, newborn babies, the very old and the very young suffered the most. Most young Greek men were with the evacuating army and had left the country earlier. The boats in the harbor from many nations had refused to pick up the fleeing refugees. Why they wouldn't do it, only God knows. Because he was a good swimmer, he reached a Japanese boat, the only nation that actually welcomed survivors.

"That was over thirty years ago and I still think of her. My little sister with her golden hair and blue eyes. Only thirteen. I hope she died. To think of her with the Turks would be worse. They are the most barbaric people in the world. They came from the East, you know; this was always Greek land. So you see, I understand what it is like to lose someone you love, so young. I still think of her all the time. She loved to sing, to dance, to climb trees like a boy." He became very emotional and suddenly hugged Michael, whose arms remained at his side. Demo patted him on his back. "We will keep looking, my friend. I promise you." If that was supposed to make Michael feel better, it didn't, but it raised his opinion of the Greek policeman. His concern did seem genuine. The staff at the hotel expressed their concern daily. Mr. Spanos, the manager at the hotel, refused to charge him for the last week. He even invited him to his home for dinner. In another time, he would have appreciated the warmth and compassion of the Greek people, but at that time, he was numb.

Michael returned to Boston grief-stricken, heartbroken. The Chief of Staff at the hospital was sympathetic, but made it clear the year's rotation had started and he was already late. If he wanted the internship, he must start immediately. He never once entertained the theory that Suzanne was dead—either by accident or by murder. If she were dead, they would have found a body. Someone had taken her, but by whom and why would remain a mystery to Michael for nine long tortuous years.

Chapter 8

CAPTIVITY
1958

After enduring five days of captivity, it was sinking in: I was *not* going to be rescued, a terrifying thought that was still incomprehensible. So I prayed—something I had not done in a long time. I yearned for my freedom, for my husband, Michael. Less important things reigned high on my list of priorities as well—simple things like a shower, clean clothing, and most of all, a cigarette. Why did I ever start smoking?

Along with six other women, I was confined to an unventilated basement room that reeked of human waste and sweat. Humidity hung in the air, and dark, clammy rings formed under the arms of my once crisp, cotton dress. For the first time in my life, I looked and smelled like a derelict.

It was impossible to think clearly or to sleep more than a few hours at a time. What I really wanted was for my mind to escape to a better place, where I could be with Michael. Where I could savor those warm memories of us together—dancing in each other's arms, making love, laughing, and even arguing.

Being imprisoned behind a locked door gave me, as well as the others, a feeling of claustrophobia. We were getting on each other's nerves. Veronica and Marilyn continued to bicker, Elizabeth and Alice remained terrified, and Bridget never stopped crying. The only one who I found to be both pleasant and intelligent was Alexandra who became my friend during those trying days.

A day earlier, in the obscurity of the early hours of the morning while it was still dark, "the goons," as we called them, sneaked us into a doctor's office for medical examinations. We were tested for venereal disease, and several of us were singled out for a "special treatment," as the doctor called it. I heard the doctor say to Kareem, *"I will send over the results as soon as I know, and tell the Frenchwoman I want my money in dollars, not drachmas or francs."*

ONE OF OUR KIDNAPPERS, whom we named "wolfman" unlocked the door and entered with Madame Boudreau, "the midget." The only bit of fun we had as prisoners was giving each of our captors a nickname, mostly made-up by Marilyn. Following the midget were Kareem and another middle-aged, fat man I had never seen before. He was dressed in a wrinkled, white linen suit, black and white spectator shoes, and a Panama hat. Something told me he was the ringleader of this whole thing. He was not an Arab, probably not a Frenchman either, but who? A Greek? He didn't look Greek. He was too tall and too fair to be Greek. Marilyn gave him the name Sid, after Sidney Greenstreet, the character actor of *Casablanca* fame. Later, I came to the conclusion that this was a renegade group of men and women who were white slavers for profit and did not represent any particular people or government. The truth, however, might never be known.

When Madam inquired about our treatment, as if she cared, we said nothing and just scowled at her.

Then, like a battering ram, one by one, she told us our fate.

"Veronica, you are diseased—you will no longer remain with the group. But the rest of you are not infected."

"What will happen to her?" Alexandra asked.

"Nothing. She will return to the streets where she came from."

The German prostitute clawed at her captors as they tried to lead her away but she fought them, and she screamed at Madam Boudreau. "You're lying! I'm clean. You just want to kill me!"

Kareem, the only Arab who spoke English drew back his fist and smashed it into her face. I saw an explosion of blood and heard the crunch of bone. She collapsed like a puppet whose strings had been broken, and they dragged her out with both her feet trailing on the ground.

I looked at my fellow captives. We each saw the fear in the other's faces. Poor Veronica's nose was probably broken. The ball game had changed. Violence was no longer just a possibility—it was a fact. Marilyn and I never got an opportunity to put a plan of escape into action. Talk was cheap but without a weapon, we were helpless, and they had just shown that they were willing to hurt us.

Madam Boudreau mumbled something to the man in the Panama hat. He nodded in agreement, and I wondered what had been said. *Had he agreed to have Veronica killed?*

She asked us, "Why would I want to commit murder over someone like her—someone worthless, ugly, and diseased?" If that was supposed to relieve our fears, it didn't. She continued speaking to us as though she were describing a list of inanimate objects. "Alice, you are a drug addict, and Bridget, you are not attractive enough for our special clients, so together you will leave for another place."

They screamed. Bridget cried, "I don't want to go. Please let me stay with the others."

Alice pleaded, "I only take drugs once in a while. I'm a diabetic. Why won't you believe me?" I don't want to become a whore."

Madam stood there, with her arms folded across her chest, showing no sympathy for anyone, even for Bridget who was more a child than a woman. Those poor girls! My heart broke for them. Most likely, they would end up in a brothel, where they would become prostitutes or a love-slave—both terrible possibilities. If looks could have killed, Madam would have been dead. We all hated her.

"The rest of you will remain together. You are the lucky ones," said Madame Boudreau. I didn't feel so lucky.

I shivered as I recalled our visit to the doctor's office the previous night where Marilyn and I had been reinstated to the status of virgins. Elizabeth, Bridget, and Alexandra did not need it. The doctor had said, "It's a treatment often done in this part of the world where men will pay a premium price for a virgin. A few stitches in the right place, and you are as you were before—a virgin." He added, proudly, that he had saved the lives of many Muslim women who for one reason or another lacked a maidenhead.

He did his work quickly and efficiently. The procedure was painful though bearable, but when Marilyn screamed, his demeanor changed and he shouted at her in a voice like gravel, "Shut up you fool! Someone will hear you."

When it was my turn, I bit my lips, promising myself I would not make a sound. I would not give him the satisfaction of knowing that he had hurt me or violated my body. I will never forget his face—sallow and doughy with hooded lids and dark eyes; steel-rimmed glasses hooked over his large ears.

BLINDFOLDED AND GAGGED, we were guided up a flight of stairs, out of a building, and lifted into a truck. We bounced along for about half an hour in silence. From the movements and the sounds that followed, it was obvious that we were in an airplane. Someone had fastened our seat belts. Once airborne, we heard Madam speaking in Arabic to several men. It was almost reassuring to hear her voice. Although she was the enemy, somehow I felt that she cared about what happened to us, even though it might just be for our monetary value. She removed our blindfolds and gags, and we found ourselves in a comfortable private airplane. Two silent men sat at the front of the plane—the enforcers. A smiling Indian stewardess (assumed by the cadence of her English) with skin the color of honey, offered us warm towels and served us yogurt, fruit, and tea. *I wanted to scream at her: Look at us! We are prisoners! But of course, she knew that.*

For a long time, we flew over water, and the sky was blue and cloudless. About two hours into the flight, land appeared. I looked out the window and studied the terrain below. It was mountainous and barren, without any greenery. To the rear of the airplane was the fading sea. *Where the hell were we?* Alexandra and Marilyn kept their composure, but Elizabeth was terrified and started to hyperventilate. Madame Boudreau gave her a pill to calm her down. It worked, and a few minutes later she was slumped over in her seat.

The next few days remained a blur. I have only a vague recollection of leaving the airplane; our food was probably drugged to make us docile. How else could we have allowed women to strip us of our clothes and remove all our body hair? After boiling a concoction of sugar, rosewater, and lemon juice, it was smeared on our bodies in a paste. When it dried, it was ripped off along with the hair. Everyone screamed from the pain. I can still hear Marilyn yelling at the two African women who held her down, "Leave me alone, you *schvatza* bitches!

Marilyn's vocabulary was laced with Yiddish and curse words, which she used with relish, mainly to entertain or shock us. However, she was in fact well-educated, and from a prominent New York family, or so she claimed. When she wasn't swearing, her diction, nasal sounding voice, and choice of words reminded me of the debutantes from my days at Radcliffe. Life as a model in the garment district and later on in magazines had drawn her to the jargon of homosexual men and immigrant Jews who ruled the fashion world.

A mix of servants, African and Arab women, chatted among themselves in Arabic, giggling and wondering what we would think when we discovered that we had to repeat this hair removal routine for as long as we maintained an intimate relationship with a Muslim man. Alexandra repeated everything they had said about us in English. We laughed at them—they were totally surprised that Alex understood Arabic.

The boss of the whole production, an Arabic woman by the look of her, told us that we must always clothe ourselves in a cloak-like garment (an abaaya) when we left our homes, that covered everything but our faces. A gauzy veil took care of that. The abaayas were black and silky, and beneath them, we wore modest clothing. The Arab women added that we were fortunate, because most abaayas were made of heavy cotton and the veils were usually much thicker. Marilyn, in her usual fashion, had a wisecrack to share. "Hey girls, aren't we lucky? We get to wear Arab couturier clothes—the latest thing in desert fashion." She said it mockingly, fully aware of our helplessness.

Madam Boudreau made one last appearance. We pleaded with her to notify our families and assured her that she would be richly rewarded, with no questions asked. I played my final ace and told her my aunt was Margaret Bowes, one of the richest women in the world. She answered, "So what. I know who she is, but she can't help you."

We gathered in an office, and she stood behind a desk in front of us, small-boned and delicate—with a veneer of steel. She held out her pack of cigarettes; two of us reached for one. Madam lit them with her lighter and Marilyn and I shared an ashtray.

"Mesdemoiselles, welcome to Riyadh, the capital of Saudi Arabia. I am going to tell you how to survive, so listen carefully. Men rule this place! This is the most extreme of all Islamic countries. They follow a conservative form of Islam, called *Wahhabism.* The rules for women are fanatical, and punishments *are* enforced. Women cannot vote, carry their own passports, travel unescorted, drive cars, or go unveiled except in private homes. Women's births and deaths are not recorded in official records. In many ways, you will not exist. They make no excuses when they refer to you as inferior—it's in the Koran. Most men and almost as many women believe it. The paradox is that there are women in this country who are wealthy, beyond any woman's wealth in the Western world, including that of Queen Elizabeth and Queen Beatrix, but even these women have no freedom."

She paused and lit another cigarette, her third. By all indications, she was a chain-smoker. I couldn't help but notice her inelegant, black dress with a high neck and long sleeves. Except for the colorful kerchief that covered her hair, she was dressed modestly.

"Earlier in this decade, a Saudi princess committed adultery and was sentenced to death. Young and beautiful, she had been forced to marry a sadistic older man. When she fell in love with a younger man, another member of the royal family, they were caught together trying to sneak out of the country. One of the requirements for a conviction is the sworn testimony of four male witnesses, or eight female witnesses, which tells you what their courts think of women. Unfortunately for the princess and her lover, the court had the required four male witnesses, and the princess and her lover were sentenced to death. The Western world was shocked, appealing to the King to have mercy. He refused. The punishment for adultery by a woman is stoning. Because she was a princess, she was spared the punishment of stoning, and shot in a parking lot. Her lover was beheaded in a public square. If they show no mercy to their own princesses, what can you expect? If you commit adultery, you *will* be stoned to death."

She stopped to drink a glass of water. I took this opportunity to ask a question.

"Madam Boudreau, why do they stone women for adultery?"

"It is a custom that probably goes way back to the days of the Jews, long before there was a Muslim religion. In all Muslim countries, it is the worst crime a woman can commit—even worse than murder because adultery always involves dishonor."

"But what makes it a death sentence?" I asked.

"Because the honor of the woman's family has been destroyed and can never be reclaimed until she is killed. Until that happens, they are all shunned and have no recourse. Any more questions?"

Marilyn stood up, strutted over to her, and said defiantly, "It's not a question—it's sort of a statement. She screamed, "You French bitch! You've ruined our lives!" Then she spat in her face.

There was a collective gasp from the group. Smirking, Marilyn sashayed back to her chair, sat down, and crossed her long legs under her abaaya, muttering under her breath, "who gives a damn about these people and their customs anyway."

Madam stood perfectly still, her gray eyes ablaze, the sides of her mouth curving downward, her chin defiant. She reached into her handbag, took out a handkerchief, and wiped the spittle off her face. She pointed her finger at Marilyn. "I could kill you for that. But then, I would not have the money that you will bring me. Think about that when some old Arab is poking his thing in you." She stopped to light another cigarette and passed them around to us again. Marilyn, a true New Yorker, had the chutzpah to actually take one from her.

"You will be presented to a group of men wealthy from oil revenues, to which there will be no end in our lifetime, or for that matter, in your great-grandchildren's lifetime. They will pay a fortune for you. If you are smart, you will make it work for you. Some are princes in the royal family. Most are seeking third or fourth wives or concubines, mistresses—whatever you choose to call them. They requested virgins only, which is a clear indication that you are to become a permanent fixture in their lives, at least until they tire of you. You could never be a first wife, or even a second; they only marry cousins from the paternal side of the family."

There was a knock on the door—we were being summoned.

"As for you, Mademoiselle Marilyn, I predict a *bad* end—no Arab man will tolerate your impudent behavior. They will deal with you—I promise you that. *Adieu,* Mesdemoiselles, and good luck."

RIDING ON DUSTY AND BUMPY dirt roads in a Cadillac with

darkened windows, the four of us continued on our journey, only this time there were no blindfolds. The air-conditioner groaned, competing with a blazing noon sun. The driver was a Saudi, as was the man sitting next to him in the front seat—the same two hoods that were on the airplane. We sat in the backseat, stuck to one another like glue. I sat next to the window, looked out, and was as bewildered as *Alice* going through the *Looking Glass*. It was a depressing sight. There was not a speck of green anywhere. Only endless miles of beige and swirling sand everywhere.

Men dressed in white shifts led camels along the roadside, which was heaped with debris of every type imaginable: worn tires, mounds of trash, rotting dead animals, and lots of camel dung.

Many buildings were under construction. The hard-hatted workers, African and Asian men, wore gauze masks over their faces to protect them from the desert sand. Caucasian men operated the forklifts and bulldozers, and other white men huddled over blueprints, pointing and shouting to the workers. Not once did I see a Saudi man laboring in the heat of that desert kingdom.

Alexandra exclaimed, "This certainly isn't Beirut or anything like it. No sidewalk cafes or elegantly dressed women."

"Oh God! Don't ask how much I miss New York," said Marilyn. "I'll never complain again when I get back to the Big Apple."

"Do you really think that's possible?" I asked.

"When they tire of us—they'll ship us back home. For Christ's sake, Suzanne! They aren't going to kill us."

Marilyn's words cheered me. Perhaps she was right. I continued to observe the surroundings. There was no order to anything. A new building, landscaped with small date palm trees, stood next to a house made of dried mud. It was obvious that this was a country in flux. Occasionally, figures that looked like penguins in their black abaayas and veils appeared on the unpaved roads, carrying shopping bags and holding the hands of their male children. They were no little girls to be seen and hardly any women. Men walked everywhere, often holding hands.

Marilyn said, "Where the hell are we, in Greenwich Village? There are queers everywhere!"

Alexandra explained. "Walking and holding hands is just their custom. Homosexuality is banned in the Koran—but it still goes on, privately just as it does in every country. I've been told by classmates in Beirut that if they are caught by the *metawain* they would be arrested and lashed in a public square."

There were many mosques—some big, some small—some magnificently decorated in colored tiles with golden domes. Minarets stood out, as they were taller than all the surrounding buildings. Alexandra explained, "That is where a religious person, a *muezzin* calls the people to pray, five times a day and everything stops. Shops close, especially at mid-afternoon when the prayers last three quarters of an hour."

The man in the passenger's seat turned around and growled something in Arabic. Alexandra lowered her eyes and stopped talking. Elizabeth had not spoken a word, and we are worried about her. Even in the heat of Arabia, I could feel her shivering as she pressed close to me. Luckily, the car was very large, and we were all thin—we sat four abreast. We passed a marketplace with crowds of people milling about. About ten kilometers later we drove to a residential area.

We approached a large Moorish styled building encircled by walls on all sides. Two tall Africans who towered over everyone opened the gates and we drove in. It must have been newly built, for I could see the beginnings of a lawn growing. It was more than a residence, or even an estate. *It must be a palace.* When we emerged from the air-conditioned Cadillac, the full blast of the heat hit me. It was as though I had opened the door of a fiery furnace. I had been to Greece in August when the temperature hovered at over hundred degrees, but this was something else—something merciless.

GUIDED INTO A ROOM THAT WAS large and opulent, I stared at the burgundy satin drapes, the golden wallpaper. The furniture was made of expensive ebony and rosewood. Everything in the room was overkill—my mother would have laughed at its gaudiness. On the floor lay the largest Persian silk carpet I had ever seen. It was the only truly beautiful thing in the room and glowed in the sunlight with an iridescent sheen of blue.

We were seated and served tea by a woman with eggplant colored skin. I had never seen anyone so dark or so graceful. She moved like a gazelle and her neck stretched even longer than Audrey Hepburn's. The ceiling fans circulated the air through the air-conditioned room. Through the French doors, we could see a swimming pool and lush gardens with red and fuchsia bougainvillea climbing the white stucco walls. The scent of jasmine from the garden permeated the room. Marilyn giggled, "The furniture looks like early Frankenstein."

I was losing patience with her. "Marilyn, this is no joke. This is for real. We are going to be sold—like cattle."

Six men entered the room through a large archway. They seated themselves on several large couches. Four were dressed in long, white, shirt-like garments which I later learned were called *thobes*. They wore red and white cloth *ghutras* with double black cords on the crowns of their heads. Only one man was young, about thirty; the others were ten to twenty years older. He was dressed in a business suit and reminded me of Nikos, Andreas's handsome friend that I had met in Greece, except that this man was taller, his complexion a bit darker and he sported a thin mustache. His eyes were jet-black and intelligent as he observed everything around him. He carried himself with a look of athleticism and elegance that was lacking in the others. *If it must be, let him be the one.*

The other man in Western dress spoke to us in English. He held four books in his hand and gave one to each of us. "This is the Koran. We live and die by this book. These are the words of Mohammed the prophet, Allah be praised." He paused, "This is the only time you will ever remove your veils to any man, except the one who becomes your master. Take them off and show yourselves, your eyes to the floor. You must never look at men directly in the eyes. It is forbidden, so remember that."

Alexandra was the first to rise. When she removed her veil and they saw her angelic face and waist length hair, I heard a series of gasps. There was no doubt that *she* was the prize. They would all want her. I stood next. The men mumbled among themselves. I was different—blonde, and blue-eyed and I knew that I had made a favorable impression. Elizabeth followed, struggling to lift her veil. Her eyes were red from crying and tears were falling down her cheeks. Her lips quivered. I heard one of the men say, "Ah! She is so young and modest." Finally, Marilyn, who towered over everyone in the room except for the handsome young Arab, yanked off her veil. Although she kept her eyes glued to the floor, her body language told a different story.

The bearded and middle-aged man who had commented on Elizabeth, swaggered over and stopped in front of her. He put his hands on her shoulders, and turned her so that her back faced the other men. He parted her cloak, reached into her dress, and felt her breasts. I tried to keep my gaze downward, but I could not. I turned my head slightly, saw his ugly face with his hawk nose and thin lips, and trembled. I was sure I was looking at the devil incarnate.

He spoke in fractured English, wanting the girl to understand him. "This one I want. Before seven days pass, she be circumcised like Muslim woman. Then she be mine. *Insh'allah.*" This was a word I would hear over and over again at the beginning of every statement, and at the end of every question. I learned it meant God Willing. Elizabeth swayed from side to side, and I thought she was about to faint.

I noticed the youngest Arab looked uncomfortable. He shifted in his chair, then whispered angrily to the man next to him.

After some haggling and shouting, they agreed on a price. Elizabeth was led away. She looked back at us pathetically as he dragged her away. She cried, "I don't want to go with him. Please, don't make me. My name is Elizabeth St. Cloud…I'm only sixteen."

I was shaken. I had read about female circumcision in my father's medical books. It was a ritual done at puberty in many African and Middle Eastern countries to Muslim girls. The clitoris would be cut out, and in some cultures the whole labia was removed. It was a brutal and barbarous procedure, as well as dangerous to the life of the girl. Its real purpose was to kill all desire in a woman so that her eyes would never seek another man. Would I ever see her again and, if I did, would she still be sane? Inside my psyche, there was a scream of protest. How I hated these men. I wondered if what was happening to us was legal, even in Saudi Arabia. I doubted it, but there loomed the fact that slavery was still legal in this backward third-world country.

The young Arab in Western attire and the one sitting next to him were father and son. They were seated within six or seven feet in front of us. I could hear their conversation, and was surprised to learn that the son spoke perfect English, though the father had a thick accent. He wanted Alexandra. Ali, the younger man, said, "Of course, father, if the Lebanese woman is your choice, I will respectfully accept her as your wife."

"Prince Kareem, you have made a wise choice," said the seller. She is from a Muslim country and not such a stranger to our customs, though I understand she was raised as a Christian."

"We will change that," said Prince Kareem. "She will give me many sons. Now Ali, will you choose one?"

He hesitated and looked surprised, as if he hadn't planned to select anyone.

"Do it my son. You have done your duty—now is the time for *your* pleasure."

"The small one with the golden hair, with eyes the color of the Arabian Gulf—she will suit me," he said softly.

I knew that Arabs were poetic, but I hadn't expected this. Although he appeared the least threatening, he was nevertheless, a stranger. Only then did I think of Marilyn. What would become of her and poor Elizabeth? At least, Alexandra and I would have each other.

WE SAT IN THE REAR of a black Cadillac. It appeared that Cadillacs were the vogue for wealthy Arab royals. A car followed us, for what purpose, I didn't know. Ali drove with his father seated next to him, a distinguished looking man of about fifty with a salt and pepper mustache and goatee. He was meticulously groomed as was his son. Both men wore dark designer sunglasses, which were not a fashion statement in this climate, but a necessity.

"We are on our way to the airport," said Prince Ali. "Once there, we'll fly on to Jeddah." Neither of us dared to say a word. At best, it was an awkward situation—at its worst, it was frightening. Our experience in the palace had left us shaken and distraught. I already missed Marilyn's feistiness and Elizabeth's sister-like dependence on us.

"My son, Prince Ali, attended Sandhurst just like England's Prince Philip, and then Oxford University at King's Church College."

I really didn't care one bit about Prince Ali's education. How dare they presume that we would be interested in the details of their lives when they had snatched us away from all we knew and loved! I thought of Michael, and my heart was heavy. *Was he looking for me? Was he still in Greece?*

In Arabic, Prince Kareem asked Alexandra a question. She replied in his language, her voice soft and lilting. Although I didn't understand what they were saying, the words sounded like water flowing from a fountain. He was so pleased, he turned around and for the first time smiled at us.

Alexandra switched back to English, probably to include me in the conversation. "Do you ride camels?"

Prince Kareem chuckled. "Of course. I grew up riding a camel. We drank their milk. We used their bodies to protect us from sandstorms. In my childhood, we rode everywhere. We used female camels for riding and the males for packing. In some ways, it was a wonderful, free life, but in other ways, harsh and difficult. I still ride a camel occasionally, but I prefer an automobile. Sometimes, we go out to the desert and stay for a few nights to celebrate a holiday. In our hearts, we are still people of the desert." He paused, "Better still, is to ride an Arabian horse. They are the finest horses in the world. The Prophet Mohammed owned fifteen mares in his lifetime and he said, 'After woman came the horse for the enjoyment and happiness of man.' He was a philosopher, a messenger of God, a great rider of horses, and I think a romantic man as well. Are we not the best riders in the world, my son?"

"Yes, father. One of my fervent hopes is to become the rider you are."

"Ali is a modest fellow. He is a fearless rider and has won many competitions. He also plays polo. He showed those Brits how to ride when he was in the United Kingdom. Do either of you ride?"

I answered; "I do a little." *I felt weak and panicky. Once again, I had forgotten how to breathe. What was wrong with me?* "Excuse me…is it possible…to have some water? I feel ill."

Prince Ali stopped the car immediately. The car following us nearly rammed us in the rear, but it braked in time.

Through a haze, I was looking at Alexandra as she bathed my

bare face with cool water. I had fainted. I was given several glasses of water but couldn't quench my thirst. This horrible climate had drained me. When my breathing returned to normal and I felt better, we continued on our journey.

Prince Kareem chattered on endlessly. His English was so heavily accented that it was difficult to understand and I missed much of what he was saying. "Everything changed when oil was found. In fact, we were searching for water. In this part of the world, water is more precious than oil. You see, we Arabs hate the desert. We love water and all growing things. It is only the eccentric English, like Sir Richard Burton and T. E. Lawrence who loved the desert."

When Prince Kareem finally stopped talking, Alexandra spoke to him in Arabic. I had no idea what she was saying.

Prince Kareem responded in English to reassure me as well, "No! Absolutely not. We do not approve of female circumcision. We consider it to be barbarous and backward. For that matter, there is nothing to fear in our household except the jealousy of my second wife, Fatima." Despite still feeling light-headed, I was relieved that *we* would not subjected to mutilation.

Alexandra looked at me and smiled through her veil, reached for my hand and squeezed it, responding sweetly to the prince, "Thank you, Prince Kareem. I am pleased with your answer. Also, I will do my best to be respectful to Fatima, and then she will not be jealous."

Prince Ali swerved the car to the side of the road, slammed on the brakes, out of the way of traffic and came to a stop. An insane mix of trucks, cars, and bulldozers, wagons of all sizes, and camels and donkeys shared the road competing for the right-of-way. There was no correct direction for traffic. In fact, an ambulance sometimes followed the car of an important person, as the likelihood of an accident was always present. Prince Ali provided us with all of this frightening information as we drove through the chaotic streets of the capital of Saudi Arabia.

Ali lit up a cigarette, and appeared nervous. He turned around and faced us. "There is something you must know. Our family must never find out that you were kidnapped. We have told them that we met in Athens at a party aboard my Cousin Abdullah's yacht, and he will ascertain this. That is the story that you will tell them, and nothing more—is that understood?"

"What if they ask of our past lives? What do we say?" I asked.

"About that, you may tell them the truth. Everything, except how we actually met. If you can't do that, tell us now, and we will make other arrangements." I thought about what he meant by "other arrangements" and decided to play along for our own safety.

"Yes, Prince Ali," I said. "I can do that. We met in Athens on a yacht. I was visiting a friend, and, after a short time, you asked me to marry you, and I accepted. Is that satisfactory?"

"As a matter of fact, it is perfect. I suppose, in the ways of your culture, I would wait before presenting your father with a marriage proposal."

"Yes. Usually, a year or two."

"How extraordinary," he replied. "I knew my first wife only as a child and never met my second one until the wedding."

"I will say that I was studying Greek antiquities, which is something that has always interested me," said Alexandra.

Prince Kareem applauded. "We will say nothing more. Your explanations are intelligent and believable."

"One other thing Suzanne," said Ali. "I want to call you Yasmine."

"Yes, if that's what you want."

"It is."

We rode in silence. *Now I've even lost my name.*

"We are going to my palace in Jeddah," said Prince Kareem. "It is on the Red Sea, and though it is humid, it is air-conditioned just like the ARAMCO compounds. (Those places where Americans who worked for the oil companies lived with their families) That is the best thing the Americans have brought us—now we can breathe on the hottest nights."

WE ARRIVED AT THE AIRPORT, which was a primitive place compared to our airports. I saw several large green and white airplanes, with the name *ARABIA,* in large script font painted on the body of the planes. However, we were not traveling on those planes. Prince Kareem owned his own plane, and much to my surprise, the pilot and co-pilot were Americans. *Oh! Thank God!*

As we boarded, I tried to make eye contact with them, but they did not look at us. In fact, they went out of their way to avoid us. They spoke to Prince Ali and I heard the wonderful sound of a Texan accent.

"Welcome aboard. We'll have you in Jeddah in no time flat. Great flying weather, as usual, not a cloud in the sky."

"How are you, Hank?" asked Ali.

"Never better sir, thanks for asking," replied the friendly American.

Prince Ali continued talking to the pilot while we got settled into our seats, which faced each other, helped by a pretty stewardess. She was an Egyptian. Prince Kareem smiled at her and said, "When are you getting married, Deena?"

"You would have to ask my father that question. Soon, I hope. If I had a larger dowry, it would have happened by now."

"What does your father do for a living?"

"He works for the government—a civil servant."

Finally, we were all belted in, and the pilot turned the plane towards the short runway. I held my breath as the plane lifted off. I let out a big sigh once we were airborne and on our way to Jeddah.

I wanted to scream to the pilots—I AM AN AMERICAN—HELD AGAINST MY WILL. But I dared not, and yet I knew that this might be my only chance. Our part of the plane was separated from the front by only a curtain, but the roar of the propellers was loud. Perhaps, if I spoke loud enough, the pilot and co-pilot would hear me.

"When we arrive," Ali said, "you will go to the women's quarters and remain there until the ceremonies take place. It will be a double wedding."

This was my chance. Should I ask the question? I was mystified as to why these two Muslim men would engage in such unethical and illegal acts such as forcing marriage on abducted women. I had to know why. I spoke as loudly as I dared and chose my words carefully, "Why do you want to marry us? We are not of your faith and this is not of our choosing."

Ali said, "Did not Saint Paul say, 'Husbands, you should be the head of your wives.' Did he not?"

He was giving me a political answer. Answering a question that I had not asked. The oldest trick in the world.

He continued, "All of our female servants were sold to us by their fathers for their wages. In time, they will be allowed to return home or marry in our country. They are from the Philippines, Sri Lanka, Pakistan, Sudan, and other countries. You see, the world over, women are the responsibilities of men. They do not have the wisdom to select their own husbands. That is why divorce is so common in America. The women have too much freedom. As for you being Christian, that is not a problem. A few Muslim men marry non-Muslim women, but the women must convert. However, you Yasmine, will be the first American to marry into our family, and I must warn you, you will be a curiosity."

Ali's lecture went on. "I loved the United States with all its natural beauty, universities and culture. But its films, music, and morals are a disgrace. Yasmine, if you were not still pure, you would not be here. I would not marry an immoral woman, nor would my father. I would not plant my seed in a garden that had many seeds in it, even one. In time, you will come to appreciate and love our ways. In Saudi Arabia, there is no drunkenness, no prostitution, and we have the lowest crime rate in the world. A man can have four wives, so he has no need of other women, and our religion protects women."

Prince Ali was clever and had an answer for everything. I discovered that he was adept with words, but he didn't really answer my question, so I decided to tackle the slave question.

"Isn't it true Prince Ali that slavery is still legal in Saudi Arabia?" I felt a chill go through my body as I saw his piercing black eyes looking back at me. Perhaps he was beginning to regret his choice of a bride.

"Yes," he said abruptly.

Prince Kareem explained, "Slavery only happens when African Muslims cannot pay their way to Mecca for their *Hadj* (pilgrimage). They sell their sons to us, we raise them in our families as "little brothers" to the princes, and they have a better life. That is how Prince Ali got his little brother. However, my brother, Crown Prince Faisal, is going to change the law. He realizes that some countries consider slavery to be backward, and we must modernize like the rest of the world."

It was then that I first learned that Prince Kareem was the son of the legendary King Abdul Aziz ibn Sa'ud. "The whole world knows of Lawrence of Arabia because of an American journalist, but who in the Western world knows my grandfather—who was a great man and a warrior?" said Ali, the king's grandson. "When T. E. Lawrence first arrived in Arabia, he said, 'The heat of Arabia came like a drawn sword and struck us speechless, the atmosphere was like a bath.' My grandfather was born to this land, dealt with this oppressive climate, united its people through battle and intermarriage, defeated the Rasheeds, drove out the Hashimites, the foreigners, the Turks and their Arab puppets, and fought his way to become the first king. Our country took its name from him."

I was spellbound by this history lesson given to me by the man I was to marry. He was no ordinary man.

At that moment, Hank opened the curtain and stood in the doorway. "We'll be at the airport in about ten minutes. I think you folks ought to buckle up." When Ali turned his head to look at his watch, Hank's eyes caught mine. He gave me just the hint of a nod. I responded with the slightest movement of my head. I prayed nobody had seen what passed between us. Just before he returned to this seat, he said, "Looks like we made good time."

He knows. He got the message. I was sure of it.

A car with an Ethiopian driver named Daniel was waiting for us and we left for the family compound. Ali sat in the back seat with us—another air-conditioned Cadillac.

A gray limousine sped past us. A lone man sat in the front driving. In the back seat sat one of the men at the palace along with Marilyn. He was slapping her bared face, and she was hitting him back. We were aghast. Prince Kareem roared with laughter, pausing only to light up a cigar. "It seems our cousin Mohammed got a wild mare."

Ali seemed less amused. "He will teach her our ways." His father laughed until the tears rolled down his cheeks. "Wait until she meets Mohammed's mother, Marlama."

"Yes," growled Ali, "Auntie will know how to handle her—that old witch." The two men looked at each other and laughed together as though they shared a private joke.

The next half-hour we all remained silent. The atmosphere was tense. Alexandra and I contemplated our future. I looked out the window and saw villas with high outer walls. Then, I saw the sea, which was a vast panorama of aquamarine near the shore and cerulean blue on the horizon. Large birds circled overhead, diving to catch their prey. I thought of the irony of it.

"The Red Sea coral reef has the richest marine life in the world, comparable only to Australia's Great Barrier Reef. I read that out of a book, but it is true," said Ali. He told us we were riding on the world's longest Corniche, which he said was seventy-five kilometers long. "It is much longer than the one in Southern France and in time, would be more beautiful, but who in the West would know that?"

I wanted to say that I agreed with him, for I had been to the French Riveria, and it was much longer, but I kept silent. Every time I spoke, I had gotten into trouble. It was imperative that he liked me. Only then, would I have a chance to escape.

"One more bit of advice, Yasmine—you must learn Arabic," said Ali. If you don't, you will be lost. The only reason that we speak English is because we are in the royal family and are the leaders of our country. How else can we do business with English-speaking people if we don't understand their language?

"Do any of the women speak English?" Alexandra asked.

"My sister Sara was educated in England and the other women in my family are tutored in English. All Filipino and Indian servants speak English. You will find that only two percent of the Saudi people speak English. For younger male members of the royal family, learning English is necessary to our survival. It is too late for the older ones, even for the king."

We stopped and Ali tooted the horn. Less than a minute later, servants opened the gates. The car climbed a hill and circled the long driveway, and we parked in front of the residence. The surface of the driveway in front of the building was covered with Persian rugs. It looked absurd. "What would happen if oil leaked on the rugs?" Alexandra asked. They both laughed.

"We'll get more," said Kareem. Ha! Ha! Ha! We have more Persian rugs than there are stars in the sky."

I thought Aunt Margaret's home was large, but nothing could have prepared me for this. It was an enormous residence, which easily covered three acres, not including the grounds and surrounding outer walls.

Bevies of black gardeners were busy working on the grounds, clipping bushes, and watering the grass and flowerbeds. As soon as the cars stopped, three servants rushed out and took the packages out of the trunks of both cars. After Prince Kareem and Prince Ali had taken us from the mysterious palace, Ali stopped at a building in the city, and after a brief time, men brought out boxes tied with fancy ribbons and put them in the cars. Alexandra and I were puzzled by it, but then everything that had happened to us was a mystery.

We entered the palace at the front entrance and walked into the large communal room that was used for prayer. A woman dressed in black came rushing towards Prince Ali and Prince Kareem screaming, "*Wallahi! Wallahi!* " She shouted a barrage of obscenities at Prince Kareem and pounded his chest with her fists. He responded with a thunderous slap across her face that sent her sprawling on the tiled floor. A trickle of blood fell from the side of her lip.

"What did you expect? I've waited all these years for sons, and what did I get? Daughters! Behave yourself, woman, or I'll divorce you."

She whimpered and then wailed a frightening sound. We were transfixed by the incident, and then, suddenly, she sprung up from the floor and ran towards Alexandra, and would have attacked her if Prince Kareem did not intervene. It was the infamous Fatima. In her hysterics, her veil had fallen from her face, and I saw absolute loathing in her glazed black eyes. She looked old—much too old to ever bear any more children.

Prince Kareem dragged her off screaming at the top of her lungs. What had happened to the polite, charming Prince Kareem? Alexandra looked perplexed, but I didn't see any fear in her eyes.

"She'll be all right. Don't let it upset you," said Prince Ali.

Another woman, also veiled, approached us. I sensed that she was young by the way she walked and held her head. In perfect English, in a soft and cultured voice, she said, "Welcome. Come with me. I am Sara."

Chapter 9

LIES AND LOVES

Sara led us to the women's quarters. I thought I had entered the pages of the *Arabian Nights*. The sight and sound of a bubbling fountain surrounded with flowering potted plants in an open-air atrium welcomed my senses. My eyes swept over a large expanse of white stucco walls and a black marble floor, partially covered with glowing silk carpets. Cages with beautiful birds of vibrant colors were singing sweetly to one another. Delicate grillwork separated the spacious rooms that were filled with lounges, tables, chests, and other pieces of furniture, their surfaces made with mosaic tiles and mother-of-pearl inlay.

We had removed our veils and young girls in their teens stared at us with curiosity. Everyone was barefaced and I was surprised to see that two of the girls dressed in jeans and white cotton shirts like my sister Jane. The others were dressed conservatively in traditional dress, most in headscarves. If anything was different, it was the heavy eye make-up and the garish gold jewelry they wore. On a coffee table, I saw old worn copies of *Seventeen*. One of the girls in jeans strutted around the room smoking a cigarette, coughing profusely.

Sara took off her veil and revealed a lovely, intelligent face with clear skin, an aquiline nose, and large dark eyes rimmed with *kohl*. She was dressed in a floor-length native dress in panels of silk—aqua and muted rust. She wore a necklace of golden coins. Her hair, a lustrous black, fell in loose tresses to her shoulders. She wore sandals. Smiling, she said to us, "It is probably not what you expected." Sara turned to the others, "Come over everyone, and meet Yasmine and Alexandra."

The first to greet us was Nina, an impish little girl of about nine dressed in a frilly white party dress. She giggled and bowed slightly to both of us. Her two older sisters, Sabatz and Noohra, stood behind her, pretending to be bored. Both had long dark hair. They wore bright red lipstick with matching nail polish; their red toenails peeked through their high-heeled sandals. Sabatz was taller, older, and better looking than her sister. Thick, horn-rimmed glasses sat on Noohra's prominent nose. Both wore blue jeans.

After introducing themselves, Sabatz asked, "Would you like a cigarette?"

We both declined (though I was dying for one), causing Noohra to say: "You don't smoke? How strange. I thought most American women smoked like they do in the films. My favorites are Elizabeth Taylor and Audrey Hepburn. But I don't like Bette Davis or Joan Crawford—they're too old and ugly. Do you play any games, cards, chess, dominoes, or backgammon?"

Two giggling cousins introduced themselves. They seemed friendlier, but left the talking to Noohra and Sabatz.

"Which one of you is to marry Aba?" asked Noohra.

Alexandra responded in Arabic.

"Let's speak English. I need the practice," said Noohra.

She looked at me next. "And you must be Ali's bride. Aba gets a young wife and my oldest brother, Ali, gets himself a blonde like Grace Kelly."

Sara had had enough. "Noohra, stop it! You are not being polite to our guests."

I was astounded that everyone spoke English, including American slang. Their knowledge of American film stars was unexpected. They said they had watched *Gone with the Wind* so many times that the film broke, and that they thought Clark Gable was very handsome.

I couldn't help but express my amazement. "I never expected any of you to speak English so well."

Sabatz responded, "It is only because we are part of the royal family, and the old English spinster, our tutor, drills us two hours a day until we're bored to death. Though I did like *Pride and Prejudice.* Mr. Darcy really loved Elizabeth and she was so mean to him.

"I'm telling you just one more time," said Sara. "Be pleasant and don't speak of Miss Woodstock with such disrespect." She turned to us. "Don't pay any attention to them. They are just silly young girls."

The girls frowned and went back to their magazines. It was apparent who was in charge. Sara was the elder sister, and I learned later, her father's favorite. Sara clapped her hands, and almost immediately, a woman dressed in a sari appeared and addressed Sara. "Yes mistress."

"Please bring our guests some refreshments." Sara said, "Make yourselves comfortable and take off your abaayas." We lifted them off and sat down on a luxurious sofa with pillows so soft that we almost sank to the floor.

During an hour of conversation, while nibbling on dates, figs, pomegranates, and peeled melon, we began to feel more comfortable. The two sisters asked us a million questions. Their curiosity was boundless. Did we drive cars? Had we ever met any movie stars? Did we go out alone with men? Did we kiss men? Did we wear bikinis as they did on the French Riviera and Beirut?

We looked at Sara for counsel. She shook her head and we remained silent. We were not there to corrupt these young Muslim girls. It soon became apparent that the two sisters were just putting on a show for us. They were like little girls playing dress-up and lived a very cloistered life in spite of the cigarettes, jeans and makeup that they donned to impress us. "Is smoking for women permitted in most homes?" I asked.

"Oh! God, no," Noohra answered. "This is a crazy place. Our father has *never* seen us smoke. He considers it to be the same as being a courtesan. But the men aren't allowed in this part of the house, so we're safe. Our mother smokes a hookah, a water pipe that we call the hubble-bubble. She doesn't really care what we do, as long as we remain within these walls and behave ourselves. She wanted sons and she never got them. That's what counts in this country—sons. They can't wait to marry us off when we reach eighteen—which isn't far off. Most girls marry much younger, but our father doesn't approve. He wants us to be educated so we can marry well."

Sara looked annoyed and changed the topic of conversation. She told us of her work at a clinic treating mothers and their children but never men. "I try to make a difference. Some women have child after child, so I teach them how to protect themselves and remain within the law. I talk to their husbands and fathers, and persuade them not to practice circumcision on the young girls of their families. I have had great success. I thank my mother every day of my life for convincing my father to allow me to go to England and study medicine. Of course, it was permitted only because my two older brothers and an aunt were there."

Abruptly, the servants vanished, and the sisters rushed to put out their cigarettes. Something was going to happen—I could feel the tension building in the room. Fatima strolled into the room wearing a gaudy ruby necklace, with a purple welt across her cheek. Her dark blue dress stretched across her ponderous breasts. The hem reached her ankles, revealing a body that was no longer young. She had no waistline, and I could see her belly bulging through her dress, one hip jutting higher than the other. We rose respectfully, not wanting any more trouble with her. I wondered if she was going to give Alexandra a few slaps now that the men were gone. Surprisingly, she smiled and acted as though nothing had happened previously. It was a fake smile. Her eyes flashed like two coals of fire.

Fatima spoke in Arabic and Sara translated. In two weeks, the weddings would take place. It was Fatima's responsibility as the family matriarch to see that everything went smoothly. We must do everything that was required, and if we did so, all would go well.

Fatima left without a good-bye, only a flick of her hand. Justine, an ebony-skinned Sudanese servant who adored Fatima and was said to have instructed her in witchcraft, trailed her. We were all relieved to see her leave, including her own daughters.

"Father will be pleased that we all can get along,' Sara said. I am going to take you to your rooms now, and you can relax before our evening meal."

Once we left, Alexandra asked her, "Is Justine really a witch?"

"Of course not. Witchcraft is against our religion. It is just servant and little girl talk. If the *mutawas* ever heard of such a thing, we would all be in trouble. Fatima is a difficult, uneducated woman, but she would not dare to defy the mutawas. Even members of the royal family can be reprimanded by these militant holy men and their religious police force."

Once we were alone, I said, "Prince Kareem is a violent man. Aren't you afraid to be his wife?"

"All men have the potential to be violent," said Alex. They are bigger and stronger, and in this part of the world, wife beating is a common practice."

"One thing I know for sure—my father wouldn't hit anyone, let alone a woman."

Alexandra grinned. "My mother managed my father beautifully—she treated him like a king. I once heard her tell her closest friend that she was a Madonna in the living room and a whore in the bedroom. But of course, don't forget, my mother is French."

ALEXANDRA AND I FOUND our room to be satisfactory. Everything was spotless though somewhat garish. The bedspreads were chartreuse satin, and a colorful oriental carpet covered the white tiled floor. The windows were small and shuttered from the inside, but one opened on to a lovely, flowered-potted balcony that overlooked a courtyard surrounded by high stucco walls. The bathroom was adequate with a porcelain sink and toilet and wonder of wonders—a shower. In the corner of the room was a chamber pot with flies buzzing around it and I wondered why it was needed. I discovered later that it was used when the water or electricity weren't working—which was often. As for the flies, in hot Middle-Eastern countries they are commonplace. Though I hated the disgusting things, after my imprisonment in that cellar in Greece, I learned to co-exist with them without going crazy.

On the two beds were the boxes from the shopping trip. We opened them, one by one. It was a basic wardrobe, two or three of everything—nightgowns, dresses, slacks, blouses, lingerie, even an evening dress, and a modest skirted bathing suit. We were both amazed. Not only was everything fashionable, but the right sizes. I was a size smaller than Alexandra, and I wondered how they knew that—another mystery to ponder.

"Madam Boudreau must have told them. She knew everything about us," said Alexandra.

"You're probably right. I wonder where that little French midget is now?" I caught myself laughing at my own misguided sense of humor. Hearing it startled me. *Why was I laughing? I should have been crying. I had a terrible secret. I was two weeks late with my period and probably pregnant.*

At the evening meal, we women sat around a Formica table, not cross-legged, sitting on the floor. I asked Sara if other families ate at a table.

"No. Most sit on the floor, but Fatima has rheumatism and when she saw a picture of a table in a catalog, she demanded one. It's hard on her back and legs to squat or sit on a low surface—"

"She wants to be like the rich Americans," said Sabatz. We like automobiles, air conditioning, motion picture films, and modern conveniences. We all do—and soon we'll have them—even fresh water. Imagine that, scientists know how to turn the seawater into drinking water. What a miracle that would be. Mrs. Woodstock told me, so I know it's true."

Fatima's brow creased and her eyes darkened when she heard her name spoken.

Fatima asked me if I knew that Ali had two wives. Sara, obviously uncomfortable with the question, translated.

"I know that I am to be the third wife, but I know nothing about the others," I answered.

"Let me tell you about them." Her eyes gleamed with malice when she spoke, "His first wife, Hagar, is his cousin and is a great beauty. They have a son and a daughter, and his second wife, Hassa, my niece, is expecting a child. Ali has a big appetite for women." Sara, looking miserable, was forced to translate.

I lowered my head and bit my lip. What did "big appetite for women" mean? Were there others besides his two wives?

Fatima turned to Alexandra, and a volley of words crossed the table. They spoke in Arabic. At first Alexandra conducted herself with dignity and spoke softly. She looked to me and switched to English. "I'll *never* cut my long hair to please her. She said that I am vain and not humble enough."

Fatima became upset and started screaming at her two daughters. "What did she say? What did the Christian whore say?"

"Mother, Alexandra said she's glad *her* hair isn't gray, *her* skin isn't wrinkled, and *her* teeth aren't yellow like yours," said Shabaz mischievously.

Again, Alex translated everything to me.

Sara interrupted and reprimanded Shabaz for lying, but it was too late. Enraged, Fatima rose from her chair, her hands fluttering, her eyes riveted on Alexandra, greasy lamb dribbling from her mouth. She took the crystal goblet from the table, dashed the water into Alexandra's face, and smashed it to the floor. A look of surprise came over Alexandra's face, and then she doubled up with laughter. She shouted, "You have never given him a son, have you Fatima? I will. I'll give him many sons." Fatima swept out of the room in a fury. Justine trailed her, but only after she narrowed her eyes at Alexandra.

All mouths plummeted. We were astonished. First, how could Sabatz be such a troublemaker? And how dare Alexandra insult Fatima. When I questioned Alexandra about her boldness, she replied, "I can handle her."

The next two weeks went by so rapidly, I barely had time to notice. We met endless female relatives who brought gifts and sweets, and who were curious to meet the "foreign brides," especially the one with yellow hair. We endured marathon fittings for our wedding gowns and trousseaux. Since neither of us had a dowry, there was much to be purchased and homes to be established.

From the men's quarters, we could hear laughter and music. Cars and even a helicopter arrived night and day bringing in guests. What was going on, I could only surmise. Sabatz was only sixteen but seemed very knowledgeable about sex. She told me that some men were hypocrites who drank alcohol and watched pornographic movies even though it was against their religion. I asked, "How do you know that?"

"I have my ways." Then she added, "For the men, all that is forbidden in our country is desired all the more. And then we have the others, which are worse. The religious fanatics that want us to stay in the dark ages and treat women like camel dung."

Slowly the secret life behind the veiled warren of women's quarters, men's quarters, and servant's quarters was being peeled away. Nothing was what it seemed.

We saw little of Fatima, and when we did, she acted as though that horrible scene with Alexandra had never transpired. Her maid, Justine, was always peering at me—the whites of her eyes were a startling contrast to her purplish black skin. Once she approached me, stared at my stomach and patted it. *Oh my God! She knows I'm pregnant.* What if she tells someone? Yet, I knew everyone except Fatima thought she was deranged.

THE WEDDING DAY ARRIVED. It took an entire morning to prepare us. Again, all body hair was removed in the ritual they called *halawa.* Once again, henna was painted on our hands, only this time more elaborately, in delicate intricate patterns. Our wedding gowns were beautiful enough for a queen, but too elaborate for my taste. Mine was blue/violet, and Alexandra's was a pale rose.

Fatima sat enthroned in a high-backed chair like a queen, directing the whole production in her strident voice. We were forced to take tranquilizers so we would remain docile. Sara assured us that this was normal, as many brides were young and frightened. She did not say that many of them were as young as eleven or twelve and were being married against their will to men as old as their fathers, but I knew this was true because Noohra and her sister had big mouths. About a dozen female relatives had gathered together to watch as we prepared for the wedding. I wondered if any of them were Ali's wives. I asked Sara. She replied, "No, it would not be proper."

At last, we were ready, and Fatima came over and brushed her lips hurriedly over our cheeks. There would be no kisses for the Christian whores. (Shabtz had squealed on her mother and delighted in telling us what she called us.) Fatima adorned us with thin cloud-like veils and gaudy pearl and rhinestone tiaras, then, stood back to give us a final look and muttered something in Arabic. She tried to force a smile, but her hands trembled; her eyes smoldered with hatred. It must have been hard for her to see her husband's beautiful young bride, when she herself was no longer young. I reminded myself that she was the matriarch and forced to take part in the wedding preparation.

I stared at Alexandra who looked radiantly beautiful, but frightened. I remembered that she was still a virgin. I was not as afraid, but I was apprehensive. I had never slept with anyone except Michael, and soon I would be breaking my marriage vows. Although it wasn't my fault, I was betraying Michael. My last thought, even in my drugged state, was of him and the child that I carried.

Sara whispered to me, "You are so lovely, my sister." I smiled at her and felt the tears falling down my cheeks. Mistaking my tears for fear, she again spoke to me. "Don't worry. Ali is a good man. He will make you happy."

In a private ceremony with only the male family members and a religious man present, I married Ali, and Alexandra married Kareem. I never once looked up into Ali's eyes until the ceremony was over, and he lifted my veil, smiled, and kissed me on the cheek. I met his dark hypnotic eyes, but I chose not to return his smile.

I met Hussein, Ali's brother. In an instant, I knew that Hussein was homosexual. I could tell from his gestures, the way he walked, and from the way he looked at another young man. Now I understood why Prince Kareem had never mentioned his younger son.

AS BRIDES WE WERE HONERED with a party just for the women and young children. We entered the large tent to the sound of hundreds of women ululating. It was deafening. They did this by flicking their tongues on the roof of their mouths, creating a sound that was a distant cousin of yodeling. This was their custom, and like it or not, we were brides of the desert. Tables overflowing with food surrounded the swimming pool, and sheep killed in our honor were part of the wedding feast. In the swimming pool, orchids and lit candles floated on the surface. Everywhere I looked, I saw candles flickering in elaborate golden candelabras. Most surprising was that beneath the abaaya, women dressed lavishly, showing cleavage, and nearly all were adorned with precious jewels. Arabia was a country where women dressed mainly to impress other women.

A belly dancer with long black hair and golden coins strung around her neck performed. Wearing only a skimpy sequined bra, her breasts over-flowed, and above her low hung pantaloons, she rolled her ample abdomen. The blindfolded musicians were men. *What a strange world I have entered.*

As she continued to shake her shoulders and hips seductively, several of the older and more obese women jumped up and joined the dancer. Their corpulent breasts and bellies jiggled, causing the other female guests to hold their sides with laughter. Though drugged, I, as well, found this hilarious and began to laugh and laugh until I cried. Although there were tears on my face, I knew that I not really laughing at all.

Sara told me that the next day Prince Ali and Prince Kareem would claim us. The men celebrated throughout the night. Then she shocked me. Fatima and other family members would examine the sheets from our wedding bed when we returned from our honeymoons, and if we were not virgins with bloodstains to prove it, we would face dire consequences. I thought the whole process was degrading, but realized that it was better than some unknown punishment. (A custom that exists to this day at Muslim hotels where the wedding night takes place.)

That last night, in bed, exhausted from all that had taken place, with the lights out, I concentrated on Michael. This night would belong to him. I relived our precious moments: the first time I realized he loved me; the New Year's eve when he proposed; our wedding day. I tried to remember the things about him I missed the most: the feeling that he was invincible and that nothing bad could ever happen to me when I was with him; the intimate look he gave me even in a room filled with people that made me feel like I was the only one present. I missed the scent of him and the warmth of his body touching mine, his touch when he traced the hollow in my throat with his fingertips, his voice calling my name when we made love. I missed everything about him and felt cheated. He was everything I had ever wanted.

I sobbed. Alexandra came and slid into the bed, snuggling up to me. "Oh, Alex, I'm so miserable. I want to go home. I miss my family and I might never see them again."

"I know. I have the same fears, but we must be strong. I think it's probably worse for you—being an American. You probably have a boyfriend, someone you love. For me, there has never been anyone; I have always been chaperoned. So I have trained myself not to love any man until I marry. That is our way."

I lied and said that there wasn't anyone.

"That is best. Remember that there is always a way out of everything. We must use whatever power we have."

"What power do *we* have?"

"Ourselves—beautiful women can get anything they want if they use their minds—and their bodies."

THE NEXT DAY when I was alone with Ali, riding to the airport in Jeddah, he spoke his first words to me as his wife.

"You were a beautiful bride. I wanted you to have your last night alone to rest and be refreshed. We will spend three weeks together so we can get to know each other."

"May I ask where we are going?

"You may ask, but I will not tell you—It is a surprise."

We boarded a small airplane, one of two belonging to the family. The pilot and co-pilot were Saudi. What had happened to the Americans?

Dressed in a lilac silk suit under my abaaya, I squirmed in my seat trying to get comfortable. I was so hot—it was probably 100 degrees. Beads of perspiration slid down my face. I was stuck to my seat. Finally, the engines started and I felt the cool air circulate throughout the airplane.

I asked Ali what had happened to the American pilots.

"I fired them. I saw Hank look at you. He was lucky he didn't get sixty lashes."

"You would have done that, Prince Ali?"

"Oh yes, without another thought. He was a weak man and I could not trust him."

"How long did he work for you?

"Two years."

"Prince Ali, I only nodded to acknowledge him as a fellow American. Is that why he lost his job?"

"Of course. It is forbidden for him to look at you and *you* are forbidden to even think of it. It must *never* happen again. I have excused you because you have not yet learned the ways of Arabs. There are many methods I can use to get what I want, and I have chosen the gentlest method because you are a bride. If there is ever a next time,

I will not be so gentle, so take care to obey me." Being alone except for the stewardess, he lifted my hand and brought it to his lips, his eyes mocking me. His mustache tickled my skin. On that same hand, a diamond as big as my knuckle sparkled in the sunlight, on the other, a golden wedding ring.

My mind was racing. *Where were we going? Would it be possible to escape? I feared him.* I felt sick, and asked the stewardess for an air bag. I vomited and was mortified. Ali held a wet cloth to my brow as I slumped in my seat, sick from the heat, the excitement and more likely, from my pregnancy.

"I am so ashamed that you have seen me like this. I must be air-sick."

"My darling Yasmine, I am your husband, and from now on we will share many things. It feels strange for me to say this, for in Saudi Arabia, love comes after marriage, but for me it is not so. I feel love for you. I admire your spirit and your intelligence as well as your beauty."

I closed my eyes and could hardly believe my ears. He said he loved me—the third man to say those words to me, but I didn't want him to love me. I belonged to someone else.

The stewardess brought me water and fresh towels. The queasiness subsided and, for that, I was grateful.

When the airplane landed at a small airport several hours later, I still didn't know where we were. I could see that it was green and lush. Nearby was the sea and a marina. Ali finally revealed our destination. He said, "We are in Turkey—a perfect place for a cruise." My heart sank. There was no possibility of an escape—Turkey was an Islamic country.

We boarded a yacht that made Andreas's boat in Greece seem like a rowboat. Alone in our palatial salon, we were served a gourmet meal of sea bass, wild rice and white asparagus. We drank champagne, and our dessert was a flaming baked Alaska. We made polite conversation, and I never spoke except to answer a question.

He looked quite handsome in his white trousers and nautical blue jacket with a silk ascot tied around his neck. He admired the pale green cotton dress I had chosen to wear because it was cooler and more casual. Just before the Turkish siesta began, Ali told me his story. He smiled as he sat opposite me, and yet, there was sadness in his eyes.

"Yasmine, my first wife Hagar was my childhood playmate and paternal cousin. We marry our cousins to ensure that all sons and daughters will be of pure blood. You will notice that I did not use the word children. In Arabic, there is no word for children. Everyone is either male or female and the two can never be equal. It is important that you understand that. Because, only then, can you grasp our culture, our religion, and our family traditions."

He sighed, leaned back in his chair, and continued his story.

"Hagar was more like a sister than a wife. She was only fifteen when we married. I was twenty and I thought I couldn't go any longer without a woman. I had not seen her since she was ten years old and I had been sent away to be educated in England. When I saw her again at our wedding, I was smitten. While it is true that she has a sweet disposition and is quite pretty, she doesn't have an original idea or an opinion about anything. The only thing she reads is the Koran. Hagar is excited about one thing, our son, Abdul, and she is a good mother to our daughter, Mira. What concerns her most is that she has only two children. Hagar has female problems that make it difficult for her to get pregnant. She is a gentle creature who is honored to be my first wife, but whether I spend the night with her or not, is of little concern to her. Unfortunately, she was circumcised and does not enjoy making love, though she does want more children, or more accurately, more sons. After five years, I married for the second time. Hagar never asked me one question about my second wife—she simply didn't care. She was used to it—her father had at least five or six wives, divorcing one to marry another. Unfortunately for her and for me as well, there was no passion in our marriage. Have you any idea how boring it is to be married to someone like that?"

I didn't know if I was expected to answer or not, but I did respond. "I can understand why you would be bored, but do you not love her?"

"Of course. I treasure Hagar. I am responsible for her and our son and daughter, and I will *never* divorce her. But Hagar does not satisfy my needs. I need more.

"My second wife, Hassa, is half-Egyptian and half-Arabian. I never met her until we married. My father insisted that I marry her. His wife, Fatima, was making his life miserable until he agreed to find a husband for Hassa, her niece, who was twenty-seven and unmarried. A disgraceful situation for a woman in an Islamic country, unless you are an exceptional woman of intelligence like my sister, Sara. He wanted peace in the family. So to please him, I married her.

Ali remained silent for awhile and I could see the anger mounting in his face.

There is a reason that she had no husband. She is jealous and unstable like Fatima. Actually she is quite beautiful, but that is the only thing about her that I find agreeable. We have been married nearly a year. I have only slept with her a handful of times, and on each occasion, she tried to claw my eyes out. She equates sex with violence. Now she is pregnant with my child, and I have an obligation to her. If she were not, I would divorce her in an instant. When I told her about you, she became enraged. Yet, she does not and never has loved me, but takes great pleasure in making my life a bloody hell. So you see, I have never been in love."

I sighed and whispered, "How sad for you."

He clasped both my hands, held them, and continued his story. "I am a man who requires love, and I think that in you, I have found what I have been seeking. In many ways, I am more Western than Middle-Eastern, probably the result of spending so much time in England and the United States. I accompanied my father to the palace because *he* was the one who wanted a wife. He had heard of a beautiful Lebanese girl who was going to be sold. Usually the women who are shown are from other countries, very young, poor, uneducated, and sold by their own families—Muslim, Asian and African girls. They frequently end up in horrible circumstances. This was the first time I had ever heard of Caucasian women being sold. When I saw Alexandra and her extraordinary beauty, I admit, if my father had not taken her, I would have. Then, you removed your veil. Your incredible eyes captured my heart first and when I saw the fear in them, I didn't want anything ugly to happen to you. You looked so vulnerable, and I knew I couldn't let you go. It was then and only then, that I decided to marry again. Do you believe me?"

"What does it matter what I believe?"

"It matters to me. I ask you again. Do you believe me?"

"Yes, I do."

He fingered his Lapis worry beads, and continued. "In our country, it is not unheard of for a man to marry a woman from another country or even of another religion. But I knew I could never find anyone like you—someone educated who would be willing to become a third wife, and live in a backwater country, even if it is floating on a sea of oil. No American or European woman would have agreed to give up her freedom and live as our women do. So when I saw you, I saw an opportunity that I might never have again. If I had met you in your world, you never would have agreed to marry me, would you?"

"No. I would not."

"I know…I will not force myself upon you…I will sleep in another room if you wish and wait until you are ready, but I am not a patient man. I would not want to take you against your will."

"You would though, wouldn't you?"

"I always take what belongs to me."

"Even if you had to force me?"

"If you didn't resist, there would be no force. I would be gentle."

For a full minute, he smoked a cigarette and looked across the table, waiting for my answer. Then he stood up to leave and walked towards the door. He turned around, looked at me and said, "Hassa resisted me because it was a game to her—a challenge. To prove to me that she still had the spirit of a Bedouin woman, to fight me was to reinforce her virtue. I didn't like it. I didn't find it exciting. It made me hate her. I want a soft yielding woman who opens herself to me like a flower. That is what I want, Yasmine."

Before he turned the doorknob, I said, "Don't go! We are married, and you *are* my husband."

If he had only known my thoughts: *this marriage must be consummated; I am a month pregnant, in a country where a child born out of wedlock or not belonging to her husband, is a death sentence.*

ALI UNBUTTONED THE FRONT of my dress slowly and deliberately, studying me. The dress slipped off my shoulders and fell to the floor in a heap. He fingered the straps of my chemise, lowered them slightly, revealing the swell of my breasts, which he kissed so lightly that I barely felt his warm lips and soft mustache. It was like a butterfly flicking its wings on my bare skin. His raven eyes were riveting. When he finally kissed my mouth, it was gentle, almost sweet. I returned it. Then he stood back and smiled at me. "Your eyes are incredible, like two jewels." He picked me up and carried me to the bed.

Beneath the sheets, I removed my undergarments. I was glad the drapes were drawn and the room in semi-darkness. He was less modest, but I averted my eyes to feign modesty, which to a certain extent was true, as I had never seen another man naked except Michael. Soon, he was lying next to me, exploring my body slowly, delicately, expertly. A fire stirred within me.

How did he know my secret places and desires? How could he possibly know what even I hadn't yet discovered about my own body? Who had taught him the art of making love? Certainly not his wives. An experienced courtesan topped my list. I cared not because he took me to a place that I had never been to before—it was not of this earth. I was ashamed to admit that not once did I think of Michael, except at the conclusion of our love making when I acknowledged that this man was the better lover—infinitely better.

The doctor had done his work well, and I bled when I was penetrated. Actually, it was more painful than my first time and although I tried to restrain myself, I cried, not just from the pain but also for breaking my marriage vows. When it was all over, the anxiety, the pain, the ecstasy, and the dreamy state that followed, Ali cradled me in his arms, and said softly, "You please me. Oh God, you please me greatly."

Later, he rose from the bed, walked over to a dresser and opened a drawer. Though the shadowy light, I could still see his naked body, lean and muscular. His chest was covered with a fine mat of hair, just enough to enhance his manliness. He slipped back into bed and switched on a lamp on the night table next to him. I sat up with the covers drawn up to my neck. He grinned. "You are shy. I like that." He handed me a velvet jewel box. It read in golden letters—Van Cleef and Arpels. I opened it. It was an amethyst necklace, bracelet and earrings. "To match your fantastic eyes," he said as he brushed my cheek with his lips.

Then he hooked the clasp of the necklace, and kissed the nape of my neck. "It's exquisite. I've never owned anything this beautiful," I lied. He ran his fingers through the spiraling curls of my shoulder length hair. "It feels like silk—don't ever cut it," he said.

I promised myself that I would never fall in love with this man, because I planned to leave him the first chance I got. Even then, with all my inexperience, with all my confusion, and with all my mixed emotions, I knew the difference between love and sex. I wanted to be in control, and that would never happen if I learned to love him. I wondered if any other woman had married two such extraordinary men within a period of only weeks, and under such bizarre circumstances. I doubted it, and if I told anyone, who would believe me? This would always be my secret.

WE DOVE FROM THE YACHT into the clear water where, beneath the surface, we gaped in wonder at the kaleidoscope of marine life—small schools of fish and multicolored coral. The first time we surfaced, he laughed and said, "You swim like you were born in the sea."

I floated away on my back, and kicked water into his face yelling, "I grew up swimming in the coldest water in the world, and loved it." We sun-bathed on the deck, my skin tanning to bronze. It was here that I first told Ali that I was a smoker. I asked if he minded.

"Of course you may smoke. But please, Yasmine, only in the proper place. Promise me, never in front of my father or other men."

"I never smoked in front of my parents either. They didn't approve and I considered it to be disrespectful."

"I can see that you were well brought up."

We ate lunch on the deck with white-coated and black-tied waiters serving us caviar, prawns, oysters, and champagne. Ali admitted he loved champagne, although he was a Muslim, but that he never drank it within his own country. He thought it best to be observant of one's religion at least part of the time than not at all. "Sometimes," he said, "the mind is weak and the body succumbs."

"I know about that. Every time I smoke a cigarette, I hope it will be my last, but it never is."

We laughed and talked for hours. He cared what I thought about the world we lived in. He talked about the children we would have. I was becoming an expert liar, but I knew of no other way to survive. What surprised me most was that I was comfortable with him. He had a way with women, and it was getting easier and easier to be myself. This life was becoming my reality and my former life, a dream.

Near the end of the third week, we sailed through the Sea of Mamara and the Bosporus Sea, and spent the day in Istanbul, an exciting and historical city that was unique because it was partly in Europe and partly in Asia. The exact dividing line was on the Galato Bridge, which connected the two continents.

First we visited the Blue Mosque. We washed our hands, removed our shoes and I covered my hair with a scarf before entering. The beauty of the interior brought tears to Ali's eyes as he kneeled and said his prayers. The floor was covered with enormous oriental rugs; the walls were aglow with blue tiles, and the stained-glassed windows shimmered with color in the soft light of the morning. It was as though we had ventured into another world, a magical blue world.

As a Christian, I was more interested in Haghia Sophia, the enormous Greek Orthodox Church that was once the pride of the Byzantium Empire. Four tall minarets loomed above its enormous dome. Upon entering, we left the hustle and bustle of the outside world and entered a sanctuary that was once the largest and most beautiful cathedral in all of Christendom. I thought it sad that it was no longer a church—the Ottoman Empire had ended that.

After our morning sightseeing was completed, we lunched at a fashionable rooftop restaurant which overlooked the Bosporus. We peered down at the harbor that was filled with boats of all sizes. We continued that day and the next with further visits to the Grand Bazaar, and then to Topkapi Palace where I saw an uncut emerald as big as a man's fist. "The crown jewels of England are nothing compared to these," I said. At the old harem, where hundreds of women, and eunuchs had lived, Ali commented, "All of those women for just one man. He must have been exhausted." We laughed trying to imagine such a scenario, but I couldn't help but think about all those sad young women locked up in a harem to satisfy one selfish man.

"I think the Turks are a somber people and have a cruel history," I said.

"My people have no love for the Turks either. During the First World War, we killed our share of them and drove them out. The Ottoman Empire was a powerful force for hundreds of years. But, of course, you must know that. It seems strange to talk to a woman who knows about history."

"Lawrence of Arabia was one of my heroes," I said.

"Not mine," he said. "The English favored Sharif Hussein of Mecca, of the Hashemites, and a descendant of Mohammed over my grandfather, Abdul Aziz ibn Sa'ud. Lawrence would have done better to go with him. In the end, it didn't matter; ibn Sa'ud drove them all out, and became the king of what is now Saudi Arabia, named after him, of course. The English and French carved up Arabia and Mesopotamia and created Transjordan, Syria, and Iraq, which they gave to the Hashemites. As if it were theirs to give. Now, one grandson of Sharif Hussein rules Jordan, the young King Hussein, and the other grandson, Faisal, became the king of Iraq and then he died and his son was later assassinated. Renegades rule that country now. Because of the mix of Sunnis, Shiites, Kurds, Christians and even Jews, they will never have peace in Iraq. Too bad, when it was called Mesopotamia, it was the cradle of civilization. My people resented the colonial powers and their meddling so much that when we were ready to look for the mineral wealth of our country we turned to the Americans."

"Lucky for both our countries."

"Americans have always respected our differences and that's why we've had a long-standing relationship. They understand that just because we wanted their modern technology, their medical knowledge or their cars and airplanes, we don't necessarily want their customs or to be friends with the Zionists in Palestine. Not at all—we do not want to be like the Americans. We are Muslim—we are Arabs."

"It's because of the oil. Your country and mine would never have come together if it were not for that."

"Of course. The oil. Some call it a blessing—others call it a curse. To most Saudis, and to me, it is God's will. If he did not want us to have it, he would not have placed it on our land. Everything that happens is God's will. Remember that, Yasmine, and life will be easier to understand. Remember, regardless of the circumstances that brought you here, that in the end it was because of God's will."

"I will try."

DURING THE CRUISE, I WAS frequently seasick, or so Ali believed. At the end of the three weeks, I told him I was late with my period and possibly pregnant. Having been a father twice before, he was not unfamiliar with the workings of the female body. He asked me some personal questions that I found embarrassing, but he was, nevertheless, concerned and so attentive and loving that I felt guilty. One night, very late, when I was sure he was asleep I wept. I was thinking of Michael. I tried to smother the sound in the pillow, but he heard me. He wrapped his arms around me and held me close. "Don't cry. I love you, my little American wife. In time, you'll learn to love me too."

I nodded, but I said not a word.

"I'll make you happy. As soon as we return to Jeddah, we'll move into our own home. After Hassa delivers her child, I will divorce her and take my child. She would be a terrible mother. I will visit Hagar as required, but I can assure you, she will not mind if I spend more nights with you." I wasn't accustomed to a culture in which women shared their husband, but in this instance, I was relieved. He added, "I will make it right, you'll see. We'll travel and, in time, you will even see your family again."

My heart stopped. All was not lost. I turned and kissed him with such enthusiasm that I startled him, and though it was not my intention, we ended up making love.

At breakfast, Ali told me that we were returning to Jeddah. He was worried about his business dealings with the Oil Company, ARAMCO, and he had to tend to some problems immediately. Prince Kareem had sent Ali to schools in the West for three purposes: at Sandhurst to learn about the military, at the University of Pennsylvania to get an MBA at the Wharton School of Business, and to become proficient in both English and French. He had accomplished all three.

Sara said that Crown Prince Faisal, who really ran the country, considered him to be one of the shrewdest businessmen in the country. He was not an Arab playboy prince like so many of his cousins.

We returned to Jeddah to a screaming Fatima who blamed her niece's miscarriage on *my evil eye.* We entered the palace of Prince Kareem merely to collect my belongings and move to our own residence. Prince Kareem and Alexandra were still away on their honeymoon in Egypt. We left Fatima sobbing on a couch with Sara trying to quiet her.

Ali seemed sad that he had lost a child, but he no longer felt any obligation to Hassa. He met with her briefly, and she spat at him screaming, "I never wanted your child anyway. Go back to your blond whore. She's bewitched you."

Quickly thereafter, Ali called in the witnesses, and repeated to Hassa, "I divorce thee, I divorce thee, I divorce thee." Once it was done, he was free of her. He gave her a good sum of money and sent her back in shame to her family in Egypt. Fatima was outraged, and I knew I had made a bitter enemy.

Ali had selected a walled-in villa on the Corniche overlooking the Red Sea. It was a quarter of the size of Prince Kareem's palace, but being smaller, it was more intimate and less daunting. It had a separate women's quarters, a men's quarters, common rooms for prayer, and servants' quarters for the seven servants, including Mary, my personal maid.

All the servants except Mary and Ali's assistant and driver, Daniel, were new, so I didn't have to worry about Fatima spying on us.

"If I could, I would spend every minute with you, but I must leave for the oil fields at Dhahran. Daniel will drive you whenever you want to go out, so you won't become bored. Sometimes, I wish we lived in Egypt and you could drive your own car and go unveiled."

"Ali. It's not your fault the laws are so strict, but in our own house, it will be much easier for me. I'm sorry you lost your baby. A human life is precious."

"It was in the hands of God." After a few final words of endearment, he left me for the first time since our wedding trip began.

I explored every inch of my new home until I knew where everything was. I even entered the men's quarters while Ali was traveling. Only one door remained locked and that was to Ali's office. Only Ali and Daniel had the key. I wondered what was in the room that Ali did not want me to see.

Ali hired an American contractor who worked for ARAMCO to build the villa. A small army of men had completed it in record time. He designed it to be similar to homes in Florida and California, so that our residence was a mixture of an Arabian exterior and an interior that was a combination of both cultures. Ali had asked me what my favorite colors were, and I told him blue and white. Now I understood why. Almost every room was white or some shade of blue or with blue accent pieces of furniture, including a sofa, covered in blue and white chintz. It was almost like being in Maine, and it gave me a pang of longing for home.

After returning from our wedding trip in Turkey, relatives left us alone as was the custom. Ali and I settled into a pattern of domestic life not too different from other cultures. I arranged and rearranged furniture, selected fabrics for curtains and bedspreads, selected bed linen and other household necessities from foreign catalogs. In Saudi Arabia, almost everything including the servants is brought in from another country.

I became acquainted with our seven servants (only Mary and Daniel spoke English) and forced myself to converse mainly in Arabic. My sentences were often limited to only two or three words strung together with a lot of hand gestures. I worked with the middle-aged Egyptian cook, Nadia, and learned how to plan the household menu to include foods that we both liked. Daniel escorted Mary and me to the souk where he taught me how to select the best fruits and vegetables. Beneath the veil, and often stumbling, I blended in with all the other women.

Ali stayed within the Jeddah area, going only to Talif, the mountain town retreat where the Royal family congregated during August, the hottest month. In Talif, King Sa'ud and Crown Prince Faisal would gather at dusk with their many brothers and sons to pray and then partake of their evening meal together. On such days, Ali usually lunched with me.

What was to be done with so much money? It was mind boggling, and it didn't sit well with the faith of Islam. Vast wealth and humble, pious people did not mix easily. The old king had managed to keep things simple when he could store his wealth in bags full of gold in a single room, but after he died, his sons needed whole buildings to store their riches. Reluctantly, the Saudis were forced into the twentieth century. Little boys who grew up in the desert, nourished by camel's milk, ended up driving sports cars. Was it any wonder that so many of them became playboys and spendthrifts like the present King Sa'ud? The old king ibn Sa'ud had had siblings of his own, over forty living sons, an unknown number of daughters, and now there were thousands of princes and princesses to be educated and supported by the kingdom. Even with so much revenue coming in from oil, it was swiftly being spent and squandered away. It was only a matter of time before King Sa'ud would be disposed and Crown Prince Faisal, his younger brother, would become king.

Five times a day, dawn to dusk, from the cone-shaped minarets, a voice called the people to prayer all over the desert kingdom. '*Allahu akbar!*' ('God is most great!') In public squares and in the mosques of Medina, Mecca, Jeddah, Talif, and five hundred miles east to Riyadh, the capital, men formed lines and genuflected in long rows of white thobes and caps. How many times had I seen Ali, his feet bare, his buttocks raised, and his forehead touching the ground with his prayer rug spread out under him? Many times, even on the yacht, during our wedding trip, the all-consuming Muslim religion was always with us. I had to make a decision soon: to embrace it or to resist it.

Chapter 10

THE BIRTH OF A SON

Were it not for Mary, my Filipino maid, I am not sure that I could have survived those early days in Saudi Arabia. She and I were about the same age, and for me to have Mary, an English-speaking servant, in my household was like a gift from God.

Her impoverished parents sent her to the Kingdom three years earlier, and in return for her services, they received a paltry stipend each month. After six years, she could return to her own country, provided she could endure the abuse and indignities that were dealt out to foreign servants. It was dangerous to work in a country that didn't respect other religions or foreign women. But, of course, I didn't know that when we first met.

Mary would teach me many things, one of which was the love of one's faith, in her case—Catholicism. Mary longed for her church, but in Saudi Arabia there were only mosques. The one acceptable religion was the strict form of Sunni Islam, known as *Wahhabism.* The desert kingdom showed little tolerance for non-Wahhabi Sunnis and Shiites, and zealously excluded the practice of any other religion.

Whenever Ali returned from one of his frequent business trips, he always brought back the latest magazines and even books from the United States, which I devoured. I read a recent copy of the *New York Times*, with a headline that read, "Governor of Arkansas Defies Supreme Court." The Federal government ordered the schools to integrate in Arkansas as well as the rest of the South. Governor Faubus of Arkansas closed the schools and reopened them as private schools as an act of defiance. Most thought that Southerners would never accept colored and white children in the same school. I had my doubts too; after all, the two races couldn't even use the same bathrooms in the South. I felt my country was in for some dark days.

Eventually, I met Hagar, Ali's first wife. She lived on the Corniche with a splendid view of the Red Sea in a house nearly identical to my own, except in décor. I found her to be a pleasant young woman who showed no outward sign of resentment toward me. She had a lovely face—cheeks that were full and naturally pink. She wore no make-up except kohl encircling her enormous black eyes, and dressed only in traditional clothing—a floor-length, bright colored shift, with a modest neckline decorated with embroidery. She wore gold hoop earrings and an array of gold bangle bracelets on both wrists.

Hagar never spoke first unless it was to her children. Ali treated her respectfully and kissed her on both cheeks when he greeted her. She would giggle, lower her eyes, and kiss his hand. Whenever I asked her a question in my feeble Arabic, she would lean forward, straining to understand me, apologizing profusely for being "so stupid." Her good manners were beyond anything I had ever experienced. Her eyes hardly ever left her children: Mira, six, and Abdul, four. Like all Arab children, they were spoiled, especially the boys, and corporal punishment was forbidden. Such a strange country—people are beheaded and whipped, but children are never spanked.

One lazy afternoon, after our siesta, Ali surprised me with the news that we would be visiting his Uncle Mohammed and Marilyn that evening. I was astonished. Visiting in mixed company even with relatives was usually reserved for holidays like the last night of Ramadam. This was to be my first visit with men and women present, and for an outsider (non-family member or foreigner) to be included in such groups would have been unthinkable—no people guard their family privacy and women more zealously than the Saudis. When Ali expressed hope that I would not be too tired to go, I said I would have gone even if I had to crawl.

We arrived at their residence, which was only three kilometers away from our home. I had expected to find a defiant Marilyn and an angry bridegroom, but what I found surprised me. Marilyn greeted us dressed in a red linen caftan with long sleeves looking quite native, and Prince Mohammed was quite dapper in an Italian silk suit.

"I'm so happy to see you Suzanne, I mean Yasmine," she said with some embarrassment at her blunder. She embraced me warmly. Mohammed stood back awkwardly. We neither shook hands nor exchanged kisses but he did smile at me.

"Forget it," I said. "It pleases Prince Ali and he says it suits me. I'm so glad to see another American. You'll never know how much."

"Me too. It's wonderful to see another Yank. You know, when we were all locked up together, you were my favorite," said Marilyn.

Mohammed, Ali's uncle, and Kareem's much younger brother was reserved but charming. Actually, he was younger than Ali, but because he was paunchy and balding, he only looked older. He was nearly twenty years younger than Prince Kareem, one of the older brothers. Like most members of the royal family, he wore a mustache and goatee. Ali was one of only a handful of family members who did not wear a goatee. A maid served me a glass of white grape juice.

Their home was palatial, and more richly decorated than ours, but not in a gaudy way. This man had taste. Beautiful wall hangings adored the walls, and the floors glowed with Persian carpets. A teak cabinet filled with antiquities from Mesopotamia was at the center of the house in one of the common rooms. Mohammed, the 22nd son of the old king (He had forty-three) was a Sorbonne educated prince who was proficient in both English and French, and very proud of his collection, but admitted that they probably should have been in a museum. A few pieces were thousands of years old. Kareem's palace with Fatima seemed ostentatious in comparison to this lovely place. Still, I preferred our own residence. It was cozy, more intimate, and more to my American taste.

Both Prince Kareem and Alexandra were also present, having arrived before us. Alexandra and I could hardly wait to talk to Marilyn alone. We didn't have to wait long. The men retreated to the men's quarters before dinner to discuss family and business problems, which among these men were one in the same.

Marilyn told us that she allowed to keep her name because it was a derivative of "Mary," which was a revered name in Islam. We asked her about the fight in the limousine.

"That was nothing. I was absolutely dying for a cigarette, and when he said no, I pulled off the '*schmutta,*' and took a butt from his pack and lit it."

"The what?" I asked.

"The *schmutta*, the rag, the friggin' veil. Haven't you known me long enough to know all my Yiddish words?"

She continued, "Anyway, he slapped me, and I slapped him back. He laughed and said, 'You're wild, but you'll learn to obey me.' I told him I'd never let a man dominate me. He laughed again and said, 'We'll see about that.' The point is, I did smoke my cigarette. He's never hit me again. We compromised and in this country, I only smoke in private homes."

"What of his other wives—what are they like?" asked Alex.

"He's got three. I only met one and she's acts like a servant. He says I'm different, so maybe that's why he finds me amusing."

"And you don't think it has anything to do with the fact that you're a gorgeous woman?" Alex asked.

"Perhaps. My only problem now is that he wants a son to join his four other sons, but he doesn't know that I managed to smuggle in my diaphragm."

"Where was it?" I asked curiously.

"That is my secret," she said slyly. "Maybe, after a few years, I'll have a child, but not yet. I'm having too much fun. You know, I've become fond of him. He's a very interesting man with a little bit of the devil in him, especially in bed, which makes him interesting. He didn't waste his time in Paris. He knows what he's doing. He owns a small plane, and has ordered a helicopter from the States, for business purposes, he says. He's been made Minister of Foreign Affairs, and even *he* doesn't know what that means. He travels a lot and, sometimes, he takes me along. We've been to Beirut, Cairo and Baghdad. Great nightlife in Beirut. He loves to gamble. He has an apartment in Cairo that overlooks the Nile River. Imagine that! I've seen the pyramids and they are amazing. Once he went to London, but alone. He still doesn't trust me, but he needn't worry. I've never met anyone in New York nearly as wealthy. I may tire of this life in time, but for now, I'm happy."

"Don't you ever plan to escape?" I asked.

"Escape from what? Modeling is not the greatest life. I know everyone thinks it's very glamorous, but it's very hard work and you have to starve yourself. In a couple of years, I'd be through anyway. I don't have any family, just my uncle, the old senator. My parents divorced when I was three. I have no siblings. I spent all my time with nannies, boarding school, and summer camps. My mother died young of breast cancer, and my father had a heart attack while having sex with his third wife who was half his age. He left most of his money to her. So being with Mohammed is not so bad. At least I have someone who cares about me, and when we travel, I get to meet interesting people. Don't worry, I'm being *good.* I gambled in Beirut and lost thousands. He just laughed. As long as I behave myself, and keep my eyes off other men, I'll be okay. However, he can't control my thoughts, and you know how naughty they can be."

We were aghast. Her life was much freer than ours, and we were amazed that she was able to pull it off. Alex suspected that Marilyn was sexually experienced and pleased him in bed. I thought it was because she was so funny and entertaining, aside from being a beautiful cover girl model.

Alexandra seemed worried. "Marilyn, do not be fooled by Mohammed. We are all new brides and they want to please us. Above all, do not dare to compromise yourself with another man. I cannot believe that you would dare to notice other men. It could cost you your life. Believe me, I'm not joking. I've heard stories that are hard to believe."

"She's right. Mary, my maid, has told me of unbelievable cruelty that goes on in some of the homes. It could happen to any of us. Please listen." I pleaded.

"Okay, I'll be careful, but I do think some of these stories are exaggerated," Marilyn replied nonchalantly.

"It was no exaggeration that we were kidnapped," I said.

I asked Marilyn if she had ever tried to call someone in the states. "No, I haven't. I know the phones are bugged. I hear a double click each time I pick up the receiver. It's the same in Beirut and Cairo. They're all bugged. He may be infatuated with me, but he doesn't trust me. He's not a fool."

"I know exactly what you mean. The only phone in our home is in

Ali's office. How about you, Alexandra? You speak Arabic. You could do it."

"Kareem warned me, that if I helped you to contact your family, I would pay the consequences. I don't ever want to find out what he meant." *Alexandra was slipping away to the other side.*

"You both worry too much," said Marilyn. "Though I do have a couple of stories to tell you. Actually, I have two vile stories to tell you. Mohammed's mother, Marlama, is a monster, so when I see her, I put on this big act. Even though she has a house full of servants, she insists that I make her tea and serve it to her. I even have to help her put on her shoes. She has the biggest and widest feet I've ever seen. She can't find any that fit properly, so she wears men's sandals. She has thick, yellow toenails that turn my stomach. She hates me, and she shows it, but she's getting old and batty and she's a little nuts to begin with. It's because of the inbreeding. Mohammed said they have a lot of health problems in the family because of it. Some of the stuff is really strange. The first two wives are always cousins. After that, they don't give a shit. The other story is tragic. I saw Elizabeth at the souk."

"What?" Alexandra asked, as I held my breath, not sure that I wanted to know. I had grown very fond of Elizabeth during our captivity.

"She was heavily veiled, but she recognized me or maybe, she heard my big mouth. You know I tower over most of the women. Those damn veils are going to kill us all yet. I'm always tripping and *they're so-o-o-o damn hot*. But I'm getting away from my story. We only spoke for a minute. She was with that bastard, and he was schlepping her all over the place. While he was bartering over some jewelry with a shopkeeper, and carrying on like a madman, she whispered to me, 'Marilyn, I know it's you.' I nodded and listened. 'I can't take much more. He's terrible—now I'm pregnant. I'm not circumcised. I threatened to starve myself if he did it to me. I may still do it—death is better than this. I heard her voice break. The poor kid was crying. Then he yanked her away with him before I had a chance to say anything else."

We were shocked, but not surprised. We had seen him buy Elizabeth and we all recognized evil when we saw it. Marilyn did say that although Elizabeth's words were extremely disturbing, she didn't sound deranged. And it was a relief to know that she wasn't subjected to that hideous operation.

A servant came and told us to go to the communal dining room, which didn't resemble any dining room I had ever seen. Our husbands were waiting. Their discussion had ended. We sat in a circle on the carpeted floor and ate in the traditional manner. We were served a dinner of lamb, baby eggplant, pilaf and hummus. Because we were foreigners, we were given our own plates and flatware, instead of just going for it, dipping into everything with flat bread like the men did. My stomach turned when I got a whiff of the lamb. Since I became pregnant, I smelled everything: perspiration, gasoline, cooked foods, everyone's breath. Ali saw my discomfit, and explained the situation. Everyone was very understanding because nothing is more revered in a Muslim country than a woman who might be carrying a son. I was brought some chicken broth with some plain rice and I hung on.

Mohammed and Kareem admitted that dining with mixed company was a new experience for them. However, as long as it was family it was acceptable. "We have to update our social habits now that we are married to educated, modern women," Prince Mohammed said.

The remainder of the evening was devoted to more business and family discussions by the men, in particular about their brother and uncle, King Sa'ud. The politics of the kingdom in Saudi Arabia had come to a boil. Prince Kareem shook his head and said his brother, King Sa'ud, was not a bad man but he was a bad ruler. The eldest son of the old king, Abdul Aziz ibn Sa'ud lacked the ruling skills of his father and simply couldn't cope with the complexities of being a world-player on the economic scene. His dealings with the Greek ship owner, Aristotle Onassis were a disaster. King Sa'ud was no match for him. Nor did he conduct his personal life any better. He had become an extravagant playboy. The number of his wives and concubines was unknown and he produced over one hundred children.

"After living here for thirty years," Ali added, "my grandfather's old friend, the Englishman Sir Harry Philby, and his Muslim wife left the country."

"Why did they leave?" asked Alexandra.

"Because he wrote articles for foreign newspapers that denounced the corruption within our country and told how our cousins and uncles were picking up their morals in the gutters of the West, getting drunk and driving recklessly, endangering innocent people. Spending money like it grew on trees. They had a habit of abandoning cars in the desert when they had a mechanical problem, and then buying another newer model to replace it. They acted like fools, and he is absolutely right. These things would never have happened under my grandfather's rule. King Sa'ud demanded an apology, and then he and all his entourage spat in the old man's face. So of course, Philby left. We will miss him and his wisdom. He was always on our side against the West, and now this," Ali said sadly.

Kareem said, "Our country is flooded with debt. In spite of all the money that rolls in, Sa'ud managed to waste it on his foolish ventures. Palace after palace, mosque after mosque. All bigger and more expensive than the last. Thank Allah, we now have Prince Faisal to run the country, a practical, pious man who has the respect of the people and the mullahs."

"Have any of you women ever heard of the Englishwoman Gertrude Bell?" Mohammed asked.

To my surprise, it was Marilyn who answered him. "You bet I have. She is one of my heroines. I read about her when I went to Vassar and took a course on the history of the First World War on the Eastern front. She was a mountain climber and she did it in a skirt, imagine that. She was an archeologist. She worked for British intelligence. She was a friend and colleague of Lawrence of Arabia and Winston Churchill and knew all the important Arab leaders, every last one of them, as well as the English generals."

Prince Ali added, "She was an amazing woman. Spoke Arabic and Turkish fluently as well as three other languages. I believe she was educated at Cambridge or Oxford, I'm not sure which.

"It was Oxford, interrupted Marilyn.

I could see from his face that he was annoyed by her rudeness, but he was, after all, a guest in his uncle's home.

Ali continued, "She loved this part of the world and left fifty thousand pounds in her will to the Baghdad museum, which she established. She died at fifty-eight in Baghdad. Unfortunately, she took an overdose of sleeping pills and killed herself. She was the first European woman my grandfather had ever met. He was astounded that her face was bare when he met her, but what amazed him even more was her intelligence. Even though she was my grandfather's enemy for a time, he admired her. (Because of her allegiance to King Faisal of Iraq, a Hashimite and son of King Hussein, who had briefly ruled part of Arabia with the blessing of the English, the French and Lawrence of Arabia.) He said that God had made a mistake and given her the mind of a man. It is also said that she boldly asked him if it were true that he had sixty-three wives and concubines. I don't know if either statement is true—my grandfather sometimes embellished his rather spectacular life."

Politely, Mohammed interrupted. "I think the women would like to spend some time alone before we end the evening."

We had been dismissed like children sent to their room; we again retired to the women's quarters for tea and sweets. "I am surprised to hear them discuss other male family members so openly and so critically, especially the king," I said. "I wonder if Crown Prince Faisal can turn the country around. If he can't, then Saudi Arabia would be open to rebellion and bankruptcy—and even worse—war. Anyway, that's what Ali says."

"Let's change the subject—it's boring," said Marilyn. "I hate politics. Ali is so charming. I think he's in love with you."

"If he is, it's his problem," I said sarcastically, out of earshot of Alexandra, who was on a balcony looking at the garden. I didn't trust Alex anymore. She was getting too cozy with her husband, and he *was* Ali's Father.

After a while, I couldn't stop yawning and could barely stay awake. I was relieved when Ali called and said, "I think it's time we left. Yasmine must be exhausted." We said our good-byes and returned home.

MARY TOLD ME STORIES about my new country. She had served in several households in a period of three years and witnessed numerous beatings and even rapes of the women servants. She said

Fatima was mean, but no one had ever been molested at the palace of Prince Kareem. She claimed that she herself had escaped with only a few slaps in the face by Fatima and her two oldest daughters. "You would not believe me if I told you what they have done to their own women. In my previous household, they drowned the youngest daughter in the family pool. She was seen talking to a man alone at the souk. Her father screamed at her. 'You have ruined our family! You have dishonored us beyond repair!' The mother pleaded for her daughter's life, but it was useless. The father replied, 'It is better to remove the one rotten apple than to let it contaminate the other apples.'"

It was hard for me to believe, but Mary swore it was true. One of the male servants had witnessed it. Mary said she believed him because nobody ever saw the girl again, dead or alive.

One frequent visitor at our home was Hussein. He was my husband's brother, so he could visit; tradition dictated that he wasn't supposed to be left alone with me, but this household was more liberal than others. He was three years younger than Ali, and better looking, almost as pretty as a woman. He was shorter than Ali, effeminate and soft-spoken with delicate features and long slim fingers. Because I was an American, he assumed correctly that I would be broad-minded about his homosexuality.

"I have spent most of my life since the age of thirteen in England, mostly at military school and then in the University," he said. "I realized I was attracted to males at the military school. It was terribly confusing, though most of the English chaps considered it a rite of passage at that age. But for me, it did not go away. I was never attracted to women."

He groaned, "Aba has given me an ultimatum, either I marry or leave the country permanently. He can be a heartless man when you have not pleased him, and I have never pleased him. He wishes that I were like Ali."

Poor Hussein. I really felt sorry for him and genuinely liked him, so I listened as he ranted against his family.

"Some of the men in this country are hypocrites—even my own cousins. They drink alcohol, watch pornography, and a few of them are pedophiles who require little foreign girls and boys to satisfy themselves—something I've never done. I don't want to give up my heritage and wealth. But I live a lie here. If I married, it would be a tragedy for the woman. She would guess soon enough and might even report me to the *mutawas*, which could be the end of me and a great humiliation to my family."

I continued to listen, but was shocked at some of the things he was telling me. My God! Weren't these the people that adored children? I guess it only applied to Saudi children.

"Can you keep a secret?" he asked.

"Yes. I can."

He confessed to having a close male friend. "I have an apartment in London, which I own and use quite frequently to be with Jeffrey. He is the son of Lord and Lady Randolph, and heir to the title and family estate. I'm afraid I love him desperately. His family is very close to the Windsor's. You know who I'm referring to, don't you?" he said.

Did he think I was an idiot? "Of course, the English Royal Family."

"Jeffrey said they're a bloody cold lot. And he says that they've had their share of fairies in their family history."

"Look, Hussein, go to London. Live your life. It's too dangerous for you here."

"I know! I know you are right, but in my heart, I belong in my own country. I don't know what to do. Aba wants an answer soon. He's even selected a bride."

I reached over to pat him on the shoulder. Did I imagine it, or did he pull away? Just then, Sara walked in.

"Yasmine! Never touch a Muslim man! They are offended by it. There are so many things for you to learn. If we were members of a traditional family, Hussein would have to wash his hands or rub them with sand after being touched by you. The only males you can ever touch are your husband, your father, your son or your brother. Brothers-in-law do not count."

Embarrassed, we both nodded, our eyes glued to the floor. I called for one of the servants to bring us some coffee: the kind Arabs like, strong and sweet. Anything to change the atmosphere—I had committed a huge blunder.

After Hussein left, Sara said, "Yasmine, our family is unusual. The women are treated well, better than in any other family with the exception of the wife and daughters of Crown Prince Faisel. Because of my mother, I had private tutors. My father allowed it because he loved her, and he wanted to please her. I was permitted to further my education in London and become a doctor because my brothers and a widowed, older aunt were there to watch over me. I was very, very lucky to be born in such a family.

"In other homes, women are barely tolerated. When a baby girl is born, it is a time of mourning. When a boy is born, it is a time of great joy. Boys are nursed two to three years, but girls, only one. Some men are cruel to their daughters and sisters, though *never* to their mothers. That is the best time for a woman—when she becomes the mother of sons, she earns the title of *Umm,* followed by the name of her son.

When I was growing up, my best friend, Anoud, a beautiful girl of fifteen, went out in public after she had colored her lips. A gust of wind blew her veil away, revealing her face on a public street. The *metawain* moved in quickly and struck her on the face with a camel whip, screaming curses at her. They are zealots, fanatics, but they more than anyone run the country. Everyone fears them—even the Saudi Royal Family. She was arrested and brought to her father. He took her home, and then he beat her so savagely that she sunk into a coma and died. In his opinion, she lost her '*ird.*' Not a thing happened to him. I have many stories like that and they are all true. Even something that isn't your fault can be misconstrued. Always be on guard."

"How can this be allowed? What is *ird*?" I asked.

"I will try to explain it to you, but I am not sure that you will understand. There is nothing in your culture that is comparable, so try to keep an open mind. All Muslim women have this thing called "*ird.*" It arrives with our birth. Upon losing her ird, the *sharaf* (honor) of her paternal family will be lost and will not be regained until *she* is punished. Her father, or her brothers, or her uncles or their sons administer the punishment by putting her to death, the only way to reinstate the family honor. Until honor is restored, there are no weddings, no family celebrations, and no business dealings—nothing. The family is shunned and cursed."

"Are you talking about the loss of virginity in an unmarried woman?"

"Yes. That is one of the worst offenses, but it is much more than that. I told you about my friend being arrested by the religious police and killed by her father. Even the *suggestion* of an indiscretion, such as being caught alone with a man, is enough to lose one's ird. When a woman is raped, the assumption is always that *she* has placed *herself* in a bad situation. That is why women are not allowed to go out alone. When you see a woman walking down the street holding the hand of her young son, she is not protecting him, he is protecting her."

I shook my head in amazement. Would I ever understand this country?

"If a married woman commits adultery, the husband will simply divorce her. His responsibility will be to deal with the seducer. Sometimes he will kill the man, or in other cases, collect a monetary payment. Her father and brothers will deal with her punishment. As much as my own father and brothers love me, they would kill me if I lost my *ird*."

"You can't believe that. It's unimaginable!"

"It's true. I doubt if Hussein has the stomach for it, but all of the other men would do it. And they would be doing the right thing. You cannot live in a Muslim country without honor."

I sat there hardly able to believe what I was hearing. Was it possible that Ali would kill his own beloved sister? Where was the love? Where was the loyalty?

She went on. "That is why when we are born, we are barely tolerated by our families. Even by our mothers. We have the ability to ruin their lives. On the other hand, our father and our brothers are our greatest ally if our husband mistreats us. And when we grow older, our sons become our protectors."

"There is so much that I don't understand."

"You will learn. You must."

I thanked her for her advice, and then we embraced. She shrugged. "I have to get back to Fatima. She is impossible since Father married Alexandra. She has become so deranged that she believes she has put a curse on Alexandra and you."

"Why me? I didn't marry her husband."

"It doesn't matter to her. Both you and Alexandra are the usurpers, and don't forget you replaced her niece, Hassa, Ali's second wife. She is convinced that Aba is going to divorce her, and she may be right, especially since she never had sons."

WHEN ALI RETURNED FROM a business trip to the United States, he brought me back the number one best seller of the year, *The Exodus.*

After I finished reading the book, I told Ali it was a wonderful book, and I was glad that the Jewish people had regained their homeland. He was furious with me, but he realized that he never should have given me the book in the first place. He had mistakenly thought that the book was about Moses, (one of the prophets that Arabs revered) being led out of Egypt, and not about the Jews returning in mass to Palestine.

I had gotten over my early fear of him and said, "Ali. Surely you realize that the Holocaust was a terrible thing and the Jews had to go somewhere?"

"Of course, I know that, but why Palestine? My grandfather said that they should have taken land from Germany. That is the Arab way. If you conquer a land, you have a right to it. Why didn't the Americans give the Jews a homeland in Germany?"

"Why would they want to live in Germany, a country that caused them nothing but death and misery? They had to have a homeland. After all, they were the chosen people and Palestine was given to them by God."

"By Allah, you know nothing. I'll tell you why they went there. The rest of the world didn't want them. The United States of America turned back a whole boatload of Jews who came from Hamburg, Germany, seeking asylum. The Americans would not accept them, nor would Cuba, and so, they were returned to Germany, and placed in concentration camps, most likely ending up dead. The benevolent United Nations, led by the United States, recognized the state of Israel in 1948, and gave them Arab land. The people who had lived there for hundreds, maybe thousands of years, could no longer live in Palestine, but a Jew from New York could."

"Ali, I wish you did not hate so much."

"I do not hate Jews! I hate Zionists! The Israelites are people of the Book, Semitic people—our cousins. Both people share one common ancestor, Abraham. We worship the same God, only we call him Allah, and Mohammed is his prophet. The Jews had Moses, the Christian had Jesus, and finally, though we were the last, we got our Prophet, Mohammed. And he went to paradise in the holy city of Jerusalem, which, thank God, is still in Arab hands. It is the Zionists who are at fault. I will get you more books which will explain the Palestinian point of view, and then you will understand." After that, I was careful not to get into any more discussions about Jews with any Muslims. On that score, all Saudis seemed united—they all hated the Zionists, which I think was just another catchall word for Jews.

That night, Ali said he had a serious matter to discuss with me. I asked him if it could wait until tomorrow.

"No, Yasmine, it cannot. According to our law, all wives must be treated equally. Hagar's father has reprimanded me for not sleeping with Hagar on a regular basis. He wants more grandchildren. If he goes to the *mutawas* and complains, I could get into a lot of trouble. I must spend every other night with her. It is the law and it is my duty."

Secretly, I was pleased. My pregnancy left me exhausted each night, and all I really wanted to do was sleep—alone. If he had to spend some time with his first wife, so be it. I much preferred to be alone with thoughts of Michael. Before he turned out the lights, he said, "My dearest, I'm glad you understand."

I smiled to myself in the dark. I neither understood nor cared.

MARY AND I SPENT THAT FIRST CHRISTMAS in Saudi Arabia, singing Christmas carols to each other and exchanging simple gifts, since she was poor and I, as yet, had no money of my own.

I had had a terrible time during my pregnancy. Wave after wave of nausea sent me running to the bathroom, but by Christmas, I started to feel better. During those early months, it was Mary who kept my spirits up and helped me. Because of Mary, Sara, and Alexandra, life was tolerable. My visits to Alexandra's home were frequent and enjoyable. Her home and household was a happy one. The servants were treated kindly and adored her. Alexandra also became pregnant, and Prince Kareem was overjoyed. He even allowed her to call her parents in Lebanon. The only stipulation was that she was to speak only of herself. She was never to mention the others or me.

Her parents were told that Prince Kareem had rescued her from some Kurdish kidnappers in Turkey, fell in love with her, and married her. It probably sounded like a fairy tale, but because she was happy and still alive, they were satisfied. Prince Kareem invited them to visit when the child was born. Because Alexandra's father was a Muslim, it was acceptable. Her family had only endured five months of torture without her; my family was possibly doomed for a lifetime.

"Kareem will give me anything I desire. He is a dear man. Everything has turned out rather well for me. I am studying the Koran, and I am beginning to value their way of life. Yasmine, it's a good way of life."

During that period, we acquired a second home in the capital, Riyadh, which was near the newly built palace of Crown Prince Faisal, who recently took over the reins of the country. His brother, King Sa'ud, was finally disposed for incompetence.

Although Ali and Daniel drove me to visit friends and relatives, they still didn't let me out of their sight. I would have called home the first chance I got if I knew how to do it. I thought of sending a letter out with Mary, but I didn't want to put her at risk. It was too dangerous for both of us. I just wanted to relieve them of their fears and tell them I was alive and well.

Alexandra and I were to go to Guy's Hospital in London to give birth to our children, which was a common practice in the Saudi royal family. Now I had a plan. Somehow, I'd go to the American Embassy in London with my baby and return to America—to my husband, Michael—the father of my child.

I don't know if it was Fatima's curse or just plain bad luck, but I experienced some bleeding, and Sara ordered me to bed for the duration of the pregnancy. Ali engaged two English doctors, a pediatrician and an obstetrician, to await the birth, which would be performed at Sara's clinic.

A shroud of despair passed over me when I lost my chance to go to London, and I fell into a depression. My body had ballooned during my pregnancy and I had difficulty putting on my shoes or getting up out of a chair. I saw my English obstetrician every few days, and I was sure that he was frustrated and anxious to return to England. I couldn't help but think of what my father would have thought of this outrageous display of indulgence. I was embarrassed by the whole ordeal, but aside from apologizing to the doctor, I kept my thoughts to myself. I had thought of telling him the whole truth about my abduction, but what good would that have done? He was there for the large sum of money he would receive for delivering my baby—he wouldn't have cared about me.

Ali tried to cheer me up by discussing names for the child—only male names. I told Ali that, while reading the Koran, I read that the Muslims revered the archangel Gabriel. Michael was an archangel also, so I asked him if it would be an appropriate name as it was one of my favorites. "I'm so pleased you are reading our holy book. Actually, Misha'al is a family name. Of course, my dear. It's an acceptable name. If it makes you happy, we will use the English pronunciation. His name will be Misha'al ibn Ali Aziz." (ibn means son of) What if we had a daughter? A name for her had never been discussed.

Nothing could have prepared me for what was coming. Although I had read and seen pictures in my father's obstetric books, it wasn't the same. When I had my first pain, I thought it was just a cramp. It continued, so I woke Ali.

He said, "It can't be. It's not time yet."

I gasped, "Babies come when they want to come." I no longer had the luxury of being depressed—labor pains can make you forget everything that has ever happened to you.

Five minutes later, another pain sucked my breath away, and then after five more minutes, another pain. When my water broke, and formed a puddle around my bare feet, I knew that this was the real McCoy. Ali was calm. After all, he was the father of two. But I was scared to death. He telephoned the doctors who resided at a small hotel near the clinic. He bundled me into his new Jaguar, with Mary beside me in the back seat, and sped down the road. He drove so fast,

I thought we would get killed. "Slow down Ali." I screamed as I clutched Mary's hand so hard that she grimaced with pain.

"I'm an excellent driver and I know this road blindfolded."

Hours and hours later, I felt myself pushing and grunting. *Was I the one making all those animal-like sounds?* A nurse was mopping my brow and moistening my lips with ice.

"It won't be much longer. You are doing well," she said.

"I am not! I can't stand it anymore!"

I saw the doctor through a haze. I felt a jab, as he injected something into my arm. I heard him say, "Now, little mother, you will go to sleep." As I drifted off, I heard him remark to the others: "We better deliver this little wog safe and sound or we'll lose our heads at Chop Chop square, but if all goes well we'll go home with a year's pay. This chap is richer than King Midas." *My mind was so muddled, but I remember thinking, why is he saying that? My father would never talk like that. I yearned for my Daddy. I was his little princess. He had told me so—many times—long ago.*

When I awoke, I was exhausted—sore everywhere—and relieved that it was over. Ali looked down at me and kissed my lips softly. "We have our son. You have made me very happy." Sara handed me my baby.

I looked at my son's face. He had Michael's eyes. His lashes curling upward to his light little eyebrows. His head covered in dark hair as soft as down. He was so little and so precious. I put my finger in his tiny hand and he grasped it—I smiled at the wonder of it. His little grip was strong.

Ali said, "He's a handsome child, long in size but a bit thin. The doctor says he's a little premature and may have to stay in the hospital a fortnight, but he's basically healthy. No lung problems, thank God."

"Yes Ali," I murmured. But my mind was with Michael, the father of my child. I nuzzled my face next to the baby, inhaling his sweet baby smell as I watched his little lips sucking air. I wanted Ali to leave.

"I think the little prince is hungry. Just one thing, Yasmine, how did you know it was a boy?"

"What do you mean?"

"You called his name over and over. Michael. Michael."

"I just knew he would be a boy, because you wanted one so badly." *I had become an expert liar.*

"Of course. You had a premonition. How stupid of me."

I opened my nightgown and offered my full breast to my infant son. He turned his head from side to side, neither of us knew quite what to do. We were both beginners but, finally, with some advice from the nurse, and even some from Ali, the baby suckled greedily, opening his eyes, and focused on me. Could he see me? I didn't know, but I understood one thing—he knew that I was his mother. Never had I felt such tenderness or closeness to anyone. It was the ultimate love—unconditional and perfect. No love for a man would ever match this. I was determined that above all, if need be, I would protect this child with my own life. If it took lies, deceptions, or even worse things, I would do it all. I would protect Michael's son with my life.

Chapter 11

THE MISSING YEARS

During the first three years of their marriage, Yasmine never once told Ali that she loved him. It would have been a deception, a total sham, and he would have known it. She still thought of Michael, but it was getting harder and harder to even remember the sound of his voice. Gradually, she began to care for Ali. It happened sometime after the birth of her second son, Rhashid, and before she became pregnant with her daughter, Sara. She awoke one morning to a revelation, which came to her in the form of a dream.

In her dream, Yasmine walked into Ali's bedroom, and he was in bed with another woman, an exotic creature, someone she did not know. Propped up on one elbow, he looked down at this woman, whom he obviously desired. Upon seeing Yasmine, he smiled demonically at her and then very deliberately leaned over and kissed the other woman. Yasmine felt an emotion she had never experienced before—jealousy. And with it, a rage, a feeling so intense, that it awakened her. Shaking with anger, she looked at Ali as he slept beside her, and sighed with relief, finally accepting a truth that she could no longer deny. She had fallen in love with Ali, and there would be no more thoughts of escaping from him

Two years and six months after her second son's birth, little Sara was born with a full head of curly dark hair and a lusty cry. Everyone adored her, particularly now that two brothers had already preceded her. Sara's birth brought joy to both her parents—this child was conceived in love.

Yasmine had changed little physically from the time she was once called Suzanne. She remained slim, but now she had the body of a mature woman, her breasts fuller and her hips softly contoured, although her abdomen remained as firm and flat as a woman who had never borne a child.

She stood out among the women of the Aziz family; most were big, lumbering women, especially the daughters of the deceased King, who had been six feet, five inches tall. They numbered in the fifties (no one knew for sure, since records weren't kept for women). Most of them had big square feet and large hands, but some of the granddaughters like Hagar, Sara, and Nina fared better and were pretty women.

That Yasmine, Marilyn, Elizabeth, and Alexandra were of different faiths and from other countries didn't diminish their status as third wives. The only thing that made them different was that three of them were American-born and that made them more a curiosity than anything else. Saudi men sometimes marry women of other faiths and from other lands, though Saudi women were strictly forbidden from marrying non-Muslims. In some religious texts, it was rumored that one of Mohammed's wives was Jewish as there was a considerable Jewish population at that time near Mecca. Islam has always welcomed converts, especially women.

All four women promised never to reveal the truth about their abductions. In time, even *they* began to accept the lies as truth—that they had met the princes at social events in Athens and London. Instructed in the Koran, each had become a Muslim.

Sura II, 221
Do not marry
Women who do not believe
A slave woman who believes
Is better than one who does not believe.

AS THE YEARS PASSED, the babies grew into childhood, nearing the time when they would begin their education. Michael was bright and inquisitive and, clearly, his father's favorite, even more than Abdul, his eldest son with Hagar. Ali loved all his children, but his feelings for Michael bordered on obsession. Yasmine was not oblivious to this, and begged him to treat the boys equally. She knew that

Rhashid was jealous of Michael: "Mother, why does Aba love Michael more than me?"

"He doesn't," she said and would hug his little body into hers. It reminded her of the unhappy times with her own mother when Rosie had held and comforted her.

"This is not America. He is the first son of our union, and that makes him special. You know I love Rhashid." As for Sara, her father loved her with all his heart, but the teachings of the Koran dictated that he must treat her differently—in all ways.

<u>*Sura IV, 11*</u>

God directs you as regards to your children. The male shall receive a portion equal to two females.

(Although the Koran was referring to inheritance, the people of the Kingdom, from the poorest of the poor to the richest of the rich, believed in every way that a male child was superior to a female child.)

LIKE MOST MUSLIM FATHERS, Ali spoiled and indulged his children, especially now that he was wealthy. Once, little Arab children of the desert led a harsh life, almost as brutally harsh as their parents' lives had been, but the discovery of oil had changed everything for most of them. Schools and medical facilities were now free, and each Saudi citizen received a subsidy and free medical care. This was not the case for thousands and thousands of workers and their families who did all the laboring and became the servants of Saudi citizens.

As many fathers did, Ali took his three sons to the camel races twice a year at Riyadh Stadium. The wild Bedouin riders rode their camels hard to the cheers of the spectators. They were exciting and colorful and the crowd screamed cheers for their favorite riders. The one thing that the children didn't like about the camels was their smell. They would wrinkle up their noses and ask their father, "Aba, why do camels stink so much?"

Ali never failed to be amused and laugh aloud. Had Prince Kareem been present, he would have probably responded by saying, "When I was a boy, I took care of those smelly animals. I drank their milk and rode on their humps. I like to see them race, but that's all. Give me a horse any day, or better still, a car."

Arabian horses were the envy of the equestrian world, and nowhere were they more loved or treasured than in Saudi Arabia. Ali and many of his cousins brought the games of squash, cricket, and polo back from England, as well as their English accent. Ali was a polo rider and played well. Each of his three sons owned a pony, and Oman, Ali's adopted Sudanese brother, taught them the art of riding horseback. In time, they would ride an Arabian horse—the dream of all little boys in the desert kingdom. Sara tagged along with her brothers, often taking a turn on the gentlest pony. But once she reached puberty, that would cease, and she would enter the world of the cloistered, veiled female.

Ali kept his word to the father of Hagar and she became pregnant and bore two more children, twins: a boy, Turki, and a girl, Nura. With four children, Ali's first wife, Hagar, was contented, as were her parents. Ali visited these children three times a week but ceased spending nights with Hagar who was busy caring for her twin babies. For Ali, two wives were enough. Many of his uncles and cousins were debt-ridden trying to provide equally for their many wives and children. Also, the constant squabbling between wives was harrowing, and Ali had no desire for more wives and more trouble.

BECAUSE ALI WAS A ROMANTIC MAN, he would surprise Yasmine with ingenious escapades. On one occasion, he told her to dress in her most beautiful abaaya and Bedouin veil and to wear nothing underneath. She wanted an explanation, but he laughed. "It's a secret." He, too, dressed traditionally in his white thobe, and on his head his red and white checkered ghutra, attached with an igaal.

It was late in the afternoon as Ali drove his sleek, silver Jaguar to the edge of a vast, open expanse of sand and rocks; there was not a growing thing or a moving creature anywhere in sight, except for Oman who was already tending Ali's horse and saddling him. Oman, a tall, handsome African, was Ali's *akhiwiya* (little brother). As was often the custom, a Sudanese slave-boy was adopted and raised to be the friend and companion to a male child of the royal family. Oman loved Ali and Ali, after his own family, loved Oman most of all.

His beautiful gray stallion, Mismaak, was shimmying, anxious to run. Ali embraced Oman. "We'll be back at dawn, my brother. Be there. *Isah'Allah.*"

Oman flashed a smile, his ivory teeth flashing, his purplish black skin glistening with sweat, emphasizing every muscle of his body even though he was dressed in a clinging white thobe. "As God wills," he said.

Ali placed Yasmine on the side-saddled horse that he had purchased in Morocco especially for her. He sat behind her holding the reins. Yasmine removed her veil and scarf and gripped the neck of Mismaak. They took off. She shook her golden hair loose. It flew wildly. She laughed, yelling, "Yaaaaaay. I'm freeeeee." They galloped over the desert sand, and the sheer exhilaration of the moment caused Yasmine to think, *never in my entire life have I felt more alive.*

"Ali, this is so wonderful. I love it. Why haven't we done this before?"

"You were either pregnant or it was in the heat of the summer. Now is the perfect season and the best time of day to be in the desert."

The vastness of the desert beyond their planned excursion frightened her; the sheer size of it was overwhelming. Foreigners called it *The Empty Quarter.* Arabs referred to it as the *Arub Al Khali* or *The Sands.* It was bigger than the country of France and all of it was barren, completely void of anything green, wet or living. Still, Suzanne found the fringes of this desert fascinating—a shifting ocean of tiny grains of sand. At dawn and at dusk, the colors on the horizon blurred—pink, purple, yellow—and nowhere on earth was the landscape more unobstructed, except for the sand dunes that jutted up like pyramids. Always, there was the underlying fear that the blazing heat and the sandstorms that rose from nowhere could kill you. However, this only added to the thrill of it. Living on the edge was exciting. Some people climbed mountains. Others explored the depths of the sea. Adventure makes one feel young and invincible, reinforcing the idea that old age with all its restraints and impediments is far into the future, when you no longer should care about such things. The irony is that you'll care even more, but you don't know that when you're young.

On the horizon, she saw a miniature configuration, like a house on a Monopoly game board. As they neared it, Yasmine shielded her eyes with her hand, squinted, and saw that it was a large tent in the middle of the desert.

Upon arriving at their destination, Ali slid off his horse, swept Yasmine up into his arms, and carried her to the tent. She smiled seductively. "Another game, Sheik Ali?"

"This is no game, love. I'm not Rudolph Valentino playing a role in a movie—this is my life—the way it's been for centuries."

Inside the goatskin tent, large, thick cushions were arranged to form a place to sleep. Carpets covered the floor of sand. Food and drink was set aside. Yogurt, ripe fruit, cooked lamb, hummus and fresh water. The aroma of spices filled the interior like a mist of perfume. A chair decorated in gold leaf stood in one corner, and on the floor next to it lay a pan of scented rose water and a neatly folded linen cloth. Yasmine eyed it and clearly understood its symbolism.

Ali stood facing her and took her face in his hands. "Now, I will show you how my grandfather and his grandfather before him made love to their women." He lifted the abaaya over her head, and stood back boldly looking at her nakedness. She was in disbelief. Muslims, by nature are a modest people. They always made love before in the darkness of night or under the covers of their bed. He said, "There is something I would like you to do, if it pleases you."

She nodded. She knew what he wanted. He had never asked her before, and she had never volunteered. He sat in the chair as she knelt on the ground and removed his sandals. Tenderly, she washed his feet and then wiped them with the linen cloth. Then, she kissed them. Between a Bedouin couple, it was a ritual, the act of complete submission and love by the woman—something that Yasmine had knowingly denied Ali. What followed after was the most erotic and romantic experience of her life. She no longer would have to play the role of the subservient one; by performing this ceremony, she made it an equal exchange. On the horizon, awash with the colors of salmon, lavender and saffron, night descended. Ali recited a Bedouin love poem to his wife.

Paradise on earth is found on the back
Of a good horse;
In the study of good books, or
Between the breasts of a woman.

His voice pulsated, "Now…my little blonde, blue-eyed savage…you really are my Muslim wife."

APART FROM THEIR INTIMATE times together, they took part in many family gatherings such as picnics and special celebrations. Yasmine sometimes wore the veil of the Bedouin woman, which revealed the eyes but covered the bridge of the nose. They could be plain or beautifully embroidered with pearls and semi-precious stones. Women of the Middle East went to painstaking care to enhance their eyes and lashes with kohl, creating a mesmerizing and exotic effect. Yasmine's bright blue-violet eyes were astonishing in a land of dark sloe-eyed women.

In Jeddah at twilight, they would gather for picnics on sites overlooking the Red Sea, which revealed an underwater wonderland of pink and purple coral. Scuba diving had become popular, and many of the young princes, home from colleges in California and Florida, brought the sport back with them.

In Riyadh, family gatherings took place at the edge of the desert where vehicles would turn on their headlights and line up at sunset. After evening prayers were said, families had their picnics under the stars. In both locations, by the sea or by the desert, carpets were spread out, covered with baskets of cooked food, dates and fresh watermelon, strong sweetened coffee, and pastries. The children happily played with their cousins, half-brothers, and half-sisters. Yasmine soon discovered that she liked Hagar, whose childlike love and trust of everyone was admired.

At these gatherings, Ali always treated them equally, never favoring his second wife. Yasmine welcomed the outings by the sea, as they reminded her of Maine. Of late, she was beginning to ache to see her family and home again.

During the month long celebration of Ramadam, they would come not to picnic, but to watch the boats arriving at the port of Jeddah. Thousands of pilgrims came to perform their Hadj (religious pilgrimage) at Mecca. Yasmine thought of it as a combination of Lent and Christmas. The holy month required fasting each day from dawn to sunset, ending at the breaking of the fast (Eed al Fitr) with an elaborate feast and the exchanging of gifts. There would be no smoking or acts of sex during this time. Mostly, Ramadam was a time for prayer, for giving alms to the poor, and for spiritual renewal. During this holiday, Ali, Yasmine, and their children would arise at dawn and pray with the rest of the Muslim household. Ali promised that when his sons were a little older, he would take them on the pilgrimage to Mecca as his father had done for him when he was a teenager.

Over the years, Yasmine learned many things, including the Arabic language, although she never lost her strong American accent. She discovered, however, that by mispronouncing the sound of a long *a* or a short *a* could mean the difference between praising or insulting a person. The culture of Saudi Arabia was entirely different from that of the West. By learning to speak and write Arabic (which is the same in all Arab countries with just slight variations), Yasmine began to analyze things differently.

Yasmine tried to remember never to compliment a person's jewelry, or an object in their home, as they would be obliged to give it to her. Politeness and hospitality were carried to great extremes, the like of which she had not seen in Europe or the United States. Nor could she openly criticize anyone directly to their face, nor would they to her. It was inconceivable. She could only reprimand servants and younger family members. When a guest entered your home, she greeted them with the words, "My home is your home." She always had to be on guard never to praise a child, which could be misconstrued as *giving them the evil eye.* If sickness or death beheld that child, *she* could be held responsible. No one would ever think of making a definite appointment, unless followed with the words, "*InshAllah.*" If God Wills. Nothing is inevitable. God decides everything.

The differences in Western and Middle-Eastern culture were incalculable, but as time passed, it was possible for Yasmine to get through a day without insulting someone.

ON BUSINESS TRIPS OUT OF THE COUNTRY, Ali slept with other women. To him, it had nothing to do with love or marriage. He loved Yasmine, but he knew that being an American, she could never understand what Hagar accepted as normal—a man's need for many women. He was an Arab, a Muslim, a prince, and he refused to feel guilty for what was normal and natural to most of the men he knew with the exception of the fundamentalists, who in his opinion were fanatics.

Ali's aging father, Prince Kareem, often sought the favor of high-priced courtesans whenever he left Saudi Arabia without Alexandra. He boasted to his male friends and relatives that when he reached the age of seventy he would remain faithful to Alexandra. He would make it a pledge during that year on his *Hadj* to Mecca.

Alexandra had borne Prince Kareem five children, four sons, and a daughter. Each time she had another child, especially when it was a son, he would give her diamonds, her favorite gem. Yasmine thought they were ostentatious, especially a jeweled tiara that was more suited for an English coronation. Alexandra giggled and twirled a finger through a lock of curls. "Yasmine, don't be a fool. What does it matter? They are worth a fortune…and no one can take them away from me…it's the law. I'm becoming a wealthy woman. I won't always be young and beautiful, but I'll always be rich."

"Alex, can I ask you a question?"

"Of course. Ask anything."

"Is your husband faithful to you?

"Probably not. But I've never actually caught him in a lie or have any kind of proof."

"It doesn't seem to bother you, one way or another," said Yasmine.

"Do you think Ali is unfaithful? Is that what's bothering you?"

"It's just a feeling—he's different lately. If he were, I'd be devastated. No. Actually depressed would be more appropriate. When you trust someone and they disappoint you, it's sad."

"The problem is—you fell in love with him," said Alexandra.

"Don't you love Kareem?"

"*Pleaseeeee.* I *like* him. I *respect* him. He's the father of my children and the head of our family. But love him, *no*. He's an old man. I loved once, before our abduction. I know I lied to you and said there wasn't anyone. My sweetheart and I did not have an affair. In fact, we were never alone and had never exchanged a kiss. Nevertheless, I loved him with all my heart. He wrote me the most passionate love letters. You have no idea how intense that kind of a relationship can be—always yearning to be touched, to be kissed, and more, and not really knowing what 'more' feels like." Alex paused, swallowed hard, and wiped a tear away with the back of her hand.

"Oh well! He had to marry someone else, someone with a wealthy father. After that, I swore that what was left of my heart would stay with me. I love my children—that's enough for me."

"I'm sorry. I didn't mean to upset you or remind you of something sad."

"Yasmine, listen to me—don't be naïve—all men cheat. The French, the Italians, the English, they all have mistresses. Men like variety. It's in their nature. Even my Papa had an affair. Mama forgave him. The important thing is that you are his wife and they are not. He loves you. Be content with that."

"Well, that's not so for some American men. I know for certain that my father was faithful to my mother."

"How extraordinary," Alexandra said, as she sipped her mint tea and smoked her cigarette from a jeweled cigarette holder. Dressed in a beautifully embroidered Moroccan caftan of emerald green, she had indeed become the enchantress that Fatima had feared.

In Saudi society, aside for allowing for four wives, there was another arrangement that was like a mini-marriage lasting sometimes only a matter of days if stated in a prearranged contract, and concubines were also acceptable. Any sexual contact outside the legal or religious process was against the law. But in other countries, this law was not always observed. To further complicate the synopsis, until 1962, slaves were legal and had no rights—more than one prince had fathered a child with an African slave woman or concubine.

(Prince Kareem's brother, Prince Sultan, one of the more high-placed sons, was a notorious womanizer and fathered a son with a fifteen-year-old dark-skinned servant in the town of Talif, in 1949. In his early years his mother raised him. Whether she was a slave or of African origin was not customarily acknowledged. He was named, Bandar, and was a brilliant child who became quite popular with some of his uncles, particularly Crown Prince Faisal. Because of the circumstances of his birth, his own father chose to ignore and even disclaim him through his childhood days. He was educated in England, and trained to fly jets in the United States. Years later, Prince Bandar would marry King Faisal's daughter, Princess Haifa bint Faisal. Prince Bandar would became the Ambassador to the United States during the Carter administration when he was only thirty years old. He lives on an estate in Virginia with his family and gives lavish parties. His whispered nickname is "the Arabian Great Gatsby." At last count, he owned seven luxurious residences. He was a close friend of the forty-first president, George Herbert Walker Bush, as well as other presidents. He serves as the Ambassador to the United States to this day, and remains a friend to our forty-third president, George W. Bush.)

FOREIGNERS FROM OTHER Middle Eastern and African countries poured into the Kingdom by the thousands to do the work for the rich and the lazy. Muslim men wanted nothing to do with working with their hands; they considered construction work and other manual labor beneath them. They would take a job that paid three times less if they could dress up and keep their hands clean. Their religion said that only the cursed dirtied their hands, as was stated in the Old Testament's Book of Genesis.

The women of the Saud family and other women married to affluent men did little more than bear children and indulge themselves in whatever gave them pleasure. They never saw the inside of the kitchen. However, since King Sa'ud's death, things were beginning to change. King Faisal, the new king was a wise, pious man and his beloved wife, Queen Iffat, an educated Arabian woman from Turkey, opened the first school for girls. The mullahs fought against it, but in the end, the school remained with many more to follow. In time, there would be more women like Sara, but for others, it would remain a boring life of visiting relatives and friends, changing their clothes three times a day to impress one another.

For ordinary women from middle-class families, this was not the case. Only occasionally was there a second or third wife, though more often there were servants, as foreign help was dirt-cheap. One wife was all most men could afford. For the poor women, it was the same as it always had been—they worked from morning to night, and many of them looked with scorn upon the women of the royal family and other wealthy families.

The Bedouin could also have four wives if he so desired. All that was necessary was to provide four tents, which then allowed him four wives and children to tend his herds. All that their religion required was that each man, rich or poor, treat his wives equally.

YEARS BEFORE, HUSSEIN had left the country after a confrontation with his father about marriage. He went to live in London. Prince Kareem couldn't follow through with disowning him, but he refused to meet with him whenever Hussein's "friend" was present. In fact, he never acknowledged, even to family members, that he knew of such a person. Hussein came home for Ramadan but the rest of the time he lived in London where he conducted family business.

The Koran addresses the subject of male homosexuality. However, it does not say how such men are to be punished.

<u>*Sura IV, 16*</u>
If two men among you are guilty of lewdness
Punish them both.
If they repent and amend,
Leave them alone.

Hussein had no doubt that in Saudi Arabia it would probably mean severe punishment and possibly death. He chose to remain in the United Kingdom where his lifestyle would be thought of only as an idiosyncrasy. There, he would have no fear of punishment or of being ostracized from society.

Other family members' lives had changed also. The years were cruel to Fatima. She suffered a nervous breakdown two years after

Kareem's marriage to Alexandra. She walked around babbling about the "Lebanese enchantress, Alexandra." A year later, she died of a heart attack. Both of her daughters, Sabatz and Noohra, married cousins—older, prosperous men. They were rarely seen, and spent most of their time with their husbands' families. Justine poisoned herself after Fatima's death to join her mistress. She died an agonizing death, laughing in Sara's face when she tried to save her. "Before the day... has ended...I will be...with my mistress Fatima...in paradise," she babbled as she clutched her belly in agony.

Nina grew into a sweet, young woman of eighteen, and came to live with Alexandra and Kareem after Fatima's death. Although she was of marriageable age, Alexandra convinced Kareem to let her have a few more years to herself. She seemed much happier and adored Alexandra. Sara never married, but continued her work at the clinic. She and Alexandra conspired together and convinced Prince Kareem to allow Nina to become a nurse. At first, he protested. "A princess does not nurse people."

Sara quickly answered. "Allah praises women who tend the sick. Did not my own mother beg you to allow me to become a doctor?" The conversation ended with Kareem's silence. Whenever his first wife's name, Mira, was mentioned, he became sad. As much as he loved Alexandra, nobody could replace his dead wife, his first love and mother of his two favorite children, Ali and Sara. He relented and Nina studied nursing in the clinic with Sara as her instructor.

Ali encouraged Yasmine to keep up with current events, especially those about America. Because English and American newspapers and magazines were available to her, Yasmine was well aware of all the news, both good and bad. She found it hard to believe that an island off the coast of Florida was now a Communist country with a dictator named Castro. Unbelievable. Hawaii had been granted statehood. She loved reading about the young president, Jack Kennedy, and his glamorous wife, Jacqueline, and shed bitter tears when she learned the young president had been assassinated. She anguished over the United States getting involved in Vietnam, and wondered if her brother Robby had gone off to fight. She doubted it. She was thrilled to see a man land on the moon. The feat made her feel proud of her country. Many Arabs believed it was a trick, and could not accept the fact that a man was actually on the moon. That wasn't surprising since most of them had never been in an automobile. For them, space travel was inconceivable.

YASMINE LIVED A LIFE of luxury and even traveled outside of Saudi Arabia, but always to a Muslim country. Depending on the time of year, she divided her time between her Riyadh palace and her less formal residence in Jeddah. She visited exotic Morocco and cosmopolitan Lebanon. She thrilled at the sight of the temple of Abu-Simble and the pyramids of Egypt. She traveled to other countries of the Middle East and Africa, but never to the United States or Europe. Ali had promised that, some day, they would go. She knew the reason. He did not trust her in a Western country.

On a vacation in Morocco, she thought about her mother, and a wave of longing and sadness overcame her. As a teenager and later as a young adult, she had had her differences with her mother, but she never realized how much she loved her until they had become separated. Although Michael had become a distant memory, her mother had not. *"Oh Mummy, I want to be with you!"* Her voice broke and she sobbed, staggering about the room in a wave of grief. What if her mother were dead?

Before she could change her mind, she decided to call home. Speaking in French, which was still better than her Arabic, she managed to place a telephone call to Maine. She heard her sister Jane's voice, "Who's calling? Is anyone there? Hello! Hello!"

Just hearing Jane's voice gave her such comfort. She shut her eyes and bit her lower lip. She desperately wanted to speak to her sister and tell her that she was not dead. But all she could get out was, "Jane," in a whisper, before someone opened the door to the hotel suite and yelled, "Mama, we're back."

Yasmine panicked and slammed down the phone. She doubted if Jane had recognized or even heard her voice. She prayed that Ali would not see the telephone call listed on the hotel bill. He would have confronted her, demanding an explanation, and possibly send her back to the United States, without her children. Once, she feared for her life; now she feared the loss of her children.

IN MAY OF 1967, the family went to East Jerusalem and they checked in at the deluxe hotel, The Jerusalem Palace. Ali accompanied the family to Al-Haram al-Sharif (the Dome of the Rock)—the place on Temple Mount most sacred to Muslims, where Mohammed had supposedly ascended into Paradise while on an Arabian stead. Yasmine went below the main floor where only Muslim women were allowed. She kissed the holy, black rock, worn smooth by the kisses of Islamic women who had been coming to this revered place for centuries. It was presumed that this was the same place where Abraham was to have sacrificed *his* son to God. Which son? Both would be leaders of two great peoples, the Jews, and the Arabs. The Jews said it was Isaac, the second son, born of his wife Sarah. The Muslims claimed it was the first son, Ishmael, born of Hagar, the handmaiden of Sarah. Because of this one question, a great divide occurred between these two Semitic people, and continues to this day.

They also visited the Al-Aqsa Mosque with its silver dome, which was much smaller than the large golden one over the Dome of the Rock. Much blood had been shed to regain this holy place. Ali said, "Palestinians fought the Crusaders, the Romans, the Greeks, the Jews, the Turks, and the English. Now it is theirs. By Allah's name, they planned to keep it."

Mary wept with happiness as she followed the Christian pilgrims as they walked the seven Stations of the Cross along the Via Dolorosa, an ancient, stone walkway traveled by the millions who had come this way. Yasmine remembered attending church on Good Friday and hearing Rev. Scott's vivid description of Christ's final journey to his death. When they reached the Church of the Holy Sepulcher, Mary knelt down and prayed for the soul of Ali for allowing her to come to this sacred place.

ONE MONTH LATER, ISRAELI BOMBERS flattened the airfields of Jordan, Egypt, and Syria. It came to be known as "The Six Day War," as that was all the time needed for the Jews to defeat the Arabs. President Nasser of Egypt had shook his fist at the Israelis for the last time when he threatened to close the Gulf of Aqaba and Israel's access to the sea. Nasser was forced to resign in disgrace. For the Arabs, it was a horrendous defeat and humiliation; worst of all, they had lost East Jerusalem and access to their third most holy place, The Dome of the Rock. The Saudis, the defenders of the faith and of Mecca, were in despair; they had lost their holy site where Mohammed had gone to paradise.

Syria had lost the Golan Heights. Egypt had lost the Sinai Peninsula. Jordan has lost the West Bank and the rest of Jerusalem. King Faisal's hatred and paranoia for the Jews intensified, and his grief was inconsolable. However, Yasmine knew that he was wise; despite his feelings, he never lost his head and sent Saudi men to fight and die in hopeless causes. His weapon of choice had always been money. No Saudi man had ever shed blood in the war against the Jews.

Ali was depressed and disgusted with his fellow Arabs for losing the war in such a short time. Where was their honor? He blamed the Americans for supplying the Jews with superior planes and weapons. He said, "The Egyptians, Jordanians and Syrians talk a bloody good game, but they can't fight and win. I'm glad my grandfather isn't here to see this. He would be ashamed."

The Jews had accomplished a great victory. Now they could again pray at the Wailing Wall, the remains of the Second Temple of Jerusalem that had been destroyed by the Romans. They reclaimed "the Old Quarter," and East Jerusalem, a piece of real estate that had changed hands many times before. Jews all over the world rejoiced, but it set in motion more war and turmoil than anyone could have imagined. (It also created a new kind of terror. Islamic groups and the Japanese Red Army based in Syria started blowing up airport terminals in Greece and Israel. and high-jacking planes.)

For the indigents, for the uneducated, and for the over educated (who could find no work because foreigners often filled the jobs) some would come to look upon the Royals and other obscenely wealthy families with scorn. It was only a matter of time before there would be trouble with the disenchanted as they grew in number. The religious fanatics filled their need—hatred of anyone who was not of their belief, especially of Israel and later on, its ally, America. The seeds were being planted in schoolbooks, in prayers, in mosques, in Saudi Arabia and in Islamic teaching schools around the world, but the aftermath, and the damage it would do, would not show up immediately. That was in the future, and it would be catastrophic for the United States as well as the rest of the world.

After the Six Day war, a dark side of Ali emerged. It seemed to come on gradually, but soon it had reached the point where even the children were afraid of him. If they did something that annoyed him, his response would be overly harsh, whereas in the past, he might have laughed it off. Such was the case in an incident involving Ali's trained and prized falcon, Winny (named after Winston Churchill). Without Ali's knowledge or consent, the boys removed the falcon's hood and were trying to untie the bird's leg from the perching post when Oman discovered them. Winny was a valuable Peregrine falcon, judiciously trained for hunting. He was also dangerous. A strike from his talon could sever a small hand. Oman loved the little boys and felt obligated to tell their father what they had done.

Ali was enraged. When he received the news, he took them to their room, slapped them across their faces, something he had never done before. He told Yasmine that they were to receive nothing to eat that evening. She pleaded with him; "They're just little boys. You are being cruel."

"Be silent! They could have been maimed. Winny could have flown away. How do you expect them to grow up to be honorable men if you continue to pamper and spoil them? They are six and seven, old enough to understand right from wrong. They must obey me."

After eight years of marriage, he had changed, and she suspected the loss in Jerusalem had something to do with it. Of late, he acted bored when he was with her, and she suspected that he was unfaithful. In time, it was confirmed. When he returned from a recent business trip to Paris, she smelled the scent of unfamiliar perfumes on his clothes, and spotted lipstick on a collar of his shirt. She showed it to him and he said it was hers. He said she had insulted him by not trusting him. But she knew the truth. She was deeply hurt and disappointed in him. She could hardly sleep and began to lose weight. Her time would come…Let him think that she was stupid and ignorant to his recent escapades.

Yasmine thought the turning point of her marriage occurred when she discovered he was unfaithful, but she was wrong, it came when he violated her.

His face was dark and distorted. "I am your husband. You *cannot* refuse me, just because it is your fertile time of the month. If Allah wants us to have more children, we will."

"No! I will not. I don't want another child now."

"I can divorce you if you deny me, and you will lose your children, forever," he yelled.

"And I will curse you, forever," she answered. He struck her with his open hand. He stared at her surprised face, and then grabbed her by her shoulders, turned her around and threw her face down onto the bed, lifted her skirt, ripped off her silk panties, gripped her hips and entered her.

"Stop! Stop! You're hurting me," she screamed. "Please, Ali. You've never done *this* before."

She moaned during the aftermath of her rape, curled up like a comma, on the foot of the bed. Later, she would remember him saying, "I'm sorry I had to do that, but you left me no choice. You *are* my wife and you *will* do what I say. But, at least now, my darling, you won't have to worry about getting pregnant."

She couldn't understand it. Her gentle Ali had changed; he had become a different man, a violent man. He had molested her in a vicious way, though she doubted that he would think of it as anything more than showing his wife her place. *She would never forget this.*

After three days of silence from her, Ali brought her an opal ring encircled with diamonds. The color of the opal was incredible, a fiery black. "I'm sorry. I lost my temper. Please forgive me." She searched his face for clues—there was no remorse in his eyes; he just wanted a peaceful home.

She looked at the ring and then at him. "If you ever hit or rape me again, I will kill myself and our children. I swear to you, I will do it."

"Don't talk nonsense. We both know you love life and your children too much to ever do that."

He gripped her by her shoulders and shook her roughly. "A husband cannot be accused of raping his own wife. And you must not speak of taking your own life or our children's lives. That is a sin. What I did was a poor choice, but it was not rape. If I had raped and beaten you as you say I did, you would have ended up in a hospital like my cousin Noohra when her husband caught her smiling at her driver. What you did was far worse. You defied my authority as your husband. That is the end of it, do you understand?" he shouted.

She nodded. He won again.

She used her only weapon and it failed. He knew her too well. She couldn't kill anyone, especially her own children. After he left the room, she took the ring and flung it across the room knowing she would never wear it.

How could she prevent another pregnancy? Sarah could help her. She would know about such things. There had to be an herbal remedy. There would be no more children born of this unholy marriage.

Chapter 12

OLD ORCHARD BEACH
1964

Six years had passed and Suzanne was still missing. Michael resigned himself to the possibility that she might never be found, dead or alive. He had exhausted every avenue of information—every possible scenario—all without success. He threw himself into the one entity that helped to dull his anguish, his medical career. He was content with his chosen profession, and residencies in both pediatrics and hematology were instrumental in his rise as a bright young star at Children's Hospital in Boston.

Summer was nearly over and he had some vacation time coming, so he went home to Maine—the best place to be on hot days and humid nights. He'd stay in his old room in Rosemont, spend some time with his parents, and meet Natasha, his brother Arthur's fiancée. He had wondered if his reticent brother would ever marry, but during the past year, Arthur met Natasha, a Russian immigrant, and fell in love. He was happy for his brother—perhaps there would be some grandchildren in the future for his parents. Babies could make a big difference in their lives.

It had been a busy week, and Michael's parents, Rachael and Frank, tried their best to make it a happy time for him, but somehow, even with the festivities of the engagement party, he still felt alone. Arthur was enthralled with Natasha, who turned out to be a pleasant young woman with a huge Russian accent and a big heart. Michael felt like a fifth wheel when he was with them; they only had eyes for each other. He remembered what that felt like. After only a few days, he missed the hustle and bustle of the hospital.

When he got the telephone call from Jane, his spirits lifted. She was just what he needed. A couple of years before, she had broken her engagement with his friend Cammy, and now Cammy lived in San Francisco and was in private practice. He had heard through the old med school grapevine that Cammy was getting married. He wondered what had happened between them, but neither of them had ever volunteered any reason other than to say it didn't work out. Anyway, he was always glad to see his sister-in-law.

"Michael, I'm so glad I caught you at home. I ran into your Mom last week and she told me you'd be in town. I've got a great idea! Let's go down to Old Orchard Beach. Louie Armstrong is at the pier Casino tonight, maybe for the last time. How about it?"

"Well…sure…That's a swell idea. I haven't been there in years. This is really taking me back. The last time I was there was with Suzanne and we—"

"Only on one condition, we don't talk about anything sad and that includes my sister. You need some fun, and so do I."

"Okay. You've got a deal."

That evening he picked her up in his black Austin-Healy, the sports car that was his pride and joy, one of the few luxuries that he indulged in. Michael had always loved cars, but only recently could he afford a car like this. It was a warm summer night, the top of the convertible was down, and the voice of Frank Sinatra singing *Come Fly With Me*, blasted away as they headed south down Route 1. This would be a special evening for them; usually it was just dinner or a movie. In the years following Suzanne's disappearance, they had become close. Each other's best friend.

After he parked the car, they walked in the direction of the pier. The town was famous for its miles and miles of white beach and crashing surf, but at night it took on a honky-tonk atmosphere mobbed with the usual Saturday night mix of tourists, mostly Canadians, and young people out on the town looking for someone to pick up. Walking past the merry-go-round, they watched the wide-eyed children riding the painted horses as they rose up and down, around and around. There was even a Roman chariot and a couple of giraffes. Michael laughed. "When I was a kid, I waited all year to come down here and ride my favorite horse—he was all white, with a blue saddle, and when I was on him, I thought I was Sir Gallahad. My family would take the train at Union Station in Portland on a Sunday afternoon, and when we arrived, Arthur and I thought we had died and gone to heaven."

"I love the music. Nothing else sounds like a carousel," said Jane.

"Did you have a favorite horse?"

"No. I got to ride the real thing. My mother preferred a beach day at Kennebunkport or Prouts Neck, so we rarely came. A couple of times my Dad took us, just to see what it was like."

"To see how the other half lived?" he asked.

"We can't help who our parents are, can we?"

Jane deftly changed the subject; "Old Orchard Beach was once a very *in* place. Did you know that President Kennedy's parents came here on their honeymoon?"

"I think I read it somewhere."

"My parents detest Joe Kennedy and his cowardly behavior when he was the Ambassador to England. I can hardly believe I voted for his son, but you know, I think he did a good job for a Democrat."

"Everyone in my family is a Democrat. And let's not forget that he was our first Catholic president," said Michael. "I liked him too. Too bad he was assassinated. Now we've got Johnson, and I think he's going to get us into deep shit in Vietnam." They walked along the boardwalk in silence remembering that sad November day in 1963 when the nation lost their youngest president. As they passed the French-fry stand, he said, "After the dance, remind me to get us some fries. Nobody makes them like they do here, and they serve them with vinegar—it's mandatory."

As they entered the pier ballroom, they looked up at the revolving crystal ball suspended from the high ceiling, shooting off all of the colors of the rainbow. It was filled to capacity with wall to wall dancers. The guys all dressed in their best and the gals with their bouffant hairdos trying to look like Jackie Kennedy in simple sleeveless sheath dresses and pearl necklaces. Louie Armstrong was belting out a familiar song, *Oh when the saints, oh when the saints, oh when the saints go marching in, oh I want to be....*

"He's still wonderful, isn't he?" said Jane.

"Yeah. I almost forgot how good he is. Let's dance, Janie."

As he swung Jane around the dance floor, her shoulder length auburn hair swished across her shining face. She wore a white linen dress that hugged her slender figure and showed off her long tanned legs. He looked at her and thought, *She's not Suzanne, but she's still lovely.*

After a set of swing music, the tempo changed and another old favorite was being sung. *I found my thrill on Blueberry Hill, on Blueberry Hill, when I found you. The moon stood still...*

He held her close. Her brow rested on his cheek, her arm around him. His firm thighs pressed against hers as they danced to the sexy and gravely voice of the incomparable Louie Armstrong.

Jane closed her eyes, inhaling his fresh clean scent. She forced herself to erase all thoughts of her sister; it had been long enough, almost six years—a lifetime ago. Suzanne was probably dead, and *she* was alive. She had loved Michael for such a long time. She ached to touch his face, to look deep into his eyes, instead of averting them when they stood facing each other. Jane couldn't imagine that he didn't feel the same way. The chemistry between them—the reflective glances, the spontaneous feelings—couldn't possibly have been so strong if it weren't mutual.

When the orchestra took a break, Michael suggested a stroll on the outdoor deck that overlooked the ocean. Once outside, the cool ocean breezes caressed them and together they looked down at the water lapping at the poles that suspended the Old Orchard Casino.

"My parents came here to dance," he said wistfully. "I don't think it'll be here much longer. It's getting old, and it's become tacky, but I'll hate to see it gone."

"I know. All the big bands and ballrooms are breaking up. Rock and roll is the sound of the future. Depressing, isn't it?"

"You were the one who said we couldn't be sad tonight," he said.

"I know. I mean this is the end of an era that was truly romantic and lovely. The innocent fifties have passed on. I don't care much for the sixties; it's too volatile for me."

"Yeah. Everything is changing: the music, family values, morality, the violence and of course, if I may be so bold, the transformation in women. They wear pants instead of skirts. They curse like men.

I've overheard nurses use swear words I haven't heard since I lived in a fraternity house. I liked it the way it was. Frankly, women confuse the hell out of me these days. I'm not sure as a gentleman whether I should hold the door open for a woman any longer. Sometimes when I do it they glare at me."

"Change is always confusing, but in the end it's usually for the best. Women are just asserting themselves a little. And you will always be a gentleman—you don't know how to be any other way."

"You make me feel like that. Even though you've become a doctor, you didn't stop being feminine. I'm not against intelligent women pursuing careers. I'm glad about that. I really am. I just wish they didn't try so hard to act like one of the guys. I love women and the things that are different about them. To be honest, I always thought women were superior to men, braver and kinder."

"Look, Michael, the moon is clouding up. I was hoping we could go sailing tomorrow, if it doesn't rain. I could pack a picnic lunch and...."

"I can't, Jane." His voice broke; he looked tortured and reached over and lifted a stand of hair off her glowing face.

"Why?"

"You know why. You feel it as much as I do. We're making small talk. Having a safe conversation, so the inevitable won't happen. So I won't say things to you that I'll regret later, even if they're true."

The music started and everyone had returned to the dance floor except them. The soulful female voice of a singer floated out to the deck. *See the pyramids along the Nile. Watch the sunrise on a tropic isle. Just remember darling, all the while, you belong to me....*

"Look at me, Michael! You know you want to kiss me. You want it as much as I do."

"Yeah, I guess I do."

Before he lost his courage, he reached for her. He heard the hushed intake of her breath and felt her body meld into his. He watched her lips come nearer and nearer, her eyes closer and closer, until their mouths met. If they had been standing naked in each other's arms, it could not have been more intimate. They moved to the music as one, their lips joined. Neither wanted the love song to end, and when it inevitably did, Michael stepped back and abruptly drew away from her. The expression on her face told it all: the humiliation, the bewilderment. He had hurt her and he hadn't meant to.

"I *can't,* Jane. Please…forgive me, I just can't do it. It's not that I don't want to, God knows, but I'm still married to your sister."

"She's gone! Face it, Michael. She isn't coming back. I loved Suzanne as much as any sister could, but I also love you. I know that you feel the same way. Deny it, if you can."

"I *can't,* but it doesn't change the fact that I'm married and until someone proves otherwise, this is the way it has to be."

"Can't you see…that I'm dying for you? Are you blind?" Jane grabbed the railing overlooking the ocean to support herself. Her legs felt rubbery.

"Don't Jane. I can't stand to see you like this. I never meant to hurt you."

She faced him. Her face was twisted with rage, her voice breaking between sobs. "Well you have! For those first two years after Suzanne was gone, I was devastated. I had lost my sister and no matter how hard I tried not to, I fell in love with you. There is nothing worse than always trying to please someone, hoping they'll look at you—smile at you, acknowledge that you exist. You couldn't imagine me as anyone…except as someone to tell your troubles to. Then a miracle happened, you began to see me…really see me, as a woman. That's when I broke up with Cammy. No matter what you say, I know you love me. If I didn't believe that, I wouldn't be standing here baring my soul to you." She broke down completely and watching it was hard for Michael.

He reached out to her with his handkerchief. "Here Jane, take this."

"Don't touch me! You're a coward! You're afraid to love me. Do you know that I've sinned because of you? I never said it or showed it, but in my heart I loved you, because you were all I ever wanted. I broke Cameron Emerson's heart and did terrible things to him—making love and fantasizing that it was you. I don't think I'll ever forgive myself for that. God knows, I didn't want to love you and I did everything I could to erase you from my mind, but nothing worked. Michael, you're like a chronic disease that won't go away, and if I don't cure myself of you, it'll become fatal."

"I never knew. I swear to you—I never knew how you felt about me, and I'm truly sorry about Cammy, but Jane, ask yourself, what if she comes back, and finds me married to you? It would be the ultimate betrayal, and she'd hate us both. What then? Could you live with that?"

"Yes, I could. I'm willing to risk it. For the last time, tell me you don't love me, and then I'll leave you alone forever."

He shook his head. "No. I can't. But it doesn't change anything. I have to think for both of us now. You're too upset."

Jane's face was blotched and mottled with tears that she wiped savagely with the back of her hand. She had gambled and lost. Things would never be the same between them—now they couldn't even be friends. One minute she wanted him to feel blameless, and the next, she hoped he was suffering as much as she was.

She shook her head in anguish, "Take me home, Michael. Now."

"I'm to blame," he mumbled. "I never should have let it go this far. I knew my feelings were changing. I've wrecked your life too. It's not fair to…."

The words were meant to push her away. Instead, they tugged her closer.

"Jane, some day, it could happen, and it'll feel right. We're both still young, and you're just getting started in your practice. I can't abandon her until I know for certain that she's dead. I made a vow, before God and my family and our friends. Please …."

Jane collapsed in his arms. He stroked her hair and held her close as she wept.

It was the last thing she wanted to happen. She cried, "Now I've lost you completely. We can't go back to the way it was."

"Yes, we can. We can *do* that. I care for you, Jane, and I want you in my life."

"You still love Suzanne, don't you?"

"I love the memory of her. I just can't escape the feeling that she's still alive and coming back."

"Michael, in spite of what I so dramatically said a few minutes ago, I will wait. You see, I have no pride left where you're concerned. I guess it's just my fate that I'll never love anyone but you."

He put his head down and stared at his feet. She was right about everything. He *was* a coward. He couldn't say the words she wanted to hear so desperately, not yet, but if he didn't love Jane, what was that big terrible ache in his heart?

"I'm sorry about you and Cammy."

"I made my own decision, and I don't regret it. Cammy deserves someone who'll love him for himself. Someone who's honest with him. Someone better than me. Are we still friends?"

"You bet we are."

"Tell me about Natasha. What is she like?" asked Jane, anxious to change the subject…to talk about anything…to stop thinking about what happened, as if that were possible.

"She's an okay gal. Kind of pretty and Arthur thinks…."

Louie Armstrong ended the evening belting out *Hello Dolly.* They knew they would never see him or anyone like him again at this dance hall. A good storm would probably bring it crashing down some day, but not this night.

"Let's go, Jane, and get those wonderful French fries I told you about."

THE SAD THING WAS, when they saw each other again at Christmas time, neither of them mentioned that night. It was as though they had let something out of a Pandora's box, forced it back in, and never wanted to deal with it again. They did remain friends—Michael had kept his word. She had offered herself to him on a silver platter, and he had turned her down. Future moves would have to come from him. Two years passed—and nothing had changed.

Chapter 13

THE PROPHECY
1967

The headline of *The Arab News* read: PRINCE ABDULLAH, MINISTER OF HEALTH DEAD. The man who groped Elizabeth at the white slave auction years before perished, along with his first wife and the pilot, in a fiery plane crash in the mountains near the town of Talif, the summer home of the royal family. At the mosque, the head mullah proclaimed that he was a good and pious man. It was a lie of course, but, nevertheless, Abdullah and his first wife, Nura, were given an elaborate funeral. In attendance were all the male members from the royal family. The women, who were not permitted to attend, shed few tears for a man they all hated. He was known as a violent man who had abused his wives, including the one who perished with him.

Since that dreadful day when Abdullah dragged off Elizabeth, he never allowed the "foreign whores" to see her. After his death, Yasmine received a hand-written note from Elizabeth inviting her, as well as Alexandra and Marilyn to her home. "Now that I'm a widow, I'm free to see you, and I want you to meet my little boy."

Elizabeth greeted her old friends with kisses when they entered the women's quarters. She had grown taller and shapelier. Her face had shed its baby-fat, unmasking high cheekbones and a defined jawline. Dressed in a floor-length black frock of mourning with a scarf covering her hair, she had become Arabic—all essence of her Western heritage had vanished.

For the first five minutes they exchanged warm greetings with the youngest of their group. Unlike them, she had been kept at home most of the time like a prisoner. The joy of seeing them was genuine and she couldn't stop smiling. Marilyn recalled their clandestine meeting at the souk years before, "You were in a terrible state, and I feared for your life."

"Yes. I remember it well. At that time, I wanted to die. Later, I learned to be a survivor." In Arabic, she introduced an elderly woman to them, as Auntie Anoud. "This is my new watchdog, Abdullah's widowed aunt. Even with a house full of servants, I can't live alone without causing a scandal. She doesn't know a word of English."

A withered old woman swathed in black squatted on the floor studying them with curiosity and skepticism. She muttered to Elizabeth. "These women have painted faces like harlots. They should not be here."

Alexandra put her head down so the old widow couldn't see her lips curve upward.

"Auntie. I can see that you're tired. Go rest while I visit with my friends."

"Yes, Umm Faisal."

The group looked at each other in amazement. Elizabeth was giving orders in fluent Arabic like a native, and dismissing a senior member of the family, who addressed her with respect as the mother of a son.

"This is what happens when you have no sons. Her husband died years ago and she goes from relative to relative. We are good to her, but without a son, she is at our mercy. Her only child, a daughter, died in childbirth along with her grandson."

Elizabeth rose from her seat, walked across the white marble floor, and stood at an open window that overlooked a garden and a gurgling three-tiered fountain. "He was a monster! The first two years were the worst. I could hardly wait for my period—the only time he left me alone. He would shout, 'Remain in your quarters. You are unclean.' It's true I wanted to die, but then I got pregnant and everything changed. Not him of course, a devil remains a devil. I changed. I had a reason to live—I was going to have a baby."

She came back and sat down when a servant brought in tea and a platter of baklava dripping with honey. She poured the tea into the delicate china cups and handed one to each of them. They helped themselves to the pastry.

"When Abdullah demanded that I be circumcised, I vowed to starve myself if he forced me into it. It worked, but after that he turned mean and violent." She lifted her shoulders, closed her eyes, and shuddered. "It was nightly rapes and beatings. I don't know how I survived. He left me with a souvenir so I wouldn't forget it. I'm deaf in one ear."

She removed her scarf, raised her long chestnut hair, and showed us scar tissue all around her right ear and upper jaw.

"When I became pregnant, he became scared and stopped beating me—the baby might be a boy. After Faisal was born, I no longer resisted and ceased to be a challenge to him. He found other victims. No female in this household, wife, servant, or even a child was safe from him."

The three women sat there horrified—he was worse than they had imagined.

"That bastard!" said Marilyn, her eyes flashing like twin emeralds. "Someone should have strung him up by his balls."

"Indeed. I should think that would have been the perfect punishment," added Alex.

"I think it would have been too good for him," said Yasmine. "Someone should have killed him."

"I nearly did. I hid a knife in my hand under the covers when I waited for him in bed. Then a miracle happened. I felt the baby move for the first time; he sent me a message—that message was *live*."

The women looked at Elizabeth with newfound respect.

A little boy ran into the room trailed by a black and white puppy.

"Ah, Faisal, come here my son." He lay his head in her lap, suddenly becoming shy. "This is my life, my little boy," she said as she stroked his hair.

In perfect English he asked, "Who are these ladies, Mama?"

"My friends."

Yasmine handed him a box wrapped in colored paper. "This is for you, little Faisal. I am your Auntie Yasmine."

"Thank you." He turned to his mother and asked, "Mama, may I open it?"

"Of course, darling." She smiled at her friends, "Faisal is seven years old and is becoming a big boy, big enough to have a pet."

He opened the box and took out a toy cement truck with moving parts.

"I love this. How did you know I like trucks?"

"My little boys adore trucks," replied Yasmine.

Faisal ran the toy along the floor as the puppy lapped his face and made him giggle. "Aba gave me this dog because he loved me. Did you know he has gone to paradise?" asked the little boy who had his mother's pink and white complexion as well as her eyes.

"Yes, Faisal, we know," said his mother. Now go back to your room and play with your new toy and that sweet little dog."

He left holding the hand of his nursemaid, Sultana.

After they were gone, she looked at us and nodded. "Yes. That is true. Faisal and his grown son, Ibraham, are the only people aside from his first wife that Abdullah ever cared about. He certainly didn't love me and I detested him. I'm glad he's dead."

When Yasmine heard the name "Ibraham," she remembered the stories that circulated through the grapevine of family gossip.

Uncle Abdullah had three other wives before Elizabeth. He divorced two of them, planning to marry another young girl, and then, while traveling with his first wife, they both died in a plane crash. The youngest son of his first wife, Ibraham, was twenty-six, unmarried, and said to be fond of Elizabeth. It was rumored, but never proven, that they may have been lovers. According to the Koran, you could not marry your father's wife. It was blasphemy.

We spoke of these rumors to her and warned Elizabeth never to compromise herself with her stepson, Ibraham.

"I am not the innocent girl I once was, and most definitely not stupid. Ibraham loves me, but not *that* way. We are like sister and brother, and he loves his little brother Faisal."

ALEXANDRA AND MARILYN left, anxious to get home before the late afternoon prayers began, leaving Yasmine alone with Elizabeth. She asked Elizabeth if she ever telephoned the United States.

"Yes, in the past month, I have called weekly. After Abdullah died, Ibraham gave me permission to phone my family. They were sure that I was dead. I invented a story that was believable. My Dad was ill, and because of that call, he's getting better. Ibraham has promised me that I'll see them. He's going to take me to America."

"Do you believe him?"

"Absolutely. He is a man of honor."

"Could I call my family from your phone? *Please*."

"I would love to say yes, but all international conversations are monitored and your husband would find out. Ibraham told me, so I know it's true. We are always careful what we say on the telephone."

"I wonder if I will ever see my family again. Mostly, I want them to know I'm still alive."

"Don't give up hope, Suzanne. I know you are called Yasmine now, but to me you will always be Suzanne." She handed me a note-pad. "Write down the name, the address, and the telephone number of your family, and when I can do this without jeopardizing you, I will contact them. I promise."

"Bless you, Elizabeth."

When it came time to leave, they embraced. "Leave this place, Elizabeth, before it's too late. I still love my husband and I have three children, so I can't leave but, oh, I do long for America."

A FEW DAYS LATER, ALI returned home earlier than usual. "Sit down. I have wretched news—it's about Marilyn."

"What happened? I just saw her three days ago."

"She was caught making love with an English chap at the Riyadh Palace Hotel. To make matters worse, she cursed and kicked the mu-tawahs."

"Foolish, foolish girl! What will happen to her?"

"When a man steals, we cut off his hand. When a woman commits adultery, and she is stupid enough to be caught by four men who will bear witness—she is stoned to death. That is the law."

<u>*The Koran says in Sura IV, 15*</u>

If any of your women are guilty of lewdness. Take the evidence of four witnesses from amongst you. Against them; and if they testify. Confine them to houses until death do claim them.

"What about the man?"

"He's a diplomat. All diplomats have immunity from the law. He's being sent back to England."

"Ali, isn't there anything you can do? She doesn't deserve to die. Why can't Mohammed just divorce her? Is it fair that the man should go free and she should die so horribly?"

"He didn't rape her. He was unmarried and not a Muslim, so he was not the one breaking our laws."

But to kill her—that's crazy. This is 1967."

"This isn't America. This isn't a country where women sleep with men other than their husbands. If he does not have her punished, the mutawas will. The hotel manager and three employees saw them in bed together—while they were actually doing it."

Yasmine was close to hysterics. "At least can you notify the American Embassy? For God's sake! She's a citizen of the United States and her uncle is a senator."

"Don't waste your tears on her. She's become a whore. Do you expect me to create an international crisis? Don't you know that your government would never allow anything to prevent them from having access to our oil? Petroleum is their lifeblood. Without it, your country and many others would fall into ruin. So would mine. They would not interfere for a *hundred* women, not for a *thousand* women. You are so naïve. I am distressed, of course, but Yasmine, there is nothing I can do."

Yasmine blinked back her tears. Marilyn had been careless in a country where even a glimpse of an ankle or an exposed strand of a hair could bring dire consequences. Marilyn had gotten more and more reckless. Alex and I warned her but she wouldn't listen. She would just laugh. It was all a game to her. She hinted about her love affairs. We thought she was kidding, exaggerating.

Yasmine screamed. "Your people are barbarians."

"Not so. My ancestors were basking in knowledge when yours were living in caves. Yes, we believe in capital punishment because it works.

"I can never win an argument with you, nor do I care to anymore I'll tell you one thing—I'm going to go to the execution."

"You will *not*," he shouted

"Yes I will."

Ali drew back his hand to strike her, as she baited him further, "Go ahead. Hit me! Give me one more reason to hate you. You, with your women and your lies."

His hand stopped in mid-air, just inches from the side of her face. It fell to his side, and his face drained of color. He swept it across her vanity table that was covered with Lalique crystal containers filled with exotic perfumes and body lotions. Everything fell to the floor, and broke into hundreds of pieces of shattered glass. The pungent smell of perfume engulfed the room.

"I never lied to you. You heard only what you wanted to hear. And you *will* obey me. When I return from Paris, I'll deal with you. From now on, you will live a different kind of life." He left, slamming the bedroom door behind him.

Yasmine remained defiant. She was going to Marilyn's execution. It was all she could do—someone had to bear witness. He didn't once say that he liked Marilyn, that she was too young to die, or even that he felt badly about it. To continue to live with a man, who was only "distressed," over the stoning of a woman they both knew and liked was intolerable to her.

Surprisingly, he didn't deny that there were "other women." It seemed to him that lying was the more troubling offense. Adultery didn't bother him at all.

YASMINE FORCED HERSELF TO GO to the place of the execution in Riyadh, (nicknamed, "Chop-Chop Square by the expatriates) on the following Friday, the Muslim Sabbath and the only day that executions were permitted.

Daniel, the Ethiopian Christian who served her husband, had become her protector, and reluctantly drove her to the vicinity of the notorious square. Even in the heat of the noonday sun, spectators had gathered, almost entirely male and all of them excited, as though it were a sporting event. Yasmine hid back in a doorway, trying not to be noticed. Daniel's handsome coffee-colored face looked tortured; he tried to convince her to leave by reasoning with her.

"Princess, you don't want to see this. It is very bad. Please, let's go. The Master would not like it. He will beat me for this."

"I will take full responsibility. I will tell him that I demanded it. She is my friend—I *have* to be here."

Even covered completely in black and blindfolded, the tall figure was clearly Marilyn. She was tethered to a post by a chain. Yasmine cringed as she heard her beg, "Noooooo! Noooooo! Let me go! I don't want to die like this."

A mass of bearded men and boys wearing white thobes and prayer caps called out a cacophony of curses: Foreign whore! Infidel! Kill her! The crowd was electrified because this was the first time in years that a woman would be stoned to death for adultery and there were rumors that she was an "American," or at the very least, "a Westerner." Something like this had never happened before. Punishments of this sort, "honor killings," usually took place behind closed doors and walled-in homes. The law was that the offended party, the male members of the woman's family, threw the first rock. Because she had no family, her husband Mohammed was the dishonored person. He appeared unkempt and grief-stricken, rather than angry. He hurled a large stone at her head with all his strength, but missed by several feet.

Yasmine gasped.

"Family members do it deliberately," Daniel said. "They try to knock the victim out so they don't suffer." Knowing that Mohammed was a good man, she believed him. He threw a second stone and this time it struck Marilyn's face. Hard rock hitting soft flesh has a sound of its own—a sickening crunch. She screamed. One after another, rocks came in a storm until Marilyn slumped to one side. Her veil had fallen off, revealing a bloodied mouth with missing teeth. She moaned, "Help, Oh God! Please help m-e-e-e-e-e-e."

A scattering of women shrouded in black on the fringes of the crowd near her screamed the worst curses, especially Mohammed's mother Marlama, "Rot in your grave, you whore of whores!"

Mohammed's face turned gray. He sank to his knees, lowered his head and covered his ears with his hands.

Marilyn's eyes rolled back in her head. Her bloodstained cornsilk hair hung in front of her face. Still not satisfied that she was probably dying, some men continued to yell and shook their fists in unison above their heads. A torrent of stones of all sizes continued to fall until they formed a mound around her motionless body. Mercifully, after almost twenty minutes, the holy man declared that Marilyn was dead. For a few minutes, as the mullah said his prayer, a hush came over the crowd and they behaved like civilized people. After he finished, the crowd started screaming again, awaiting the next execution, even though it was a commonplace execution, a beheading.

Daniel led Yasmine back to their car. When they reached it, she leaned against the rear fender and vomited. The combined horrors of the stoning and the brutal heat had rendered Yasmine helpless. Daniel stood watch over her as she retched and heaved. He gave her his handkerchief. "Take this. That was a terrible thing to see." She nodded dumbly, almost in a trance. Daniel's eyes scanned the crowd looking for the dreaded religious police as he prodded her into the car out of sight.

On the drive home she kept seeing the faces of the men and boys at the execution. They had loved it! They actually found joy in someone else's death. In all her time in Saudi Arabia, she had never seen a happier group of people. They even fired rifles into the air to celebrate, just as they did at weddings.

Somehow, she thought, she must find a way to get back in Ali's good graces, and convince him to take the family on a holiday to England. In an English-speaking country with an American Embassy, she would have a chance to escape with her children.

She cried all that night wildly beating the pillows with both fists. Mary tried to comfort her, but nothing helped. She was beyond reason. Sara was called and gave her a sedative. Before she drifted off, she remembered Madam Boudreau's words from years ago. *If you commit adultery, you will be stoned to death.*

The next morning, Alexandra visited and listened to Yasmine describe in detail the execution, and how she despised all those who participated.

"Yasmine, I will miss Marilyn and I mourn her death, really, I do, but nothing will bring her back. Her suffering is over. We both knew that something bad would happen to her eventually. She was always a risk taker, always testing herself, to see how much more she could get away with. It was like an addiction or a game to her. We told her again and again of the dangers, but she persisted."

"Madam Boudreau predicted it. Do you remember what she said the last time we saw her?"

"Of course, and you and I took her advice. Marilyn did not."

"We'll miss her. She was so funny and I loved her impersonations and her stories and…."

"Yasmine, I have something important to tell you. I know the timing is bad, but I have…a secret and I'm torn between my loyalty to my husband and my love for you. You are like a sister to me. Promise never to tell anyone who told you."

"Perhaps it would be better if you kept it to yourself."

"No, it's about you and your life. If I tell you, maybe you can change your fate."

"You're scaring me, Alex. What is it?"

"Ali plans to take another wife."

Alex waited for the words to sink in and then saw the look of surprise on Yasmine's face. It was the last thing she had expected to hear. She knew Ali was growing weary of her complaints and wanted more children. His passion for her had waned in the past year. Sometimes days would pass without him touching her, and when they did have sex, it was rushed and not like making love at all. He knew her feelings on this subject. She had told him, "I would never tolerate another wife."

"Do you know who it is?"

"Yes. You've met her. She's that young girl whom we had tea with several months ago with Sara. You know, the one we said was so beautiful, with that sweet laugh, the one who never dresses in Western clothes even though she's well-educated and her mother is French."

"You mean, Jirhan?"

"Yes. The plans are already being made."

"But, she's barely eighteen. She's more like a child."

"Some child! Face it, Yasmine. You're thirty-four. By Saudi standards, that's old. Promise me, you'll never tell Ali I told you."

"Don't worry, I won't."

"What are you going to do?"

"Nothing for now. I have to think about it."

She dared not tell Alexandra of her plans. She knew Alexandra couldn't keep a secret. She had just proven it.

Two months later, she received a letter that was delivered to her by hand from one of Elizabeth's servants. She opened the envelope.

Dear Suzanne,
By the time you read this letter, I will be gone from Saudi Arabia forever. You were right about Ibraham. We love each other. I'm sorry I had to lie to you. We are going to California and will be getting married. Ibraham has been taking money out of the country for nearly a year. He went to college at Berkley and loves America. Now that his father is dead, he is free to leave. Please believe me, we never were intimate in the kingdom. Together, with my son, we will become a family, and I'll be close to my parents and two brothers. I'll contact your family and tell them everything. Don't give up hope. My love always, Elizabeth

After reading the letter, Yasmine said aloud, "Good for you, Elizabeth! Good for you! At least, one of us has escaped from this insane place."

Yasmine never got a chance to put her elaborate scheme into action. Three months had passed since Marilyn's execution and destiny intervened in a cruel way. Ali had been away on business trips most of that time.

"Yasmine, dear sister," said Sara. I want to do some tests on Michael at the clinic. He may be anemic. He seems listless and he is very pale."

"Yes, I noticed that, and the other night he had a nosebleed. Should I be worried?"

"Yasmine, as a doctor, I sometimes assume the worst. I don't want to scare you, so let us just see what the tests tell us."

His grandfather, Prince Kareem, was so concerned that he personally drove them to the clinic. Oman said Michael didn't want to ride his pony because he was too tired. Michael was never too tired to ride his pony. That was a huge red flag. After repeated blood tests in the clinic, Sara's diagnosis was that Michael had Leukemia. The prognosis was grim—there was no known cure.

Only once before had Yasmine thought her heart would break—when her father died. This was worse. She was frantic and helpless. This wasn't supposed to happen. Her treasured child, Michael's son, was dying and he was only eight years old.

"I'll make the arrangements at the Queen's Hospital—you must leave immediately," said a worried Sara.

Prince Kareem telephoned Ali in Paris. After he had been given the dire news, Ali said, "Take my family, with Mary, and meet me in London at the Claridge Hotel."

In London, the diagnosis was concurred. Ali was strong, resolute and loving. "Be brave, darling. Everything will be all right." He held her upright when her grief nearly brought her to her knees. The English doctor advised them to go to the Children's Hospital in Boston—the foremost research hospital and battleground for treating Leukemia. Their spirits rose when he said a new experimental treatment was available for critical cases.

The war between Yasmine and Ali ended. Now as parents, they had become compatriots: their enemy, this dreaded disease—the battlefield, Boston. Ali's optimistic nature was contagious. Even little Michael perked up when he saw his father, "We are going to America," Ali said to his little son. "Your mother's country—and the American doctors will make you well again."

Only days before, it had been her fervent prayer to go to the States, and now it was coming true. She would have gratefully remained in Saudi Arabia with an unfaithful husband, rival wives, and an unforgiving religion for the rest of her life in exchange for her son's life.

Chapter 14

BOSTON
1967

In the doctors' lounge, the voice on the intercom announced, "Dr. Conti, you are wanted in the Emergency Room." His eyes brightened as he looked up from his newspaper and set aside the sports section of the *Boston Globe.*

"Duty calls. It's time to go," he said as he rose to his feet.

Dr. Vanessa Brooks, glanced up at him, smiled, and said, "See you later, Mike."

Dr. Conti rushed to the E. R. knowing that a few minutes could mean the difference between life and death. Practicing medicine had become his life—the only thing that gave him a reason to get out of bed every day. Saving children from death or making their lives better was his reward. Working in the world's best children's hospital and being considered one of the top specialists in childhood Leukemia was something he had never imagined. Residencies in both hematology and oncology had prepared him well to battle Leukemia and other less lethal blood diseases. Even though it was still an incurable illness, he felt that they were on the brink of discovering a cure.

After nine years, he still anguished over his wife's disappearance. If still alive, she would now be thirty-four. If she had perished, he would have grieved, but eventually there would have been someone in his life. He wasn't married. He wasn't divorced. He wasn't a widower. He was stuck in time, bound to a woman whom he thought to be alive. How he knew was a mystery even to him, but he knew that she was *somewhere.*

In 1958, when Michael returned from Athens after Suzanne's

kidnapping, he hastened to her family's side in Maine. Everyone was devastated over Suzanne's disappearance, especially her mother who retreated to her bedroom certain that her vivacious daughter was gone forever.

After seven gut-wrenching days in Athens, waiting for the Greek police to find her, Michael had to return to Boston to begin his internship—he was already nearly a week late. He worked hard, harder than anyone, and he welcomed the long hours that most interns grudgingly accepted. Each day he pushed himself to the limit until he was completely exhausted—only then could he sleep. If not, he relived the whole nightmare, and it always came out the same way. *He was to blame.* Why didn't he go down to the shopping arcade with her? He had always gone with her before. Or why didn't he say: "Suzanne, we'll buy some gifts at the airport." Why? If he had made either of those choices, she would still be with him. He'd still have his wife and probably a family.

SUZANNE'S MOTHER RESIDED in a nursing home, nearly incapacitated, suffering the last ravages of dementia, which recently was given a new fancy name: "Alzheimer's Disease." Suzanne would have been surprised to learn that after her disappearance her mother and Michael had become close. Little remained of the elegant, proud woman she had been at their wedding. Although not yet sixty, she looked a decade older—a white-haired, fragile, lethargic woman who rarely made eye contact with anyone, and spoke even less. However, for some reason, she always responded to Michael whenever he visited her. Sitting in her wheelchair with a silly grin on her face, clutching her doll—she would stare at him and say, "Suzanne loved you, didn't she." It made Michael sad and angry—this was another dreaded disease with no cure.

Jane pursued her career as a practicing neurologist in Portland. Her profession became her life. She lived at Cornwall with a new live-in housekeeper, Mrs. O'Neil, a recent widow. Rosie had died suddenly of a stroke after faithfully caring for Edith Mason for over five years. Upon her death, the family reluctantly agreed that Mrs. Mason would be better off in a nursing home. Charles retired at age seventy and went to live with his bachelor brother.

While in Cape Elizabeth, weather permitting, Jane and Michael took the boat out for a sail or walked together along the beach. Under Robby's tutelage, Michael had eventually become an accomplished sailor. Losing Suzanne had formed a strong bond between Michael and Jane, especially after her brother Robby had drifted away.

After graduating from Yale, Robby spent about five years working in a bank with an impressive title and a small salary, and then drifted into the world of the rebellious sixties generation. For a time, he lived in the Haight-Ashbury district in San Francisco with all the other "hippies" and early protesters of the war in Vietnam. After that, he went to live somewhere in Canada. Robby's lawyer kept Jane informed, but because of the lawyer-client relationship, he never gave her an address. It was enough for Jane to know that he was well.

After Old Orchard Beach, when Michael and Jane nearly succumbed to a love affair, they remained resolute to keep their relationship close, but platonic. Somehow they managed it and continued to remain each other's best friend. But, more and more Michael realized that he had been a fool—he should have let it happen. After all, how many times can a person fall in love in a lifetime?

MICHAEL HAD EMPATHIZED WITH Jane and his friend Cammy when they broke their engagement. He knew how it felt to be alone. They had dated for nearly two years, and Jane probably would have married Cammy were it not for him. Cammy had vanished from their lives when he left Boston and moved to San Francisco. He missed his old pal, but realized that it had become an awkward situation—after all, Jane was his sister-in-law. Later, he found out that Cammy was married, and practicing in San Francisco.

Elena's life flourished. Her marriage to Keith was a happy one that produced three daughters. Keith owned his own accounting firm in Portland, but Michael only saw them two or three times in the past nine years. Out of curiosity, the last time he saw them was at his Cousin Jim's wedding at the St. Peter's Italian Catholic Church during the past year. Jim owned his own landscaping and stonework company and had become quite successful. He was marrying Elena's cousin Grace. Out of curiosity, Michael asked Elena, "What's become of Lorna?"

She stammered, "Oh Lorna, she's around. We get together now and then. Billy's a workaholic, so Keith and I don't see him much, but our kids go to each other's birthday parties. You know what I mean."

He wanted to scream, "No, I don't!" but politely answered, "That's nice."

He wasn't surprised that they remained friends. They were two of a kind. He never believed that Elena was a real friend to Suzanne any more than Lorna was. In his book, Elena was a phony, and not really anyone's friend. If Suzanne didn't call her first, she would never have heard from her. She was a taker, not a giver. And Lorna was worse—she was lethal. Her main objective had been to knife Suzanne in the back at every opportunity. Everyone spilled the beans after Suzanne disappeared. Lorna's favorite comment was she couldn't see what Michael had ever seen in Suzanne except for her money. If they had been his friends, he would have dumped them early on—but Suzanne's naiveté had always been her biggest fault—unlike her sister, Jane, who could read people like a book.

The petty jealousies and intrigues that had occurred years before now seemed insignificant and childish and hardly worth thinking about. After all, it was just "female stuff." When he was young, he never danced around all that kind of crap. If he had a problem with another guy he confronted him head on, and if the problem was serious enough, he decked him. Now that he was a man, he had become more Gandhi-like and used passive resistance. The hospitals had become a great training ground for him.

He doubted if either Elena or Lorna gave a damn, or thought about what happened to Suzanne. Like everyone else, they were busy with their own lives. To everyone, except family members and a few close friends, Suzanne was history.

How many times had he heard that it was time to move on? The last time was a few months earlier when he was in New York City, having a drink with his old buddy, David Bennett. David settled in New York City, having become the premier lawyer in the nation representing athletes. Nobody could make the deals he could. He and his wife Mariam, another contract lawyer, had become very rich, and lived in a penthouse on Fifth Avenue on the Upper East Side with a terrace and a spectacular view of Central Park—the Metropolitan Museum less than a one minute walk away.

They met in a favorite hangout for lawyers who had made "partner," not far from David's office on Madison Avenue. The small bar had dark walnut walls, leather couches, and winged chairs and spelled class with a capital C. Crackling logs glowed in the fireplace, throwing off shadows and warmth throughout the room.

David pleaded his case. "Mike, you've got to get on with it. Suzanne's gone. I know that hurts, but think about it. It's been nine years. Look! I know a great gal. She's Mariam's cousin, Annalise, a real looker with a brain, and she lives in Boston. She'd be perfect for you. Why don't you at least meet her? I promise you, you won't be disappointed."

Michael was uneasy, and looked around for the waiter, repeating the words he had spoken so many times before. "I understand what you're saying, Dave, but I'm not interested in meeting anyone."

Awkwardly, David continued. "Okay buddy, maybe I crossed the line. Let's talk about something else. I was wrong to bring it up. You're my best friend—you knew me when I didn't have two cents to rub together, and you backed me up when that big *bubaluke* at the North School called me a Jew-boy, itching for a fight."

"You could have taken him, Dave. He was all mouth."

"But the point is, I didn't have to fight, because you were my friend, and he knew it. You were the toughest kid in the school."

"It was all make-believe. I was just as scared as anyone. I just didn't show it. When you've got an Italian father, you don't go home crying more than once."

"Yeah. My Dad used to say, 'try reasoning.' Some of those guys were kept back so many times they had to shave twice a day by the time they graduated from grammar school. Remember when Babe Tevanion flattened the principal?"

Mike laughed. "How could I forget that—he deserved it. That sadistic son-of-a-bitch whacked more than one little kid's ass with that big stick. Babe did good—too bad he had to go the reformatory for it. Or, how about Sissy Delaney when she took on the whole boys' school patrol except for us—we chickened out. Did all that stuff really happen, or did we dream it?"

"It happened, Mike. I saw Sissy a few years back when I was in Portland. She's a salesgirl at Porteous; she doesn't wear tight sweaters anymore, but she still looks good enough and she turned out okay after all. She's married to a fireman and has a couple of kids. Those years were the greatest part of our education. They prepared us for anything. Just think, if we grew up in the suburbs in those early years, we wouldn't know shit."

"We actually had a pretty good childhood. No complaints from me."

"Look, old buddy, the rest of your life can be good, too, if you let it. I want you to be happy."

"I know you do, and I appreciate it, but believe me, I'm okay. I do have friends, including women." Michael finally got the attention of the waiter. "Make the next one a double, please."

David almost commented about Michael's drinking, but thought it was best to leave that one alone. He figured that the poor guy had a reason to drink. "I wish I could tell you how much, but boy, did I get a deal for Sandy Dillon, the new pitcher for the Yankees. He gave me box seats for the season. How about going to a game with me next time you're in town?"

"Sure Dave. I'd like that. I miss sports. It was once a big part of my life."

"You were one hell of an athlete. You could have been a pro if you'd gone to a different college."

"Yeah maybe, but then I wouldn't have become a doctor."

THE ONLY OTHER PERSON aside from Michael who actually believed Suzanne was still alive was Margaret Mason. She followed every lead, spending thousands of dollars on private investigators—even calling on the State Department and the White House. She was equally as friendly with the Johnson administration as she had been with the two previous presidents, Kennedy and Eisenhower. Her wealth and philanthropy were legendary, and she was one of the most well known women in the United States.

Margaret's two brothers eventually lived up to expectations. Thad, her younger brother, became an ambassador under Kennedy, in spite of the fact that he was a Republican, and Buddy was the president of the largest bank in New York City. If a famous family like the Bowes clan, with all their connections to powerful people, couldn't find out what happened to Suzanne, who could?

Suzanne's disappearance had devastated many lives: Robby had run away; Michael's personal life was on hold; Uncle Hubert had lost some of his gusto; and Jane wrestled with feelings of guilt and grief. Before Rosie died, she had grieved as though she had lost her own child, and Charles couldn't even mention Suzanne's name without a lump forming in his throat. None of them would ever be the same. Even Edith Mason, in one of her rare coherent moments, would say, "My little girl is lost."

However, one person's life was better—that of Michael's older brother, Arthur. He married Natasha, and they had two adorable children, Ivan and Mary, born a year apart. They were the joy of the Conti family. Michael's parents had become grandparents, and he, an uncle. He liked Natasha, a pleasant but ordinary young woman who made his brother's life extraordinarily happy.

MICHAEL KNEW THE LAW, that if after seven years a spouse remained missing that person could be declared legally dead and the marriage ended with rights of inheritance. Michael never considered it before—primarily because he felt that Suzanne was still alive, and the last thing he wanted was her money. Now he made enough of his own. But it was time to move on—to have Suzanne declared legally dead. It was long past seven years. There was Jane to think about—if she was still as enamored with him as he was with her.

After Suzanne's disappearance, he actually remained celibate for a very long time, but, ultimately, his need for a female prevailed, but not with anyone he loved. He knew several women from the hospital who found him attractive. He never pretended that it was anything more than a mutual exchange of companionship and sex. He never promised anyone anything or uttered the word "love" to another woman. The two women he cared for most were Dr. Vanessa Brooks and Jane. Both remained platonic relationships.

Vanessa was different from anyone he had ever known. She had a whimsical side that made him laugh as no one else could. She wasn't beautiful or even pretty, because of her slightly prominent nose, but she was striking. Her jet-black hair hung straight to her shoulders. Wide set dark eyes, milky skin and the wide slash of her red mouth were a startling combination, and she was never mistaken for anyone else.

On Christmas Eve, 1966, Michael invited Vanessa out to dinner. Jane had left for a cruise in the Caribbean on Margaret's yacht. His own parents and Arthur's family went to Miami Beach for a week in the sun. It was his parents' first vacation outside of the Northeast. All of his male friends were married with families, though several did invite him to Christmas dinner. He declined. It was too painful.

He and Vanessa dined in a quiet candle-lit French restaurant, enjoying a gourmet meal of veal, risotto, and baby asparagus, washed down with a bottle of dry white wine. Dessert was *Crème Brulée* topped with whipped cream. As they sat there lingering over their second cup of coffee, waiters kept smiling at them and looking at their watches. *It was Christmas Eve.* Unexpectedly, Vanessa invited him to her apartment for a nightcap, something that she had never done before. He hesitated, but, why not? He dreaded returning to his small, lonely bachelor apartment that overlooked the Charles River. It was as impersonal and cold as a hotel room.

"Sure. They want us out of here. I could use a nightcap."

Vanessa's apartment in Cambridge was unpretentious but cozy, filled with antiques, several large framed photographs—one of a smiling baby, a real fireplace, hanging houseplants, a glittering Christmas tree, and two fluffy Persian cats named Mutt and Jeff.

"What do you think of my nest?"

"Very nice. It's so inviting. It reminds me of the boyhood home of my cousin, Jim Aliberti. His Mom loved plants and always had cats. All it needs is the smell of home-made bread baking."

"Not from me, I don't cook. But I'm glad you like it. Let's have a brandy," said Vanessa.

"To us," she said when they clinked their snifters, and settled back into the comfort of an over-stuffed Victorian sofa.

Michael and Vanessa shared an interest in politics, movies, and often discussed the news of the day, and lately a lot was happening. Sipping her drink, she said, "Would you ever have thought that we'd have race riots here in Boston, because of bussing? Here, of all places. It was no surprise in Birmingham, after all, that's the South."

"I'm not surprised. Boston has always been bigoted. It used to be against the Irish, then the Italians. Now it's their time to fight for their rights."

"Well, it's so wrong. They can fight in Vietnam, but they can't go to a school with white kids," replied an indignant Vanessa.

"I agree with you. As for the Vietnam War, you know my feelings; we have no business being there. They beat the French—they could beat us, too. After all, it's really a civil war and we should stay the hell out of it. It drove my brother-in-law, Robby, to Canada. We don't know for sure, but that's our guess."

"Would you go if you had to?"

"Sure, I'd go as a doctor in a minute, but not to fight. Just to save lives."

That was what Michael liked about Vanessa. She was a safe date. They would talk about anything except their personal lives. That had always been off limits. Some women were nosy, but not her. He knew nothing about her past, except that she grew up in West Virginia.

After about an hour of small talk and another brandy, Vanessa startled him with a question. "Mike, I have a couple of things I want to ask you. I've wanted to for a long time. What do people really think about me? Do they think I'm weird because I became a surgeon? Do they think I'm a lesbian? It's important for me to know."

"I'm brave—I'll tackle the lesbian one first. You know, Vanessa, any unmarried woman over thirty is considered fair game, especially in a hospital."

"So what you are saying is 'yes.' You have heard rumors."

"Gossip, yes. But nobody knows for sure."

Vanessa grinned—wickedly. "Aren't you curious? Even a little bit?"

"Nope. It doesn't matter to me. We've known each other a while and you've always been a good friend. We're buddies, so what difference does it make?"

"I'm not sure if I should be flattered or offended by your answer, but for the record, I am *not* a lesbian."

"I didn't think so, but I didn't want to make a mistake and say the wrong thing."

"Okay. Now, how about being a female surgeon?" she asked.

"You're sort of considered a pioneer—especially in a brand new field like pediatric surgery. You know, most women doctors go into specialties dealing only with women and children, and never with a scalpel."

"True. I'm only one of four female doctors in the whole hospital, but who's counting, and the only one in the sacred domain of the macho surgeon. You see, for me, anything but surgery would have been selling out, especially since a field like pediatric surgery became a reality. When I think that once they operated on infants with regular scalpels and other oversized instruments. Now, we have miniature ones for tiny babies and those wonderful magnifying glasses that have changed everything. It's so exciting—I can't believe I'm doing it. If that's weird, then I'm guilty."

"Not in my book. You're an inspiration to other women. I've heard great things about you from the nurses, and the doctors as well, including the surgeons."

"Well, not all of the nurses. Some of them resent me and they're not afraid to show it. I think it's strange that women should want other women to fail, but it's not surprising. Even my own mother wanted to hold me back. Every time I mentioned graduating from high school and maybe even going to a junior college, she would say, 'Forget that nonsense, girl. We ain't got no money for any goddamn college. We ain't rich folk.' She never looked at me the same way she looked at my oldest sister, who gave her two grandchildren. Linda was a part-time beautician married to a miner with a ninth grade education. That's her idea of a perfect daughter. I never went back home after Ma died. If she had lived to see me go to college, she wouldn't have thought anything, except that I wasn't pretty enough to get a husband."

"I doubt that," Michael said kindly.

"Oh, God, who knows?" Her voice quivered. "Maybe I gave up too much just to prove I could do it. It took thirteen years of my life to get here. Once in a while, especially at a time like Christmas Eve, I wonder if I made a mistake."

"Tell that to all the children that you've saved, and their grateful parents."

Michael stared at Vanessa as if he were seeing her for the first time. He knew she'd probably hate herself the next day for revealing so much about herself. She was always a private person. So was he, but because she was so honest, he decided to tell her his story.

"Other than a few people, I've never talked to anyone about Suzanne." He knew he could trust her so he told her the whole story, and she listened until he was finished.

"I guess I'm the hopeless romantic who lost his wife and has spent nine years pining away. It might help to know that I've had second thoughts about my life too. Am I throwing my life away waiting for someone to come back who's not alive? But then the next day, I say, maybe today is the day that Suzanne will be found—that my wife will be returned to me."

"After all this time—you still love her, don't you?"

"I don't know…I remember how it was…and it was wonderful. If time had stood still, and we both felt the same way, yeah…I would still love her."

"That's double talk, Michael. There's someone else isn't there?"

"There is, and she's a very special person. The only thing I know for sure is that I've had an obligation to Suzanne. But it's been long enough. If she's not found soon, I'm ending it legally."

"Good grief! If you only knew the rumors about you, which I will not repeat, you would be shocked. I feel terrible for you. I don't mean pity, I just mean, why should such a terrible thing happen to a nice guy like you?"

"Perhaps I wanted too much, was too ambitious, wanted a girl who was out of my league. I wanted it all, and I got zapped."

"You didn't do anything wrong. This is America. The land of dreams and you just happened to fall in love with a little, rich and slightly spoiled princess if I read you right. That's not a bad thing. You know something? I think we both should stop living in the past." She inched closer to him on the sofa nearly spilling her drink. "I'd like to get drunk, reaaaaally drunk, and the hell with what I say or what I think, or even what I do."

She was flirting with him, and that troubled him. He didn't want to spoil a four-year friendship with a woman he liked and respected, but didn't love.

"You know, I haven't gotten drunk since I was molested, no, actually the proper word is raped by my father at seventeen, and I haven't had sex with anyone else—ever. Are you shocked?"

"Of course. What an awful thing to happen to a young girl. I'm so sorry." He felt uncomfortable—where was this going?

"What a story that would be around the hospital. Prim and proper Dr. Vanessa Brooks—a victim of incest. After he was through with me, I got so drunk I thought I was going to die. I was never so sick in my life. It was moonshine, and nobody drank more of it than my Pa, especially when my mother went to the hospital for a cancer operation. I don't even know what kind of cancer, except it was in her belly—nobody told me anything. That dirty old man couldn't go one week without screwing someone. Didn't you ever wonder why I never went home for a visit?"

"Frankly, Van, I never really thought about it. Too wrapped up in my own problems, I guess. Example, Christmas Eve, 1966 and we're both alone."

After Ma died, I took my younger sister, Eva, and left West Virginia. It was just a matter of time before he did it to her too. At first, Eva remained with my maternal grandparents until I got settled in Boston. Before I left, I told them the whole story. Grandpa wanted to take a shotgun and go shoot Pa's head off—he had some temper, but my Grammy just said, 'bad things happen sometimes.' After I got my own place in Boston, they sent Eva to me. I never went back, and I don't regret it."

Michael listened in rapt attention as she continued her story. "After my sister graduated from high school, she married a decent guy, an electrician in Lowell, and is now the mother of an adorable baby boy. That monster father of mine didn't get a chance to ruin her life, though he did manage to ruin one more. He married a young girl, only sixteen, three months after Ma died."

During the past half-hour, her southern accent had crept back into her voice—the words became drawled, stretched out long and slow. "My first name isn't Vanessa, it's Patricia Lee. My last name was Bracket. How's that for a white trash name? Even the colored people felt sorry for my family, though not for Pa. They hated him—the bigoted son-of-a-bitch. Brooks is my mother's maiden name. I didn't want his name."

She stopped long enough to lift the brandy bottle off the coffee table and fill her empty glass.

"I finally got lucky. I had a guardian angel—my one-room schoolteacher, Miss Emery. She was some kind of domestic Peace Corps person from up North. I was only one of three in my grade; she spent a lot of time with me telling me how I could make my life better. I was smart and eager to learn, but I never dreamed I could graduate from college…much less become a doctor. She believed in me. I told her what my father had done to me when she found me sobbing outside the school the morning after. She cried and that wonderful young woman gave me two hundred dollars to buy some decent clothes and a bus ticket to Boston. I think she came from a rich family. She also gave me the name and address of her brother in Boston who was looking for a mother's helper. He was a professor of anthropology at Harvard."

"Van, I never knew. Nobody did. You certainly don't talk like a country girl from West Virginia. You always spoke as though you went to some fancy boarding school," he said.

"Elocution lessons from Professor Emery, my employer. One of the first things he said was, 'We'll have to rid you of that atrocious accent.' He was *my* Professor Higgins. He and his wife Abbie pushed me into college—no, more like forced me into it. At first, I lived with them and then later, I worked days and got a dumpy apartment near Roxbury so my sister could live with me. I took night classes to cover the subjects I missed in high school. Later I took courses that were more difficult. Harvard loves us little girls from Appalachia who have a few smarts. When I was ready, I applied as a full time student. Not only was I accepted, but I was offered a scholarship as well. The rest is history."

By this time, Vanessa was on her fourth drink. She moved closer to Michael, placing her hand on his inner thigh. He was uneasy and wanted to leave, but he couldn't figure out how to do it gracefully. Suddenly, it occurred to him that he had been misunderstood. She thought he was referring to her when he implied that he might be in love with someone else. Her riveting dark eyes swept over him without any pretense.

Michael could have gotten up and walked away. He liked her immensely, but this wasn't supposed to happen. Later, he would wonder why he had ever said, "Van, I need you. I have for a long time." Even as he uttered the words, he knew it was the alcohol talking and his desire for a woman who wanted him, but nothing prepared him for what followed.

All the years of stored up need and unfulfilled passion rose to the surface, and Vanessa kissed him with an intensity that excited him. They dropped from the divan to the carpeted floor, frantically undressing each other. Like a wild animal that was mating for the first time, she cried out, "love me harder, more, more." She arched her body, her flowing black hair spread out on the carpet like a fan. When he looked into her dark eyes, he completely forgot Suzanne—or Jane. He saw only Vanessa. When it was over he buried his face in the softness of her hair. Later, in her bedroom, he held her as she wept and whispered, "It's all right, Van, I'm here and I'm not leaving." He didn't want her to think that having sex was just about lust, so later that night, he made love to her again, and did and said all the things that good men do and say when they supposedly love a woman.

The next morning he was ashamed. He had said things that weren't true. He dreaded facing her, but, when she awoke, she surprised him with a mischievous smile. "Mike, thanks for last night. I know neither of us meant a word we said. We were just plain tanked and lonely. I never knew it could be like this, you know…the sex part. I hope there are some other men like you out there. I want someone to love me the way you loved your wife."

After that, they became a couple of convenience, occasionally spending a night together, but love was not and never would be in the cards for them. In the spring, they vacationed in Bermuda. They scuba-dived and motor-biked in the daytime, and under the stars, they danced to calypso music. When they parted, they hugged. "That's the best vacation I've had in years." said Michael.

"Me, too. In fact, it's the only vacation I've ever had. Thanks for showing me how to play, Michael—and for being so patient. Next time, you can teach me how to ski."

AT SUMMER'S END, Michael telephoned Jane. She invited him to dinner. They hadn't seen each other for a couple of months. As he drove through the gated entrance of Cornwall, it began to rain hard and the darkened clouds and rumbling thunder promised a turbulent evening.

Jane greeted him at the door with a peck on the cheek. "Hello Michael. It's nice to see you. Wait until you see the incoming tide—it's wild out there. All because of the full moon." She hung up his raincoat and then led him into the large living room, a wall of glass that faced the ocean. "I haven't seen waves that size in a long time, and the wind is really kicking up," said Jane.

"It looks like a nor'easter."

"It's that time of year," Jane said.

"How's the new housekeeper?"

"She's an excellent cook, a pleasant woman. However, nobody can take Rosie's place. But she did cook us a wonderful lobster stew, and baked a scrumptious apple pie before she left for the weekend."

After dinner, they sat in the living room, nursing their coffee, watching the rain come down in sheets as the wind danced the outdoor furniture around on the terrace. Logs sparked and crackled in the over-sized granite stone fireplace. Michael eyed the mortared mantle anchored with two valuable Ming porcelains, thinking they were worth more than he would ever earn in the next twenty years.

"I know what you're thinking, Michael. They should be in a museum, and they will be some day, but not quite yet. Not until Mother is gone."

"I agree. Your mother loves her antiques."

"That she does."

"It was a great dinner. Thanks so much. I enjoyed it."

"I'm glad. I don't like eating alone. Usually, a book is my dinner companion."

"I've been doing a lot of thinking and have made an important decision—I'm going to have Suzanne declared legally dead."

It came unexpectedly, and it was something she thought she'd never hear, but she answered calmly even though her heart was beating out of chest. "It's time, Michael. You've done everything you could to find her, but she's gone. You have to get on with your life. Maybe Vanessa will be the answer."

"Vanessa?"

"Haven't you been seeing her recently?" asked Jane.

"Well, yeah, but I've known Vanessa for years. She's one of my best friends. If I could share my life with anyone, it would be—"

She cut him off. "You called the play, Michael, not me."

"I guess I'll have to live with that. Next June will be ten years that she'll be gone, and I want to—"

"I repeat, no promises, Michael. When you're free and it's for real, then speak to me—if I'm still in love with you."

It was awkward. She wouldn't let him speak his mind, so he changed the subject to the ongoing inclement weather, and welcomed the flash of lightning and the roar of thunder as the lights blinked on and off.

"I hope you don't lose your electricity," said Michael.

"Not much chance of that. We have a back-up generator."

"How's your practice going?"

"It keeps me busy—I hardly have time to breathe. Most of my patients have Alzheimer's, Parkinson Disease, and Multiple Sclerosis. Also, quite a few stroke victims, but I prefer the incurable neurological diseases. I'm learning a lot, but sometimes I wish I'd gone into research."

"Never too late. You're still very young." He squeezed both her hands. "Go for it, if it's what you want."

As Jane helped him on with his raincoat, she caught a whiff of a new scent—he had changed his after-shave. Probably something Vanessa had given him. He was so close she could feel his breath on her cheek as he spoke. He still wore his wedding ring, and the sight of it annoyed her. As he dashed down the long stone walk to avoid getting drenched in the downpour, he turned, waved, and gave her one last brilliant smile.

She watched as he drove his Austin-Healey out of the circular driveway, its engine growling. She stood there watching the rain pound the driveway, thinking how much she would miss him if he were no longer part of her life. Loneliness swept over her. The house was roaring with silence. Once it was filled with voices and laughter—where had everyone gone?

Disheartened, she staggered back into the black and white checkered foyer, and collapsed at the bottom of the elegant staircase weeping. "Damn you! Damn you, Michael!" He was the only man she had ever loved, and now she might lose him to Vanessa. He said she was only a friend, but why *now*, when he was dating her, and traveling with her, was he considering this legal process? Didn't he know how much that had hurt her? Was he afraid to tell her that he was in love with Vanessa and planning to break it to her gently?

Years before, she could have married Cameron Emerson. After many proposals, she finally agreed to a lengthy engagement so she could finish medical school. She was swamped with her studies, and he was a resident at Mass General. Jane wasn't certain she was ready to marry, but he said he loved her and was willing to wait. She thought she'd fall in love with him. Everyone else had.

Cammy wasn't called *the golden boy* for nothing. He was educated, handsome, devoted, and from a fine family. Even Mummy could find no fault with him. Why did he choose to fall in love with her, someone so ordinary looking, when he could have had anyone. Though not married, Jane had no regrets or reservations about being his lover. She was not Suzanne who viewed life like a fairy tale. They were not teenagers and both were pragmatic by nature. Making love seemed an innocent enough experience when, as medical professionals, they witnessed daily the ugly underbelly of life—birth and death, and all that happened in between. Cammy had a swimmer's body—broad shoulders and a slim waist. He was a sexy man, and she easily became aroused whenever she massaged his back, her hands feeling the hardness in his muscled arms and shoulders. Then he would roll over and his lapis blue eyes would draw her in, mesmerizing her. Although he was physically beautiful, passionate, yet gentle, not once, did she ever make love to him, ever tremble in climax without closing her eyes and fantasizing that she was with Michael.

"JANE, LET'S GET MARRIED. Next week, next month, even next year, but I must know when. There's no reason for us not to marry. We love each other—we should be married. My parents keep asking me when it's going to happen. "You do want to marry me, don't you, Jane?" Cammy asked.

The dreaded moment had come—the time to tell him the truth. She had put if off for months. She remembered the conversation verbatim, and not a day went by when she didn't wonder if she had made the biggest mistake of her life.

He had come for the weekend, while her mother visited her sister in Greenwich. He kept pressing her for an answer as they sat together on the leather sofa in the library. "Cammy, I do love you, but not enough and not the way I should. I never planned to tell you or anyone else." Her words came in a rush…"I'm in love with someone else."

Cammy leaped from the couch his face paled and his broad shoulders fell. He looked at her in disbelief. "But, how? Who is it?"

"Please. Let's just end it. I don't want to tell you."

"You have to tell me. When did all this happen? You owe me, Jane. You owe me an explanation. I gave you two years of my life. I have a right to know."

It's Michael…my sister's husband. Isn't that pathetic? She's been missing for four years and I don't think she's coming back alive. I feel awful having such thoughts and I've tried to get over him. I thought I could make myself fall in love with you, but it didn't happen."

"So *that's* what it is. Why didn't I see it?" He paced the floor of the library shaking his head in disbelief.

"How long have you been in love with him?"

"For years. Incidentally, Michael doesn't know how I feel about him. I've not been unfaithful to you."

"At this point, what difference does it make?"

"I'm sorry, Cammy. I never meant to hurt you. I wanted to fall in love with you, but it didn't happen."

"You already said that. It hurt enough the first time. I can't compete with Michael. He's in love with a dead woman and you're in love with a fool. I feel sorry for both of you. You just threw away our future. We could have had everything—a home, a family, a life together." He added sarcastically, " Oh yeah, I forgot. You don't love me. According to you, all those times we made love, it was just an act. You were pretending. Forgive me, if I don't believe you. Frankly I'm tired of waiting for you to grow up, so I'm going to accept a position in San Francisco, and get on with my life, and try to forget you."

"Oh, Cammy, please—"

"Don't worry, I won't tell Michael. For old time's sake, tell me, do you think he loves you?"

"I think so—I hope he does, but he's never actually said it. It's just a feeling I have." She avoided his eyes, knowing that after he heard those words, his pride would never let him come back. She wanted him to leave—to get angry—to save himself and get a life with someone else. She loved him enough for that, and because he was her first and only lover—she knew she would miss him.

"Oh! I see. My friend Michael can't decide. He's too cowardly to love his dead wife's sister, but he has no problem sending off romantic vibes to my fiancée. My dear Jane, Michael *does* have a problem, and so do you. You deserve each other." He walked towards the front door, took one final look at her, and said, "Good-bye, Jane."

"Wait, here's your ring —"

Cammy didn't hear her, nor would he care. The slam of the door rang in her ears.

She remembered every word, including the note she enclosed when she returned his ring. She could have been happy with Cammy. It wasn't as if she didn't have strong feelings for him, and she knew that they would have grown in time, if she had given it a chance. Michael would marry again, but not her. If he had wanted her as much as she wanted him, it would have taken place by now.

Now years later, she was still waiting for Michael and wondering how she could have been such a fool.

FOUR NIGHTS LATER, MARGARET MASON called Michael from her New York apartment and said that a miracle had happened.

"Suzanne was found!"

For a few moments, he was speechless. When he tried to talk, the words wouldn't come. It was the kind of feeling one experiences when something horrible or something wonderful happens and it's too much to grasp.

When he recovered his voice, he said. "Oh God! She's alive.

Thank you, Margaret. I knew there was a reason I waited all these years."

For nearly a decade, Margaret's private investigator circulated Suzanne's photograph together with a promise of a reward to airports, hotels, embassies, and taxi companies. Finally, the concierge at the Claridge Hotel in London spotted her. He couldn't help but notice the beautiful blond American wife of a Saudi prince, and their entourage of servants and children.

At first, Margaret said only that Suzanne was alive. After he regained his composure he said, "Bless you for all you've done. Thank you for calling me with such wonderful news. I still can't believe it's true."

With reluctance, she proceeded to give him the terse version of the circumstances that brought Suzanne to London. Her eight-year-old son was stricken with Leukemia, and he was in a London hospital. Suzanne was there with her Saudi husband and their other two children. Margaret heard the anguish in his voice. "Oh! Jesus. It can't be true. It's too much," he said. He tried to muffle the sound of his anguish, as he put his hand over the mouthpiece as his body heaved with sobs.

"Michael, are you still there? Please, dear boy, answer me."

"I'm here. I just can't talk now...It's a lot to absorb. Goodbye, Margaret, I have to think—"

"I'm so sorry. Try to get some rest."

Michael knew it was *his* son. The boy's name was Michael and the age was right. Christ! Margaret said she had an Arab husband. He couldn't help but think it might have been better is she had never returned. He had no idea how he would handle any of it.

Because of the investigator's information, Michael knew that he had time to prepare for the meeting. *He* would be the doctor they would see. He shuddered when he thought of his son being the victim of a killer disease like Acute Lymphocytic Leukemia. After he put the phone down, he grabbed a towel left on the kitchen counter, buried his face in it, and collapsed to his knees. He cried as he hadn't done since he was a young teenager. Not since he missed that foul shot in an overtime game, when his team lost the championship, and his father had called him a loser.

Chapter 15

SECRETS
1967

Nearly a decade had passed since Suzanne was last in America, now torn apart with racial riots in the largest cities, and growing anti-Vietnam War demonstrations. At tumultuous college campuses, militant, angry students chanted "*One, two, three, four, we don't want your fucking war!*" It was hardly like 1958, when Eisenhower was president, and college students lived in single sex dormitories, cheered at football games, and did nothing more outrageous than getting drunk at a fraternity party.

Suzanne reclined in the first-class section of the British Airways jet—her mind in a tailspin. Below her, she watched the twinkling lights of towns and cities submerged in darkness. After all these years, she was returning to America—but to what? She forced down a glass of white wine and nibbled on a cube of cheese that didn't seem to want to go down. She was too upset to eat, and nothing seemed to calm the butterflies within her. The wine didn't help. This was little Michael's last chance. If they couldn't help him in Boston, he would die.

The voice on the intercom announced, "Due to the coastal storm we've experienced, there's been a strong tailwind. We'll arrive in Boston in about ten minutes—a half-hour before schedule. Boston has heavy rainfall, but the temperature is a comfortable sixty-four degrees. We apologize for the bumpy flight. We hope you'll fly again with British Airways."

Nervously, Yasmine shook Ali. "Wake up! We're near the airport. We'll be landing soon." His eyes snapped open.

Mary rushed to put the children's seats in an upright position; their seat belts were already fastened. It had been a rough flight, as high winds and sheets of rain had rocked the aircraft for the past hour. It was typical late September weather in Boston—the aftermath of a hurricane that had come up the eastern seaboard.

When they disembarked, Ali carried Michael, weakened from several nosebleeds on the trip across the Atlantic. Mary trailed him, lugging a sleepy little Sara.

"Am I going to die, Aba?" said Michael.

"Of course not. You're going to get better. We're taking you to the best children's hospital in the world."

Rhashid held his mother's hand and added, "Allah will make you better. He can do anything."

Ali looked at Rhashid's sad eyes and smiled in spite of himself. "Yes little one, Allah will help your brother."

An ambulance awaited them. Yasmine climbed into the back of the vehicle beside her son and introduced herself to the driver and the two attendants. She placed the briefcase, which carried all of Michael's medical records, onto her lap, and listened with fascination as they talked. It had been so long since she had spoken to other Americans, particularly Bostonians who almost, but not quite, sounded like Mainers. It felt good to be home and to once again breathe crisp cool air and feel rain fall upon her face.

Ali left the airport in a limousine with Mary and the children to check in at the Ritz Carlton Hotel. Later, he would join her at the hospital.

THE ADMITTING NURSE WAS sweet and kind. "Is there anything I can get for you, a glass of water, or maybe a cup of coffee?"

"Thank you. I don't need anything."

"The doctor will be with you shortly," said the young nurse, dressed in her white starched uniform, white stockings and twin peaked nurse's cap.

Suzanne sat on the bed, tracing her finger on Michael's colorful pajamas. "Look! There's Winnie the Pooh. He's all over your pajamas. You remember his stories, and how much you loved them?"

"Yes, I was a baby then. I'm scared."

"I know...It's scary to be in a hospital, but remember, this is a special hospital, just for children, and I'll be here with you—all night if I can."

"Please don't leave me, Mama."

"I won't. Try to sleep."

Although Michael fought against it, his eyelids finally stopped flickering, and he rolled onto his side, and fell asleep.

Suzanne heard the sound of the door opening—her eyes strained to see the shadowy figure standing in the darkened doorway. The light from the hall emphasized his silhouette—a tall figure with a familiar stance. She felt the life drain from her as she caught her breath and held it. Was her mind playing tricks on her?

He carried a thick folder in his hand and was dressed in a white doctor's coat that only slightly surpassed the pallor of his face. Tentatively, he closed the door, trying to gather his thoughts before speaking. Although he had expected her, and had prepared himself for this meeting, it was incredulous to believe she was alive until he saw her with his own two eyes.

"My God! It's you, Michael!"

"You were expecting someone else, I presume?" His words were mocking—the voice, glacial.

His eyes darted from her to the sleeping child, and then back to her—feral eyes that pierced her heart—eyes as unyielding as steel. His mouth cut a slash on his somber face. *It was unimaginable, and yet, there he was!* He had regained his color, and pain and disappointment were etched on his handsome face. He had changed little physically. He had filled out and gained a few gray hairs at the temples that took the glint out of his raven hair. But his mouth had lost its sweetness—his chin had become inflexible. There was nothing left of the boy she once knew.

"You've come back. I knew you were alive, even when almost everyone else said you were dead. I'm glad I was right."

"Yes. Michael, it is me." Her voice caressed his name. "I had no idea that *you* would be the doctor."

"I don't suppose you did."

"Please, Michael, I have to speak to you—alone, not here."

"Whatever you say."

They entered an unoccupied private room, squaring off, each scrutinizing the other.

She began. "Before we talk about our son, we must clear up a few things. All I need is fifteen minutes. Agreed?"

"Yes. That's best. There are things that have to be said. Questions that need answers. Dealing with Leukemia is a nightmare and I know what you've been going through. After we finish our conversation about *us*, he'll get my full attention."

"He's sleeping now, anyway. Are you *okay*?"

"Does it matter?"

"Of course it matters! You were…you are…my husband."

"Which is it, Suzanne, past or present?"

His voice changed—it had become more agitated. She tried another approach.

"Have you remarried?"

"No. Did you think I would be?"

"Frankly, I didn't know."

"I took a vow, and I married you for life. A vow you didn't take as seriously as I did."

"Look, Michael, let me explain. I was abducted against my will, sold like a slave, and…."

"Save it, Suzanne! Your friend Elizabeth called Jane and told her everything, the whole story, about the abduction, the slave market, your marriage to some so-called prince, but obviously, she didn't know about the husband back home, did she?"

"I never told anyone, especially my husband, Prince Ali. *Michael is trying to reduce the tragedy of my life to a mishap.*

His eyes darkened, the muscles rippled across his jaw. "This little boy who is so sick, do you even *know* whose son he is?"

"He's yours! He's the image of you. He was born exactly nine months after that night in Athens when you asked me if I wanted to have your baby. You do remember that night, don't you?"

I'm not likely to forget such a memorable occasion. A guy doesn't forget the first time he deliberately tries to knock up a woman, even if she is his wife."

"Don't be cruel! I know you're furious with me, but that can't be helped. Everything I did, I did for our child, to keep him safe and alive."

At that moment, the young admitting nurse opened the door and peeked in. "Oh! Dr. Conti, I'm sorry I interrupted—I was just checking—I saw the door was closed and wondered why—"

"I'm *trying* to have a private conversation."

She blushed a deep red. "I'm sorry, doctor."

"No. I'm the one who should be sorry. I was rude, and you did the right thing," he said his voice softening. The nurse nodded and left the room, closing the door behind her.

"I have to ask you a question. Suzanne, explain to me, make me understand, why, during all those years, you didn't try to contact me. Somewhere, sometime, there must have been an opportunity."

"I have no definitive answer for you. How can I explain tapped telephones, letters read by government officials, the language problem, and always the fear of being found out. If that happened, I was as good as dead, and so was our child."

"Why? Did you actually think someone would kill you?"

"If not death, maybe sold to other men who in turn would sell me again until I was too old or too dead."

"But that's *not* what happened to you, is it?"

"I was lucky."

"Lucky? Well, understand this. While you were so lucky, I was grieving, so much so that I wasn't sure I wanted to live. And, all the while, you, my own wife, were being fucked by another man—of another race—an Arab!"

"Michael, please let me...."

"Don't you dare interrupt me again...Remember how I waited for you until our wedding night? Do you know what a virile young man endures trying to restrain himself? He suffers and he does it because he respects the girl he loves and he doesn't want to get her pregnant. Now, after waiting nine more years, my *virgin* bride returns with three children married to a goddamn Saudi prince, and I'm supposed to forgive and forget. Well, guess what! I don't. It would have been better if you had never returned. You destroyed my life! Do you understand, Suzanne, you destroyed my life!"

Suzanne's breath left her. Never before had he used such lan-

"I know…it must be hard for you, Michael."

He squeezed his fists into two clenched balls. His eyes blazed as if he had gone mad.

"It is. You think you can waltz back into my life, tell me your sad tale, and I'll buy it. You are still the same spoiled brat who could attend any college, get any guy you wanted, including gullible me, and show up with your millionaire prince and expect me to forgive you, like nothing happened. My cousin Jim warned me about you years ago, but I didn't listen."

He smashed his fist into the wall.

Terrified, it occurred to Suzanne that he might strike her next, and she cowered, putting her hands up to protect her face.

Shocked and ashamed of himself, his anger spent, his right arm dropped to his side. "I'm sorry…I'm so sorry…I promised myself I wouldn't act like a raving maniac. You still have the ability to make me crazy. You just don't realize what you did to me."

Opening and closing his swollen hand, he looked down at his bruised knuckles—it didn't appear to be broken.

"Michael, did you hurt yourself?"

"I'm okay. I'm sorry I lost my temper."

Michael, I would have contacted you if I could have. I'm sorry it ruined your life, but I suffered, too."

"You don't look as if you suffered."

"Oh, I've suffered all right. You just can't see it. That first week when I was still a prisoner in Athens, all I thought about was escaping from that hellhole where they kept us. A couple of weeks later, I knew I was pregnant, and that changed everything. After that, the baby became my first priority. Ali married me thinking I was a virgin, but I tricked him. I'm glad I did it—it saved our son. If I weren't a virgin, I could have ended up in a brothel somewhere in the Middle East, like some of the other girls who were abducted, but when Prince Ali saw me…."

"Enough! *Please*, please…I don't want to hear what happened between the two of you. It's like driving a knife through my heart."

"All right, I won't. After the baby was born, I was terribly depressed, and I did the *only* thing I could do, I named him after you.

Michael, you mustn't hate me; I was a victim of a terrible crime. You must recognize it for what it was and stop blaming me."

"Okay, okay...I don't hate you. I know it wasn't your fault that you were abducted. It's the years following it that bothers me. No letter. No call. No nothing."

Weary and beaten, she replied, "Perhaps you are right, after all. Maybe, I wasn't clever or strong enough."

"All right. That's a beginning. Now let's talk about our son. I know he's mine. I remember pictures of myself at that age. I read the records—I know his birth date. Did you ever think of me and how much I had missed?"

"All the time. I knew if I kept my head, someday I would see you again. I never dreamed it would be like this. I know you don't want to hear *his* name, but I'm begging you not to tell him we're married. According to Saudi law, he is the only legal parent of my three children. I could lose them.

"It's not as if I have a choice. I'll keep your secret for now."

Suzanne watched in horror as the floor rose up to meet her. When had she slept last? When had she eaten? Two long strides and Michael caught her in his arms before she hit the ground. She collapsed to her knees as he knelt and held her. Long, hard, wrenching sobs convulsed her body. She clung to him—her heart pounding. Her breasts melded into his chest, and he felt a longing sweep over him. He stroked her tangled golden hair and kissed her wet cheeks, and when she guided her soft mouth to his, he was defenseless.

"You love me...You love me still...I know you do," she whispered.

He parted her lips with his tongue, forcing his mouth into hers. She offered no resistance—she wanted it as much, or even more than he did. She hungered for that kiss. To her it was the most human, intimate and telling of all expressions of love. Caught up in the twin feelings of longing and desire, they got lost in time—back to when they were newlyweds. It was wrong and they both knew it. It was no longer just about the two of them, there were other lives to consider. Gently, he eased her away, silently cursing himself for succumbing to her helplessness, which had always drawn him in like a magnet.

"We can't do this; not the way things are."

"I still love you, Michael. You care about me too. I know that now."

"I did once. But, you mustn't confuse weakness with love. I can't handle this right now…I'm sorry."

"Look at me! Don't you still love me?"

"I won't lie to you, Suzanne. I always promised to tell you the truth. I just don't know. I loved you once, but now things are different. I do apologize for calling you a spoiled brat—you were never that, at least not completely."

"Thank you. Apology accepted. Tell me about you, Michael. In all those years, haven't you made love to other women?"

"Not for a very long time, but, eventually, I did. I've even thought of marrying again."

Her eyes narrowed and her lower lip quivered.

She lifted her chin. "Michael, we've changed. I couldn't expect you to not have someone in your life. I'm sorry I flung myself at you. It won't happen again."

"That's better. Wash your face—your eyes are red. Our child is more important than we are, and I have a job to do. I'm going to examine him. He's the one who matters, not us. As difficult and as impossible as it seems, I'll keep your secret…for now. It will be hard for me. You know how I feel about deception."

She walked into the bathroom and splashed her face with cold water. *She thought that when they met, all would be forgiven. He would understand. He would figure out a way to make everything come out right, like magic.* Now she knew none of this would happen. When she came out, silence floated between them like an invisible barrier. Eventually, she found the courage to ask the questions that tormented her.

"Michael, what about our child? Is there any hope? Is there any treatment that—"

"WAKE UP, SWEETIE." Suzanne shook her son gently. She snapped on his beside lamp as he rubbed his eyes, yawning. Effortlessly, he awakened, as though he might have been only dozing. He smiled weakly at his mother, relieved that she was still there.

She returned the smile and stroked his burning brow. "Dr. Conti is an old friend of mine, and he wants to examine you. You'll get better and, before long, you'll be on your pony again."

"You promise?"

"Have I ever lied to you?"

"No. You told me it's wrong to lie."

"Let's take a look, little guy, and get to know each other. Is that okay?" asked the doctor.

"Are you going to stick a needle in me?" he asked.

"No. That's not my job. I'm not a needle sticker."

"Then, it's okay.

Michael lifted the weak child into a sitting position. He couldn't rise without help. After removing his pajama top, he placed the stethoscope on his thin chest and back. Satisfied that both the heart and lungs were functioning normally, he took the child's wrist in his hand and checked his pulse. It was weak, but still steady. Then he took his temperature, and stared with alarm at the thermometer, which had reached 103 degrees. He continued his examination, checking the child's body for bruising or swelling.

When he concluded the examination, he said, "That's it, kiddo. I want you to get a good night's sleep, because tomorrow, we'll be starting your treatment. You look like a tough little guy. Has anyone ever called you Mikey?"

"No, I don't think so."

"Well, that's what *I'm* going to call you, if it's all right with you?"

"I guess so."

"Do you mind if I give you a hug?"

"No, I don't mind."

Michael held him close and prayed as though God could hear his silent prayer or the primal scream within him that could have shattered the glass in the windows.

"Goodnight, Mikey. Sleep well."

"I'll see you tomorrow, Suzanne, and I promise that I'll do all I can."

"I never doubted that. Thank you, Michael."

Once her son was asleep, Suzanne switched off the lamp. A cot was in the room that wasn't there before. Someone was very thoughtful—perhaps the sweet-faced nurse or, more likely, Michael.

She took off her suit jacket, stretched out on the cot, and pulled a blanket up to her chin. She tried to sleep, but her thoughts were so startling, that every time she closed her eyes, she saw Michael's face. His words rang in her ears. "*I loved you once, but now things are different.*" Fatigue eventually prevailed and she fell asleep after being awake for almost two days.

After several hours, she sensed she was not alone in the room and woke up. It was Ali, slumped in a chair beside the bed—his tie askew, his top shirt button undone, his face unshaven. He barely resembled the impeccably groomed man she had always known.

She spoke softly, so as not to awaken the child. "I'm scared, Ali. I wish I could change places with him."

"I know. So would I, but that is not possible. Did you see the doctor?"

"Yes, I met him. I'll tell you what he said."

Once outside of Michael's hospital room, in the dimly lit hallway, she continued. "Dr. Conti has an outstanding reputation in both research and treatment. Some of his recent patients have gone into remission for a time—with blood platelet replacement and new experimental cancer drugs. I already signed the papers giving them permission to use them although they could be dangerous. Nobody knows the long term side effects."

"Leukemia is fatal. I'll settle for a long-term anything."

Suzanne paused, weighing her words carefully. She made a decision to acknowledge that she knew Michael. It had its risks, but she knew it would be impossible for her to act as though she didn't know him.

"It's really an extraordinary coincidence. I know Dr. Conti. We both grew up in Maine, and I socialized with him when we were both students in Boston."

Ali's black eyes flashed. "What are you saying?"

"That he was a boyfriend, one of several, none of which were serious."

"Were you lovers?"

"No! You know better then that."

"Have you ever kissed him?"

"Yes, I did."

"Am I supposed to be pleased that our son's doctor was your old boyfriend? Or perhaps it is destiny that he is the one. He even has the same name, which is quite a coincidence, or maybe it's not. Perhaps the name of someone you once loved was special to you and you gave it to our child."

She refused to be drawn into his trap. "Could you possibly have forgotten what those early years were like—when I learned to love you? Dr. Conti is part of my past, my schoolgirl past. You're my future, you and our family."

"I'm sorry. Forgive me. Tell me what he said."

"Our little son will have to endure a painful bone marrow test that will—"

Prince Ali listened to all the grim details. "At least, here in Boston, they are doing something and not telling us to take him home to die. I've arranged for a private nurse to stay with him. We must go back to the other children and get some sleep. I can see that you're bloody worn out. Let's leave now—while he's sleeping."

"I promised him I'd stay. He'll be frightened if I'm not here."

"He'll probably sleep all night. I hired a private nurse to stay with him. It's best for you come back to the hotel. You need to sleep."

As they walked down the darkened corridor together, she clung to his arm. They looked like all parents of sick children—worn out and desperate.

Michael sat hidden in his cubicle at the nurses' station. His eyes followed them until they turned a corner. His jealousy festered. In spite of everything, he knew he couldn't rid his heart of Suzanne entirely. Only time could do that.

Apart from Ali's slightly darker skin, this man with Suzanne could have been taken for anyone from a southern European country like Spain or Greece. He was in his late thirties, of average height and weight with a full head of dark hair. There was nothing unusual about him, except for the silky sheen of his tailor-made suit that filled out his back perfectly and the beautiful woman who clung to his arm.

Wearily, Michael rose from his desk, walked into the semi-darkened hospital room, and observed his sleeping son. He studied every characteristic, marveling that this beautiful child was his. His small face was a mirror image of his own when he was eight. The eyes though rimmed with purplish circles, were *his* eyes. The fluid curve of his chin and the hairline with its distinct widows-peak were like his own. But the mouth belonged to Suzanne. He bent over and kissed his son on the cheek, swallowing hard, trying to keep from crying. He failed and wept silently, as men do, mulling over the likely possibility of his son's death.

He heard a voice say, "Dr. Conti, I'm Mrs. Freeman. The agency called me in for private duty."

He wiped his eyes in embarrassment. What would she think of a doctor who cried over his patient? It was so unprofessional. She was solidly built with glasses, gray hair, kind eyes, and a voice that was soft and little girlish.

"Mrs. Freeman, watch him closely and give him plenty of fluids. If anything changes, call Millie, the head nurse, and she'll call me. Remember—call immediately if his condition deteriorates."

"Oh yes, Doctor, I will. You can be sure of that."

ONCE HE REACHED HIS apartment, Michael kicked off his shoes, yanked off his necktie, snapped open a can of beer, and dialed the telephone. He tipped his chair back, rested his feet on the top of his desk, and viewed the moonlit Charles River as the phone rang. The moment he heard her raspy voice, he knew she had been asleep.

"Hello. Dr. Mason here."

"She's here. I've seen her."

"Oh, my God, Michael, what did she say? How did she look?"

"Suzanne said many things. It seems we have to play a little charade so Prince Ali Baba doesn't know who I am. You asked how she looked—tired, but still beautiful."

"How is the boy?"

"He's very sick. Suzanne is almost hysterical, and I can't say I blame her."

"Did she ask for Mother and me? Does she know Mummy's in a nursing home?"

"No. We only had a few minutes, and I spent most of it either raging at her, or discussing the boy's condition. You know, it's all so weird. When I look at her, I know who she is, and I want to say, 'Suzanne, I'm so glad you're alive' and I want to hold her and tell her how much I missed her. Then I remember that she never tried to contact any of us, and I hate her for that."

"Michael, you remember what her friend Elizabeth told me. They couldn't call out of the country. Try not to be bitter. I have a feeling that, in the end, everything will resolve itself. One other thing...everything that happened or might have happened between us must end. You were right all long...she was alive...and how you knew must be interpreted as an omen or maybe a warning for us mortals not to interfere with destiny. I'm going to hang up now. Try to get some sleep."

"I wish you were here with me so I could tell you face to face what I've learned about myself today—what I was afraid to find out."

"What are you talking about, Michael?"

"I'll tell you when I see you. I haven't been fair to you all these years—that's going to change. I was afraid that I still loved Suzanne. I don't Jane ... I love you...only you."

"Goodnight," she whispered.

Jane returned the phone to its cradle, her hand trembling. He loved her, not Suzanne, not Vanessa, just her. She wept tears of both joy and disappointment. It was all so bittersweet. Her sister was alive! Not dead or maimed, but alive and well. For that, she was thankful. She couldn't help thinking that their lives resembled a Greek tragedy: a mother demented, a brother lost, a nephew dying, a sister married to two men, one of which she, Jane, loved more than her own life. A writer of fiction would probably avoid a scenario so complex and unbelievable, but this was the reality of her life.

Through the window, she saw dawn looming—a red ball on the rim of the horizon. Leaves on the trees were turning color. Fall had arrived, and it always made her sad with its shorter days and longer nights, its birds in flight, heading south. Everything that came from nature would sleep through the winter and then: the long, long wait for spring. She heard the sound of the sea crashing on the inlet—it was high tide. Today was Sunday—she could stay in bed as late as she wanted, relishing Michael's last words—*I love you, only you.*

LYING IN HER SUMPTUOUS king-size bed at the Ritz-Carlton in Boston, Suzanne stared in the dark at the logs blazing in the fireplace, unable to sleep. Ali slept beside her, snoring. She kept seeing Michael's contorted face, his facial expressions changing from ice to fire. Meeting him unexpectedly was traumatic, and though his appearance rekindled a passion that was long dormant, his anger and coldness had jolted her. She had not expected it. She had thought that when they did finally meet, he would look at her with disbelieving eyes and sweep her up into his arms. It never occurred to her that he would judge her so harshly. She conceded that he had a right to be angry, but he didn't know all the facts, all the raw emotions and fears she had endured. If only it had been just the two of them, without children involved, she would have returned to him in an instant, and she would have made him love her all over again. One thing was for sure: he would not easily forget that last kiss.

She had survived and prevailed because she was strong. She never expected to fall in love with Ali. She had hoped that she could have withstood their marriage with indifference. But how could she spend thousands of nights sleeping next to a man like Ali and not learn to love him. How could she have known that it was possible to feel love for two men at the same time.

YASMINE AND ALI RETURNED the next morning to Michael's hospital room, and found his bed surrounded by a group of young men. Harvard medical students, interns, and residents watched in awe as Dr. Michael Conti, the new boy wonder, reviewed Michael's case history. He would point his finger at some luckless soul. "You, Dr. 'so-and-so,' what's your diagnosis?" A mix of fear and respect showed on their faces. After all, he held their future in his hands.

Young Michael's parents remained in the doorway listening, learning of the many types of Leukemia. Dr. Conti told the group that Michael's disease was Acute Lymphocytic Leukemia. Aware of Mikey's age and intelligence, he chose his words carefully. The last thing he wanted to do was scare the boy. He emphasized treatment and remission in his recitation. If anything, he was upbeat.

Ali studied Dr. Conti. That he was confident, even arrogant, was apparent in his manner. He was also gentle. He saw him holding his son's hand and smiling at him when he referred to Michael as "Mikey" to his students. Every once in a while, there was an outburst of laughter, which put the child, as well as the anxious students, at ease. Someone had put a Red Sox cap on Michael's head and it was obvious that he was delighted, in spite of his discomfort. One of the residents told him that Ted Williams, who was the greatest hitter of all times, had one just like it.

"I know who he is. When I get better, I'm going to a baseball game. My mother promised me!"

Suzanne saw several of the younger students look uneasy—every person in that room except Mikey and Prince Ali believed he was going to die. She was a doctor's daughter and knew the score. Ali had faith that the Almighty could change anything. As they left the room to continue rounds, Dr. Conti smiled at Suzanne in recognition and nodded to Ali. "I'll see you two later after rounds."

As much as he fought it, a wave of jealousy swept over Michael when he observed Ali with Suzanne. The intimate looks exchanged between them were hard to watch and it bothered him.

"Quite a handsome chap, your Dr. Conti," Ali said curtly.

"He's not *my* Dr. Conti. He's our child's doctor. You promised, remember." Without another word, she entered Michael's room, sat on his bed, and kissed his forehead, hoping the fever had subsided. "Hello darling, how are you? You look better this morning."

After Michael Conti finished seeing his patients, he hurried to the doctor's lounge to prepare for his meeting with Prince Ali. He had to be careful, one wrong word and he could give Suzanne and himself away. He could not stop thinking about her. Today, she was dressed in an unmistakable white Chanel suit with a black braid trim. Her long blonde hair was pulled back in a chignon. S*he's her mother all over again.* He could not help noticing the huge diamond ring on her finger. She had not worn it the night before. What had become of *his* small diamond ring, the one his parents paid three hundred dollars for, the one he gave to Suzanne when they became engaged?

Michael had been a convincing actor all his life. Once again, he would play his role. Prince Ali would never know that he was anything more than the boy's doctor—at least, for now. At Bowdoin, and later at Harvard, he pretended to not be offended by the comments about pushy Jews and ignorant Italians, pretending to go along with Waspy professors and doctors who treated him like he was a guinea pig, an accident who should have been born with a last name like Jones or Smith. He had always been the underdog, but as usual managed to come out on top. He didn't have all the credentials required to get a girl like Suzanne, but in the end, she married *him.* Even now, she was not legally married to that mustached, swarthy Arab millionaire in his Italian silk suit.

Vanessa Brooks walked over carrying two mugs of coffee, one obviously for him. They were alone in the lounge.

"Hi, Mike. Haven't heard from you in a while. Is everything all right? You don't look well."

"Stop playing doctor, Van. I'm a big boy. Just a little tired." He grinned, trying to act normal. "I've got to run. The parents of one of my patients are waiting for me."

"Do you mean the prince from Saudi Arabia who is richer than King Midas, with the beautiful blonde wife?"

"Ahhhh, I see the hospital gossips are at work."

"Well, they do stand out, even here. Who is sick, their child?"

"Yes, Leukemia. A son, eight years old."

"The wife isn't a Saudi, is she?

"No. She's an American. In fact, I've known her since she was sixteen years old."

"Your childhood sweetheart from Maine, and you let her get away. You're slipping, Michael."

"No, I was waiting for a certain beautiful brunette. You know the one I mean? The one who knows when I need a cup of coffee, even if I haven't got the time to drink it." His words were cheerful, but the tone was somber.

"I'm sorry about your friend's son. It's tough when it becomes personal."

"Yes, it is. I'll take a rain check on the coffee. It smells delicious. Thanks anyway."

After he left, she cursed herself for reminding Michael of the past. *I am Stupid! Stupid! Stupid! How could I hurt him like that? Why would he be interested in another woman when he was so in love with his missing wife? Why didn't I remember?*

When Dr. Conti entered Michael's room, they were waiting for him.

Suzanne introduced them to each other, and referred to Ali as her husband.

"Sir, how would you like me to address you?"

"I have many titles. Officially, I am Prince Ali ibn Kareem ibn Sa'ud, which I admit is quite a mouthful. Prince Ali will be sufficient, and my wife is to be addressed as Princess Yasmine.

What a pompous ass, thought Dr. Conti.

"Really, Ali, we certainly don't have to be so formal. I told you I know Dr. Conti, and he always called me Suzanne."

"Your name is no longer Suzanne, it is Princess Yasmine." His words hung with ice.

"Dr. Conti, please call me Suzanne."

Michael felt like he was in the middle of a war. He didn't like the way Ali bullied Suzanne, and was forced to bite his tongue, though he admired Suzanne for standing up to him.

"Prince Ali, can we go to the visitor's lounge? I prefer to talk to both of you privately."

Once seated in the lounge, he explained what the procedures would entail—the transfusions, the bone marrow test, the drugs used, and the need to wear masks when entering his room, etc. "His immune system is fragile, and we have to protect him from infections. In fact, he did have a fever, but I'm not overly concerned about it. We brought it down some from last night. If he continues to improve, he'll remain in the hospital for a number of weeks, and after that we'll treat him as an out-patient."

"Can you save his life?"

"Your son has the most lethal type of Leukemia. Unfortunately, it has always been fatal. I'm sorry. I wish I could give you something more, but we don't know how to cure it yet."

"But, they told us in London you have a new experimental treatment," said Ali.

"Exactly. That's all it is—experimental. I told Suzanne yesterday. In a few cases that we can't explain, patients have improved. A few are still alive."

"Are you a religious man, Doctor?" asked Ali.

"In my own way I am, but I believe more in the power of medicine—science is my domain, not theology. Though certainly, faith has its place, too."

Ali said, "When I was a baby, I contracted Typhoid Fever during an epidemic. Most died. Everyone thought I would die, too. My father took me riding on a camel for many kilometers to find a doctor. He never did find one, but I survived, without a doctor, and without drugs. I am, by nature, an optimistic person, and so I look forward to my son's recovery—he is in the hands of God. If modern medicine could contribute to his recovery also, I would be most appreciative."

Michael shrugged, not knowing what more he could say to a man who refused to accept the inevitable.

"We are staying at a hotel with my other two children and their nursemaid. Since you say that we'll be here for a long time, do you think that we should find a house?"

"Yes. Children need a place to play. You may be here for months. I could recommend a real estate agent who could find you a rental home, and of course, you'd need to rent a car."

"You are very kind, Doctor," Suzanne replied. "I think that's an excellent idea."

"My dear, Yasmine, please, I make the decisions. I prefer to buy a home. I don't like rentals. I'll also buy an automobile. I like my own things."

"You can always send it back to join your collection of six other automobiles," said Suzanne.

Michael was anxious to leave before he lost his temper. He now better understood what Suzanne had been up against.

Michael loosened his collar. He felt as though it were strangling him. "I think I should leave. I have other patients to see, if you'll excuse me, please."

Once he was out of hearing range, Suzanne turned her full fury onto Ali. "You insufferable, egotistical man! To think you could talk to Michael like that and to embarrass me in front of him! He's an old friend. Why *can't* he call me Suzanne? It *is* my name. I don't mind being called Yasmine in the Kingdom, but not here.

"I'm sorry. I never meant to offend you."

"And another thing, his suggestion to rent a house was meant well. Must you belittle everyone? Is it so important to you to let everyone know you are a prince and can buy anything? God, how obscene!"

"Are you finished?"

"For now." She dared not say anything more. In another minute, she would have revealed to him that Michael was her husband and that *he* should be making the decisions about *his* son.

"We'll discuss this alone, not in a public place. People are looking at you."

They glanced at several startled faces, including a woman with tears streaming down her face, no doubt another mother of a sick child. Together they walked into the hallway and continued their argument.

"I don't know, Ali. I'm back to being a free American woman who speaks her mind, and I'm not sure that I can ever again be Yasmine. I've been lost for years and I've found myself again. When I return to the hotel, I'm going to call my mother.

"We'll see," he said calmly. Inwardly, he was seething. In his country family squabbles were private. Never like this.

"I want my family now!" she cried. "I need them, now, more than ever, and you won't stop me!"

He guided her to a nearby unoccupied hospital room, shut the door, and held her in his arms. "You must calm down! I am not a monster. I was going to suggest that you call them as soon as we returned to the hotel, but you didn't give me the opportunity. Call your family. It is time. I hesitated before because I was afraid I would lose you."

"How am I to explain nine years of silence?"

"Tell them the truth—and let them decide for themselves."

"Everything?"

"I leave that to you. Surely, you realize if I hadn't come along, you might even be dead now. I'm not looking for your gratitude, but you must be able to see by now that everything turned out for the best."

"You stole my life."

"You little fool! I saved your life. I didn't kidnap you. I rescued you. I loved you from the beginning. I still do."

"Really. Then tell me why you were planning to take another wife."

His mouth fell open. "How long have you known?"

"For weeks. Were you also planning to divorce me?"

"No, no! I never would have gone through with it or even considered divorce. I was so angry with you. All that chaos with Marilyn. You refused to have any more children, and I thought it was because you no longer loved me. I will never take another wife. You must believe me."

"I'll try, but this is not the end of it. We'll discuss it later."

"Let's spend some time with Michael when he returns to his room, and later on at the hotel, make your telephone call and do anything else you want to do. We'll even rent a house if that is what you want."

"I am so confused and anxious. I don't know what I'll hear. Mostly I'm worried about my mother. She has never been well emotionally."

"Yes, Suzanne."

"You called me by my given name."

"I've been thinking about what you said. I see no harm in it, at least when we're in the States. But, Suzanne, you must remember that you are my wife, a Muslim wife, and must defer to my wishes. When you don't, I become furious."

"You must meet me part of the way. It's our only hope if we are to have a life together. Sometimes, I forget how good you can be. It's almost like you're two people. Please try to be the old Ali, the one who captured my heart and made me love him."

Upon returning to Michael's room, they found him awake and reading a comic book. There were tubes in both arms, and his coloring was normal, not flushed like the night before. He smiled when he saw them. "You know, I really like Dr. Conti. He likes me a lot, because last night when he came in to see me, he kissed me and he was crying. I could feel his tears on my face. I was half-asleep, but I remember. Why did he do that?"

"I don't know, dear. He probably just feels sad because you're ill, and I am his old friend."

Ali said nothing, but a strange look came over his face as he looked at his son and then at his wife.

He knows. My God, he's figured it out!

He continued to stare at her until she thought she might confess to everything, when a nurse walked in with Michael's lunch. They remained with him while he picked at his food, but like most children, he ate his ice-cream cup.

"Darling, you must eat more. Is there anything we can get for you that you really want?"

"No, mother. I'm so sleepy."

Ali was strangely silent. She knew that he was suspicious, but of what? He couldn't possibly have guessed the truth.

After lunch, Michael was scheduled for tests, including a WBC, to count the white blood cells. The nurse told them it would be best for them to return in the late afternoon when the tests were completed.

"As soon as we complete the blood tests, we can start the transfusions," said the nurse.

"Nurse, is it possible that they could use my blood?" asked Ali.

"That's up to the doctor. Your blood will have to be tested, as well, and —"

Suzanne froze. She knew that she and Michael were type O positive and Ali was AB negative. The child would be their blood type, not Ali's. They always kept a supply of blood for Ali at the hospital in Jeddah because his blood type, as well as his father's and siblings', was rare.

"Ali, I need a breath of air. I'm going to take a little walk—I'll be back soon."

"Wait for me. I'll come along, too."

"No. Please, I want to be alone for a few minutes."

"All right, love," he said cheerfully, as he continued to talk to the pretty, young nurse.

She hurried from the room, grabbing her jacket before she left. As she passed the nurses station, she saw Michael writing in his cubicle. She asked the nurse if she could speak to Dr. Conti.

When he saw her, one look at her eyes told him something was dreadfully wrong.

"It's Ali! He wants you to use his blood. It's AB negative. He'll find out!"

"Calm down, Suzanne. I run the show here. He'll never know if I don't want him to. I made you a promise. I'll keep it."

"I know I've asked a lot of you, but I don't know what other choice I have. I'm afraid of Ali and what he can do if he finds out Michael isn't his child."

"This isn't Saudi Arabia. This is a hospital, and here, I'm the one that has the power and the control. Don't worry—he won't find out."

"Thank you, Michael. What a relief!"

SUZANNE AND ALI RETURNED to the hotel where the children were anxiously awaiting them. They were getting bored with the hotel suite, though Mary had taken them for walk in the Boston Commons to see the ducks. Ali kissed Sara and ruffled Rhashid's thick head of dark curls.

"We'll play some games. How about dominoes? Your mother has to make a phone call."

Suzanne went into the master bedroom and closed the door, her eyes fixed on the telephone. She poured herself a glass of white wine, lit up a cigarette, and with a trembling hand dialed the number of her home in Maine.

She listened to the sound of the phone ringing, hoping someone would answer. She had waited for this exact moment for so many years. Anticipation and fear, coupled with her pounding heart, made the waiting unbearable.

"Hello, Dr. Mason here."

It was Jane's voice. For an instant, Suzanne was speechless.

"Hello. Is anyone there?"

She gathered her courage. "It's me, Suzanne."

She heard Jane gasp.

Chapter 16

SISTERS

Hubie and Margaret Mason sat in front of the fireplace of their bedroom in twin chairs that were slip-covered in a flowery chintz of pink roses and green vines on an ivory background. Above the mantel hung Margaret's beloved painting, Van Gogh's, *White Irises*. Over the years it had become priceless. Heat and smoke from burning logs would never rise from this hearth. A red Chinese fan stood guard.

The click of Margaret's knitting needles had grated her husband's nerves during the early years of their marriage; now he no longer heard it. As he drank several cups of his morning coffee, he scanned the *New York Times*, checking his largest stock holdings first, the obituaries second, followed by the world's news and his favorite columnists. If all this was the main course, on Sunday the dessert was always the crossword puzzle.

"Hey, Honey. Who wrote *Stardust*? His last name is Carmichael, but I can't remember his first name. It has four letters and ends with 'y'."

"Try Hogy," said Margaret.

"Thanks, Maggie."

Margaret Mason nodded; her coppery hair had become more steel gray than chestnut, but the years had not dulled the radiance of her eyes. After twelve years of wedded bliss and bluster, she still managed to amuse and fascinate her husband.

A phone rang, ending the click, click, click, of her knitting needles. Although Margaret was a sophisticated and astute businesswoman, she continued to enjoy knitting scarves that no one ever wore. "Keeps me calm," she'd say when anyone asked why she kept making them. Margaret held the phone to her ear and announced to her husband, "Your niece, Janie, is coming over. She spoke to Suzanne last night, and she still can't believe it."

"Who can? Tell her to hurry—I want to know everything."

TEN MINUTES LATER, A BREATHLESS Jane burst into their bedroom. Her face was flushed with excitement. "I got the call last night, but it was too late to come over. Wait until you hear. The very first question she asked was about Mummy and Robby."

"Oh my, that must have been tough," said Margaret.

"I told her everything—about Mother getting Alzheimer's and Robby living in Canada. Of course, she was shocked and sad—who wouldn't be? I hated being the bearer of more bad news. God knows, she has enough turmoil in her life."

"What the Christ is she going to do about her situation with Michael?" asked Hubert, his head shaking with bewilderment. "Are we supposed to pretend that they aren't married?"

"Yes. That's what she wants. Michael is going along with it, at least for now. It's terribly complicated—it's not just about that sick little boy who is Michael's son, it's also about her two other children. If Prince Ali finds out, and bear in mind, he's the only one who has legal custody of those children under Saudi law, he could leave her and take those children away forever."

"Jane, dear, I'm forgetting my manners. Pull up that chair over there and join us. How about some coffee, or maybe tea if you prefer?" asked Margaret.

Hubert leaped up and pushed the chair under her. "Sit down, Janie."

"Thanks. No coffee though, I've been up for hours. In fact, I had an emergency at the hospital at about six a.m. and got home about an hour ago."

"Tell us about the boy," said Hubert.

"It's all bad. You already know about the Leukemia and the prognosis. That hasn't changed. As predicted, Michael is his doctor, and we can only imagine what he's going through. He has to *pretend* that this isn't his son, and he has to *pretend* that Suzanne isn't his wife, and he has to *pretend* that he doesn't hate her Saudi husband."

"I'd hate him, too, if he stole my wife."

"The whole thing is bizarre. You know, as bad as it is for Suzanne, I think it's worse for Michael," said Margaret. "He can't express his grief or expect sympathy from anyone."

"Tell us about 'him,' this prince Ali," snapped Hubert. "What's he like?"

Jane, dressed in old faded jeans and a Shetland sweater, kicked off her sneakers, curled her long legs beneath her and sunk deep into the soft pillowy boudoir chair. She sighed. "It's complicated, and I don't really know much about him. He's well-educated, fluent in English, of course very wealthy, and from what Suzanne told me, an attractive man. Beyond that, I don't know anything."

"Well, what are her feelings?" asked Hubert. "About everything."

"I'll quote Suzanne as near as I can remember: 'Jane, I'll say it once so you won't ask me again. I don't know my own mind yet. I'm still uncertain about Michael and seeing him again rekindled old feelings that I thought were gone forever. I love Ali too, but I just don't know if I can continue to live like a prisoner in a land where women are third class citizens. It's not living with him that's so bad, it's living in a country with such archaic laws.' Those aren't exactly her words, but they're close enough."

"In other words, she doesn't know what the hell she's doing," said Hubert. "I'm glad Robert isn't here to see this. His first grandchild is probably going to die. His daughter was kidnapped at the happiest time of her life, and now this dilemma—what a mess." He shook his head in disbelief, picked up his pipe, packed it with tobacco, and lit it, as he always did when he wanted to unwind. For Hubert, tobacco worked like an anesthetic that calmed him down. "I'll be back—I'm going out on the balcony. No need to stink up the place." He got up and left the room.

Jane continued. "Suzanne knows that her friend Elizabeth called and gave us all the details of the abduction, so we didn't rehash that. She has a diary with her. She wants me to read it. She said that after I read it, I'd understand everything."

"What did she say about Michael?" asked Margaret.

"They had quite a scene. She said he feels betrayed, and that just about killed her. She thinks he doesn't believe her when she said she couldn't get a message out to us."

"Do you?"

"I think, subconsciously, she didn't want to deal with it because she was afraid of the consequences. Before the child was born, she said she thought her life was in danger, and later, after she had three children, it was the fear of losing them that kept her from trying to get out of the country."

"What about you, Janie? What are you going to do about Michael?" asked Margaret.

"I don't know what you mean."

"Yes you do. You love each other."

Until now, Jane had never discussed her true feelings about Michael to anyone except Cammy. "Has it been that obvious?"

"Yes, it has. Jane, we all have secrets, or at least we think they're secrets, but you *can't* hide love. You don't see your faces when you're together, but I have. Suzanne's not the same person anymore either. She's been someone else's wife for a long time, and more importantly, she's a mother. I can't see her giving her children up for Michael."

"When I told her I had become a doctor, she was so pleased, she cried. Funny, she didn't cry about the tragedy of her little boy's illness. She probably doesn't want to face it. The worst thing that can happen to a person is going to happen to her. When you lose a child, a part of you dies, and you never laugh the same way again. The pain is so raw that it never goes away completely. Many times it destroys the marriage. Just looking at each other is a daily reminder of their shared grief. I've seen it happen."

"Yes. I've heard that."

"What do you suppose she would think if I told her that Michael and I fell in love after all she's been through?"

"I don't know, but you should tell her. Denying your feelings isn't going to make her son well, or change the past. You must stop allowing yourself to be a victim and make things happen that are good for you. Michael's going to need someone now—more than ever, and the world isn't going to come to an end if you tell her the truth."

"You make it sound so easy and it's not."

Hubert returned with an implacable look on his face, mumbling under his breath.

"What is it Hubie? Spit it out!" demanded his wife.

"I don't know about you two, but I'll be damned if I can meet that rag-headed Arab. You can't trust them. Where the hell has she been all these years—probably in a harem with his other wives."

"He's an English-educated prince, and besides, they can only have four wives at a time," said his niece.

"Bullshit! Only a few years ago that fat King Saud had to give up his throne to his younger brother, King Faisal. He had a harem and about a hundred kids. He almost bankrupted the country with his crazy spending. They're hypocrites. Alcohol is against their religion, but they drink like fish. I know—I've met some. They act like children and make damn jackasses of themselves. One asked me right out where he could get a young blondie to take home, like she was some kind of Barbie doll."

"Oh, Hubert, they're not all like that. Every country has its fools. You have to remember that it takes time to change. Not too many decades ago, they were one of the poorest countries in the world."

"Now thanks to American ingenuity and having oil on their land, they're so rich they could buy up the whole stock exchange and still have cash left over. Not only that, when they go to war, they switch alliances when their side is losing. You can't trust an Arab."

"Calm down, you old goat! You'll give yourself a coronary."

Jane listened and wondered how much was prejudice and stereotyping, and how much of it was true. She had a lot of questions for Suzanne.

As much as she wanted to see Suzanne in person, she had decided to wait until Michael and her sister resolved their differences. She could not face Suzanne until then. If her nephew's condition turned critical, she would go regardless, but for the time being, she would wait.

AT THE HOSPITAL, the treatment began, and Suzanne watched

helplessly as her child suffered pain that no child should have to endure and no mother should have to witness. As they poked and probed his body, Michael cried out pitifully as they administered more transfusions, more intravenous drugs and more spinal punctures. One bout of nausea followed another. His skin became a mottled network of purplish bruises. Suzanne's soothing voice was always at her son's ear. "Don't worry darling, this is going to help you. Mama's here." Suzanne never left his side. Ali couldn't bear to watch.

Michael's observation of Ali altered his opinion of him, but only as a father of a sick child. Although he could hardly stand the sight of him, he did empathize with Ali. He was as distraught as any father he had ever seen. He retreated to the lounge and smoked pack after pack of cigarettes. He paced the hallways. Michael saw him sitting by his child's bed fingering worry beads, wringing his hands, and mumbling in Arabic, "*Allahu akbar*."

"What's he saying?" asked Michael.

"He says that God is most great. If he honors God enough, perhaps He will hear him and not take his favorite son."

"And who is his God?"

"There is only one God, Michael. He is also called Allah, but it is the same God that Christians and Jews worship. If we didn't all believe in the same God, it would be impossible for me to be Muslim."

"How ironic that he prays for my son and loves him more than his other sons."

"He may not be, biologically, but as much as I don't want to hurt you, he is Michael's father in all the ways that really matter."

"I realize that."

"Tell me the truth, Michael, has his blood count improved at all? Is he any better?"

"No. I'm sorry. There's been no change. Do you know how many times I've said that to other parents? I never knew how awful it felt. Now I do. The doctors and nurses that treat children learn early in their careers that they must distance themselves from their patients and their grieving parents. It's a form of self-preservation, but still, I have to admit there were times when I broke down and crept away somewhere and had a good cry. There were always certain children who could break your heart, as little Michael has broken mine."

"So it's hopeless," she said as she looked back at him with the saddest eyes he had ever seen. As he watched her, he could see the panic building in her face as she struggled to breathe normally. The stress was overwhelming—she began to hyperventilate.

"Suzanne, take long deep breaths. Inhale, and hold it for ten seconds. Exhale slowly, very slowly. Hold it again for ten seconds, then do it all over again. It's called square breathing, and it has the same effect as inhaling from a blown-up brown paper bag. It will calm you down."

She kept her frantic eyes focused on his and followed his instructions. He held her hands and guided her through it until her breathing returned to normal.

"I'm so glad you were here. It's never happened to me before—it was frightening."

"I know."

"I'm okay now. Tell me, will he suffer?"

"We can take care of the pain. I promise you. Most children just drift off until they're comatose. It will be like going to sleep."

"How long does he have?"

"A week. Maybe a little longer."

"Should I tell Ali?"

"Honesty is always the best policy, or so I used to believe." *He couldn't believe he said that at a time like this.*

"He refuses to believe that Michael will die," Suzanne said. "He expects a miracle. I think that in these circumstances, I am stronger than he is. I have to be, I may be pregnant again."

Michael couldn't stop himself from envisioning them having sex and it filled him with disgust. *It was an unholy, bogus union and he still refused to accept the fact that Suzanne actually loved the Arab.* He remembered their wedding night when Suzanne first gave herself to him. Was it really nine years ago? If they had remained together, would she be carrying *his* fourth child?

He wasn't benevolent enough to congratulate her, so he ignored her revelation. "Our son is our last connection. I have no claim on you anymore. I'll file for a divorce, and I promise you Ali will never know. This nightmare has to end for everyone." He was thankful that they had the privacy of his office and that they were completely alone—most likely, for the last time.

"Michael, there were so many things I was going to tell you. I even thought, somehow, we might get back together again. I still love you, you know, but I belong with Ali."

Michael's shoulders sagged. "I feel like the best part of my life is over. Those two short weeks we had together, as husband and wife, will always be the most treasured memories of my life. We were so young and in love, and it can never be like that again, with anyone. I want to hold you one last time," he said as he reached his arms out to her. She ran to him.

She fit into him like a missing piece of a puzzle. She was as familiar to him as a part of his own body. They kissed, tenderly, lovingly. They clung to each other for a long time, neither wanting to be the first one to let go. They both knew that whatever they said to each other would have to last them a lifetime. This time it was Suzanne who had the strength to pull away first.

"You were the best thing that ever happened to me, kiddo," he said. I promise you, I'll never forget you, ever."

"You better not. I once thought we had a lifetime to spend together and we'd grow old spoiling our grandchildren, but it was not to be. Michael, I know *now* that I'll never get beyond the memory of loving you. When I draw my last breath on this earth, and close my eyes forever—I want your face to be the last one that I see."

She left quickly, her heart breaking. Michael's face was a mask of frozen anguish that eventually melted into tears. He stood by the window, staring out of it, wondering how his life had turned into a saga much like a Greek tragedy. Everything that needed to be said between them had been said. It was over.

TO EVERYONE'S ASTONISHMENT, several days later little Michael rallied. No one was more amazed and happier than his doctor. Mikey greeted him with a big smile, and showed him a tooth that had fallen out. Dr. Conti told him that in America, children put their teeth under their pillow, and a tooth fairy left money.

"I know that. My mother told me. And you know what? I've already gotten some money. See, I have two missing teeth." He grinned and showed the two empty gaps on the sides of his mouth. "I bled a lot, but it stopped. Not like when my nose bleeds." His color was better, and he was eating again and watching television. He had discovered Captain Kangaroo and Mister Green Jeans, and like all children, loved them. Michael was even tempted to let him go into the children's playroom, but feared exposing him to an infection.

Suzanne was glad she had withheld the doctor's dire prediction and not told Ali that the end was near.

Ali was exuberant and told anyone who would listen that he had known that his son would recover. "I have faith," he said. "I pray five times a day."

Mikey had improved to the point that Suzanne called Jane, as she had daily, and said to expect her and Ali within the week. It was only a two-hour drive. They would spend a whole day together, and, most important, see Mother.

After having a long, thoughtful conversation with Ali, he agreed with Suzanne that they should take care of some things that were bothering her. He suggested they meet with a lawyer and settle things legally, so she no longer would be worried about the future for herself and her children. She was flabbergasted that he was so eager to accommodate her. She had expected anger and distrust.

The next two days, except for lunch and a quick visit to the hospital, was spent in a lawyer's office. So many legal papers were transacted that it kept six office workers busy typing. All of the provisions that Suzanne requested of Ali were fulfilled. Once processed, no country with a just legal system could defer them, or so the lawyer claimed. Suzanne eyed his law degree on the wall. Dennis Ellis Burnham graduated from Yale Law School in 1948, when she was fifteen years old. It was two years before she had met Michael—a lifetime ago.

Ali signed his name to everything at the lawyer's office. She knew he was wealthy, but never did she suspect that so much money was involved. In a Swiss bank account, millions were deposited in her name, along with additional millions for each child. There were papers drawn that would grant Suzanne the right to divorce Ali, and leave Saudi Arabia, awarding custody to each parent for six months of the year. Neither expected the divorce papers to ever be processed, but it gave Suzanne a sense of peace that she had never known before. Now she knew for certain that Ali wouldn't risk taking another wife with such serious consequences.

Ali was congenial and non-confrontational and said that in many ways it was just a marriage contract—he must live up to his responsibilities and she must live up to hers.

When Suzanne called Jane that evening and told her everything, Jane listened, but still had her doubts as to the validity of the legal proceedings. Who was this lawyer who made such promises? Was he an honest lawyer who would protect Suzanne's interests, or was he bought off in a ploy to trick Suzanne into returning to Saudi Arabia? Suzanne's naiveté had always bothered her.

When they arrived in Maine in two days, Jane would be ready. Margaret promised to consult with her team of lawyers, which included a specialist in international law, to find out the truth before it was too late.

Chapter 17

CAPE ELIZABETH

For the first time in almost ten years, Suzanne sat behind the wheel of a car and felt resurrected—exhilarated. She controlled the speed. She chose the direction. She had not made many life-changing decisions in nearly a decade, and even the simple task of driving a car felt like a rebirth of her spirit. She was alive again. When she neared the exit of the Maine Turnpike, she turned to Ali breathlessly, "I can't believe we're almost there. It won't be long now."

"You know, you really are a splendid driver. You shift the gears quite smoothly."

"My father taught me how to drive a car and how to handle a sailboat. If I'm a good driver, it's because of him."

"He succeeded admirably."

Within twenty minutes, they turned east off Route 77 and drove down a paved road until they reached the grounds of the Mason estate. Suzanne's heart raced as she drove through the open gates—over the narrow bumpy dirt road that sloped down a hill, running through wildflowered pastures dominated with an abundance of goldenrod. On the rise, the house came into view.

"Cornwall" stood majestically as it always had since her grandfather converted it from a modest summer cottage into the most imposing house in Cape Elizabeth. Everything was the same—the big White House, the black shutters, the Ionian columns, the ivy clad chimneys, the sea in the backdrop. Borders of crimson and golden mums and towering trees of maple and oak blazed in full color, along with the delightful, but unruly, bittersweet vines that scaled the southwestern side of the house. The wind had given the sea a chop, and it sparkled in blue and white, matching Suzanne's fiery Kashmir sapphire earrings. The deafening roar of the incoming waves at high tide and the smell of salt reminded her of her childhood and it filled her with remorse. She hadn't realized how much she had missed it, or how incredibly beautiful it was until now.

"I am sorry that you were taken away from all of this...I really am," he said.

She fought the lump in her throat, as she turned off the ignition. She didn't want to think about what might have been.

They spied Jane in the garden, wearing a big straw hat and large sunglasses, carrying a basket that was filled with sunflowers. When Jane saw Suzanne, she dropped the basket, flung her hat into the air, and raced towards her.

"Ya—hoooooo! Suzanne!" she called, and in an instant, they were wrapped in each other's arms. For several minutes they stood there, clinging to each other, sharing hugs and kisses, not quite believing that it had all come true. Ali stood aside and watched, not wanting to intrude on their intimate reunion. He was surprised that they looked nothing alike—although Jane was a striking woman. She reminded him of the cinema star Katherine Hepburn. She was tall and extremely thin, with an angular face, dressed in black slacks and a man's white shirt, a red sweater tied over her shoulders. Perched on the top of her head were her large sunglasses.

"Jane, I want you to meet my husband, Ali," said Suzanne.

"Prince Ali, I hope you're not going to be offended if I kiss you on the cheek."

"Of course not. But let me be the first to do so." He kissed Jane politely on her cheeks, even though one of them had a smudge of dirt on it. Both cheeks were streaked with tears.

Several things about her struck him; she was taller, younger and fresher than her sister, yet the wide-set eyes were the same. Jane's were more green than blue and the unruly mane of hair that she tied back carelessly with an elastic band glowed a fiery Sienna red in the sunlight. He thought her fascinating, despite the fact that she obviously cared little about the latest fashions or pampering herself.

"Welcome, Ali. I'm so happy your son is better. Sue keeps me updated on everything when we talk on the phone."

"Thank you for being so kind." He looked out at the sea. "The view is incredible. Really quite breathtaking."

"Yes, the Maine seacoast can be addicting. Many summer people come to vacation here, and a few never leave. Take care that it doesn't happen to you."

"I'm afraid I could never adjust to your cold winters, though spending a holiday here is tempting."

"I'd like that," said Jane. "The housekeeper is off today, so we have the house to ourselves, except for Aunt Margaret and Uncle Hubert, who'll be joining us later. I've got you to myself for now. I'm sorry I'm such a mess—I was so nervous I thought some gardening would help me relax." She squeezed Suzanne affectionately as the three of them walked the stone path leading to the terraced patio and entered the house through the French doors into the large living room.

"You know, even though I prayed for this, I never really expected it to come true," Jane said. She closed the mullion paned French doors to shut out the roar of the incoming tide. Ali spoke so softly that it was difficult to hear him.

"It should have happened years ago, but I was afraid of the outcome. I didn't want to lose Yasmine, I mean Suzanne. I've never called her Suzanne until a few days ago, so you'll have to forgive me."

Suzanne screeched with delight: "It's the same! Just the same! You haven't changed anything." She ran to the foyer, and like a child did a mock pirouette, then peeked into the library, and finally ran back into the living room laughing. Seating herself in her father's favorite chair, her eyes darted around the room, absorbing everything. "Oh! Look at Mother's portrait. You moved it from the library. She was so beautiful! And, Daddy, how I've missed him." She picked up a photograph from the baby grand piano and handed it to Ali. "Wasn't he handsome?"

"Your parents are both handsome people. Now I can see where you get your beauty."

Jane left the room and returned minutes later with refreshments.

She had washed the dirt from her face, and brushed the frizz from her hair until it shone. The elastic band had been replaced with a pony tail clip.

"Prince Ali, you must have some apple cider. Maine is famous for its apples. I think you'll like it." As she poured the cider, she reflected: "I'm so glad you came. And it's wonderful that Michael has improved. It's like a miracle."

"Yes, it is." After a few sips, he smiled. "This is an excellent beverage—very refreshing."

"Would you mind terribly if Suzanne and I went upstairs together for a few minutes? I'd like to speak to her about our brother, and to show her some documents I've received from his lawyer. While you are waiting, you can look at some family albums. Our mother has documented every photograph, so you'll see Suzanne through all the years of her life."

"That would be splendid." He rose until they started up the stairs, and then sat down.

They dashed up the staircase together, tittering. "Your prince has exquisite manners, and he's quite dashing. I didn't expect an English accent."

"Oh yes. He was educated there—first at Sandhurst, the military school, and then later at Christ's Church College at Oxford. Finally, he got his MBA at Wharton's School of Business."

"Rather impressive credentials."

Once they got to Suzanne's old bedroom, Jane shut the door and leaned against it. "I have to talk fast because I have a lot to say. First, don't worry about pictures of you and Michael. I've removed every trace of him. Margaret and Hubert know the score, so don't worry about them either."

"When you handed him those albums, you scared me half to death. You are still a troublemaker."

"And you still have your sense of humor. I've missed you terribly," said Jane.

"Me too, I never thought I'd see this room again. You didn't change anything."

"I couldn't."

"Thanks for saving it for me."

"I've got great news, Robby's coming," said Jane. "I haven't seen him in over two years. His lawyer contacted him and told him you were found. He's going to risk immigration and come over the border. He's married and expecting a child in three months. Can you believe our little brother is going to be a daddy? He burned his draft card, so he still has major problems. He'll be in Boston tomorrow. Isn't that terrific?"

"Yes it is. I'm dying to see the little brat."

"He knows the drill, too, so don't worry, he won't give you away."

"Jane, I've waited so long for this. It's overwhelming. Seeing Michael again was unimaginably difficult, and trying to explain everything was a torture—for both of us. He said some terrible things to me. I didn't know that he was capable of so much resentment and hatred. He's bitter, but I understand why. He feels cheated. We both do. After all, when you lose the love of your life, it's not easy to pick yourself up again. The last time I saw him, we made our peace though it was very sad. It was the end of something magical. It would have been less painful if he only had remarried."

"Yes, It's been a long lonely time for him. He called this morning and said that it's over between the two of you. I guess it's the only way it could have ended."

"You two have gotten pretty chummy."

"Yes. We have become close over the years," said Jane.

"We never had any real chance of a reconciliation. If only it had been between Ali and Michael, *you* know which one I would have chosen."

But that was the mystery of it, Jane didn't know which one Suzanne would have chosen, and she doubted if Suzanne herself really knew. Even if she did, would she tell her the truth?

Suzanne continued: "I'm sure that he still loves me though he kind of hinted that there was someone in his life, and he was thinking of marrying again. At first, I thought he was just trying to make me jealous, but after thinking about it, it may be true. Do you know who the mystery woman is?"

Although Jane intended to tell her sister about them, she hadn't expected it to be now and she was not the least surprised that Suzanne still thought she was the queen of the roost. Other things needed to be explained, so not wanting to lie, she said, "Let's save that question for a few minutes—it's a bit complicated."

Suzanne, normally impulsive and anxious by nature, sensed that something was wrong, but she let it go.

"You've aroused my curiosity, but I guess I'll have to wait." She shifted the conversation back to herself. "Did Michael tell you I'm pregnant?"

"Actually, he did. I can't believe you're the mother of three children with another one on the way."

"Yes, and it's brought me closer to understanding our mother and what she went through raising us essentially alone, with Daddy always working. Ali is away from the country almost as much as he is at home. Michael told me that you and Dad had suspected that she had dementia even before I married, but nobody told *me*."

"What was the point? We didn't want to spoil your wedding. What could you have done anyway?"

Suzanne sighed. "Spent more time with her, I suppose. Been more understanding. Poor Mummy."

"Suzanne, there's something I have to tell you. Now that you and Michael will be getting a divorce, you have a right to know."

"You can trust me. Are you going to tell me that there has been women in his life after all?"

"No, that's not it. If anything, he never gave up hope. Of course, there were women, but not anyone he loved. For a long time, you were the only one for him. It's really more about me…You see…I'm the mystery woman."

"You!" Her eyes narrowed to slits and she looked at Jane with surprise, as though she was seeing her for the first time. It was a look that Jane would not soon forget—a feral one.

Jane paused, jolted by Suzanne's fury, but continued while she still had the courage. She remembered Margaret's words. *If you want something, you have to make it happen. She couldn't turn back now.*

"I've loved him for years. Not when you married him of course, at least, I didn't realize it then, but later I did. We've been very close in every way but one…we've never been intimate."

Jane reached for Suzanne's hand but she drew away.

"*Please* Suzanne. Try to understand. *I love him. He loves me.* I'm sorry it was such a shock to you."

"What's one more shock when your life has been shattered as mine has?"

"I know you feel deceived. Michael said you would."

"What about me? I'm the queen of deception. I can't possibly judge you or Michael. It was wrong of me to scream at you." She opened her purse, took out her diary, and placed it in Jane's hand. Her face softened, "I'm sorry I got angry. I just didn't expect it. Read this Jane, and you'll know everything about my life these past nine years. Keep it for me, but don't ever show it to Michael. It would hurt him deeply to read how I fell in love with Ali."

"I will, and I promise you, he'll never see it. Can you forgive me for loving Michael?" said Jane, her eyes begging for atonement.

"What the hell! Of course, I forgive you. I've learned one thing in this life—we don't choose the people we love—it just happens."

Jane rushed into Suzanne's arms, and they held each other close. Jane felt a surge of relief. She could breathe again.

When they returned to the living room, they found Ali engrossed in one of the many albums stacked on the coffee table. He held one book up to Suzanne and showed her a picture. "Is that your father? He looks just like our Michael."

Suzanne looked at the picture and was surprised. "You know he *does*. That's my Dad when he was a little boy. I never connected our son's looks to him, but I think you're right."

"Well, I guess it's only fair that one of the children took after your side of the family. The other two have my coloring and are not as tall as Michael. Though, he was small when he was born. But of course, he was premature."

"You say he was premature?" Jane said. "How much did he weigh?"

"Only five pounds. He stayed in the clinic about a week longer than our other children did, but when he came home, he was fine. He certainly gained weight fast enough, and, as you can see, now he's quite tall for his age."

Suzanne remained silent. *Let them think he was premature. She knew he was full term—just small at birth. She remembered the night he was conceived.*

"All the Masons and Merediths are tall," said Jane. "Suzanne is the runt of the family."

"Well, one thing he definitely inherited from me is my rare blood type, AB negative. When we return to the hospital, they want me to give more blood. There's a shortage of it. I've always known his blood type. Most of my family has it, and Sara confirmed it years ago. We always keep a fresh supply of it at Sara's clinic and in Riyadh as well. What if there were an accident and—"

"Does Dr. Conti know you have the same blood type?" Suzanne asked, her heart beating like a drum.

"I don't know. I suppose so. They tested me several days ago, and yesterday they took blood from me. Said that I'd have to give more in a few days. Is something wrong, Suzanne? You look ill."

"No, I'm okay, just excited. Jane and I are going upstairs again for a minute. I need a few aspirin. I'm getting a splitting headache."

"Sure. I'll keep looking at the pictures. I like seeing you as a child. Your mother wrote interesting comments about the photographs. I'm getting to know your family, even if it's only through family albums. Take your time."

When they returned to Suzanne's old bedroom, Jane stared at her sister who sat on the edge of the bed with her head in her hands.

"What's wrong Suzanne?"

"Everything! What have I done?"

"What are you talking about?"

"Little Michael is Ali's child! He has to be—his blood is AB negative. Michael and I are both O positive. I've been so wrong. Whenever I looked at the baby, I saw Michael's face. It never occurred to me that the baby inherited some of his grandfather's features. You know, the widow's peak, the tall stature, and the same color hair. Even Mummy commented on it. She said I was probably marrying Michael because he reminded me of Daddy.

"I can see how you could have been confused."

"After I married Ali, I was queasy all through the cruise in Turkey and weeks late with my period. I was sure I was pregnant."

"Maybe you were seasick and were under so much stress that you missed your period because of it. It happened to you when Daddy died, and then again, about a month before your wedding. Don't you remember?"

"Now I do. I'd forgotten that. It's all beginning to make sense. All these years I've carried this tremendous guilt, and for nothing."

"If what Ali says is true, then there are no doubts. It's kind of complicated to explain medically," said Jane. "It's not always possible to prove conclusively who is the father is, but it is possible to prove who isn't. Two people with type O blood could never have a child with type AB. I wonder if Michael knows yet? He'll know instantly if he studies the blood report."

"Jane, it was meant to be. This is just another example of why Ali and I belong together. All these years I never figured it out. Because the baby was born eight months after I married Ali, I was sure he was Michael's, but the truth was, he was Ali's child all along."

"Suzanne, when you get back, you must tell Michael immediately if he doesn't already know. My God, he thinks that it's *his son* that's dying of Leukemia...Darn it! I didn't mean to say that, it just slipped out. Forgive me."

"You just said what we all fear. The best we can hope for is a remission." She tightened her lips, determined not to cry.

"Perhaps it will happen—after all, he has improved. And if the worst happens—you're a strong person and you'll survive it. Michael is a compassionate doctor and he'll not allow your child to suffer. Trust him. I'm going back downstairs. Freshen up and join us when you're ready. I'm calling Margaret and Hubert. We'll have a tea party. Okay, big sister?"

"Okay. I'm glad you'll be with me through all of this." After Jane left, she flung herself on the bed and sobbed, muffling the sound, and dug her face into the chenille bedspread. She wept for all of them, for herself, for Ali, for Michael and for the child they all loved who was fighting for his life.

UNCLE HUBERT EMBRACED SUZANNE. "My darling girl. I sometimes thought I'd never see you again."

"That's because you're a pessimistic man," said Margaret. "Hubie Mason. I told you a million times, we'd see that swell niece of of yours again. I was right, wasn't I?"

"Maggie, have you ever been wrong?" replied Hubert, mischievously.

"Yes. When I married you, so shut up, my dear."

"It's heavenly to be together again with my family," said Suzanne, ignoring Hubert and Margaret's playful bantering. Hubert turned down the tea that Jane offered. He mixed himself a scotch and water, and stirred it with his finger.

Ali observed the people who were part of Suzanne's life. They were markedly different from his own family, so much so, that they could have come from another planet. *How could a man be a man in a country like this? The women were frighteningly opinionated.*

"Prince Ali, I would like to ask you a question. Supposing you tell us how she came to be in your possession?" asked Hubert not even trying to disguise the sarcasm in his voice.

Ali was jolted. Suzanne shuddered, thinking how rude this would be considered in Saudi Arabia. Direct questions were never asked, and never of a guest visiting in your home.

"I don't know how much you know, so I'll start at the beginning. I bought Suzanne as if I were buying an animal—the deed was wrong, but the motive wasn't. Only Allah can judge me. It was 1958—slavery was legal in Saudi Arabia, although it almost always involved Africans, but white slavery went on, too—generally ignored as long as it didn't involve our own people."

Hubert glared at Prince Ali but kept his mouth shut. He couldn't stop the voice in his head that said, *Arabs made a business of slavery—way back when they captured Africans and sold them to white men to send to the Americas.*

"When I first saw Suzanne, frightened and vulnerable, I merely wanted to save her—to protect her. I knew what could happen to her. So I married her, and she became my third wife. Marriages and divorces are easy for a man to obtain in a Muslim country, except for the first marriage, so it wasn't an enormous sacrifice or financial burden on my part. I didn't expect to become as attached to her as I did, but it happened. After several years, she learned to accept me as her husband without any reservations. You have to understand that this is very difficult for me. Muslim men do not discuss their wives or their feelings for them with others. It's a matter of respect." He looked at his wife. He knew that this was painful for her as well.

"I denied her the right to contact her family, even though I promised her that in time she could. I watched her constantly, and I knew that once there were children, she would be bound to me forever, or as long as I wanted her. The only defense that I can offer is that I was afraid I would lose her if she contacted her family. I can see now that I was wrong."

"Ali, there's another thing we must explain," said Suzanne. "Marilyn Moore, the missing model and niece of Senator Moore was abducted along with me. She was my dear friend and I cared for her deeply. She died in a horrible, gruesome way—stoned to death in Riyadh before hundreds of people for adultery. Although it was true that she had broken the law, she didn't deserve to die in such a horrible way. It was then, after that abomination, that I decided to plan an escape, but little Michael got sick, and my priorities changed—in ways I never dreamed. Someone should tell her uncle, so he'll finally know what became of her."

Ali fixed his dark eyes on Suzanne as he struggled to hide the anger that was smoldering within him. *She was going to leave him and take his children away.*

Margaret exclaimed, "That poor girl! We had hopes for her too, but now that's ended. I don't think the State Department will make much of a stink. They don't want to lose all their oil connections with the Saudis. Forgive me, Prince Ali, but I call a spade a spade. Your country is still in the dark ages. So please explain to me why they killed her in such a brutal way?"

Though Ali hadn't expected to defend *Sharia* law or the customs of his country, he did, nevertheless, feel compelled to do so.

"Mrs. Mason, a couple of decades ago, the people of my land lived under the most primitive conditions of the Middle-East—no industry—no agriculture—just camels and dates. Any structures that we built were of dried mud or from coral hacked off the reefs in Jeddah. The death rate for children was horrendous. By the time the Second World War ended, Arabia had leaped a couple of centuries and all because of oil. Now, twenty-two years later, we enjoy wealth and potential wealth the likes of which the world has never witnessed. By the twenty-first century, our control over the economy of the world will be felt everywhere—and nowhere more than in the United States."

"*In a pig's neck,*" muttered Hubert to himself.

Ali continued his diatribe. "Wealth is not our greatest treasure—Islam is. We are the guardians of Islam for all Muslims with our sacred cities of Mecca and Medina. That will never change. The Koran and Sharia law rule our lives in ways that Christians and Jews could never understand. Islam is not just a religion—it is a way of life. We have a saying, 'There are good Muslims and bad Muslims, but there are no non-believing Muslims.'"

"Prince Ali, you still have not answered my wife's question about Marilyn Moore," interrupted Hubert.

"Yes, I was getting to that. Sharia law decrees that a woman is stoned to death for adultery, but only after the testimony of four male witnesses, which is almost impossible to acquire. Stoning hasn't happened in years, and to my knowledge, never before to an American. Yes, we behead murderers, rapists, and other criminals. Losing your head or even your hand for stealing is a big deterrent, and we have little crime. Your country is filled with prisons. Many of your young women act like whores. If you call my country living in the 'dark ages,' so be it. I don't condone stoning, but I don't condemn it either."

"Well, that's quite a story," said Hubert.

"You were actually thinking of escaping?" Ali asked Suzanne, his dark eyes flashing.

"After the stoning, I thought I could never bring my children up in a country so barbarous."

Ali's mouth fell open, "What were you going to do?"

"Try to convince you to take the family to England for a holiday, and once there, take refuge in the American Embassy with the children. But I didn't have time to do anything because of Michael, and now, things have changed, and I feel differently. There is nothing more important to me than keeping our family together, but we must make some changes such as the ones we discussed at the lawyer's office."

Ali was dumbfounded, and muttered, "Unbelievable, to think you would have taken my children away from me."

There was a long pause in the conversation, and Margaret knew she had to do something to change the atmosphere. "I don't know about the rest of you, but I need a drink, a stiff one." Hubert had collapsed in an easy chair and looked shell-shocked.

Ali forced a smile and said, "Muslims have another saying, 'Whatever happens, is God's will.'"

"We do, too. 'What will be, will be.' Prince Ali, I want you to know that it took a lot of guts to confess to everything. But the bottom line is that you did not kidnap her, someone else did. You saved her. Fortunately for her, she is here, alive, and with us, most likely, because of you. Let's drink to that."

"Yes, Aunt Margaret," replied Jane. They all joined in the toast—even Ali, who admitted that he was not a perfect Muslim, for he did enjoy an occasional drink of Scotch, a habit he had acquired while living in the United Kingdom.

"I think we ought to go now—I'm anxious to see Mummy," said Suzanne.

"And so we shall," said Jane. "Aunt Margaret has invited us to dinner. Her new chef, Antonio, is superb."

Upon receiving the invitation, Ali smirked at Hubert who puffed on his cigar that was imported from Harrods now that the U. S. had banned cigars from Cuba. He continued to eye him with suspicion. *You may have charmed the women in this family with your elegant speeches, but you don't fool me, you Arab son-of-a-bitch.*

Chapter 18

REUNIONS

Jane chatted to Suzanne and Ali as she drove to Wateridge, the state-of-the-art nursing home where Edith Mason resided. She was fully aware of Suzanne's anxiety: shifting in her seat, fidgeting with her bracelets, barely noticing the changing landscape with new houses popping up everywhere. Cape Elizabeth was no longer the exclusive domain of the homes and summer cottages of the rich.

For Suzanne the ride seemed to last forever, and yet it could not end fast enough. Her last memory of her mother was on her own wedding day. She looked exquisite: a middle-aged beauty who defied her years, wearing a designer dress with her trademark hairdo—silvery blonde hair tautly drawn back into a chignon. Now, what would she look like?

Jane doubted that her mother would even notice Suzanne. She hadn't recognized her in nearly a year. Jane never got over the hurt when she looked into her mother's eyes and saw only bewilderment. It always hit her in the pit of her stomach, and yet each time, she hoped for a miracle. *Please, Mummy, this time remember me.* She had witnessed her mother's gradual deterioration; but for Suzanne, the change would be traumatic. Mother was only sixty, but looked more than ten years older. Alzheimer's was a cruel disease that destroyed the mind and body, slowly. It was equally cruel for the victim's family who had to watch the long good-bye.

Along the driveway that led to the nursing home were blazing hedges of burning-bush that had turned about the same time as the fall equinox.

The main building was more like a country style inn than a nursing home, with its gray shingles, wide porch, and white wicker furniture. Suzanne believed that her mother would have approved of the elegance of the surroundings.

Suzanne, Jane, and Ali climbed the broad granite steps to an impressive entrance with double doors anchored with redwood tubs of petunias and geraniums. An old man dozed in a hammock on the porch with a copy of *Time* resting on his chest. His eyeglasses had slid down his nose. Upon the cover of the magazine was a picture of Martin Luther King.

After entering a large, airy solarium festooned with hanging plants of ivy and philodendra, all eyes turned to them. At the information desk in the center of the room, sat a pretty young woman dressed in a pink uniform. Women in their seventies and eighties sat in clusters, wringing balled handkerchiefs in their hands—sharing their problems, both real and imagined. All were dressed in old women's garb: white-laced shoes, beige support stockings, and floral cotton dresses. Amidst the group sat a solitary man with tremors, aged beyond his years by some insidious disease. Another resident was crying; opposite her sat a tiny colored woman seemingly lost in a large wheelchair, old and wrinkled like a prune staring blankly into space. Those women whose minds were still intact dismissed the trio, as though they were invisible.

A plump, breathy nurse greeted them. "Oh, Dr. Mason, how nice to see you! You've brought some visitors. Your mother will be so pleased."

"Hello, Francine. I'd like you to meet my sister and her husband."

One old lady, upon hearing the word "doctor," stood up, grumbling, and started following them.

"Doctor, I want to go home! I don't belong here." The statement was addressed to Ali, the assumption being that *he* was the doctor.

Francine, trained by profession, doled out affection equally, and guided the woman back to her chair. "That's not your doctor, Gladys. He's coming another day. Now you go back with the girls and have a nice time."

Francine returned, apologetic for the intrusion, and after the introductions were made, she said, "Mrs. Mason is having a so-so day.

She did eat all her lunch, but she seemed tired, so she returned to her room."

"Thanks, Francine," said Jane. "I'll call you if I need anything."

Jane turned to her sister. "Just remember, this is the best place for her. It will be a lot harder for you than it will be for her."

They entered the private sitting-room/bedroom suite and saw their mother sitting in a rocking chair with her eyes fixed on some unknown entity outside the picture window. In her arms, she clutched a yellow-headed rag doll that once belonged to Suzanne. "Mother, someone is here to see you. Someone you haven't seen for a long time—it's Suzanne." Her mother did not respond.

Suzanne gulped. *This must be a mistake. This can't be my mother, but of course, she knew it was.* Her mother's blonde hair had turned completely white; the outline of her head showed through a halo of thin hair. She was well dressed, even wearing costume jewelry, but this was not the woman she remembered. She looked so *old* with her thin tissue-paper skin. Only her electric, blue-violet eyes remained unchanged. Her aristocratic nose was sharper, her face, gaunt. Her lips were coated with a bright red lipstick that her mother would never have chosen. Her eyebrows were gone; a thin pencil line had replaced them. Suzanne made a mental note to remind her sister to buy a soft pink lipstick for her mother and a brow brush that would make them look more natural.

Suzanne squatted in front of her and held her mother's thin, elegant hands. "Mother, it's me, Suzanne."

For a moment, there was nothing, no recognition, and no eye contact. Then very slowly, her mother looked up at her, squinting, her eyes gradually growing brighter with recognition. She mouthed her daughter's name, but there was no sound. She tried again, and this time, her hoarse voice, although croaked, was audible. "Suzanne!" She dropped the doll and held out her arms.

"Yes, Mummy, it's me."

"Where…have you been?"

Suzanne burst into tears and embraced her. "Oh, Mummy, you *do* know me. Thank God! I've missed you so much. I've waited so long to see you."

Astonished by her mother's response, Jane rushed off to get Francine. When they returned, the nurse was dumfounded. "Well! Now, I've seen it all. I've never heard her speak more than two or three words since I came here."

"Mother, this is Ali." He came forward sheepishly and kissed her hand.

"It's who?" She skewed her eyes and said, "Where are my glasses?"

Francine opened the drawer on the night table, retrieved her glasses, and placed them on Edith.

"Who's he?"

Jane laughed, "Now, that sounds like Mummy."

"I am very happy to meet you," said Ali who seemed amused.

She ignored him, and clung to Suzanne's hand. "Don't leave me again. They stole my pearls."

Jane whispered to Suzanne, "We got her a fake necklace, but she won't wear them." Hoping for another miracle, Jane said, "Mother, do you know me? I'm Jane, your other daughter."

"No, you're not! You're a nobody, just someone to wait on me." Jane's looked away in despair, but the others saw her mother stare at her again in confusion and then she said the single solitary word that meant the world to her younger daughter, " Jane."

"She knows me. Thank you, Mummy. What a gift you've given me."

Suddenly the blue eyes lost their luster; Edith turned her head back to the window, and rocked her chair with renewed vigor. Francine picked up the doll and put it back in her arms. "She's decided that she's had enough talking for one day, isn't that right, Edith? It was nice to hear your voice so loud and clear."

"I think she's angry because I put her in here," said Jane. "I had to. After Rosie died, I couldn't keep anyone—Mother was too demanding. Maybe she spoke to me today because I brought you, and subconsciously, decided to forgive me. Who knows what goes on in the mind of an Alzheimer's patient?"

"I thought she barely spoke."

"She doesn't. It isn't the voice that is gone, it's the part of the brain that tells her to speak that is gone. But sometimes, when they see a certain person, it acts like a short circuit, and you've seen what can happen."

"Will it happen again?"

"I don't know," Jane said. "I think you were the trigger."

An hour passed. Suzanne showed her pictures of her children and even recited some familiar poetry to their mother, but nothing seemed to jog her memory back. She remained locked in her own solitary world. During this time, Ali wandered outside the grounds, having a cigarette.

After thanking Francine for taking such excellent care of their mother, the sisters kissed their mother good-bye. She stared out the window at the birds. *Who were these women who put their lips on my face; I didn't even know them.*

Suzanne took one last look around the room; the fresh flowers and all the silver-framed family pictures, including one of herself on her mother's favorite antique bureau. Even the afghan at the foot of the bed was a familiar sight. Her mother was surrounded by all the things she loved. Her Monet painting hung over her sofa. "What is that painting doing here?" Suzanne said. "It's worth a fortune."

Jane whispered, "Don't worry. It's just a copy, but she stares at it, so we know she remembers it."

They left the room, continuing their conversation. "At least she isn't suffering," Suzanne said. "But, oh God, I'd give anything to hear her nag me one more time."

Jane sighed. "Poor Mummy. She's had a hard life. Dementia, regardless of the disease, is worse than cancer—not to be able to communicate or to make another person understand that you love them or even to say a final good-bye. People who think dying is the worst thing that can happen to them, don't know anything about life. My heart breaks for her every time I see her. I wonder if we'll get Alzheimer's, too."

Suzanne shuddered. "I don't want to know."

"Me either."

"And one other thing. Tell them to tone down the make-up. It's not Mother. She would hate the way she looks."

"It's nice to have you back, my big bossy sister."

"Ditto."

THE NEXT VISIT WAS THE CEMETERY where their father was buried. An urn filled with fresh white roses stood in front of the rose-colored granite headstone. The inscription read, "Robert Alden Mason, Beloved Husband, Father, and Brother," with the dates of his birth and death. The engraving below read, "He would rather light a candle than curse the darkness."

"Wasn't that what the president's wife, Mrs. Roosevelt was quoted as saying?" asked Ali.

Jane replied, "I wonder how many Americans would know that?"

"Ali loves American history," says Suzanne.

"Then, you probably would be interested to know that our father was a descendant of John and Priscilla Alden, one of the Mayflower settlers. There are some other descendants of the Aldens that live in Gorham, Maine, not far from here."

"The Mayflower must have been a gigantic boat. There are so many people that make that claim," said Ali.

"In our case it's true," answered Jane curtly.

Suzanne knelt at his grave and laid a bouquet of sunflowers next to the roses. Her voice wavered, "I'm here, Daddy. I love you." On the brink of tears, she stood up with her hand resting on the headstone.

"He was the best father anyone could have. He died too young," said Suzanne as she walked away, peering over her shoulder for a final glance of her father's grave. Ali watched and thought the Bedouin way was better—an unmarked grave on the edge of the desert. Why relive a place of sorrow again and again?

MARGARET AND HUBERT presided over an early dinner, which the chef had prepared. Margaret told Antonio to be sure not to serve pork. Muslims, like devout Jews, did not eat it. They sat in the lavish dining room with all the gleaming silver and the crystal glasses filled with Hubert's finest wine. In between courses, Suzanne recounted her visit to her mother. "I'm relieved that I saw her and that she knew me, but it was tragic to see Mummy like that. She seems to have shrunk in size and has become so frail. When she was herself, she was always so capable and strong-minded."

Ali felt at ease with Jane and Margaret, although he was still wary of Hubert. Unlike most Muslim men, Ali was not uneasy in the company of women. After all, he had spent almost half his life in the West. After dinner, he was surprised when Hubert offered him a brandy and a cigar, and even sat down next to him in the living room. They talked of world events and, eventually, about the influence of oil from the desert kingdom on the rest of the world. To Hubert, Ali sounded pompous; he could no longer remain silent, and after a few brandies, he spoke her mind.

"You know, Prince Ali, you told us of the primitive conditions your country was in when Americans developed your petroleum industry, but tell me where would your country be today if it were not for the United States? Probably still riding camels and living in tents in the desert? Is that a fair question?"

"That may be true, Mr. Mason, but when Texas goes dry, where will your country and the rest of the industrial world be without the oil from Saudi Arabia and the other oil producing countries of the Middle-East? Just remember that the desert of sand called Saudi Arabia is sitting on an ocean of oil and —"

Jane sat there quietly. She began to understand why her sister was attracted to this man. He was dynamic and, though he spoke softly with a clipped English accent, he was a skilled communicator with an analytical mind who knew exactly how to dominate a conversation without being a bore.

Suzanne remained silent and thoughtful, wondering if she should have admonished her uncle for asking such a rude question. Once again, her family had insulted Ali. But if he was angry, he did not show it. The differences between Michael and Ali were enormous. Both men were highly intelligent. Both were passionate about their beliefs. But Michael's emotions were always on the surface. He was quick to anger and even quicker to forgive. Ali's emotions often remained dormant, smoldering within him. He was a calculating and unforgiving man. Once you had lost his good favor, it was gone forever. He had ruined many a man, both foreigner and Arab. He gave only total loyalty to his family, and even then, cautiously.

"I guess we'd really be at the mercy of your country when our oil goes completely dry," said Margaret. "You're right about that, unless we learn to develop wind and sun power, or discover new sources of oil. Maybe it's under the sea as well. Did you ever think of that? Any country that can put men on the moon can find a new source of energy. Don't ever underestimate the good old United States of America."

"Mrs. Mason," Ali said, "I would never want you for an adversary because you would probably win. Your theory about oil being under the sea is interesting. I've never met a woman quite like you."

"I'll take that as a compliment. My father used to say it wasn't natural for a young girl to ride a horse as well as I did. I won a slew of blue ribbons. I could have made the Olympic team if there hadn't been a Second World War. My other specialty was business—I was good at it. Better than my two brothers. Some men don't like strong women, but not my Hubie."

"Don't be so sure of yourself, Maggie," said her husband.

"Hush up! Incidentally, Prince Ali, it was one of my people who found Suzanne when you checked into the hotel in London."

"I'm very glad that you were successful in your search for your niece."

While Ali continued his conversation with her family, Suzanne asked to be excused. "Would it be all right if I called a friend on the telephone. Someone I used to be very close to."

"Of course, my dear. We'll continue our little talk while you make your phone call."

"Thank you, Auntie."

"Are you calling Elena?" Jane asked.

"I know what you think of her and you're right. But old habits die hard. I need a break from all this serious stuff, and Elena is so gossipy, and so much fun. She really never harmed me, you know. She wasn't malicious like Lorna, and I've known her forever."

Suzanne left and went into another room, out of range of the living room, to first telephone the hospital. Michael was continuing to do well, and with this news, she felt less guilty for leaving him for the day. Then, she looked up Elena's number in the telephone book and dialed it. It rang four times, and was answered by a man. In the background, she heard the sound of children's voices.

"Is this Keith?"

"Yes it is. Who is it? You sound familiar, but I can't place you."

"It's Suzanne, Elena's old friend. I'm back in the world of the living."

"Jesus Christ, Suzanne! I thought you were dead. Hey! I'm sorry I said that, but you took me by surprise. I'm glad you're still alive and obviously in good health. At least you sound like it. Elena still talks about you and the old times. Hang on. I'll get her right away. She's not going to believe this." She heard him call, "Hey, Honey, come here." Seconds later, she heard Elena's voice.

"Holy cow! Sue, is it really you?"

"Yeah. I'm back for a while."

"God, I'm so happy. Where have you been? "

"I'm home at last, and although I can't see you this visit, I just had to talk to you. I've so much to tell you." Time had stood still. Elena was the same. It was as though they had seen each other the previous week. They talked for about twenty-five minutes. Suzanne told her everything. Elena brought her up to date on her life.

"I just realized that you're a princess, like Princess Margaret!"

"Not exactly. There are thousands of princes and princesses in Arabia. Don't forget, Muslims can have four wives, and that creates plenty of royalty. It's just a title. It doesn't mean we are connected to any of Europe's royalty. So forget the princess stuff. I'm still just Suzanne, Okay?"

"Sure. By the way, do you want me to bring you up to date on Lorna?"

"No. I don't mean to be rude, but I'm not particularly interested. She's ancient history."

"I don't care! I have to tell you. I must."

"Tell me what?"

"Lorna's husband ran off with a lawyer from his firm."

"Did a woman finally join that stuffy old law firm?" asked Suzanne.

"No. That's what I wanted to tell you. He ran off to Key West with a man."

"Holy Shit!"

"Now that's the Suzanne I remember," laughed Elena.

"I'm flabbergasted. I really am."

Everyone was surprised. The other lawyers, their friends, even relatives. Who knew? He was pretty macho except when it came to dealing with Lorna.

"Elena, it's been so good talking to you. I have to go now."

"Suzanne, I'm going to church to say a rosary for your little boy. I'm going to pray like I never prayed before."

"You always were the religious one. Thank you."

ALI ROSE FROM HIS CHAIR. "Are you ready to go back to Boston? It's getting late."

"I'm sorry I took so long. You're right. We must go. I want to be at the hospital early to see how Michael is doing. I called the nurse's station, and he's having a real good day."

"I've coming to Boston with you," said Jane. I was planning to drive down tomorrow afternoon, but Ali invited me. I can pack in five minutes."

"Oh, I'm so glad," said Suzanne. "I can use the moral support and you'll get to meet your two nephews and little Sara.

Margaret grabbed Suzanne's hands and squeezed them. "I'll be thinking of you for the next few days, and don't be surprised if we come down to see that boy of yours."

Leaving Hubert and Margaret was difficult for Suzanne, but it was a pleasant surprise when Jane decided to return with them. Robby was flying into Boston the next day. After all those years, the three siblings would be reunited.

Once they had left, Hubert and Margaret refilled their tumblers with aged Scotch whiskey and switched on the television to watch *I Love Lucy*. Even though it was a funny, neither laughed much. Margaret had just received a distressing phone call.

"I just don't have heart to tell the girls the news," said Margaret.

"That son-of-a-bitch *knew* when they went to that lawyer's office that none of those documents would hold up in Saudi Arabia," said Hubert, his hand trembling so badly he could hardly hold the glass.

"Richard Davis conferred with three other lawyers, two of them experts on international law," said Margaret. "Saudi Arabia only recognizes one kind of law, Sharia law. Women do have inheritance rights, but forget the rest. It's all a sham. Do you think I should tell

Suzanne?"

"What the hell good would that do? Do you actually think she'd stay here and let her children go back without her?"

"I just hope she can trust Prince Ali. I think he does love her."

Hubert was not persuaded. "You know what I think of him and his kind."

"I hope you're wrong, pumpkin."

"You still have your connections at the CIA, don't you?"

"You promised me you'd never discuss that. You know it's a secret," said Margaret.

"You could have the bastard killed and have it look like an accident. It would solve everybody's problems. We'd get Suzanne home again—for keeps. You know you can still go to the Director and get it done. Christ, Margaret. You were one of their top agents. They owe you. If the *New York Times* only knew that one of the richest women in America was a spy. Who else could go where you went without raising an eyebrow? What a story that would make."

"Hubert, stop talking nonsense! Someone might actually believe you mean that instead of just letting off steam. If you don't shut up, I'll have *you* assassinated! That part of my life is over. Finished. I never want to hear you mention it again. Now let's watch Desi and Lucy. Maybe we'll still get a laugh or two out of it. I could use one."

Chapter 19

RESOLUTION

Jane peeked over her blanket and stared into the eyes of her niece, Sara. The four-year-old grinned at her, clutching a large book with a picture of a West Highland Terrier on its cover.

"Auntie Jane, Auntie Jane, this is the story of a lost dog with a broken paw, named Bonnie, who couldn't find her way home." Her round black eyes were huge with excitement. It's my favorite story. She's like Mama's old dog, Daisy."

Jane lifted her head off the pillow, leaned on her elbows, and looked around the room in the daylight.

"Hi, sweetie. I remember Daisy. We had another dog named Jack, too."

"You had two dogs!"

"Yup."

"What does 'yup,' mean?" asked Sara.

"It's what people who live in Maine say when they mean to say 'yes.'"

"I know all about Maine. It's where Mama came from."

"I loved to read when I was your age. I wish I had a child who liked books but I don't have any children."

"Why? Why not?"

"That's a good question. Perhaps someday, the baby doctor will send me one. Meanwhile, I have you," she said, as she reached out and touched the tip of Sara's button nose. Sara gave Jane the widest grin she had ever seen, and her eyes twinkled with mischief.

Behind Sara stood Rhashid, a head taller. His skin was a shade darker than that of his little sister. Despite his downcast eyes and obvious shyness, he mustered a friendly greeting to his aunt, not needing any coaxing from his nursemaid.

"Good morning, Auntie Jane. Mama told us stories about you. She said you are a doctor like Auntie Sara."

"Yes, I am a doctor, Rhashid. Your mother is my older sister, and we have a younger brother named Robby, your uncle."

This time he looked at her directly—his eyes brightening, "Mother said that he raced on the ocean in a sailboat, and that you went sailing all the time."

"Yes, that's true. I still go sailing and I hope we can do it with you sometime."

"Don't forget me, Auntie Jane," said Sara, jumping up and down.

"I won't. I promise."

Standing aside patiently, a petite sloe-eyed woman introduced herself.

"Doctor Jane, I am Mary, the children's nanny. I'm so pleased to meet you."

"Hi, Mary. Glad to meet you too."

Mary, outfitted in a brown skirt and a yellow sweater, was very pretty. Her olive complexion had a slight coppery tinge. Her features were delicate and feminine. Jane guessed her to be under thirty.

"Come on, children. Let's leave your aunt alone so she can get dressed. If you need anything, Doctor Jane, just ask."

"Oh, Mary, I do have a question. Where is my sister now?"

"Still sleeping. She's exhausted. But, she'll be up and ready to go in about an hour. Then, you can have breakfast together. Would you like a coffee now, to help you wake up? I know…I can tell…You are not a morning person any more than your sister is."

"You got that right—but how did you know?"

"You talk with your eyes half-closed like Princess Yasmine."

"Do I really do that?"

"Yes, but please forgive me for my boldness." She looked embarrassed as to what she considered a faux pas. She must remember that she was a servant, and this was not Princess Yasmine, who had become her friend and confidant.

"I'm taking the children out to the Commons to feed the ducks. If they aren't there, we'll just take a walk."

As they left the room, she heard Sara ask Mary, "Why does her hair stick out so funny?"

"Sssssssh. She hasn't combed it yet."

Jane laughed to herself. Through the blinds, the morning sunshine cast strips of light on the beige carpeted floor. The room was large and well appointed. There was an adjoining sitting room with a fireplace. The bathroom was large and luxurious.

She stretched her arms outward and yawned, still tired from the night before.

Jane stood under the shower longer than usual as it beat life into her, rethinking the telephone conversation she had had with Michael the night before.

"Yes, when the opportunity presented itself, I told her about us. She would have found out eventually. It was awkward, and I felt a little guilty, but I'm glad I did it. All and all, she took it quite well."

"I think it was better coming from you. And now, Jane, you and I definitely have a future together...we do...don't we?"

"That's something we have to talk about face to face, Michael. I'll be in Boston tomorrow."

"Okay, it's been on hold all these years—a little longer won't make any difference."

"Good-by, Michael." *Why did he sound so unhappy? Something was wrong.*

"Before you hang up, Jane, there is one other thing...I'm still rattled, but it's beginning to sink in...Michael isn't my son; he's the Arab's." He still couldn't say Prince Ali, without the sound of it grating on his nerves. "There are no doubts. They have the same blood type AB negative. I'm type O, positive. It's his child."

"Yes, I know."

"But how could you?"

"It's a long story, but here's what happened. Suzanne thought he was yours because—"

He listened. She heard him sigh a few times.

She felt compelled to tell him the circumstances that led Suzanne to believe that it was his child. She simply wanted him to understand that her sister never deliberately lied to him. It was simply another cruel twist of fate. The conversation was brief, as it had taken place just minutes before she left for Boston with Ali and her sister.

"Tell Suzanne for me that I understand how it could have happened. Any reasonable person could have come to the same conclusion. Besides, she doesn't need any more problems. Things aren't going well here."

"You mean with Mikey?"

"Yeah. He's getting worse. He's not critical yet, but it won't be long. I'll see you tomorrow. Okay?"

"Sure, I understand. Goodnight, Michael."

Jane brooded over the obvious serious change in her nephew's condition, as she left the steamy shower and patted herself dry. The shock of seeing herself naked in a full-length mirror confirmed to her once again that she was too thin. No matter how much she ate, she never gained weight. There were no show-all mirrors anywhere in her home. She rubbed herself briskly with a soft white towel. Before she finished, she heard a knock on the door.

"I'm up, Janie. Coffee's waiting."

IT WAS MIDNIGHT WHEN THEY had returned to the hotel the previous night. The day in Maine had been an emotional one, a roller coaster ride of highs and lows.

Although the penthouse suite, which overlooked the lush landscape of Boston Commons, was spacious and sumptuous, it was all done tastefully, bearing the trademark look of the Ritz-Carlton. Flaming logs crackled in the fireplace, casting dancing shadows on the walls.

A bellhop carried Jane's single suitcase into her suite, and stood there awkwardly until she pulled a few bills from her wallet. Ali stood in the archway of the room and glared at the bellhop for his blunder. *Didn't he know that he was a member of the Royal Family of Saudi Arabia*?

The sisters tiptoed into the children's room and, for the first time, Jane saw Rhashid and Sara. Tears came to her eyes. Cherubic Sara clutched a teddy bear close to her face, and Rhashid lay uncovered on his back, revealing the handsome silhouette of his face. She felt a startling feeling of closeness and love—they were of her blood—the first, she hoped, in continuing generations of Masons and

Merediths. She wished her parents were here to see their first grandchildren. She ached to touch them. Suzanne sensed her hesitation and whispered, "Go ahead, Jane, give them a kiss. They won't wake up."

Her lips brushed their warm, soft cheeks; she inhaled their soapy scent. They were beautiful children, especially Sara, with her hundreds of long black lashes resting on her plump cheeks. She and Suzanne closed the door quietly when they left the room. Now she understood why her sister did what she did. Suzanne had told that her children were her life.

THAT MORNING, UPON WAKENING, Suzanne smiled to herself remembering and savoring the previous night. For the first time in weeks, Ali and Suzanne made love. They needed to draw strength from one another, especially Suzanne, who at first, wanted only to be held, but she needed more—they both did. When she cried out, Ali swiftly covered her mouth with his hand. "Shhh, my love. Someone will hear you."

She nodded her head, as her body convulsed with pleasure, and for a few minutes, she enjoyed total peace and fulfillment. "I love you, Ali. I love you so," she whispered.

"I know you do."

The sleepiness that usually followed lovemaking came quickly, and she escaped the painful reality of her life, slipping into a merciful slumber. It was preferable to taking sleeping pills, which of late had become a nightly habit. Ali didn't approve of them.

AFTER FINISHING BREAKFAST, Jane accounted in detail to Suzanne her nighttime conversation with Michael: he now knew beyond a doubt that he wasn't the father of Suzanne's child. He accepted it without blaming anyone. Suzanne listened, grateful that Michael understood the bizarre circumstances that led her to believe that he was the father of her child. A heavy burden had been lifted from her shoulders.

"He also knows that I told you about us…you know…about loving each other. Is it really okay?"

"Yes. I thought we covered that before. Muslims believe that everything happens because God wills it. Others call it destiny. Whatever it is brought us to Boston for a reason. Actually, for more than one reason: Now you and Michael are free to have a life together. My little boy may or may not go into remission, and I've learned my place is with Ali and my children. The only thing I have not or could not resolve was to tell Ali the truth about my marriage to Michael. If I did, It would destroy his honor—and that would destroy him. I'll live with the lie because I have to. Believe me, Jane, I do love my husband."

"Even though he raped you. And cheated on you. And is thinking of marrying again."

"Tell me, little sister. What choice do I have? I'll lose my children. He promised me that he wouldn't marry again and I believe him. He was only violent once in almost ten years, so you see, it wasn't a pattern. He's not a monster. Most likely, there will be other women in his life. Leopards don't change their spots, and I'm not a fool, you know. But as strange as it might seem to you, I do love him in spite of everything. There's something about him that's continuously exciting and I need that. He's never boring. I still love Michael and always will. He was my first love and nobody forgets their first love. But Ali is my husband and the father of my children. We belong together.

Even though she had doubts, Jane wanted to believe that Suzanne actually loved Ali for himself and was not just being a sacrificial lamb trying to keep her family intact. In any event, it was Suzanne's decision. However, she did have one other question for her sister.

What if all that stuff at the lawyer's office was just a bluff, and you can't come home again, ever?

"Then I'll find a way. The secret of power in Saudi Arabia for a woman is to have a strong male ally. If not my husband, than it will be my son or sons. You haven't seen the last of me, yet. I can tell you that for sure."

As they traveled to the hospital in a stretch limousine, Jane commented, "You certainly live in style, Suzy."

"Compliments of the hotel when you rent the penthouse. When do you think we'll be seeing Robby?"

"Once he arrives at our hotel and checks in, he's coming directly to the hospital," said Jane.

"He's going to stay in our hotel?"

"The very same. Of course, he's doing it under an assumed name. Even has a passport to go with it. The Canadians are glad to help. They don't think much of the war in Vietnam either. Imagine Robby being a husband and soon, a father!"

"Love does strange things, even to our brother," said Suzanne. "If I hadn't come back...how much longer would you have waited for Michael?"

"Something has come up that's about to change my life for the next couple of years. He would have had to make a life-changing decision soon in any event. Now he'll have to make it sooner," said Jane

Suzanne did not press for details. If her sister had wanted to tell her about her mysterious plans, she would have.

An hour later, they joined Ali who had gone to the hospital earlier, in the visitors' lounge, Little Michael was scheduled for a transfusion. While they sat there making small talk, Dr. Conti entered the room, white-coated and grim-faced. Something was different; they could sense it.

"Are you all right Michael? You don't look well," said Suzanne.

"I'm okay. It's not me I'm worried about—it's your son."

Suzanne's face paled. "Tell us, what's happened?"

"We're losing him...he's drifting off. We couldn't do the transfusion because he's too weak." He sat down next to them trying to find the right words, but there were none. "He's being transferred to Intensive Care as we speak."

Ali's face was ashen and he sunk his teeth into the back of his knuckled fist until he almost broke the skin. The two sisters looked at each other in horror.

"Someday, there'll be a cure—perhaps a bone marrow transplant, but it's years away—still in the earliest stages of experimentation. You must prepare yourselves. He has maybe a day or two, perhaps a week."

Ali's hand trembled as he lit up another Camel. Heaped in the ashtray in front of him was a pile of butts, most of which were his. He stared past Dr. Conti—unable to comprehend, much less to accept, what he had just heard.

Suzanne's hands flew to her face. "Oh, God, no!" she cried.

After about ten minutes of questions and what-ifs, the mood was broken when a tall, blonde, trimly bearded man, strode into the room. He was dressed in jeans and a denim shirt and was carrying a duffel bag. There was no mistaking him. It was Robby.

In an instant, he embraced his sisters. His voice broke when he spoke. "I know I've been wrong staying away, but I'm here now. When I heard about you, Suzanne, and your son being sick, I knew the time was right. I've been an irresponsible coward. Not about Vietnam, but about my family."

"You're here now and that's what counts," said Suzanne. "I love you, Robby, and I don't think I've ever told you that before."

Independent of the sad circumstances, there were smiles as well as tears on everyone's faces.

"Oh, Robby, we've missed you so much," exclaimed Jane.

Robby spied Michael. "Mike, how are you, old buddy? Have you learned to skipper a boat yet?"

"Maybe a first mate, but not a skipper. *Does he ever think about anything but sailing and Vietnam?* It's nice to see you again, Robby." Robby leaned forward to hug him, but Michael stepped back and extended his hand. He felt Ali's eyes on them—he needed to be careful. *Don't blow it now.*

Robby was still the joker. He laughed nervously, eyeing Ali, not knowing quite what to say to him. Suzanne introduced them, and they shook hands.

Michael had done what he had to do. Now he needed to be alone for a while and compose himself for what lay ahead.

He changed into casual clothes, which he almost never did, and rode the elevator down three floors, walked out of the main lobby, past the hospital shop, past sick children and their parents, past nurses and doctors, until he was outside the hospital. He paused, tightened the laces on his sneakers, took several deep breaths of an Indian-summer breeze, and jogged briskly away, trusting that his headache would be gone before he returned.

For some reason, his mind wandered back to when he was a fourth-year medical student and he was working a thirty-six hour shift that was ending at eleven that night. He was exhausted and annoyed when the head-nurse woke him from his catnap and asked him to look in on a patient who was dying.

"Damn her. I gave him morphine for his pain—what more can I do?"

He walked quietly into the dimly lit, semi-private room, observed one empty bed and, in the other, his patient, a man in his late fifties who was dying of cancer. Before he could say anything, the man spoke to him.

"Doc, I got no one I can talk to about this. No real family. Everytime I bring it up with one of the nurses, they change the subject, like I ain't gonna' die."

His eyes were set deep, his cheeks hollowed. The gray pallor of death was on his face.

"Are you in pain, Mr. Collins?"

"Not much anymore."

"Then, tell me what it is I can do for you."

"Talk to me! Ask what it's like to be dying. Ask me anything."

Michael knew that this was a minefield in the medical profession. Never become intimate with your patient, and God forbid, never tell him that there is no hope. *The hell with the rules. This could be his own father.*

"Okay, Mr. Collins."

"Doc, call me Barry, *please*."

"Okay, Barry. Tell me, what does it feel like?"

He sighed, stroking the bristly whiskers on his unshaven face. "It's like an inner tube that has a slow leak and you can feel your life goin' out of you, and even if some doctor didn't already tell ya' what's happening, you'd already know, but you want to talk about it.anyway."

"Are you afraid?"

"Shit. I ain't afraid to die, but dying *alone* is hard. Mostly, I'm curious. Ya' know, Doc, I was a merchant seaman, and I saw the world. This is the last adventure I'll ever take, but I need a little help."

Michael looked at his watch. It was eleven o'clock—his shift was over—Suzanne was probably waiting for his phone call. He took the man's emaciated hand, covering it with his. "I'll stay with you, Barry."

"You're gonna make a great doctor someday, young fella'. Thanks."

Two hours later, after talking about a divorce, about being a bad father, about screwing women of every color on five continents, Barry Collins drew his last breath, and young Michael Conti was going to become a doctor for the best of reasons—compassion.

He didn't know why he was thinking of that night. Perhaps it was because it was the first time he actually saw a patient die. Others had died, either before or after his shift, but never when he actually was by their bedside, and never had he met a patient who was so eager to talk about his own demise. Michael felt that it had been a lesson. He knew that some of his patients would not make it, but when they didn't, he would be there for them until the end. It was especially important for the suffering children who had become his little friends as well as his patients. He and the nurses who had worked with him bonded and were known as "Michael's Angels." Together, they took care of these sick children who lived their brief lives so courageously. Now they would do the same for Suzanne's son, the child that should have been his. This beautiful little boy that loved life so much: who wanted to see Ted Williams hit a homer, who wanted to ride his pony again, who had Suzanne's sweet mouth. Michael finished his run, drenched in sweat. He returned to the hospital with a renewed strength and faith, believing that God had chosen him to ease the way for little Mikey. With that conviction reinforced in his mind, he was at peace with himself. In addition, he was relieved that the pounding in his temples had finally ceased.

WHEN THE END CAME, it was merciful and swift, like a candle flame that flickered and then went dark. With his brother Rhashid snuggled next to him on his bed, and his sister Sara offering her favorite stuffed animal to him, wondering why he didn't open his fluttering eyelids, and with Mary standing in the corner of the room fighting back tears, little Mikey left the living like a whisper.

"He's gone," said Dr. Conti, who swallowed hard to keep his professional composure, even though his own heart was splitting in two.

Ali shrieked in Arabic, and threw himself across his son's body. His grief was beyond anything that Michael had ever witnessed of another father. A nurse brought in a sedative and a glass of water.

"Take this, Prince Ali. It won't bring him back, but it might help you to get through this," Michael said.

"No-o-o-o! No-o-o-o! I want to feel the pain!" he screamed. Ali fell to his knees by the side of the bed, barely coherent. He wailed openly, his emotions a floodgate of sorrow, as he pulled at his hair as though he had gone mad. There was no "stiff upper lip," attitude among Arabs when they lost their loved ones. The cultural differences were enormous. Sara and Rhashid cried as children do, mostly because Aba was acting like a crazy man, and they did not fully understand the finality of their brother's death.

Michael was overwhelmed with empathy as he watched Suzanne cover her son's still warm face with her kisses. *Why wasn't Ali man enough to be strong for his family? Michael understood his grief, but he couldn't dismiss his weakness.* Once, Suzanne looked up at Michael, and through a shroud of tears, her eyes searched his. *Why is this happening?*

Later, Suzanne sobbed quietly and rocked back and forth in her chair, while Jane and Robby comforted her. Mary had removed the children from the room, afraid that they would see their mother fall apart as their father had.

"I can't believe he's gone. My darling little boy is gone. What will life be without him?"

They came to remove the body from the room, and Ali fell apart once more as they covered little Mikey's face with a sheet.

"Listen to me, Ali! He's not in pain anymore. He's in paradise," Suzanne said.

He nodded in agreement, his face, twisted with grief. Suzanne wrapped her arms around him and held him like a little boy. Watching them, Michael felt like an intruder.

"We must go back. His soul must rest in peace," Ali cried.

Michael remembered that Muslims, like Jews, buried their dead before sundown or as soon as possible. Soon they'd be returning to Saudi Arabia. Before leaving the room, he whispered in Jane's ear, "I'll wait for you. We have to talk."

When he entered the doctor's lounge, he found Vanessa still in surgical garb sitting there. "Is it over?" she asked.

He sat down wearily. "Yeah. I'm afraid so. I've never felt more helpless. I tried everything, but we lost him."

"You know, Michael, you aren't God. You did your best. It was a long shot from the beginning. Have you ever seen a kid survive that damn disease? I'll never get used to seeing children die. Suzanne was your friend, so it's much more personal isn't it?"

"She's more than my friend. She's my wife."

"Oh, Jesus! Michael, I didn't know. A part of me suspected something—the way you looked when you said her name. This must be awful. What can I do to help you?"

"Just be my friend."

"You got it."

It had been a sad farewell for the Mason family. There were many hugs, kisses, and tears. Jane promised that her mother would continue to get the best care, and Ali said that Jane and Robby would always be welcome to visit Saudi Arabia.

"I'll come back. I promise you," Suzanne said as she hugged them for the last time.

As they left the hospital, loading the small casket into a hearse, Michael stood with Jane and Robby. For the first time, he shook Ali's hand and brushed Suzanne's cheek with his lips. He whispered in her ear as he pinched her lobe, "Good-bye, Suzy Q, I'll never forget you."

Suzanne gave him a look that tugged at his heart and she didn't seem to care if Ali was watching or not. Jane saw that look too and knew that no matter what occurred, nothing would ever sever the love that existed between Michael and Suzanne.

Several hours later, the jet was airborne, and Ali, Suzanne, Mary, and the children were on their way back to Saudi Arabia to bury little Michael. They were returning to their country, to be with Ali's family, and to return their son to his final resting-place in an unmarked grave in the desert on the outskirts of Jeddah.

Throughout this tragedy, Jane stood by her sister and never once lost her composure. But watching Suzanne drive away was overwhelming. Robby understood and hugged her. "As soon as all the crap is over about Vietnam, I'm coming back to Maine with Adele and our child. We should be a family again."

"I know," she sniffled. "Tomorrow, we'll leave for Maine, but tonight, let's have dinner with Michael at the hotel. I hope you have a jacket and tie."

"I'll borrow something from Mike. We're about the same size. I'm going back to the hotel and take a nap, I'm pooped," said Robby. "You're in good hands with Mike. See you guys later at the hotel, and Mike, don't forget to bring my clothes."

He walked off in the direction of the parking lot, and they were left alone for the first time since Jane came to Boston.

"Robby hasn't changed much," said Michael. "Still walking to his own drumbeat."

"He'll change. Nothing builds character like paying the family bills. We had a long talk about Vietnam. He's not a coward, you know. He really believes in what he's doing and he certainly doesn't blame the Americans who are fighting there. Just the old men who send them to fight."

Michael didn't look convinced. Even though he didn't believe in the war either, he wouldn't have run off to Canada. "Let's go get something to eat. I want to talk," he said. Jane nodded, and they walked a few blocks to a diner and sat in a booth looking at each other soberly.

"Michael, it seems like a dream. Everything that has happened is so unbelievable, and it occurred so fast, I can hardly grasp it all."

"It's been a nightmare." He studied her face, noticing that it had become a more interesting one with age, though she still was a very young woman. She wore the same old schoolgirl ponytail, but her cheekbones and chin had become more defined. Her green eyes were more scrutinizing and intelligent. Being with her felt comforting and familiar. Over the years, she had become part of him.

"Will you really be able to put Suzanne behind you? I'll no longer settle for being second best," said Jane.

"You were never second best at anything."

She knew in her heart that he couldn't answer the first question without lying and that was something he never did. "Yes, I was. We both know it. Suzanne was always the star."

He laughed. "She always thought *you* were. You two are a mutual admiration society."

"Answer the question. Can you put Suzanne behind you?"

"I loved her a long time ago, but I've loved you longer."

He still hadn't answered the question and she knew now that he never would.

A waitress came, and took their order: one milk, one coke, two sandwiches, liverwurst and onions on rye for Michael, and chicken salad for Jane. Neither was very hungry, but life goes on.

"Jane, how many times have we done this? You know, getting together to talk things over regarding other people's problems and misfortunes—my Dad's heart attack, Robby, your mother, and now, all of this. I just wonder if we'll ever get around to talking about us. I'm thirty-five years old, and what do I have to show for my life except my career? When is it going to be *our* time?"

"That's what I want to talk to you about. Something has come up that's important to me. I want to take a leave of absence for two years to go to Africa."

"What? Where the hell is this going?"

"Calm down, and hear me out." She reached out across the table and grabbed his wrist.

"There's an organization called 'Doctors Who Care' that excites me. Michael, I'm weary of taking care of people with incurable diseases. I want to go somewhere where I can make a difference. Where there is a desperate need for doctors. Can you understand that?"

"What about *us*?"

"I haven't changed my feelings for you. It's not about that—it's about a new beginning for us. Of course, I wouldn't go without you, but I wish you'd think about it. You know how much I love you, Michael."

"Play fair."

"I am. It would be the best thing in the world for us. Imagine seeing most of our patients get better. We could make such a difference. It's only for two years. Think of it as an adventure—to go to Africa. Didn't you ever read Hemingway? Haven't you ever dreamed of it?"

"Hey, Jane, it wouldn't be any picnic. What if you had a baby?"

"Babies are born in Africa every day. You could deliver your own child. My Dad did."

He grinned mischievously. "I haven't asked you to marry me yet."

"But, you will."

"What about your mother?"

"Michael. Her disease is devastating. It could go on for a very long time, but it's comforting to know that she's being cared for so well at the nursing home. And, I'd be only a plane ride away. I've already spoken to Margaret and Hubert. Mother still has her sister Marie who visits twice a month. They'll watch out for her."

The waitress returned with their lunch.

"Anything else, folks?" asked the apple-cheeked waitress who only had eyes for Michael.

"We're all set. Thanks," he said returning her smile.

"What are you going to do about us?" asked Jane.

"How do you feel about Mexico?"

"Never been there."

"How about a month's vacation—enough time for a quickie divorce and a wedding—before we leave for Africa," said Michael.

"Michael, did you just propose to me?"

"You know I did. How about it, doctor, should we go for the whole shebang?"

"You're not very romantic. I was hoping for at least a flower, if not a ring."

"You can have the entire world if that's what you want. I'd never say no to you about anything."

"Okay, prove it. Take me home with you."

"All these years I never said what was in my heart, never really told you how much I love you, how much I need you, but when we get back to my place, I'm going to show you."

For the first time in Jane's life, she was speechless.

Crossing the Atlantic Ocean, the aircraft bearing the inscription "Arabia" in green letters, climbed to thirty thousand feet on its flight to Saudi Arabia. It had been sent by King Faisal to bring the family home. It carried five passengers, five crew members, and one coffin containing the body of a child.

Suzanne knelt at the rear of the plane resting her tear-stained face on the casket. She needed to stay close to him. Part of her wished for death to end the sorrow that was wrenching her heart. There were no words that could ever make it better. No miracle worker, no surgeon, not even God could take this pain away. She sobbed when she thought of her little son being buried in some god-forsaken corner of the desert, and she wouldn't be allowed to attend her own son's funeral. Being a Muslim woman was hard and she knew none of her family in America would ever understand this. How could they, she didn't understand it herself. After a few hours, Ali would relieve her, and she would return to her lifeline, her children.

In remorse, Ali sat in his seat, his cigarette curling smoke. Although Mary was reading to the children across the aisle, he didn't hear her. He was lost in a maze of memories and events to come. After the funeral, when the mourning period was over and his heart stopped aching for his beloved son, he would return to Paris to his bride, the eighteen-year-old, Jirhan, daughter of a wealthy Saudi businessman and his French wife. Once Yasmine accepted her place in their family, and gave birth to their fourth child, he would bring Jirhan back to Saudi Arabia to live.

Yasmine had disappointed him. She was going to take his children away from him. She made him go to lawyers and make ridiculous promises and sign bogus papers. She had looked at that Conti fellow with lust. If she had not been pregnant, he would have beaten her. Even now, anger consumed him. Still, she was the mother of his children, and they were united in their grief. He would retaliate in ways she would never dream. In the end, she would be a better wife. She, with her sparking, jeweled eyes, he loved most of all; despite the fact that he fought against it, and it mocked his honor as a man.

His thoughts returned to Jirhan; he felt himself harden. He closed his eyes recalling her shyness, her young smooth face, her small, firm, cone-shaped breasts, and the long dark hair that held not one strand of gray. There was nothing like a young woman—absolutely nothing else compared to it. His father had known it, so had his grandfather, and the Prophet Mohammed as well. This was their religion, their heritage, their duty. In time, there would be many more sons born to the House of Saud.

AUTHOR'S NOTES AND ACKNOWLEDGEMENTS (REVISED FOR SECOND PRINTING)

Beyond The Memories is a work of fiction, and all of the characters stem from my imagination. I chose the town of Cape Elizabeth as a setting because of its natural beauty, but took great liberties with its geography and residents. In my mind's eye, I have combined Cape Elizabeth with its lighthouses, rocky seacoast, and Scarborough's sandy beaches, and Falmouth Foreside, where most of the grand estates were located, and created a town that exists only in my novel. My description of Portland and Old Orchard Beach are as I remember it. All historical information about the city of Portland came from the book, *Portland*, by Greater Portland Landmarks, Incorporated.

I don't know who the valedictorian of Portland High School, class of 1950 was, but I know it wasn't my fictional character of Michael Conti. Although, it is true that the Portland High School basketball team of 1950 did, indeed, win the Class A state championship. It's challenging to combine true events, ordinary and historical, mix in a little fantasy and see what happens.

I have traveled to all of the countries referred to in detail with the exception of Saudi Arabia. Everything that I have written about Saudi Arabian history, its geologic makeup, the Koran, Islamic women, the Arabs, Sharia law and customs have come from years of extensive research. Sometimes, I changed the time frame, placing them either before or after their actual occurrence. (Such as the execution of the Saudi princess that took place after the date I mentioned.) Other examples are the luxurious and careless life style of the Saudi Royal Family which really came into play in the late seventies when the price of oil soared, and not entirely in the time period that I write about.

Prince Ali and Prince Kareem and their families are fictitious and their lives do not reflect on anyone, living or dead. However, when writing about real people such as the first king of Saudi Arabia, King Abdul Aziz, ibn Sa'ud, and others such as King Faisal, King Sa'ud, Queen Iffat, Prince Sultan and Prince Bandar, I relied on research from such books as Robert Lacey's, *The Kingdom*, *The Arab Mind*, by

Raphael Patal. *The Saudis*, by Sandra Mackey, and *Nine Parts of Desire*, the sub title, *The Hidden World of Islamic Women by* Geraldine Brooks as well as hundreds of other sources—books and articles.

Slavery in Saudi Arabia was legal until the early sixties. However, to what extent the trafficking of women existed or to what degree, is unknown as Saudi Arabia is one of the most closed societies in the world and the private life of the royal family is guarded zealously. Did any American woman ever marry into the Saudi royal family? Honestly, I don't know. This is fiction. In no way do I intentionally demonize or insult Islam, which is the religion of millions of people. All religions are equally good, when practiced according to their dogma and not to the interpretation of the extremist element of their religion.

The idea for the novel came about after hearing about an actual kidnapping. While a medical student at Harvard in 1958, a relative of mine told me of a classmate's wife being abducted in Istanbul while they were on their honeymoon. She was never found. I have wondered about her for years. Where is she? What happened to her? Was this educated, privileged young woman alive or dead? Ultimately, years later, I wrote this novel. I changed the location of Istanbul to Athens because I was more familiar with Greece than Turkey.

I have no adequate words to express my gratitude to all of my family, especially my children, Greg, Philip, and Andrea for their support and encouragement. Although my mother is no longer alive, I do remember her saying after reading the first draft, "I knew you could write but not like this." However, she was my mother, and I can only hope that you the reader will be as generous with me. I, a little girl with big ears, heard much of the chatter in the fictitious barbershop in my father's shoe repairing shop at the base of Munjoy Hill. My Dad, Dominic Candelmo's nickname was also, "the Sheik."

I want to thank the talented team of Joan and Philip Candelmo for their contribution in line editing, and designing the book cover. They have been with me through the beginning. Christine Kourapis, a friend and former English teacher was the first to go over a rough first draft and lead me in the right direction. Constantine Markides, who believed that fewer commas were better, was my final proofreader, and although he never intruded on my voice or my story, he made it better than I ever thought it could be.

I learned more from Stephan King's book, *On Writing* than I ever learned from any other book on writing with the possible except of *The Elements of Style*, by William Strunk Jr. and E. B. White. In my opinion, the other books are both a waste of time and money—and I've read enough of them to know that. However, there are some good books out there on editing.

I am indebted to Dr. Kerry E. Kimball for his invaluable advice on the psychological effects of being abducted and other suggestions that were helpful when dealing with characters that experienced life-changing trauma in their lives. I am most grateful to my bother-in-law, the late Dr. Angelo J. Eraklis, a pediatric surgeon at Boston's Children Hospital, who told me about the tragic disappearance of the American girl, and also for describing for me in layman's terms the prescribed treatment for Lukemia in 1967 long before there were bone marrow transplants, and for his many colorful stories about becoming a doctor. Nancy Sferes, R. N., a nurse for children with cancer, was also helpful. Katherine Eraklis kept me honest on the layout of Harvard and Radcliffe and on which side of the Charles River certain buildings were located. And finally to my late husband, Paul for traveling with me innumerable times to Greece, its many islands and Asia Minor, (Turkey) and exposing me to the people, the land and the culture of his ancestors. I came to love it as much as he did.

Others who took time out from their daily lives as readers were Evangeline Getzen, Jennifer Steele, Lorraine Reinsold, Doris Wood, Rose Goodell, and Donna Towle. Layla Kargar, a senior in high school and my only Muslim reader read the book as well. To all of them and anyone I might have missed, thank you. And most especially to Josephine Ristick, who kept coming back again and again for more chapters to read—her enthusiasm was contagious and encouraging. It kept me going when I considered giving it all up. A special thanks to Sandy and she knows who she is and for The Book Review in Falmouth for being the first to feature my book in the window of their bookstore. Thanks to you guys, I'm on my second printing.

Norman Mailer has been quoted as saying that writing a novel is like jumping out of an airplane without a parachute. He was right, but the ride down was glorious.